Graveland

Alan Glynn is the author of three previous novels: *Bloodland*, described by the *Sunday Independent* as 'a cracking conspiracy thriller worthy of Le Carré', was awarded the Ireland AM Crime Fiction Book of the Year in 2011. It was preceded by *Winterland*, described by John Connolly as 'timely, topical and thrilling' and by the *Observer* as 'an enthralling and addictive read'. His 2001 debut, *The Dark Fields*, was released in 2011 as the movie *Limitless*, which went to number 1 at the box office on both sides of the Atlantic.

Praise for *Bloodland*:

'Ripped from tomorrow's headlines, *Bloodland* is irresistible. An exhilarating thriller from the heart of the global village.' Val McDermid

'There are ... echoes of John le Carré, *24* and James Ellroy here, but Glynn's talent is all his own, and his ability to ratchet up the tension is eye-popping ... I've not read such a multi-layered, expertly plotted portrayal of arrogance, greed and hubris for a long time.' *Guardian*

'An intelligent, well-written and compelling thriller . . . while *Bloodland* makes some serious points, it never forgets that a good thriller is there to entertain the reader as well as to make her think – and this is a very entertaining book.' *Irish Times*

'Glynn's ability to take these big themes and distil them down to the seedy personal stories, and motivations of the protagonists, is the key to why this novel hypnotizes the reader . . . Many have termed *Bloodland* as the political thriller of the year, and perhaps they are right as the furious pace wraps the reader into a trap, one that requires introspection and a curiosity to investigate what lurks beneath our headlines a little more closely, not unlike an Adam Curtis polemical documentary, and equally surreal.' www.shotsmag.co.uk

By the Same Author

The Dark Fields/Limitless
Winterland
Bloodland

Graveland
Alan Glynn

faber and faber

First published in this edition in 2013
by Faber and Faber Limited
Bloomsbury House
74–77 Great Russell Street
London WC1B 3DA

Typeset by Faber and Faber Ltd
Printed and bound by CPI Group (UK) Ltd, Croydon CR0 4YY

A CIP record for this book
is available from the British Library

ISBN 978-0-571-27545-8

For E, R & C

Graveland

One

In early 2001, having saddled the pharmaceutical giant with huge debt and cut its workforce by a third, Vaughan's Oberon Capital Group sold Eiben-Chemcorp for a profit of $457 million. It appears, however, that Oberon did this in the full knowledge that an R&D scandal involving leaked samples of a trial 'smart drug' was brewing at Eiben. What is more – and is perhaps more shocking – they then shorted the buyer's stock in order to make a double killing on the transaction.

House of Vaughan (p. 23)

I

Jeff Gale leaves his building at 8.15 a.m. It's a Saturday morning and Seventy-fourth Street is quiet. A taxi glides by. Across the street an old lady stands with her poodle waiting for it to take a dump.

The sun is shining, but it's still a little chilly.

Jeff limbers up. He puts in his earbuds, taps on his iPod and takes off for Central Park, which is three blocks away. As usual, by the time he gets to Madison Avenue he has pretty much clicked into gear, running in sync with the music and staying ahead of his anxieties, none of which will make it with him as far as Fifth, let alone the entrance to the park at Seventy-second Street.

He'll gather them up again on his way back.

One by one.

This renovation kick Felicia's on, for instance. How unnecessary it is, and how he's had to pass his resentment off as indifference. Simply because he hasn't got the time or the energy to deal with it.

Or *her*.

Which is nothing, of course, in comparison with the next anxiety – being at the helm of Northwood Leffingwell. What a bizarre, unending fever dream *that's* turned out to be, his shift from the number two position at the New York Fed not exactly proving to be the best-timed career move in Wall Street history.

What with all this supposedly long-overdue reform loom-ing.

De-reg, re-reg.

It's a joke.

But as for the *next* anxiety, don't even go there.

He swallows.

The girls, what else? Is he spoiling them, screwing up their chances of having a normal childhood? Is *Felicia*? Will the girls ever have the motivation to accomplish anything in their lives, given that they're incredibly, obscenely wealthy? They're not out of place at Brearley, that goes without saying, but they are a bit (a lot) when they visit North Carolina, where Jeff's orig-inally from, and where they must seem pretty exotic to their subprime cousins.

Mean little Manhattan rich girl bitches.

It's with the angled lens of Fifth Avenue widening just ahead of him that Jeff remembers he didn't take his pill before coming out. It's still sitting on the shelf of the medicine cabinet in his bathroom.

Damn.

Felicia distracted him with a catalogue of marble samples for the vestibule.

Verde Guatemala or Nero Marquina.

But what's he supposed to do now?

The music alone's not going to cut it. This weird, minimalist European jazz a guy at the office turned him on to isn't working at all this morning. Without the medication, it's just too much, too jangly, too grating.

Crossing Fifth, he tugs at his earbuds, pulls them out.

Without the medication, in fact, running itself is too much.

He only *does* it to get out of the house. That's because work, as excuses go, tends not to fly this early on a Saturday morning, not in normal circumstances anyway, whereas a run in the park does.

Plus, he has a gym at home that he never uses, so this is actually good for him. He just doesn't enjoy it. That's why before leaving the house he usually takes an anti-anxiety pill, which he then washes down with a counterintuitive triple espresso.

His secret formula.

Other guys he knows in their forties *love* running, and tennis, and lifting weights.

Jeff would prefer to be working.

Jeff would always prefer to be working.

But on he trots – two blocks south, then into the park, and around to the left – lumbered now with all of this unfiltered crap in his head.

As he passes the playground – which is already pretty busy, despite the hour – he imagines having Elena and Jordan at his heels, imagines them still being small enough to head in there for a quick go on the climbing pyramid or the swings.

Ellie and Jojo.

His precious girls.

When did they get to be so big?

At a steady pace, he makes his way along East Drive, down through the Dene. Other runners flit past. Sunlight flickers through the trees to his right and reflects against high apartment-building windows to his left.

Verde Guatemala or Nero Marquina.

It's insane.

There's also been talk of gold fittings for the main bathroom.

She's going to *ruin* the place. Make it look like the Donald Trump-inspired fuckpad of some lowrent Saudi sheik. Which he can't allow. If only on the grounds of taste. Though actually, in these days of the deferred stock option, the twelve million dollars Felicia has pencilled in for the job may well end up being needed elsewhere.

The cash bonus no longer a given.

Heading sharply downhill now, he builds a little momentum.

New structures.

For a new paradigm.

At which point he glances up and sees them. Two runners, twenty yards away and closing in.

In front of him, though.

Directly in his path.

Jeff's not an expert or anything, but he knows there's an etiquette here, something about – what is it? – following the counterclockwise flow of . . .

'*Hey*,' he says, almost before he thinks it, New York indignant.

But nothing.

No reaction.

He glances around, not all the way . . . enough, however, to realise that they're down in a little hollow here – granite apartment buildings high to his left, OK, but *very* high, and not much now to his right either, just a steep clay mound leading up to some patchy dry grass.

The two runners are very close. He swerves to avoid them. They swerve, too.

And meet him head-on.

'*HEY.*'

The collision, the distribution of force, is uneven – *they're* prepared, Jeff isn't. He falls and hits the path, sideways, hurting his arm. He immediately swings around and looks up, trying to focus, somehow imagining that what he'll be seeing is faces.

Recognisable, explicable.

But all he sees instead – barely recognisable, and far, far from explicable – is an extended arm, a gloved hand and the grey barrel of a gun.

*

The delivery arrives. It comes in two pallets, fifty cartons to a pallet, two units to a carton. That's two hundred new LudeX consoles, three quarters of which are on pre-order, meaning they'll have fifty units on display.

Fifty.

These will sell out within minutes, literally, which in turn means the rest of the day is going to be a living nightmare – apologising, explaining, the two things you're never supposed to do. But whoever said *that* clearly never worked in retail, be-cause it'll be 'I'm sorry, we're sold out,' followed by 'We only got fifty units in,' *all* fucking day.

Frank Bishop signs for the delivery and starts hauling the cartons from the receiving area into the already overloaded stockroom. As the manager, he gets to do this – come into work early on a Saturday, before eight, and strain his back in such a way that he'll be in pain for the rest of his shift, and probably for a lot longer than that. The two young sales guys will be in at nine, but that's too late, the stuff has to be ready to go when the doors open – and since he was recently instructed to cut twenty hours a week from payroll there's no one else here to do it.

It's his responsibility.

In the loosest possible sense of the word, of course.

Because Frank Bishop knows what responsibility means, he's had plenty of it in his day, and doing *this* job? Getting LudeX consoles onto the shelves of a PalEx store in a suburban mall in upstate New York in time for a 9 a.m. onslaught by an army of pimply geeks? That barely qualifies.

But Frank is happy to have the job. There's no question about that. At forty-eight, and in the current climate, he could just as easily have landed on the scrapheap. There are days when this certainly feels like the scrapheap, but most of the time he just gets on with it.

He has bills to pay.

It's as simple as that, his life reduced to a monthly sequence of electronic bank transfers.

College fees, allowances, rent, utilities, car, food.

Fuck.

Close his eyes for a second and Frank can be right back before any of this got started, twenty-five, thirty years ago – a different world, and one in which this degree of a financial straitjacket was something he only ever associated with his parents, with that whole generation.

It wasn't going to happen to him, though. Not a chance.

But then who paid for him to go to college? Exactly. And arrogant little prick that he was, he took every bit of it for granted, never once imagining, for example, that his old man might have had other things he could have been doing besides working his ass off holding down two jobs he more or less hated.

One of which, ironically, was not unlike this one.

Frank exhales loudly, no one around to hear him, and reaches down for another carton.

He carries it into the stockroom and adds it to the pile by the main door.

Back then, as well, it was all about possibilities opening up – relationships, career moves, the *world*. Now it's the opposite, possibilities are closing down all around him. The world? Forget about it. Career moves? He's lucky to *have* this job, and there aren't any others out there waiting for him. As for relationships, well . . . unless it's paid for or virtual, that ship's *sailed*.

Frank exhales again, even louder this time.

Is there anything less attractive than self-pity?

Not really, but at least he knows how to bitch-slap it back into place whenever it gets out of hand. Because the truth is he doesn't really feel sorry for himself at all. He has two kids that he adores, and even though they're both off at college now, he is completely and utterly defined by them. The world of twenty-five years ago, for all its breathless sense of expectation, of the open road ahead, didn't have *them* in it. This one does, and that's all that matters. This one, for all its oppressive sense of disappointment, of the economic jackboot in the face, is infinitely superior.

When he has carried in the last carton, Frank rips one open. This will be his first look at the new, long-awaited LudeX upgrade.

Like he gives a crap.

He takes a unit box out and turns it over. The sight of the Paloma Electronics logo, the powder blue stripe, sets off a tiny ripple of anxiety in his brain.

Paging Dr Pavlov.

But what does he expect? This is a Paloma *store* after all. The logo is everywhere. Damn thing is even sewn into the collar of his shirt.

It's just that he associates it with . . .

He was going to say *defeat*, but that'd be overstating things.

He puts the unit down.

Wouldn't it?

Maybe, whatever, yes, no.

Self-pity snapping at his heels again, Frank decides to hit the accelerator. He gets on with unpacking the units and stacking them on shelves. He makes coffee and takes a couple of Excedrin for his back.

Just before nine Lance and Greg show up.

They're nice guys, friendly, reliable, and a lot more savvy about all the tech stuff here than he is, but at the same time there's something about them that he doesn't get. It's a sort of dumb, unenquiring compliance, a lack of . . .

He doesn't know, but when he was their age –

Yeah, yeah.

Walking across the main floor, Lance says, 'Yo, Mr B.'

Greg points at the LudeX display and says, 'All *right*, let's do this.'

The launch of Paloma's LudeX upgrade today is a big deal. But for the real action you'd have to go to their flagship store in Times Square. That's where the hardcore gamers will have been standing in line all night, where the cash registers and card machines will be humming steadily all day, and where staff members will be under intense pressure to exceed sales quotas and push service extras.

Up here at Winterbrook Mall it'll be a more sedate affair, and considerably shorter. Outside in the main gallery there isn't a line exactly, though clusters of certain usual suspects are beginning to hover. When they open the doors at nine, there'll be a rush to get in, followed by an intense flurry of activity, but by ten o'clock it'll all be over – thanks to that jackass at corporate who saw fit to only send him a lousy fifty units on top of the preorders.

What kind of a sales strategy is *that* supposed to be?

Frank doesn't care, though.

By mid-morning he's on autopilot, daydreaming again – about his previous life, about Lizzie and John, about . . . *whatever* really, that Asian woman who works at the Walgreens on the lower level, the four-cheese pizza at Mario's, local cancer services even, not that he needs them or anything, but you never know.

Just after midday his attention is diverted by something he sees on TV – sees on multiple plasma screens lining the back wall of the store. It's a Fox News report.

He stands staring at it, reading the crawl.

Happy to be distracted.

In Central Park, a jogger has been shot dead.

In cold blood.

What gives the story a little twist, though, Frank soon sees, an extra kick – what will allow perfect strangers to make eye contact with one another throughout the day and express disbelief, shock, or even a hint of schadenfreude – is that the victim has been identified as the CEO of a big investment bank down on Wall Street.

*

'Holy shit.'

Ellen Dorsey glances from the small TV screen behind the counter to the old guy sitting next to her. She shakes her head. The old guy nods in acknowledgement. Picking up his coffee cup, he says, 'Too good for the bastard.'

Ellen makes a snorting sound. She then finishes her own coffee, pays and leaves. Out on the street – Columbus at Ninety-third – she is conflicted. The plan had been to go home and get back to work, but now she's thinking . . . crime scene. It's only twenty-five blocks away and across the park, a short cab ride. By this time, of course – what is it, almost one – the whole area will be cordoned off and there won't be anything to see, she knows that, but her instinct tells her this is going to be a big story, and nothing beats first-hand experience of a crime scene.

Besides, it'll be in the bank. If necessary. For later.

I was there.

You can also pick up on stuff walking around, details, vibes.

But as she throws her arm out to stop a cab, Ellen remembers just how much work there is waiting for her at home, and how soon it's due. A five-thousand-word profile of no-hoper GOP hopeful Ratt Atkinson. To be extracted from a mountain of notes, interviews and archive material spread out all over her desk.

For Monday morning.

The cab pulls up. She hesitates, but gets in.

You always get in.

Anyway, *Ratt* Atkinson? That kills her every time she hears it, or has to write it, which today and tomorrow will be plenty.

The article is one of an informal series she's doing for *Parallax* magazine on the degraded nature of the modern presidential bid. It started with a bang, that piece she wrote with Jimmy Gilroy a while back on the John Rundle fiasco. Since then she's covered a couple of other crash-and-burn candidates . . . but really, at this stage, is the idea wearing a little thin?

She's just not sure.

The cab turns left at Ninetieth and heads for the park.

The point is, Ratt Atkinson, rock-solid middle-aged white-guy former governor of Ohio, hasn't crashed or burned yet, and Ellen figures he won't have to bother. His name will do it for him. Sooner or later. It'll have to.

Campaigns have stumbled on less.

But is there a *story* in it?

The cab cruises through the park, comes out at Seventy-ninth and heads down Fifth. Ellen gets out at Sixty-eighth.

As expected, the crime scene is a disappointment, yellow tape and surly cops blocking access at every approach. But also as expected, there is a mild carnival atmosphere on the periphery, as joggers, passersby and tourists congregate in small improvised groups to stare and make comments – and more often than not out loud, some of them cranky, others smart-alecky, little vocal tweets posted on the thickening early afternoon air. There are a couple of OBU trucks lined along Fifth, and one camera crew can be seen wandering aimlessly around, looking – Ellen supposes – for a decent vantage point.

They're too late, of course.

Ellen wanders aimlessly herself for a bit. She takes out her phone and does a quick check. A lot of actual tweets are being posted about Jeff Gale. This isn't surprising, though. A murder in Central Park would be pretty unusual in itself these days, but add in a high-profile victim and you've got yourself an instant trend. Ellen thinks about it. The only information out there is that Gale was jogging, and that he was shot.

She looks around.

But why would anyone shoot a jogger? Not for their iPod. Not even for their wallet. Not in Central Park. Not these days.

Not *shoot* them.

So who did do it, and why?

Unless there's a quick explanation forthcoming, this is a story that's going to burn up a serious amount of media space in the next few days. There'll be intense speculation about it, because Northwood Leffingwell is a Wall Street behemoth, one of the Too Big to Fail brigade. But even if it turns out that where Jeff Gale worked had nothing to do with why he got killed, it's inevitable that where he worked will form a significant part of the narrative.

Anyway.

It already has.

Ellen checks the time on her phone.

Ratt fucking Atkinson.

It just annoys her that *this* feels like a real story, and that she's right here, where it happened, but that for all she can do about it she might as well be one of those French tourists over there. Ellen's not a beat reporter, and hasn't been for many years. What she specialises in these days is longer, slow-burn investigative pieces, and mainly for *Parallax*. She's also quite well known, and has a bit of a reputation, built up over years, as a polemical, potty-mouthed, uncooperative *bitch*. So even if she wanted to report on this, it's unlikely that anyone – cop, city official, fellow hack – would talk to her.

But anyway, report on what? The story's over. She's wasting her time. Even that camera crew there seem resigned to it and are setting up a generic shot now – East Drive in the background, steady stream of joggers, fine, but not one of them laid out dead on the asphalt.

Ellen looks at her phone again. She could make it over to Central Park West, pick up a cab and be home in fifteen, twenty minutes.

She glances around one last time, then starts walking. But at about the five-yard point someone calls out, 'Hey, wait up.'

She turns back.

'Ellen?'

A guy is walking towards her, early thirties, overcoat, shades, mop of curly hair. Could be anyone. She's actually pretty bad on people – faces, names – unless it's someone directly related to whatever she's working on at the time.

'Yeah?'

The guy arrives, hand extended. 'Ellen, how are you?' Sensing her hesitation, he adds, 'Val Brady.'

Oh.

Yeah.

The reason she didn't recognise him straight away, apart from the fact that they haven't met in a while, is that he's one of the few journalists she hasn't ended up fighting with – this guy, and Jimmy Gilroy, and maybe one or two others. It's the ones she doesn't get on with that she tends to remember.

'Val. What's up?'

He nods his head back in the direction of the cordoned-off area. 'Just another day at the office. You?'

'No. I'm . . . I'm just passing. I heard, though.'

'Pretty wild, isn't it?'

Val Brady is a reporter for the *New York Times*, and a fairly reliable one. A couple of years ago they shared information on a story, some big pharma-related thing, as she remembers. He was scrupulous about it, careful, didn't let his ego bleed into the proceedings.

She liked him.

'Yeah. Any clue about what happened?'

Brady takes off his shades. He looks around, then looks back at Ellen. 'He was shot at point-blank range, in the forehead. They didn't take his wallet, which apparently had a couple of hundred bucks in it, or his iPod. And no witnesses.' He points up at the apartment buildings on Fifth. 'The cops are going to check over there, the high floors, see if anyone was looking out of their window. But given the angle and stuff it's a long shot.'

Ellen considers this. 'Surveillance cameras?'

Brady shakes his head. 'There are a few in the park, but not back there, and they're mainly used for detecting after-hours activity.'

'What about the bigger picture, is there anything known to be going on, I mean with Northwood, or . . . ?' She laughs. 'Jesus, listen to me. I sound like your editor. Sorry.'

'You're fine. It's an obvious question. And to answer it, no, not that I'm aware of, not yet, anyway.' He pauses, and fiddles for a bit with his shades. 'So, Ellen, what are *you* up to these days?'

She explains. Presidential candidates and why so many of them tend to implode.

'OK, yeah. I read that piece you did on John Rundle a while

back, the whole Congo thing, the stuff with his brother. It was amazing.'

Ellen grunts. 'It was pretty spectacular material, you have to admit. Though I kind of feel like I'm scraping the bottom of the barrel now with Ratt Atkinson.'

Brady laughs. '*Ratt*. Jesus.'

'I know.' Ellen pauses. 'I actually came down here because it felt like there might be some . . . action. Is that pathetic?'

'No, but are you sure you're remembering what it's like to be a news reporter? Real action is pretty hard to come by. It's usually like this.' He indicates behind him. 'The afters, yellow tape, endless waiting around.'

Ellen nods. 'Sure. Of course. I remember.' But still. 'Sometimes it's about instinct. You get a hard-on for a story and . . . I don't know.'

Brady smiles. 'A hard-on, huh? Nice. Well, let me look into it, ask around, and if anything interesting shows up, why don't I give you a call?'

Is he hitting on her? She doesn't think so. And she's hardly his type. Small and lean, with shortish dark hair, Ellen doesn't really think of herself as anyone's *type*. But as if to clarify matters, he holds up his hands. 'Look, Ellen, I'm a big admirer of yours, have been for years. All those pieces for *Rolling Stone* and *Wired* and *The Nation*, and then your stuff for *Parallax*? I mean . . . shit.'

It's easy for Ellen to forget that her reputation isn't all bad, that it can sometimes extend beyond a roll call of character defects, that she *has* a body of work behind her, and stuff that someone like Val Brady here might actually hold in high regard.

'OK,' she says, going with it, 'thanks.'

In the cab a while later, she tries to do a little rearranging in her head. Ratt Atkinson she can dispose of today, at a push. It's not a complicated story, all the details have already been fact-checked, and it'll tell itself, really.

That'll give her time tomorrow to read up on Jeff Gale.

And on Northwood Leffingwell.

She looks out the window of the cab, Amsterdam Avenue flickering past, and realises something.

It's been a while, but she's excited.

2

'So, how *is* the old man?'

Craig Howley watches John Kemp wince a little as he says this, but there's really no other way for him to put it.

They both know what he's asking.

Howley looks around, surveys the room. At least they're not talking about Jeff Gale any more. 'He's fine, you know. Not as young as he used to be. It's nothing specific, just a gradual . . .' He pauses, catching himself up. 'He's fine.'

'Yeah.'

James Vaughan. Chairman of the Oberon Capital Group. Eighty-four years old, born a week before the Crash. Which turned out to be a good omen actually, at least as far as his old man was concerned, because later that very week the same William J. Vaughan shorted a pool of stocks on a downtick and cleared over a hundred million dollars.

All these years later and what's changed?

'He hasn't stopped working or anything,' Howley says.

'Oh sure, of course.' Kemp has a knowing look on his face. 'Guess he wants to go out with his boots on.'

'No, but really, John, I mean it.' An edge in Howley's voice now. 'He's still chairman and CEO. He's still running things.'

Kemp nods along, but doesn't pursue it. It's a cocktail party, Saturday evening, East Hampton.

There's a time and a place.

Which is just as well, Howley thinks. Because it's bad enough to have a little *WSJ* prick like John Kemp fishing for gossip about Jimmy Vaughan, but here? With *these* people?

He moves along, glass in hand, mingling. Never his strong suit. Jessica is working the other side of the room, tireless as ever in promoting her latest gala benefit for the Kurtzmann Foundation. Howley admires the ease with which she carries herself in any setting. Although he's now the number two at Oberon, and thus one of the top financial dogs in attendance this evening, he still considers himself more of a Pentagon guy than a Wall Street guy. He could effectively buy and sell half of the people here, but he doesn't feel like he's one of them.

At the same time, and given the rumours about Vaughan's health, he knows that the question of who will ultimately take over at Oberon is one of the hot topics of the moment.

And that everyone assumes it's him. Or at least assumes that *he* assumes it's him.

Which he does.

So he has to be careful what he says, and to whom.

Because with Jimmy Vaughan you don't ever assume anything. You just keep working, making connections, cutting deals, bringing it home.

Naturally enough, Howley does hope it's him. Being brought in last year as COO is one good indicator, and a very clear public endorsement, but what he believes should be an even more reliable indicator is his actual working relationship with Vaughan. Complex and of many years' standing, it's a relationship that has benefited both of them hugely, a recent example being that thanaxite supply chain they set up out of Afghanistan. It's been a cordial relationship, too, and generally free of bullshit, which Howley puts down to the fact that he's not intimidated by Vaughan, and never has been.

'Craig.'

Howley turns.

'Terry.' Hasselbach. Another little prick, hedge fund guy. 'How are you?'

'I'm good, yo.'

Howley groans silently, covers it with a smile. He's twenty-five years older than this guy, just as Jimmy Vaughan is twenty-five years older than him. Which isn't a problem, not in relation to Vaughan, he doesn't think about it, but guys like this? Buffed, mouthy Adderall-heads, still in their early or mid-thirties . . . he doesn't know, what is it? Anyway, they get talking – stock picks, dream deals – and within minutes two or three others have joined in.

And Howley realises something.

For all their cockiness and walls of money, these guys are looking to *him* as some kind of an oracle. It's clearly the Vaughan factor, a sprinkle of stardust from the old man – who you don't let down, by the way. He drops you into the number two position at Oberon, you'd better *believe* you're some kind of a fucking oracle – believe it and behave accordingly. At the Pentagon, it was a little different. There was always room for ambivalence, room for creative ambiguity. And expectations were different as well, less concrete, less performance-driven. In private equity you either make money or you lose it, and that's it.

Who has the stones, who doesn't.

'Where am *I* looking?' he says, and tilts his head to one side. 'Well, I'll tell you one area, it's not the only one, but . . . health

23

care.' This gets a muted response from the hedgies. What, no inside track on the latest DARPA-funded robotics program or new advanced precision-kill weapons system? Apparently not. Howley raises his glass to his lips, taking his time. Then, 'Thirty years ago you know how much of our GDP was devoted to health care? Three per cent. Now it's heading for twenty. Think about it. You've got a whole generation of baby boomers coming to retirement age, and remember' – he waves his left hand around, to take in the room, the beachfront, the Hamptons – 'this is the wealthiest generation of people we've ever seen, not just in US history but in the history of the entire fucking *world*. So you think they'll spare any expense when it comes to their artificial hips and knees and whatever? When it comes to, I don't know, stem cell therapies and assisted living technologies? No? Me neither. It'll be whatever's required, and that's going to mean more and more of GDP getting channelled into health care.' Everyone nodding now. 'So in *my* view, over the next ten, fifteen years, investments in the sector will do pretty well.'

This isn't some big secret or anything, but coming from *him*, with his signature delivery – conspiratorial, almost whispered – it very much sounds like one. It's certainly enough to please the assembled pack.

Howley glances over at Jessica. She's deep in conversation with some chunky, hatchet-faced woman he doesn't recognise. A member of the board of trustees, no doubt, or the wife of a principal donor. He looks at his watch. He'd like to get out of here soon.

'So, Craig,' Terry Hasselbach says, 'what's this I keep hearing about an IPO?'

Howley turns and glares at him. The IPO story isn't a big

secret either, far from it, there's been plenty of speculation about Oberon going public in recent days – but it's not something he's willing to discuss, not with these guys.

He peers into his glass and swirls what's left in it around. 'Speaking of rumours, Terry,' he says, looking up, 'did I read somewhere lately that you were a nosy little cocksucker?'

No one reacts to this for a moment.

Howley keeps looking at him.

Then Terry Hasselbach laughs. It's a weasely laugh, but it breaks the tension. To move things on, someone brings up Jeff Gale.

Again.

The subject has been unavoidable all day.

'They're saying he might have been into some mob guys for –'

'Oh what, gambling debts? Get out of here. That's ridiculous.'

'No, that it was an escort thing, some agency, and that after Spitzer and all they didn't want to lose –'

'No way. Besides, a mob hit in Central Park? Fuhgeddaboudit.'

Everyone laughs.

Except Howley, who's looking at his watch again. He knew Jeff Gale – not well, but he knew him, saw how the man operated, could read him like a book, read all his moves. Gambling and escorts? It's about as far as you could get from a plausible explanation for this.

That's what bothers him, the seeming randomness of it, the casualness.

He glances across the room and catches Jessica's eye.

Ten minutes later they're in the car and on the way to dinner at Mircof's in East Quogue.

*

Sitting alone in a booth at Dave's Bar & Grill, Frank Bishop sips his second Stoli. It usually takes more than one for that exquisite hot-coals-in-the-belly sensation to hit, but it's coming now, he can feel it.

Slowly, he takes another sip.

Blue. Icy. Viscous.

This is the sweet spot, all right, portal to a brief sun-kissed season of illumination and understanding. It won't last very long, a few minutes at most, but that's fine. In a while he'll order some food – chicken, fries, plenty of carbs, a club soda – because if he orders a third Stoli he'll only order a fourth and then a fifth and that'll be it for the night. He won't eat and he'll get stupid and sloppy. He'll end up feeling like shit and be hungover all day tomorrow. Then, before he knows it, it'll be Monday morning again and *he'll be back at work*.

For now, though, it's Saturday evening.

He holds up his glass of filmy liquid.

To the LudeX console upgrade, and a long, strange day at Winterbrook Mall.

He takes a sip.

Frank used to be an architect.

It was up to a couple of years ago, and *for* a couple of decades, designing office buildings and airport terminals, frozen music, he ate, drank and slept the stuff. Worked for Belmont, McCann Associates and had an office in Manhattan. But now?

Now he manages an electronics store in a second-tier mall in upstate New York.

WTF.

It's not as if he's the only one, though. A dozen others were let go at the same time, and most of *them*, as far as he knows, are struggling. The younger ones, still in their twenties, either take it on the chin and go off in an entirely different direction, or they obsessively hone their résumés and send them out to anyone they've ever come into contact with, co-workers, class-mates, contractors, people they meet on fucking Facebook. The older ones, like Frank, mid-forties and beyond, either manage to hang on by trading their experience and skills for much reduced salaries, or they take anything at all, whatever they can get, retail, driving a cab – it doesn't matter, really (ex-cept for the serious damage this will do to their marketability if they ever want to get back in the game). Frank is one of these and he figures the damage is already done. The idea of getting back in the game is remote to him anyway, a little intimidating even.

This job he got as a favour. It was through an old connection, a middle-management guy in Paloma he dealt with when Bel-mont, McCann were doing their new regional headquarters over in Hartford. And he only got it because it was Winter-brook Mall. If it'd been anywhere else, chances are he wouldn't have been hired. Like Dave's Bar & Grill, which is beside it, Winterbrook Mall is a relic of the 1980s, morning in Mahopac, and will very probably not survive this recession. In fact, it's hard to know what's keeping the place afloat right now. It's vast, but more often than not deserted, with a distinctly creepy feel to it, especially at night when you could imagine B-movie zombies emerging from behind the fake backdrops of some of the empty retail spaces to search for stragglers and lost shoppers. However, Winterbrook's biggest problem lies two miles down the road in the shape of the sparkling and relatively new Oak Valley Plaza Outlets Center.

That's where it'd make sense for Paloma to have their store, but if they did, Frank would be out of work.

He looks into his glass.

The truth is, he's hanging on by a thread here. There are over eight hundred Paloma stores across the country, and this is probably the only one he'd be able to hold down a job in. And that's because – with the exception of today – it's probably the only one that's empty most of the time.

Which suits Frank just fine.

Not because he can't do the job, or he's lazy, it's just that dealing with people, customers, members of the public . . . he's not cut out for it. Heavier footfall than the store gets and he'd more than likely crack up. It might take a while, a few weeks, a month or two, but he wouldn't last – there'd be an incident with someone out on the floor, he'd raise his voice, they'd file a complaint, and who'd end up with their second pink slip in as many years?

For the moment, though, this position he's got at ghostly, creepy Winterbrook Mall seems secure enough.

Which is a big relief.

He finishes the drink and orders some food.

Because as long as he's able to meet his basic financial obligations, as long as he's able to –

Phone.

Vibrating in his pocket.

He pulls it out and looks at it. *Lizzie*. Pretty much on cue. 'Hi there.'

'Hey Dad.'

Tone alert.

'You OK?'

'Yeah, I'm . . . I'm fine.'

Lizzie's at Atherton and even though she got a scholarship it's still costing him a fortune. She wants to be a web . . . something, he can't remember what exactly. He finds it hard to keep up, to stay in the loop, especially the tech loop. When she was starting out, he was all over it, but that was two years ago.

'So . . . what's happening?'

'Not a whole lot. I just wanted to hear your voice.'

Frank looks up, slowly, and out over the dusty, wood-panelled expanse of Dave's Bar & Grill.

Hear my voice?

'You can hear my voice any time you want, sweetheart, you know that.'

He swallows. Was that the right thing to say? Lizzie is extremely smart, but she's hard work sometimes, and you have to know what you're doing. When she was small, he and Deb had to choose their moments with her. She could be charming, too, of course, and some of the stuff she came out with would blow your socks off. Unfortunately, Lizzie's teenage years are a bit of a blur to Frank, because after the divorce he burrowed down and didn't do much else besides work. Then, a year or so before he was laid off, things changed again, and he started making more of an effort to see both her and John. It seemed like a new phase, a new era – college looming, Deb married to someone else, their early lives together as a family in the house in Carroll

Gardens receding like a brittle dream. Lizzie hadn't changed, though, not really, and her renewed presence in his life, her occasional attentions – emails, phone calls – sustained him in a way that he hadn't expected.

'I know, Dad.'

Silence.

Well, at least *that's* settled.

'So,' he says, trying again. 'Saturday night. What are you up to?' But why does he want to know *that*? Doesn't he worry enough about her as it is? With nothing at all to go on? Now he's fishing for *ammo*?

'No plans. Just working. I've got a paper due.'

He'll settle for that. Moving his empty glass around the table like a chess piece, he proceeds to tell her about his day, the LudeX upgrade, the early torrent of excited geeks, the subsequent stream of disappointed ones. Trying to make it funny. But at a certain point he realises she's not laughing, and then guesses she's probably not even smiling. Which is when he remembers that Lizzie hates hearing about his job. It freaks her out. She thinks of her old man as an architect who works in Manhattan, not as some loser sales guy in a suburban mall. Either that or she's racked with guilt about what he has to do to keep her and her brother in their good schools.

Actually, he doesn't know what she thinks. They've never really talked about it. It's what he imagines she thinks, what *he'd* think.

What he *thinks*.

'Have you heard from John?' he asks, interrupting himself, changing the subject. John's at grad school in California doing a master's in genetics and microbiology and only surfaces every few months for a little air.

'Yeah, I spoke to him last week. He's good. Still seems to be with that German girl, Claudia, is it? They'll be getting married before you know it and moving to Frankfurt or Berlin or someplace. You up for some German-speaking grandkids?'

This is news to Frank, though it makes sense. John was always the quiet one, straight as an arrow. 'Sure. Why not? Though it's a pity he didn't hook up with someone Spanish or Italian. Better food and weather.' Stupid joke. He pauses. 'There's the Bauhaus stuff, I suppose. Mies van der Rohe and Walter Gropius, and Le Corbusier, although I think Le Corbusier was Swiss.' He's rambling here. He stops. In the silence that follows there's a strange –

'Lizzie?'

Nothing for a second, and then, 'Yep.' But it's more of a gulp. She's *crying*.

'Lizzie? What is it?'

Out of the corner of his eye, Frank sees the waitress approaching with a tray. He doesn't look at her directly but holds up a hand, to wave her away.

'Lizzie? Sweetheart. What is it?'

He holds his breath, to hear better.

'Oh, it's nothing... I'm just...' She snuffles loudly and clears her throat. 'You know.'

Does he? He looks at his watch. He could be up there in two hours. 'Are you OK?'

'I'm fine, just a stupid hormonal bitch.' More recovery noises. 'I'm sorry, Dad.'

'Oh, Lizzie, *don't*...'

Even though she's not there – in front of him, physically –

Frank's need to reach out for her right now and hold her is overwhelming. It even makes him feel a little sick. Any display of vulnerability on Lizzie's part has always cut through him like a knife.

When she was four years old, or maybe five, she –

Jesus, Frank.

'Lizzie, do you want me to come up there?' he says. 'I could easily make it in a –'

'No, Dad. Come *on*.' She's laughing now, or at least pretending to.

And so it goes.

Later, driving along the back roads to where he's renting an apartment near West Mahopac, Frank replays the conversation in his head, looking out for clues, a reason, something to explain why Lizzie was so upset. He spins various theories out, elaborate ones, simple ones, but in the end he just doesn't know.

And, sadly – experience tells him – he probably never will.

*

All through the afternoon and early evening Ellen Dorsey works on the Ratt Atkinson profile, trawling through his eight-year gubernatorial record and clacking out three and a half thousand words of boilerplate magazine prose. At about nine o'clock she decides she's had enough, that she can do the rest tomorrow. She then switches her focus to the Jeff Gale story. She's had the TV on in the background the whole time and for the last hour or so has been checking Twitter – and semi-psychotically, every three or four minutes at least. But there don't seem to be any developments, none that she can see from the screen in the corner of her living room at any rate. On Twitter, predictably, there's plenty of the usual idiotic comment and meaningless bile to keep things ticking over.

She flicks around a few of the news websites, but it's the same everywhere.

TOP BANKER SHOT IN CENTRAL PARK.

That's it, no details, no explanations, no theories even.

The thing about instant news is that it's, well, *instant* . . . but nowhere near fast enough. It's addictive, but you're never satisfied. Ellen works hard at what she does – but the inescapable fact here is that she works for a monthly publication.

A periodical.

Both of which terms sound like Victorian euphemisms for something else entirely.

Parallax magazine has been around for more than forty years and has a reputation – it's known for its investigative reporting, its long-form pieces and its uncompromising, ballsy attitude. Max Daitch, the latest in a long line of the magazine's fearless editors, and the one Ellen has mostly worked with, is indeed fearless, but even though he's young – younger than she is by three or four years – he's been heard to quote H. L. Mencken and is really just a couple of sandwiches short of wearing a bowtie. Which means that her habits in recent years have been shaped by this traditionalist, analogue regime, even though her instincts remain resolutely progressive and digital. Her MO for *Parallax*, for example, has been to burrow, slowly, patiently, sifting through mountains of information with a view to building a 'case'. But these days, no longer in her thirties, what she'd prefer to be doing, and got to do briefly with Jimmy Gilroy back when the John Rundle story broke – and felt she was maybe *trying* to do earlier today when she went down to Central Park – is identify a breaking story . . . find a curve, get out ahead of it and stay there.

A change of pace.

You can't force it, though.

She tidies her desk for a few minutes, rearranging stuff and clearing a little space. Then she sits back, puts her feet on the desk and phones her sister. Michelle lives in a beautiful split-level colonial in the suburbs of Philadelphia, is married to the financial controller of a fair-trade import company and has two exceptionally bright kids. Which is fine, for Michelle . . . but the thing is, every once in a while Ellen needs a vicarious *hit* of all this, of the supposed normality of her sister's domestic setup, so she gets Michelle on the phone and pumps her for information, stuff about the house, about her and Dan, about the kids – what they're doing at school, what medications they're on, how many boxes in the pages of the DSM they're currently ticking. But when Michelle tries to turn the tables on big sis, Ellen clams up, declaring same old, same old.

Same apartment, same obsessive workload.

Same lack of social skills, same monthly subscription to *Bad Mood* magazine.

It's become a routine, but a curiously comforting one.

After she gets off the phone with Michelle, Ellen orders up Thai food. While she's waiting, she grabs the remote and surfs around the cable news channels. The only thing giving the Jeff Gale story a run for its money today, in terms of high-end prurience, is the Connie Carillo murder trial. On at the moment, some MSNBC talking head is reviewing the week's evidence. 'Look, it's simple,' he's saying, 'she clearly needs a lifeline, because even though no motive has been established yet, she just, I don't know, *radiates* guilt . . .'

The *she* here is Constance 'Connie' Carillo, daughter of Senator Eugene Pendleton and ex-wife of mob boss Ricky 'Icepick' Carillo. A powerful soprano, Connie was about to make her debut at the Met in *Salome* when her husband of the time, investment banker Howard Meeker, was found naked on the kitchen floor of their Upper East Side apartment with a carving knife stuck in his chest. Connie was immediately charged with his murder, and since the trial started a couple of weeks ago, the court proceedings have been broadcast live every day, with updates, highlights, commentary and wall-to-wall analysis. In media terms, it's been pretty much full-spectrum dominance.

But this being a Saturday there's something of a vacuum to fill.

So Jeff Gale's timing couldn't have been better.

And although Ellen, like most people, has been following the trial pretty closely, she has no difficulty now in dropping it for *this*. She presses the mute button and throws the remote onto the sofa. She goes back to her desk and starts digging up anything she can find on the 'gunned-down' banker.

As she reads, she jots some notes on a loose sheet of graph paper.

Born in Carthage, North Carolina, forty-seven years ago, Jeff Gale majored in psychology and economics at NCSU and then got an MBA at Harvard Business School before going on to do stints at Morgan Stanley and Wells Fargo. After five years at Citigroup he was appointed vice president of the New

York Federal Reserve, and then, just in time to see the company clock up losses of nearly $4.2 billion, he took over as CEO of Northwood Leffingwell. Amid embarrassing lawsuits over the bank's foreclosure practices, as well as SEC claims that statements he made to Congress may have misrepresented Northwood's health, Gale's tenure at the bank was not an easy one. More recently, however, things seemed to be looking up, with the bank's share price finally crawling out of the single digits.

Gale was married and had two teenage daughters. A *Forbes* profile describes him as obsessive and detail-oriented. Standard stuff, then, and fairly tedious, but it's a brand of tedium that Ellen has grown used to over the years. It's part of her stock-in-trade – wading through data and looking for patterns, glitches, the one thing no one else sees.

She goes through some photos of Gale now, on Google Images, but doesn't see anything of any interest at all, apart from the fact that he was about five ten, pale and balding.

She looks over at the TV. They keep going back to the crime scene in Central Park, recycling the few precious, banal facts that are known about the case. Ellen finds all of this frustrating. If she were working on the story herself – for a paper, say, like Val Brady is – what would she be doing now? Would she be on the phone to this or that contact? Would she be camped outside Jeff Gale's house?

Maybe.

But if so, wouldn't she need a little more to work with, a lead, something concrete?

When the food arrives, Ellen gets a beer from the fridge and sets up at the kitchen table.

She eats in silence, staring over at her desk.

Something bugging her.

What is it?

Ever since she did that piece on John Rundle with Jimmy Gilroy a year and a half ago, nothing has been the same. He called her up out of the blue one afternoon, this diffident, inexperienced Irish journalist, and within a couple of days she was involved in the fastest-moving, most exciting story she'd ever worked on. Senator John Rundle, sniffing out the possibility of a party presidential nomination, was found to have lied about a trip he made to the Congo on behalf of his brother, Clark, CEO of engineering giant BRX – a trip on which a private security contractor just happened to go postal in a tiny village and massacre nine people. As if that wasn't enough, Clark Rundle was subsequently indicted for murdering the owner of the private security company *by bashing the man's brains in with a fucking laptop*.

She and Gilroy led on every aspect of the story, scooping all other news outlets, and then drawing the whole thing neatly together for the next issue of *Parallax*. It was a thrilling time in her professional life, a definite high point, but these days she can't shake off the suspicion, even the fear, that she was perceived to have gone too far – and that she'll never be permitted to go that far again.

Why, and by whom, remains a mystery, but she's been around long enough to know that certain people just don't like people like *her*. Over the years she's been harassed, followed and offered money and had her various accounts hacked into. This feels different, though, more subtle. Recession notwithstanding, *Parallax* has lost a *lot* of advertising revenue recently, and for his part Max Daitch hasn't seemed quite as fearless as he once did. Maybe it's her imagination, maybe not, but the atmosphere around the office has had a weirdly muted feel of late.

As for Jimmy Gilroy, Ellen doesn't know. He sort of disappeared *into* the story in a way she's rarely seen. He was of the opinion that what they did together only scratched the surface, and from what she understands he has spent the last eighteen months immersed in a follow-up piece, excavating the background to the original story, but sinking ever deeper into it, travelling to London, Paris and the Congo.

Getting lost, chasing ghosts.

She pushes the remainder of her food aside and finishes what's left of the beer.

But does she envy him this for some reason? Maybe. She certainly envies someone *something*. What that is, or might be, exactly, she doesn't know. On consideration, though – and looking over at her desk again – she knows it probably isn't the Jeff Gale story.

Or shouldn't be.

And as if to confirm this, her phone rings.

She picks it up and looks at the display.

Val Brady.

She hesitates, but lets it ring out. Then she waits for a moment and checks to see if he's left a message.

He has. 'Hi, Ellen, Val Brady here. Er . . . nothing really, I just thought I'd check in with you, seeing as how we were, you know . . . talking today. Funny thing about this story, it's . . . it's *flat*, there's nothing there. I've talked to a lot of people since this morning, associates of Gale's, people who knew him well, people who could even be classed as adversaries of his, in a business sense, but it all comes across as so fucking *boring*, you know? He does, they do, that whole world. I mean, these people don't go around shooting each other, that's for sure. So maybe it was just one of those random things.' He pauses. Ellen looks over at the window, out at the darkening, orange-washed street. 'Hey,' Brady goes on, 'I just feel bad that that hard-on of yours had to go to waste, you know. Maybe next time.' Another pause, during which she can feel the recoil from his brain exploding. 'Listen, Ellen' – this quickly – 'I'll talk to you again, OK? Take it easy.'

Poor bastard, he couldn't resist it. *Or* make it sound like he was one of the boys.

But –

Something weird.

She walks over to the window and stands there looking down, thinking . . . what if he's wrong? What if he's wrong about all of it?

His approach, his conclusion.

Some people walk by on the other side of the street, huddled into their coats, laughing.

A yellow cab passes.

What was it he said . . . the story was flat and they were all so boring?

And then it hits her.

Of course.

None of that is the *point*, is it?

She turns back around and glances at the TV, where for the hundredth time today they're showing the scene down in Central Park – the yellow tape, the guys in baggy white suits, the photographers, the media pack, the onlookers.

That's the point.

She walks towards the corner of the room, staring directly now at what's on the screen.

Calculating . . . extrapolating.

And suddenly she's sure. It's as real as a headache.

This is going to happen again.

3

If Alice Harvill Holland weren't iced right now on Triburbazine, this dinner would be a lot less bearable than it is. She hasn't been able to eat, though. Not properly, anyway. She's had a few morsels, a pickled beet, some of the smoked yucca, a fried plantain, but that's all. And it's such a shame, because the food here at Bra is usually so exquisite. She can't drink, either. With Triburbazine you absolutely can't drink.

Unless, of course, that is, you'd prefer to. Before slipping into a coma.

And a nice one . . . deep, thick, lasting.

To sleep, perchance to dream.

She picks up her Veen.

But you make your choices.

She looks over at Bob. He's talking nonstop, and has been since this morning when the news broke. Jeff Gale this, Jeff Gale that and Jeff Gale the goddamn other thing.

She knows it's all very shocking, but right now 'shocking' is a bizarrely relative term.

The other two – their guests, the Spellmans – are happy to let the great Bob Holland dominate the conversation. Toby Spellman is a wuss in any case, and Lynn is clearly afraid of Alice, won't even look at her.

So the dynamic at the table isn't great.

'He was going to turn things around for Northwood,' Bob

is saying, 'no doubt about it, it was just a question of time.' He forks a roasted scallop into his mouth and chews, impatient to go on talking. 'He'd gotten all of that SEC shit behind him, the hearings were over and most of the MUI documentation had been shredded. Far as I could see it was a clean slate going forward.' He shakes his head. 'Absolutely tragic.'

Alice glances at Lynn. She's a brittle creature, pretty in a grotesque sort of way. Trying too hard, and yet not trying hard enough. What is she, thirty-six, thirty-seven? Wait till she hits fifty. If she makes it that far.

Alice is fifty-two.

Unbidden, an image floats into her mind of Lynn stretched out naked on a marble slab, writhing, all pale and skinny. It's not a sexual image. God forbid. More like something cold and scientific, a specimen, a bacterium wriggling in a Petri dish.

She exhales loudly.

Bob is still talking.

More food arrives.

A cigarette would be nice at this point. Pity she doesn't smoke.

'Yeah, but listen, Toby, it's simple.' Bob raises an index finger. 'Profit outsourcing, *that's* the key to this thing, always has been. Low overseas tax rates . . .'

And on it goes.

Pork belly, snapper, mango, coffee.

People gliding past, greetings from across the room, fluttering fingers, flushed faces. Music that's barely identifiable as music, more like some chilly blue vapour rippling down her spine.

Without warning, Lynn turns to look at her, wide-eyed,

smile sharp as a blade.

'Alice,' she says softly, 'are you OK?'

Oh yes.

Alice nodding it, *oh yes, oh yes.*

Eventually, the dinner draws to a close. They get up to leave, are given their coats, shuffle out onto the broad, breezy expanse of Columbus Avenue. And here, standing under the sidewalk canopy, waiting for their car to pull up, and gazing south over a bobbing river of yellow cabs to an elegant redbrick apartment building on the other side of the avenue, Alice Harvill Holland comes to a curious realisation. Dr Engdahl prescribed her the Triburbazine for anxiety and nausea, both of which she's been suffering from lately, and on what has seemed like an industrial scale – but it's as if he knew she'd need something even stronger, somehow knew she'd need more protection . . . the pharmaceutical equivalent, say, of Kevlar, or a plutonium suit, or just plain cotton wool, but miles and miles of it, wrapped around her, endlessly, soundlessly, layer after layer after layer.

But why? For what?

For *this*.

She sees it all in slow motion, and doesn't move a muscle, doesn't feel her heart rate increase by a single beat, doesn't *flinch*. The two figures rush forward, one raising a gloved hand and pointing it at her husband's head, the other efficiently elbowing Toby Spellman in the abdomen and pushing him to the ground.

Lynn's hysterical scream and the gunshot come in the same moment. The scream lasts a good bit longer, though – enough to soundtrack the violent sideways lurch of Bob's head, the ripping apart of his face, his backwards collapse on to the sidewalk and the rapid retreat down the block, through the panicking, parting crowds, of the two . . .

The two . . . what's the word?

Perps.

Yes, that's it.

She looks around, speckles of blood everywhere now, on the sidewalk, on her own dress, even on Lynn's contorted face, a part of Alice wondering if some of this isn't maybe more than blood, if it isn't lumpier, gristlier, if some of this isn't, in fact, tissue from Bob's brain.

And the man had a serious brain. When they met, over twelve years ago, he was day-trading in his shorts from the apartment he'd lived in with his first wife – who left him *because* he was day-trading, and to the exclusion of all else. It took him a few years, but he made over twenty million dollars at it, partnering up with some equity guys and then starting his own shop.

The rest is history.

They didn't call him Exponential Bob for nothing.

But here, tonight, that's all over. His second wife gazes out from under the canopy of a restaurant on Columbus Avenue, and it's quite a scene . . . Bob dead on the sidewalk, Toby Spellman crouched down next to him, Lynn Spellman having a sort of epileptic fit while still standing . . . Alice herself frozen, like a model, posing for a photo long after the photographer has gone.

All around her now the nighttime colours and textures of the city are stretching, and in every direction, like pizza dough or chewing gum. There are sirens, too, rising, piercing, closing in. But a few moments later, when the police arrive, something happens. The adrenalin in Alice's body kicks in, *digs* in, starts going to work on what's left of the Triburbazine.

'I'm Detective Brogan,' she hears a voice saying. 'With the NYPD.'

She turns and looks into the man's pasty Irish face.

'I understand this is your husband,' he says.

She nods.

'Can you tell me his name, who he is?'

'Yes.' She stares down at the body. 'His name is Bob Holland.' She starts to shake at last, and uncontrollably, her hands, her arms, even her voice. 'He works on Wall Street. He runs a . . . a hedge fund, Chambers Capital Management.'

Two

The photo dates from some time in the summer of 1972 and shows Richard Nixon, Bebe Rebozo, Adnan Khashoggi and a forty-three-year-old James Vaughan on a yacht in Key Biscayne, Florida. Jacqueline Prescott, who later went to work for Vaughan, can be seen in the background holding a cocktail shaker.

House of Vaughan (p. 59)

4

Most mornings, by the time he gets to the office, Craig Howley has already done about two hours' work. On Mondays, it's more likely to be three. This is because James Vaughan insists on kick-starting the week with an 8 a.m. meeting of senior investment and consulting staff to review all Oberon deals either in play or on the table. Howley will get up at five, therefore, and pore over any relevant files or documentation, and continue doing so through breakfast and in the back of the car on the way to the office. He believes it's essential to get ahead of any perceived curve. Vaughan himself seems able to pull this off instinctively, without any apparent effort – certainly without having to get up at 5 a.m. and probably without even having to look at a single quarterly report. Which is kind of annoying. But it's part of his thing, of what makes him the great Jimmy Vaughan.

On his way up in the elevator, Howley anticipates the usual sniping and goading that goes on at these meetings, as different people seek to impress Vaughan by championing or attacking this or that deal. He also anticipates a lot of speculation, some of it informed, most of it hopelessly uninformed, about what happened over the weekend. At first, the general perception – the story, if you will – was that the Jeff Gale killing in Central Park on Saturday morning was an isolated incident. It was a random shooting, and as such, for the victim's family, a terrible tragedy.

But the killing of Bob Holland twelve hours later on Columbus Avenue changed all of that.

Now, it seems, the two incidents are linked.

Now, as a result, this possible link has *become* the story.

As Howley emerges from the elevator car and into Oberon's steel and glass reception area, he is joined by Angela, his PA. Efficient and fiercely loyal, Angela is a brunette in her late forties who has worked for Howley since his early days at the Pentagon.

'Morning, Ange.'

'Mr Howley.'

They proceed towards the central conference room, and as Angela takes his coat and briefcase, she discreetly informs him that Mr Vaughan has just called in sick.

'What?'

'Just now. It was actually Ms Prescott I spoke to. She passed on the message.'

Jacqueline Prescott is Vaughan's PA, and has been since Angela herself was probably in kindergarten.

'What's the matter with him?'

'She didn't say exactly. Under the weather, something along those lines.'

In the twelve months he's been at Oberon, Howley doesn't think he's seen Vaughan miss a single one of these Monday morning sit-downs.

'Well, well.'

'Ms Prescott also said that *Mrs* Vaughan would like you to call her after the meeting.'

Howley nods.

Hmm.

What's that about?

A moment later, arriving at the door of the conference room, he feels a twinge of apprehension. It's strange. He's chaired a thousand meetings in his day. What's different about this one?

No point being coy. He knows what it is. He'll be the most senior guy in the room. Which also means that for the next sixty minutes or so he'll effectively *be* the Oberon Capital Group. And that's bound to ignite more succession talk, fuel the chatter he knows has been going on for some time.

Without Vaughan in the room, too, the dynamic will be different, it'll shift, and that's always unpredictable.

'Ange, get me a green tea, will you? Decaf.'

He's already had coffee and doesn't want to overdo it.

He steps inside. Everything in Oberon's main conference room – recently renovated according to specs laid down by Vaughan – is white, or on a spectrum, snow, ivory, alabaster, vanilla. The room's only saving grace, for Howley, and no doubt for the rest of them, is its spectacular view over Central Park.

'Morning, gentlemen.'

Clearly, word has spread that Vaughan won't be making it in today, and there's already a certain tension in the air. Seated around the table are the heads of the various industry-specific investment groups, as well as the CEO of Lyndon Consulting, a firm that works exclusively with Oberon to assess performance levels and devise rationalisation plans.

Howley gets straight into it, deciding to make no reference to Vaughan's absence. This sets a tone, and within a matter of minutes – and somewhat to his surprise – he feels a growing confidence. They discuss proposals to buy a Phoenix-based electric utility operator, a chain of British health food stores and an equity fund that manages $35.6 billion on behalf of two Swedish pension schemes. Views are expressed, relevant data is presented, figures are pored over. And Howley *listens*. He defers, solicits further information, and then outlines a provisional strategy for each of the deals. The whole thing goes very smoothly. Afterwards, as Howley is chatting with the CEO of Lyndon Consulting about 'poor old' Bob Holland, one of the group heads comes up to him and shakes his hand, doesn't say anything, just gives him a very firm handshake that seems to speak volumes. A few minutes later, two other group heads approach and ask him straight out what his position is on the IPO question.

This is a tricky one.

Filing for a public ticker is not necessarily the panacea that some people think it is. High-profile private equity firms have offered in the past, started well and then seen their share prices plummet. It'd also involve opening the company's books to public scrutiny, and as a Pentagon man that's something Howley would find particularly distasteful. In fact, he's pretty much *ad idem* with Vaughan on this, but at the same time he's aware that that's not what *these* guys want to hear.

'Look,' he says to them, just above a whisper, 'we're in a volatile phase here, so let's take it one step at a time, OK?'

This is sufficiently cryptic and conspiratorial to mean anything and everything – and, crucially, nothing. It seems to satisfy them.

When he gets to his office, Angela already has the call in to Meredith Vaughan. Personally, he'd have waited a bit, but he's not going to argue. Angela only ever acts in his best interests.

It's Meredith that's the problem.

He can't take her seriously. She's forty-six years younger than Vaughan – a man who's already been married five times – and yet she acts, and expects to be treated, like she's the First Lady. She's very attractive, he supposes, but that's hardly relevant.

'Meredith, hi.'

'Thanks for getting back to me, Craig.'

And then there's that awful come-hither, pussycat voice of hers.

'No problem. How's Jimmy?'

'He's not too bad, a little tired. I think he's got a mild chest infection or something.' She pauses. 'I wasn't going to let him go in today.'

'Of course not.' Howley is about to say something here about calling a doctor when he remembers that Vaughan sees a doctor every single day – his own personal physician, no less, a man employed to monitor a serious blood condition Vaughan has, along with anything else that might come up.

Such as a mild chest infection.

'But listen, Craig,' Meredith says. 'Jimmy wants you to come for dinner tonight. Is that OK?'

This is not a question. Or an invitation.

'Sure.'

'He just wants a quiet chat.'

Code for don't bring Jessica.

'Of course.' Howley knows the routine here. Vaughan needs to eat early. 'Seven good?'

'Perfect. We'll see you then.'

We?

After he puts the phone down, Howley looks at his desk, at a big report on it that he has to read for an upcoming symposium he's addressing on opportunities in the clean energy sector.

Wind turbines, solar power, shale gas.

He reaches for the report and skims through a few pages. He's distracted, though, and his eyes glaze over. He glances out the window and replays the meeting in his head.

It was subtle, not much you could put your finger on, but he was right – the dynamic here at Oberon HQ has indeed shifted.

*

Ellen Dorsey wakes up tired. Technically, she got plenty of sleep, but it wasn't the restorative kind, not by a long shot. It was more like eight hours of enhanced interrogation, but without any actual questions or clear notion of what her interrogators might have wanted her to reveal. It felt like one continuous garbled dream based on what she'd been doing over the previous sixteen hours – online research mainly, plus one or two brief phone calls (no more, solely because it was a Sunday) and a quick trip down to Bra on Columbus Avenue, with assiduous note-taking throughout, countless pages of them scrawled on loose sheets of graph paper.

She hadn't slept well on Saturday night either, partly due to this heightened sense she'd had of what she might wake up to. And when she did wake up to something, to the Bob Holland killing – the Sunday morning newsfeed already engorged with it – she felt there was no route back.

She felt this was *her* story.

However irrational that may have seemed. And impractical.

And now, on Monday morning, mainly impractical.

Because as a news item it's covered, everyone's on it – it's not like she's got a jump on the story. In addition to which the new issue of *Parallax* will be out on Thursday, so anything she might come up with in the next twenty-four or forty-eight hours would be too late anyway. And next month's issue, in news-cycle terms, may as well be a century away. There's always the online edition, but it's not exactly a premium site for breaking news.

Even if she had any to break.

Despite all of this, Ellen feels energised.

She emails in her copy for the Ratt Atkinson piece and then heads out for some breakfast. Over coffee she goes through the papers, where it's wall-to-wall Jeff and Bob. The pattern of coverage is pretty much the same everywhere, as it has been since yesterday morning – an outline of what happened, a profile of each victim and some editorialising. The outlines are sketchy, because not much seems to be known, the level of detail in the profiles depends on which paper it is, and the editorialising is remarkably consistent – all of them reaching more or less the same, and perhaps obvious, conclusion, i.e. that Wall Street bankers are being targeted by a group of highly organised domestic terrorists. A single reference is made to a months-old report detailing concerns within the intelligence community that al-Qaeda operatives in Yemen may have been planning attacks against certain leading Wall Street institutions.

And beyond that, just yet, no one seems willing to go.

No mention is made of any possible connection with the Occupy movement, and very little is said about what – or *who* – might be next. In the blogosphere, predictably, things are a little different. Convenient lists are drawn up, after-the-fact manifestos are posted and each-way conspiracy theories are for-mulated.

When she leaves the coffee shop, Ellen takes the subway to midtown, walks around for a bit with her earphones in, listen-ing, thinking, and then stops by the *Parallax* offices to see Max Daitch. With the new issue almost – but not quite – put to bed, the place is fairly hectic.

'Hi, Ellen,' Ricky, the features editor, says as he passes her in the hallway. 'Got the Ratt piece, thanks. Cutting it a bit fine, though, no?'

Ellen shrugs.

A deadline's a deadline.

In Max's office, there's a meeting in progress, some minor crisis. She stands in the doorway, and waits.

Sitting at his desk, partly hidden behind piles of books and papers, Max looks tired, under siege. Standing in front of the desk, in a semicircle, are three young tech guys.

Two beardies, one baldy.

Lots of jargon.

Max doesn't stand a chance.

The magazine's website is fairly primitive, barely on the grid, in fact – no Twitter feed, no YouTube channel, no mobile app, no Facebook page even – and that's more than likely the source of the problem here. Max claims to be a technophobe and a Luddite, and he probably is, but he'll also argue in private that no one has yet worked out a convincing business model for any of this stuff. If he was going to commit the magazine to a digit-al future, he'd like to feel that the range of possible outcomes wasn't limited to either financial self-harm or institutional sui-cide.

'Well,' he says eventually, dragging the word out, and then exhaling loudly, 'I don't know, do I?' He gets up. '*You* fucking figure it out.'

End of meeting.

Ellen steps back to let the boys pass.

Max remains standing and then waves Ellen in. 'What's the matter with me?' he says. 'I'm not even forty, and I can't get a handle on this shit.'

'You were *born* forty, Max. I wouldn't worry about it.'

'I *have* to worry about it. These pricks are at the gate. It's all very well me taking a stand, old man shakes his fist at Twitter, but how long is that tenable? Sooner or later –'

'*Get* a handle on it, Max. It's not hard.'

'Yeah, yeah.' He sits down again. 'So what's up?'

'Jeff Gale. Bob Holland.'

'What about them?'

'In case you didn't know, Max, someone shot them both dead over the weekend. I'm interested in who and why.'

'No shit.' He leans back in his chair and swivels from side to side. 'What about Jane Glasser?'

This was to be Ellen's next subject in the presidential hopefuls series, the congresswoman from West Virginia whose own staff members were recently caught on a video posted on YouTube calling her 'the she-devil'.

'Yeah, I'm on that, but . . . this is *news*.'

Max groans. And she knows why. It's the same argument as before, the same argument as always. *Parallax* calls itself a news magazine, but does that mean anything any more? The phrase is almost archaic, like 'fax machine' or 'long-distance telephone call'. The issue that's coming out on Thursday, for instance, has some good stuff in it – a piece on China's new megacities, and an interview with Alexandre Desplat – but for the next four weeks the magazine will sit on newsstands and coffee tables across the country blithely unaffected by anything *new* that actually happens.

'I know,' Max says, 'I know. We have to ramp up the online side of things. I *know*. In fact, I should call those three guys back in here right now, shouldn't I? Give them the green light, give them the *keys.*' He pauses. 'But you know what? It wouldn't make any difference.'

Standing there in front of him, listening, Ellen is torn between going, *Yeah, yeah, Max, whatever*, and leaning across the desk to slap him in the face.

He winces. 'Don't look at me like that, Ellen. Not *you.*'

Then she feels bad. They go back a long way and have never fallen out, which for her has to be some kind of a record. 'What is it, Max?'

He turns away for a moment and gazes out the window. Then he says, 'Do you know who owns *Parallax* these days, Ellen?'

She's about to answer, but hesitates. *Does* she know? Maybe not. As a contributing editor, she should know, and certainly did know at one stage – it was Wolper & Stone, and was for decades. But then Wolper were bought out by MCL Media. Wasn't that it?

And now?

'Isn't it MCL?'

'Sure, yeah, but who owns *them*?'

Penny dropping, she clicks her tongue. 'Oh.'

Max leans forward. 'Last year MCL were bought out by the

Mercury Publishing Group, who are owned by Offtech . . . who, in turn' – he squeezes his eyes shut for a second, as though in pain – 'have just been bought out by Tiberius Capital Partners.'

'Fuck.'

'Exactly.' He leans back in his swivel chair. 'Let the asset stripping begin.'

'Oh, Max.' She feels even worse now. And stupid. For not having known. *Parallax* survives almost forty years as an independent organ, a supposedly fearless voice in print journalism, and then in the space of two or three years it disappears into a Russian nesting doll of corporate ownership.

'They could switch us out like a light, Ellen, any time, and they're going to, it's simply a matter of when.' He taps out a drumroll on the edge of his desk. 'So listen to me, start asking around for work, OK?'

'Jesus.'

'I mean it.'

'*Max.*'

'Don't worry. You'll be fine. Anywhere you go will be lucky to get you.'

'That's not what I meant.'

'I know. But I'm just being realistic. You said it yourself, what's happening out there is *news*. Once opened it has to be consumed immediately. Or it goes off. Or needs to be refrigerated.' He looks up at her. 'Something like that.'

When she gives it a little thought, Ellen isn't surprised by any of this. It's a combination of things – the current climate principally, but also the curious, gradual fact of Max's diminished fearlessness. The Luddite thing, she believes, is part affectation and part defence mechanism. But what she really believes, and can't satisfactorily explain, and definitely isn't ready to articulate just yet, is that since she and Jimmy Gilroy wrote that piece on Senator John Rundle eighteen months ago, this magazine has been more or less doomed, with Max's own doom – professionally speaking, at any rate – an unfortunate and inevitable piece of collateral damage.

She holds his gaze for what feels like a long time.

But there's only one way forward here, and it applies to both of them.

'So,' she says eventually, 'you want to hear what I've got?'

'Yeah. OK.' He draws a hand across his thinning hair. 'Shoot.'

Ellen pulls a chair over, sits down and starts telling him about how she spent the weekend – about her quick visits to the two crime scenes, the first in Central Park, the second on the sidewalk outside Bra on Columbus Avenue. She describes how she met and spoke with various people at these locations, and then got follow-up texts or phone messages. She lists the different subjects she spent most of yesterday researching online, anything from algorithmic trading to real estate litigation to forensic ballistics. 'And from all of *which*,' she says, summing up, 'I did manage to extract at least one interesting and possibly relevant observation. It's something I haven't seen a single reference to yet, not anywhere, though I'm sure it's only a matter of time before there'll be one.' She pauses. 'Or maybe not. You never know. But it *is* weird.'

'What is? What's weird?'

'OK, look, everyone's saying that this is the work of terrorists, right? And maybe it is, but an assumption is also being made, and it's based on nothing as far as I can see –'

'What assumption?'

'That these terrorists are highly organised and professional, and that therefore the two shootings were carried out by the same people. Now maybe there's an official narrative being put out for some reason, that's always possible, I don't know . . .'

'But?'

'Well . . . from talking to different people, and putting it all together, *my* understanding of it is that Jeff Gale took a clean shot to the forehead, and no one saw the perps, whereas Bob Holland had half his face and head blown off on a busy sidewalk with literally dozens of people watching.'

Max nods slowly. 'Different MO.'

'Completely. The weapons were different, that's clear from the ballistics, even to me . . . and the psychology of it was different. I mean, look at the whole approach.' She hunches forward a little more and lowers her voice. 'So that can only mean one of two things – different perps, with no connection, or the same perps, but they're a bunch of clowns and are making this up as they go along. Either way, what we're being fed at the moment is clearly a line of bullshit, and this story isn't even two days old.'

*

By the time Frank Bishop gets to work on Monday morning the feeling he's had since he woke up – a low-lying sense of dread – has intensified considerably. It's not a full-blown panic attack, not yet, but he suspects he's getting there. And he tries to pin it down, to locate the starting point, the catalyst – because there usually is one, a specific moment when you see or hear or even just remember something, and it's like a change in wind direction or a sudden shift in temperature. Was it a dream he had? He can't remember. When you wake up feeling this shitty it usually *is* a dream, an insidious wormhole into some forgotten corner of your unconscious.

Though now that he thinks about it he actually went to bed feeling shitty, so . . .

What did he do yesterday? Nothing. It was a Sunday. He slept half the day and flicked through the pages of the *New York Times* and watched TV.

Oh . . . that was it. He remembers now.

He watched part of a documentary on some cable channel about Frank Gehry, and it reminded him of how his own career as an architect has turned to dust. What bothers him is not the alternative life he has ended up leading, here in Mahopac, and at Winterbrook Mall, so much as the stuff he never got around to doing in his original life, professionally speaking, at any rate – the civic buildings, the bank offices, the bridges . . . the grand unrealised projects. *That's* what bugs the crap out of him whenever he thinks about it. Which, to be fair, isn't that often. But when he *does*, like last night, and now this morning, the feeling tends to linger and thicken.

He waits until Lance has arrived before calling the regional manager. The place is quiet, and they'll be lucky if three or four people wander in all morning. Though given the state he's in today, Frank doesn't want to take any chances. He talks to this guy at the same time every Monday, to go over numbers and staffing issues, and while it's a perfectly routine call, it's never that easy. Only in his late twenties, the regional manager is a bit of a jerk and clearly perceives himself to be on some 'upward trajectory' within the Paloma management constellation.

Frank gets all of this and plays along. He's not an idiot. It's part of what he has to do if he wants to keep getting a paycheck every month. But he doesn't have to like it.

'Frank, my man,' the regional manager says when the call is put through, 'talk to me.'

'Saturday,' Frank says at once, emphatically, and as if that's all that needs to be said – one word, nothing else, not even the guy's name.

Which is Mike.

'Saturday? What do you mean, Saturday? I don't understand, Frank.'

'I mean, Saturday, *Mike*. Fifty units of the LudeX.' Then, instead of a judicious edit, he lets the tape roll. 'Jesus, what was that meant to be, some kind of a fucking joke?'

'I *beg* your pardon?'

Hesitating, Frank looks out over the stockroom from his little office in the corner. No contingency plan here, it would seem. Though whatever this is, it didn't just happen. *Something* is spurring him on. It feels like anger, but if so, what's he angry about? Not the LudeX situation, that's for sure. He couldn't give a shit about the LudeX situation. Is it his increasing dread, then, his anxiety, but redirected somehow, transmuted into this belligerent little snit he seems to be having? Maybe, but he's confused and doesn't feel entirely in control.

'It was insane,' he says. 'We were turning customers away all day.'

'We allocated –'

'Oh come on, allocated. That's ridiculous.' He leans back in his chair. 'I don't know, do you people sit around all day thinking this shit up? *Allocated*.'

There is a short silence. Then, 'Frank, have you been drink-ing?'

Frank laughs at this. 'No, *Mike*, I haven't. It's a little early in the day, don't you think? But is that all you can come up with? I've been *drinking*?'

'What the –'

'Because I question your fucking *judgement*?'

'Jesus, Frank.'

There is another silence. Frank presses the back of his head against the wall. He's being reckless here, and he isn't sure why – why now, why like this. But what does strike him is that in terms of tone, whatever about content, there's no reason why *any* conversation between himself and Mike shouldn't un-fold in precisely the way this one has. It's what should be nor-mal. His being deferential to Mike, on the other hand . . . *that's* what's absurd. At the same time, if he doesn't climb back through the looking glass, and pretty quickly, he's going to be in serious trouble.

'Listen to me, Mike,' he says. 'What I –'

But he freezes. He can't do it. Not at the moment.

'*Frank?*'

'Let me call you back later, OK?'

He puts the phone down.

After a couple of seconds, he gets up out of the chair and starts walking across the stockroom, expecting the phone be-hind him to ring at any second. He hopes it doesn't, and ac-tually suspects – on the basis that Mike must have been as relieved to end the conversation as he was – that it won't.

He goes outside to the loading area and takes a few deep breaths.

Anyway, this probably isn't a situation Mike would be all that well equipped to deal with – disaffected staff member getting confrontational, using abusive language. He might be trained for it, in theory, but given his age it's unlikely he's had any direct or relevant experience. With jobs so hard to come by these days, people tend to be more careful in their behaviour.

Frank stares out over the vast, largely empty parking lot to the rear of the mall.

So . . . what was *he* thinking? What was on *his* mind?

With jobs so hard to come by and all.

He doesn't know. Could this be a turning point, though? A tipping point?

Maybe.

But to what?

In the absence of a cigarette to smoke, or a soda to drink, he takes out his cell phone and scrolls down through his list of contacts.

He stops at Lizzie's number.

He didn't want to call her yesterday, because that would have been too soon after their conversation of the night before. No doubt today is still too soon.

But he's worried about her.

He makes the call. No answer.

Leave a message.

He doesn't.

What would it be? I'm worried about you? I love you? It makes my heart ache just to say your name?

With his stomach jumping, he puts his phone away, turns around and goes back inside.

On his way up in the elevator, Craig Howley straightens his tie. He'd have liked a little time to freshen up before coming here, but it was a busy day. Hectic actually. The worst part was the two hours he spent on a conference call with three executives from struggling Asian hotel chain Best Pacific – a company whose senior and subordinated debt Oberon recently acquired, an act that then necessitated Oberon shedding the chain's pension fund along with seventeen hundred of its employees.

Tough, yes, certainly, but what planet were these people living on? Barking at him over the phone wasn't going to change the basic facts of the situation.

Vaughan's absence didn't help much either, it has to be said.

The elevator door slides open.

At which point Howley remembers just where he is, and what he's in for here. The foyer to James Vaughan's Park Avenue apartment is a palace of onyx and alabaster, a *trompe l'œil* cathedral. Howley has lived on Park himself – though a good bit farther up, and it was at least fifteen years ago, different job, different marriage, different life. He currently lives in a handsome townhouse on Sixty-eighth, but this place is simply of a different order.

'Meredith!'

And there she is – sculpted purple sheath dress, crimson lips, coruscating eyes, raven black hair. Gatekeeper, keeper of the flame. Howley more or less hates this woman, but he has to admit that he has a weird, tingly kind of crush on her at the same time. He couldn't imagine having sex with her, wouldn't want to in a million years, nor could he imagine even having a meaningful conversation with her, but there's something there, something that renders – not her, actually, but *him* incomprehensible.

'Craig, how *are* you?'

And the pussycat voice. Over the phone, it's like a joke. In person, it's more like an intimidating sex toy, black, solid, shiny.

Unknowable, but in your face.

A lot of people, Howley included, have expended a good deal of time and energy speculating about the nature of Vaughan's relationship with this woman. Of course, the knowledge that five fairly formidable wives preceded her only complicates matters. Howley himself knew Ruth, who stretched back into the early nineties, and who at the time seemed like a perfect lady, smart as a whip and rake thin – a victim of cancer, sadly, but also, in many people's eyes, the calculating *bitch* who took over from Megan, his eighties wife. To those in the know, however, Vaughan's *real* wife – the way people have a *real* president, the one they grew up with, and that in a strange way defines them (LBJ in Howley's case) – was Kitty. She stretched from the early eighties right back to the mid-fifties. She was the sweetheart, the mother of his children, the woman behind the man. The first two wives, the early ones, Howley knows nothing of. He assumes they were probably a bit like this one, sexy, distracting, ill-advised.

'I'm good,' he says, mwah-mwahing her. 'Kept on my toes, you know, with the boss out sick and all.'

'The *boss*,' she says, mock dismissively, and leads him along the main hallway. To Howley's surprise, they head for the kitchen. He's been to the apartment many times before and has usually been led into the library or straight into the dining room. This is his first visit to the kitchen, which is huge, brightly lit and fitted out with cabinets and surfaces of brushed steel, black chrome and polished marble.

Vaughan is seated on a high stool at a long counter. He looks small and frail. There's a bowl of something in front of him. He glances up.

'Craig.'

Howley approaches and nods at the bowl, which contains some kind of soup or chowder. 'Getting a head start there, Jimmy, are you?'

Vaughan shrugs. He's wearing a bathrobe and hasn't shaved. Howley has never seen him like this before, never seen him out of a *suit* before.

'Yeah,' he says. 'What are you gonna do? Sue me? Mrs R there will fix you something if you're hungry.'

Howley looks at him. *If he's hungry?* Of course he's fucking hungry. He's been working all day and was expecting dinner. He glances to his left. Mrs Richardson, Vaughan's longtime cook, is busy over at the sink scrubbing something, a baking tray or a pot. Howley looks back, hesitates, and then says, 'You know what, I'm good, thanks. I'll eat later.'

'Suit yourself.' Vaughan indicates a stool on the other side of the counter. 'But sit with me, will you?'

Howley pulls out the nearest stool and sits down. A little farther along the counter, an open copy of the *New York Post* is lying next to a can of Dr Thurston's Diet Cherry Cola. Meredith slides onto the stool in front of the paper, hunches forward and starts reading.

'So, Jimmy, how are you feeling?'

Vaughan makes a face. 'Lousy. I've got ten different things

68

wrong with me.' He takes a slurp from the bowl, then glances up at Howley. 'Believe me, you don't want to know.'

And he's right. Howley doesn't.

But at the same time it'd be useful to know what they're dealing with here. Vaughan looks pretty awful, it has to be said – pathetic, really . . . stooped, unshaven, pale, dribbling chowder. It's hard to imagine a route back from *this*, and to something like a vigorous investment committee meeting or a tricky client lunch at the Four Seasons. It's shocking how rapid the deterioration has been. The old man seemed fine on Friday.

'Are we going to be seeing you back at the office any time soon?'

The moment Howley says this, he regrets it.

'Jesus, Craig.'

Because it's not as if Vaughan has been out sick for weeks. He's missed a single day. It just felt like a very *long* day.

'No, I meant . . .'

'Ha,' Vaughan says, his spoon suspended over the bowl, 'either you can't handle the pressure or you're itching to rearrange the furniture in my office. Which is it?'

Howley tenses. He isn't comfortable having a conversation like this in the kitchen, with Meredith there, and the cook listening in. 'Jimmy –'

'Just tell me, should I be worried?'

'Look, I, er –'

Vaughan cracks a smile, a sour one. 'Oh, *relax*, Craig, would you?' He shifts his focus back to the spoon. 'I was just kidding.'

'Right.'

The next mouthful of chowder Vaughan takes has a chunky piece in it that requires chewing. The chewing goes on for quite a while and Howley becomes exasperated. He's just about to ask why he was summoned up here in the first place when Meredith slaps her hand down loudly on the countertop.

They both turn to look at her.

'These *people*.'

Howley tilts his head to get a glimpse of what she's reading. It's a two-page spread covering the Connie Carillo trial. In between blocks of text, he can make out pictures of Judge Roberts, Ray Whitestone and Connie herself.

Vaughan puts his spoon down. 'What's the matter, sweetheart?'

She flicks the back of her hand against the spread.

'*This*. I've had enough of it. They're like vultures.' She shakes her head. 'Poor Connie.'

Vaughan shrugs. 'What do you want? It's a murder trial.' He turns back to Howley. 'You been following this, Craig?'

'As much as anyone, I guess. It's hard to avoid.'

'Yeah, tell me about it. Meredith here was at Brearley with Connie. Isn't that right, Mer?'

She tenses. There is silence for a moment. 'Just because I was at school with her doesn't mean –' She stops and slides off the stool. 'Oh, what would *you* know? Finish that slop there and take your medication, would you?'

She grabs her soda roughly, spilling some on the countertop, and storms out of the kitchen.

'My word,' Vaughan says, picking up his spoon again. 'What's eating *her*?' He takes another sip of chowder. 'So, Craig. What do you think? Is Senator Pendleton going to take the stand?'

Howley can't quite believe the way this is shaping up. It's certainly not what he had in mind. Nevertheless, he looks around, thinking . . . Connie Carillo, Pendleton. He heard something about the trial this morning. People were discussing it in the elevator.

'I doubt it,' he says eventually. 'Too much exposure. It's the *name*. If she was still a Pendleton, then maybe, but I figure the old man's going to let her fry.'

'Yeah,' Vaughan says, 'but if she fries, he's finished anyway. In fact, he's *already* finished. Connie screwed her old man over years ago by marrying Ricky. I mean, what, we're going to elect a governor who's got an ex-son-in-law with "Icepick" for a middle name? Please.'

'I don't see why not,' Howley says. 'These days? It'd take a lot more than *that* to crush Gene Pendleton.'

'Maybe, but it's not over yet. I think there's still a bunch of stuff to come out. That campaign funds thing, for instance, with Meeker . . . the missing checkbook.' He pauses, then coughs. 'There's also this guy at the moment, the doorman, what's his name?'

Howley hasn't seen enough of the coverage and is out of his depth here. A missing chequebook? The doorman? He has no idea what Vaughan is talking about.

He shakes his head.

'Mrs R?' Vaughan then says, turning awkwardly. 'The doorman, the guy on at the moment, what's his name?'

Mrs Richardson looks up from the sink and clicks her tongue. 'Joey Gifford.'

'*Thank* you. Yes, of course.' He takes another old-man slurp of chowder and quickly wipes his chin with a napkin. 'And let's not forget the question of method, the carving knife.' He pauses, looking up. 'Not exactly an icepick, but hey.'

Howley remains silent and gazes at the tiny splashes of cherry soda on the countertop. Sticky and crimson, they look like speckles of blood.

'Anyway,' Vaughan says, 'Ray Whitestone is going to have a ball working the various angles.' He puts his spoon into the bowl and pushes it aside. 'Case is made for him.' He reaches into the pocket of his robe and takes out a silver pillbox. 'It's got everything,' he goes on, more slowly now, concentrating, his mind fixed on getting the box open. 'Politics, sex, the mob . . . Wall Street, grand opera. You couldn't make it up. Right, Craig?'

Howley nods. What else is there to do?

The old man clears his throat. 'Get me a glass of water, Mrs R, would you?'

She does.

Over the next couple of minutes, and in silence, Vaughan takes his various tablets. When he's done, he stands up, ties the sash of his robe and nods at the door. 'Come on, Craig, let me walk you out.'

Walk him *out*? He just got here.

Resigned, Howley nods at Mrs Richardson, who's standing at the counter now, scrubbing at the soda stains with a spiral wire brush.

On the way out, Vaughan starts coughing. It escalates, and to get it under control he has to pound his chest with the palm of his hand. Howley finds this alarming.

'You OK?'

'Do I *sound* it?'

After he's regained his composure, and as they're crossing

the foyer, Vaughan turns and says, 'So, Craig, tell me, what do you make of these shootings over the weekend?'

Howley exhales loudly. He doesn't know, and at this point he doesn't really care. He's more concerned – or, at any rate, baffled – by Vaughan's behaviour. It's clear that the old man is unwell, and very frail, but also that he's as sharp as ever, and as calculating. The fact that they haven't discussed either the succession question or the proposed IPO is no accident as far as Howley is concerned. This other stuff, the Carillo trial, the shootings . . . Howley sees it all as smoke and mirrors, a form of misdirection.

Sleight of hand.

Or *is* it?

In truth, he can't be sure. Because the thing is . . . could Vaughan have actually forgotten what he'd called Howley up here to discuss?

It can't be discounted as a possibility.

'I don't know, Jimmy,' he says, eyeing the old man warily now. 'I refuse to believe any of this conspiracy stuff in the papers. There's no mystery about it, really.' He shrugs. 'It's simple. The murder rate goes up in a recession.'

Vaughan shakes his head. 'I think you'll find the most recent stats contradict you on that one, Craig.' He starts coughing again, but manages to contain it this time. 'Big drop in violent crime, five, almost six per cent last year alone.'

OK, whatever, Jesus.

'Well, Jimmy, what do *you* think?'

This is what he wants, isn't it?

Vaughan presses the button for the elevator and the door whispers open. 'Whatever this is,' he says, 'I think it goes pretty deep.' He holds his arm against the elevator door to keep it open. 'It could be some form of, I don't know . . . bloodletting.' He looks very weak all of a sudden, and a little spaced. 'I don't think we've seen an end to it.'

Howley nods and steps into the elevator cab.

It goes deep? Bloodletting? An *end* to it?

He's not quite sure what the old man is talking about. But maybe – it occurs to him – just *maybe*, the old man isn't sure either. In fact, maybe he's losing his marbles. Maybe this is the end of an era, or the start of a new one. Howley has a quick vision of himself steering Oberon to a successful IPO, and then beyond, to his own rightful place at the table, CFR, Trilateral, Bilderberg, whatever – the old man, meanwhile, stuck here in the apartment coughing his lungs up, fumbling with tablets, sucking his food out of a straw, and watching endless coverage on TV of some tawdry celebrity murder trial . . .

Howley turns around.

Maybe he *should* think about rearranging the furniture in Vaughan's office, because chances are this decrepit old bird in front of him now won't be leaving home any time soon.

Unless it's in a box.

'OK, Jimmy,' he says, looking out from the overly ornate interior of the elevator cab. 'Good night.'

'Yeah, Craig, old sport,' Vaughan says, but quietly, a sudden and unexpected glint in his eye. 'I'll see you in the morning.'

5

At the counter in her local diner, sipping coffee, waiting on a bagel and cream cheese, Ellen flicks through her notebook, the most recent few pages of it. But there's nothing there. It's all doodles and arrows and mini-mindmaps and word lists – hieroglyphic shit in her own handwriting that soon even *she'll* be unable to decipher. This is what happens when you lose the thread of a story, or can't find the shape of one in the first place.

She puts the notebook down and stirs her coffee. There's no reason to, it's black and unsweetened, but she does it anyway.

One of the little diner-y things people do.

Like shaking the packet of sugar before you open it, or chewing on a toothpick.

She glances up and down the counter.

Skinny guy in a business suit perched on his stool at one end, burly construction worker spilling off his at the other.

Where's Norman Rockwell when you need him?

The bagel arrives, and she starts into it, eyeing the notebook, unwilling to let this go. Since expounding her theory yesterday to Max Daitch, Ellen has made little or no progress. Probably because it wasn't much of a theory to start with. What was it she said? Different perps, no connection, same perps, bunch of clowns?

Something like that?

Or *that* specifically.

The counter guy is passing, and she holds out her cup for a refill.

The official line hasn't changed in the last twenty-four hours either. Maybe there's hard evidence somewhere that she's unaware of – or maybe it's a carefully engineered consensus, or maybe it's just intellectual laziness, she doesn't know – but the continuing and remarkably consistent media assumption seems to be that a group of domestic terrorists, as yet unidentified, was responsible for the two killings. Within those parameters, there is a modicum of theorising, and the usual lingo is deployed – jihad, radical, global . . . battlefield . . . threat level. Repeated reference is now also being made to that earlier report about intel analysts picking up noises in Yemen relating to possible targeting of Wall Street executives.

But what strikes Ellen most is that there hasn't been a single mention anywhere, at least not that she can see, of the differing methods used in the two shootings, and of how weird that is, and of what it implies –

Quick sip of coffee.

– namely, that the shootings may well have been separate and unconnected, which would also mean they were random and coincidental, thus rendering all of that speculative Homeland Security-speak in the papers and online pretty much irrelevant. The alternative scenario is that the shootings were indeed connected, at least circumstantially. For the moment, the how and why remain unknown, but what the differing methods would seem to imply is that maybe there *was* no method, or very little method, and that the perps were simply amateurs.

As far as Ellen is concerned, if it's the first, there's no story here worth pursuing. It'd just be two routine homicides. But if it's the second –

She takes her last mouthful of bagel.

– there is.

So she's going with the second.

With the amateurs, the clowns.

The lone wolves, the stray dogs.

Because if that's what these guys *are*, amateurs, and not a highly organised terrorist cell – not pre-installed units, not strings of code in some elaborate phase of video gameplay – then there's no reason why she or any other moderately intelligent person shouldn't be able to get inside their heads, work out what they're up to, second-guess them even.

She twirls the coffee spoon between her fingers for a moment.

Is that being overly ambitious? Perhaps. Wouldn't be the first time, though.

She looks around.

Regrouping.

OK, most parties with an interest in this – Homeland Security, the FBI's Joint Terrorism Task Force, the NYPD, CNN, Fox, the *WSJ*, the *Times*, half the blogosphere – are just assuming that these perps are experienced professionals, possibly with a background in the military or in special ops. Little Ellen Dorsey, on the other hand, and based solely on a fucking hunch, has decided otherwise – that they're newbies, isolated and largely clueless.

It's not much of a competitive edge, and maybe she's deluding herself, but it's all she's got.

She pays and leaves.

And there isn't much of a window here, because if she's right about this, it's bound to become apparent to everyone pretty quickly – one more development is all it'll take, and that could happen at any time.

Walking back to her apartment, she decides that with the lack of any intel on the perps, the only other likely route into the story is through the vics. Why them? Who were they? What did they have in common? Did they ever meet, or cross paths professionally? And if so, does this tell us anything?

She gets home, clears some space on her desk and settles down to work.

Over the course of the day she trawls through dozens of business websites, gathering and collating references to the two men. She reads profiles, magazine articles, blog posts, anything she can find. She prints out some of this stuff, pinning loose pages of it onto various corkboards around the apartment and laying others out on the floor. She moves quickly from one spot to another, highlighting passages with a red marker as she follows a line of thought, swirling and daubing red streaks on paper like a hopped-up Jackson Pollock. She spends a good deal of time on the phone and writing emails, putting out feelers, questions, requests for information.

She doesn't eat anything. She drinks a lot of coffee.

But none of this really gets her anywhere. Because although it turns out that Jeff Gale and Bob Holland had quite a lot in common, there's a predictability to it all, and a banality. They both served, for instance, on a couple of the same boards; they were both members of the same golf club for a while, and they both had former wives who went to the same high school. She finds gala charity events that they both attended and infers a certain degree of casual social contact between them, at lunches, openings, the occasional weekend in the Hamptons.

But what she doesn't find, or stumble upon, is any kind of sinister nexus between Northwood Leffingwell and Chambers Capital Management. She finds a nexus, all right, but it's the bigger one – the one that links them all together, the banks, the hedge funds, the private equity shops. She knew this – of *course* she did, it's axiomatic now – but it still comes as a shock to see it laid out like that in such unequivocal terms.

And it's no help really.

Because it doesn't tell her anything.

By late evening she's tired, addled from too much caffeine, her brain engorged with terabytes of useless information. In an attempt to reverse this, or at least to calm it – to calm what she considers her attention surplus disorder – she takes a long, hot, fragrant bath. Lying there, in the flickering candlelight, she listens for the weird sounds that her building tends to make occasionally, or that tend to ripple through it – bumps, thuds, muffled voices – and that for some reason she can only ever seem to hear at all clearly from here, from the bath.

Not that she wants to particularly.

But it has become a routine, a little ritual for unwinding, for emptying her brain after too many hours at the keyboard.

Delete, delete, delete.

Ten minutes in, however, and she's *thinking* again, speculating, unable to help herself. If these guys aren't jihadis – and she doesn't for one second believe they are – then what are they? *Who* are they? The Tea Party? Occupy Wall Street?

She shakes her head.

The Tea Partiers want to *be* the bankers, not to kill them, and the Occupiers are too woolly and amorphous for anything as decisive and proactive as an assassination programme.

So she keeps coming back to her first instinct on this.

They're amateurs.

Stray dogs.

Doing their own thing.

And where do people like this find inspiration? Where do they get their ideas from? Where do they meet, and hang out, and exchange information, and *chat*? Her heart sinks.

The fucking internet, of course.

She stares at the tiled wall in front of her.

What's she going to do? Instigate a *search*?

Without the full resources of an Echelon-style intercept station or fusion centre, Ellen knows very well how pointless this would be. She pulls the plug and gets out of the bathtub. She dries off and puts on sweats and a T-shirt. She orders up pizza.

Not having eaten all day.

She turns on the TV. Even there they've sort of given up and are discussing instead the witness currently on the stand in the Connie Carillo murder trial.

Joey Gifford.

The celebrity doorman.

Jesus wept.

The thing is, for all she's got, for all she's pulled out of the hat, she may as well give up too, and sit around like the rest of them, waiting for the next target, the next vic. She flicks through a few channels, but doesn't want to watch anything. There's no one she wants to talk to, either. She checks Twitter on her phone and glances at the time. Pizza won't be here for another fifteen minutes. She looks over at her desk.

It couldn't *hurt*.

Three hours, the pizza, a bottle of wine and two bananas later she's still at her desk, bleary-eyed, near to tears, scrolling down through forums, discussion groups and comment boxes. Each new post she reads, or thread she follows, seems to hold out the promise of something, an insight, an angle, a revelation even. In discussing stuff like fractional reserve banking, the creation of the Fed, the Glass-Steagall Act, Keynes, the Chicago School, subprime, securitisation, the bailouts, there'll be an initial hint of reasonableness, a striving for clarity – for the holy grail of a coherent *point* – but sooner or later, and without fail, each contribution will descend into ambiguity, internal contradiction and ultimately gibberish.

On some sites things can get pretty heated and shrill, especially when they focus on the bankers themselves, on the voracious, lying, bloodsucking *zombie motherfuckers who've effectively been RUNNING THE COUNTRY FOR THE LAST HUNDRED YEARS ...*

But it's at about 3 a.m. that she comes across something she thinks is significant. Though she can't be sure, because by that stage she also suspects she might be hallucinating.

It's deep, deep into the comment box of an archived blog post on a site called Smells Like Victory. She doesn't remember how she got here – through what circuitous route, or when exactly she veered off topic – because the post itself, go figure, is a half-scholarly account of the effects railroad construction had on the economy of pre-Civil War America. The discussion in the comment box leads with a fairly polite disagreement about the relative importance of railroads over canals in the antebellum North, and this soon degenerates into a testy spat about how unsuited the 'heavy' imported British locomotives were to the supposedly 'lighter' American-engineered track systems. But after close to a hundred comments – and as is so often the case these days, online *and* off – the subject somehow ends up being about the current crisis. A comment is posted claiming that the likes of Cornelius Vanderbilt, Jay Gould and John D. Rockefeller shaped modern America, and pretty soon a discussion is in full swing about the relative merits (or demerits) of the nineteenth-century robber barons over today's one-percenters.

After a few more posts, someone called Trustbot37 says, 'People forget that back then these guys were hated every bit as much as the bankers are now. I mean, Gould was routinely referred to as the Mephistopheles of Wall Street.' Sans-serif says that Trustbot37 is missing the point here – that OK, sure, people resented these Gilded Age fucks for their money and their fifty-room summer 'cottages' in Newport, but at the same time they *admired* them and essentially approved of what they were doing, which was building up huge new industries and transforming the country in a thousand different ways. Whereas today, Jesus . . . today people are incandescent with rage at what they see as the wanton *bleeding dry and tearing down of this same great country.* John Fuze says we should bring RICO charges against these bastards, that that's what the damn thing was enacted for back in 1970, to combat organised crime, and what is the Great Global Debt Bubble if not the most highly organised crime in human fucking history . . .

It goes on and on like this, and with multiple references – of the kind you see pretty often now, even on mainstream sites – to pitchforks, tumbrils and guillotines. Then someone called ath900 takes up the theme and runs with it, but without the grim jocularity, without the slightest hint of irony. 'Look,' he says, 'these people need to be eliminated for real, and it needs to be systematic. If it was up to me I'd start with someone from each of the three pillars of this rotten temple, i.e., from an investment bank, a hedge fund and a private equity firm. I'd do it like that, make a statement – just pick three institutions and pop the top guys. Maybe do a test run, start with some of the second-tier outfits – say, Northwood Leffingwell, Chambers Capital Management and Black Vine Partners . . .'

Ellen stares at this last sentence in disbelief.

Then she scans the screen, looking for a date.

The comment was posted over a year ago.

ath900?

She reads his last sentence again, then the whole comment. She goes over the five or six comments that precede it and skims through the five or six that immediately follow it. It seems to be his only contribution. And within three or four comments anyway the discussion has moved on to a fine-point dissection of a recent SEC fraud settlement.

She goes back.

Pop the top guys?

Holy shit.

She slumps in her chair, hand still on the mouse.

It's the middle of the night, muffled Upper West Side traffic noise outside, muffled techno beats coming from the guy next door. In a state of shock and frost-brained exhaustion, Ellen lets her gaze slide from the screen to the debris around her on the desk – scribbled notes, empty wineglass, oil-stained pizza box, shards of crust, banana peels, crumpled napkin . . .

Then she shakes her head and shifts forward in the chair

again.

It may well transpire that she's wasting her time here, but she has to keep going. This is only the beginning. There's so much more to find out.

Like who ath900 is.

She moves her hand from the mouse to the keyboard.

Like who the *fuck* – more crucially right now – the top guy at Black Vine Partners is.

6

'It's a hotel,' Scott Lebrecht says, glancing out of the car window, Harlem flickering past. 'In Marrakech. I stayed there a couple of years ago.'

The assistant clacks on his laptop.

'The . . . Mamounia?'

'Maybe. Go on.'

'Er . . . traditional Moroccan riads, seven and a half thousand square feet, each with its own courtyard, terrace and pool.' He pauses. 'Ten grand a night? Just under.'

'Yep, that's it.'

'You want six nights, early June?'

'Yep.'

'Got it.'

Clack, clack.

'So, this British journalist, she's at what time?'

'Eleven,' the assistant says, 'right after the event.'

'Tell me about her. Is she cute?'

'So-so. Petite. Fortyish.'

'Hmmm.'

'Not *my* type.'

'Who gives a fuck what your type is, Baxter? Jesus.' A pause. 'I could do petite and forty, no problem. So long as she's got a halfway presentable face.'

'Well . . . she's got good bone structure.'

'Right.' Lebrecht rolls his eyes. 'Who does she work for?'

'*Sunday Times*. Of London. Business section. She's on the private equity beat.'

'They have a PE *beat*? How fucking sad is that?'

'She's doing a piece on the increased pressure CEOs are under these days from their private equity bosses. You know, to perform, to succeed.'

Lebrecht laughs out loud at this. 'To perform? Damn right. They be my *bitches*, nigga.'

'Maybe not the line she'll be expecting, but –'

'*Shut* up.' He takes out his phone and starts fiddling with it. 'What line should I give her? The unvarnished truth or some kind of scented bullshit?'

'I'd go with the scented bullshit. In a piece like this she's bound to find someone who'll break ranks, but there's no reason for it to be us.'

'Right.'

'So . . . ?'

'What? You want me to rehearse? Fuck. I don't know, er . . . we manage companies efficiently and profitably, we deliver higher returns, not just for the wealthy but for pensioners as well.'

'Good.'

'*And* we create more jobs than the stock market. Sure, CEOs are under pressure, but when was that ever *not* the case?'

'OK.'

'Excuse me?'

'I said that's OK.'

'It's OK?' Half turning. 'It's fucking *OK*? What's that meant to be, Baxter, your seal of approval or something? I know you're experienced, you've been around the block a few times, but I can do this shit on my own, you know. Jesus.' Turning back. 'Could do it in my sleep.' Distracted now, composing a tweet.

I'm on a panel this morning at this year's –

On a panel soon at this year's . . .

He glances out the window.

Hundred and Tenth Street, at last. John the Divine. Central Park.

Global Equities Conference . . . in Manhattan's . . .

At Manhattan's . . . Herald Rygate.

At the Herald Rygate.

How many does that leave?

Sixty-one.

The things we do for love.

Thirty-four.

Tweet.

A moment or two later, Baxter puts a hand up to the side of his head. 'Er . . . I've got Teddy Schmule for you.'

'Oh.' Lebrecht shifts in the seat and adjusts his earpiece. 'Yo, the Schmulemeister.'

'Scottsdale. What's up?'

'Nothing. I'm in New York, at a conference. I'm down for a nine-thirty slot, panel discussion. Couple of things after that, then I'm heading out to the coast. You get Shem Tyner? Are we good?'

'Meh. We'll see. You've got to play a long game where Shem is concerned.' He pauses. 'Shem is Shem, you know.'

'Yeah, but Teddy . . . tell me he's at least read the script. That he's psyched.'

Teddy Schmule snorts at this. 'Oh, he's psyched all right, and he *loves* the script. It's just that by the time he gets through with

87

it . . . well, you might have a hard time actually recognising it.'

'Fuuuuuuck.'

'Shem always does this. It's one of his things.'

'We don't have the *time*.'

'The one thing you've always got in this business, Scott, believe me, is time.'

'No.' He clenches his fist and bangs it against the window. '*No*. Fuck him. We can scale it down, go with someone else, someone who's hungry. This is my third time out, Teddy, and I feel it, it's the big one. I'm not going to let a little shit like Shem Tyner take the reins.' Shaking his head. 'No way. This is a Black Vine production.'

The pause that follows is long and weary.

'OK. Let me get back to him.'

'You do that, Teddy Schmule.'

Outside, they're canyoning into midtown. A few moments later, they pull up outside the Herald Rygate.

Reaching for the door, Lebrecht pauses and turns to Baxter. 'OK,' he says, 'so I've got *this* thing now, right? Then Reet Petite. Then . . . where am I having lunch?'

*

Frank Bishop checks the time, drains his coffee and heads for the bathroom. Over the course of four or five minutes in there – quick dump, hands, teeth – he doesn't look in the mirror.

Doesn't look at himself.

Not even once.

Is that weird? Maybe, but it's become a habit lately.

It seems easier.

Avoidance.

In the car on his way to work, however, there's something he can't avoid. It's been bugging him for the last two days.

He stares at the road ahead.

After his little snit on Monday, he never got back to the regional manager, and the regional manager never got back to him. And that has to mean trouble. What kind of trouble exactly, Frank is unwilling to contemplate.

But it's not just that.

It's the humiliation.

A further run-in is inevitable – on the phone, face to face, whatever – and he's dreading it. This is because he knows he cannot win, or come out ahead, without grovelling, without begging to keep his job. And all for what? Because he didn't feel like taking shit from some pimply-faced little motherfucker at head office? Because he decided to speak his fucking *mind*?

So it would seem.

The other source of anxiety for Frank this morning is Lizzie. He hasn't heard back from *her* yet, either. He called again yesterday afternoon and left a brief message. Then, a while later, he thought about sending her a text.

He's thinking about sending her one now.

But he knows that in Lizzie's book that would probably qualify as harassment.

He's sure she's fine. She wasn't fine on Saturday evening when they spoke, he knows that, but Saturday evening is probably ancient history already as far as she's concerned.

He takes the wide bend at Cedar Bay Drive, and the enormous, creaking mall heaves into view.

He gets to the parking lot, turns in and crosses its vast,

mostly empty expanse. He finds a space near the main entrance. On his way inside he takes a detour to the Walgreens on the lower level to get some Excedrin and maybe make eye contact with that gorgeous Asian woman who works there, maybe even get served by her.

Kickstart his day with a little squirt of serotonin.

But it's not to be.

He doesn't see the woman anywhere and gets served instead by a skinny black kid called Felix.

*

It's just after nine thirty when Ellen Dorsey rolls over in the bed.

Shit.

She didn't fall asleep until nearly five, her muscles knotty and aching, her head buzzing with facts – with the *fact* of these facts.

The weight of them.

And as her eyelids grind open now, these facts are first to greet the light. His name is Scott Lebrecht. He's thirty-three. He's from Philadelphia. He's worth a billion dollars. He's the CEO of Black Vine Partners.

He's on a hit list.

He's next.

She sits upright in the bed.

Or at least that's how it all seemed last night.

She looks across the room, through the open door, her desk in the living room partially visible.

No matter how she spins it – that it was random, a coincidence, the kind of spooky but ultimately meaningless shit the internet throws up all the time – there's no escaping the key fact here: two of the three people mentioned in that post are already dead.

Popped.

So it's only logical to assume that before long number three will be, too.

She slides off the bed.

She puts on a pot of coffee, tidies up, takes a shower and gets dressed.

Through all of which she grapples with the central dilemma here.

Shouldn't she be passing this on to the police? Isn't she required to by law? If she doesn't, and something happens, wouldn't she be an accessory?

It's a tricky one.

Because it's not as if she's protecting a confidential source and could be subpoenaed for discovery.

Who was your source, Ms Dorsey?

The internet, Your Honour.

Sipping coffee, she reads the comment again, more than once. Foreknowledge of a crime. Is that what this is?

She vacillates.

It is, it isn't. It might be, it might not. The notion is plausible, the notion is ridiculous.

She massages her temples, to ward off an incipient headache. Outside, it's overcast, dull and grey. Is it going to rain?

She looks from the window to the floor.

Actually, she decides, the notion *is* ridiculous. Jeff Gale and Bob Holland were killed twelve hours apart. This is four days on from that and Scott Lebrecht is still alive. There's no discernible pattern here. So, seriously . . . who would *take* her seriously?

No one.

She looks up.

The thing is, she can talk herself out of this, no problem – but deep down she wants it to be true.

Not even deep down.

She gets up from the desk, walks around, stretches.

But then . . . let's say it is true, that there really is a story here, what happens then? First, she'd have to bring Max Daitch in on it, and he'd have to run it by legal. Chances are that a fear of civil or even criminal liability would stop the whole thing dead in its tracks right there, with the lawyers advising Max to pass the info up the corporate chain or possibly straight on to the police.

So . . . what? She just hands it over? Before she gets a chance to work it, even a little?

Raindrops start pelting against the window.

She sits down again and reaches for the coffee. She'll give it some thought. Go over her notes.

Fifteen minutes.

Black Vine Partners.

Scott Lebrecht . . .

He founded the company six or seven years ago with the assistance of two guys from a New York-based hedge fund called Reilly Asset Management. They provided Lebrecht with a substantial chunk of capital and a revolving line of credit, which he then very successfully used to focus on investments in the power and energy sectors. More recently, he has set his sights on Hollywood by creating Black Vine Media and signing a five-year production deal with Sony Entertainment. So far, this has only led to his involvement in a couple of poorly received mid-budget thrillers, but Lebrecht is said to be very determined and is busy raising finance for a third, considerably more ambitious project.

He also has a reputation for hanging out with the talent – dates with actresses, courtside seats with the boys, who-knows-what in the private jet. In photos, he comes across as something of a jock, blond and burly, not exactly good-looking – at least not preternaturally so, not the way some of his new A-lister friends tend to be – but he does have an energy about him, and a certain charm.

That's what it says here, anyway.

In her barely legible 4 a.m. scrawl.

She flicks forward to the next page.

Lebrecht has a ferocious temper, serious commitment issues, a severe nut allergy and a 'rad' collection of sports cars.

He has a two-year-old son in Florida he apparently refuses to acknowledge.

He has over ten thousand followers on Twitter.

Ellen stops.

She reads that last bit again. She swivels in her chair.

Hmmm.

She reaches for the keyboard, logs on to Twitter and finds him.

He appears to be an avid tweeter.

One thousand two hundred and fifty-seven so far. Been at it for about a year.

She scrolls down through some recent ones.

Awesome celebration last night with my Jenkintown brohims. #achingintheplaces

A leader leads for a reason. Try to jump ahead of him and all you'll get for your trouble is lost.

Tough negotiations on the Salertech buyout, including that ninth inning zinger, but we prevailed. Kudos to all concerned.

She goes back to the top.

His last tweet. It was one hour ago.

On a panel soon at this year's Global Equities Conference at the Herald Rygate. The things we do for love.

*

Craig Howley wonders if Vaughan is going to make it into the office again today. He looks at his watch.

Nearly ten.

Isn't that pushing it? Even for the old man?

He showed up yesterday, having pretty much thrown down the gauntlet the previous evening, but if Howley thought *Monday* was long . . .

Jesus.

The old man came in looking his normal self – back in a suit, groomed, dapper – but everything was painfully slow, his movements, his speech.

His reaction times.

It was a good thing they had nothing on, no visitors or important meetings.

Howley catches Angela's eye through the glass partition, but she shakes her head.

He swivels in his chair and gazes out the window at

midtown, and at his allotted shard, here on this side of the fifty-seventh floor, of Central Park.

Should he call Meredith? Show his concern? Not that that's really what it is. What it *really* is, he knows, is impatience. Because ever since Monday's early meeting, and the way he was approached afterwards by the various group heads and senior managing directors – not to mention Vaughan's quip later on about rearranging the furniture in his office – Howley has been in a sort of waking fever dream of anticipation.

He doesn't have any illusions, though. He fully understands who and what James Vaughan is, and that no one can replace him or occupy quite the same space he has occupied in Washington and elsewhere for the past sixty years – more, in fact, in a *way* . . . if you go back, if you include his old man, William J., and *his* old man.

Fuck.

But replace him as head of Oberon? Howley could do that, no problem.

The thing is, in a long and distinguished career, Vaughan has had many more strings to his bow than just the Oberon Capital Group. He worked under Jack Kennedy, fought with Johnson, switched to the Republicans, got into bed with Nixon, did a stint at the Agency under Bush. He was always there in the background during Reagan's two terms, and it was the same again later, during Dubya's two. Without once being elected or appointed to public office, the man has exerted enormous influence, and mainly by operating in the interstices between federal agencies, private contractors, consulting firms, lobbyists, think tanks and policy institutes.

Not that the private equity side of things has been too

shabby. After more than forty years in the business, Vaughan can boast that Oberon has achieved compound annual returns for its equity investors of something in the region of fifty-seven or fifty-eight per cent.

Which is staggering.

Howley gets up from his desk and goes over to the window.

So keeping a show like that on the road would certainly be enough for *him*. It's what he wants and knows he'll be good at. He spent long enough at the Pentagon shaping the acquisitions programme and influencing which weapons systems were bought, not to mention being one of the instigators of the great outsourcing land grab that saw contractors move in on logistics and support services. And now, on *this* side of the so-called revolving door, he has proved equally adept at wooing and acquiring these same companies.

But not just them, as it turns out. He has been phenomenally successful at parlaying his considerable political clout into hard equity across a whole range of sectors – pharmaceutical, energy, telecoms, real estate. Plus, Oberon have expanded, they're everywhere now, in Africa, Asia, China, and with the company sitting on stockpiles of cash the prospects for deal-making have never been better.

It's what Vaughan hired him for. The two men go back, they get on. It was a clear succession strategy.

But these things rarely go smoothly. Of the major buyout firms that are still run by their founders, most of them have no strategies in place at all for handing on the reins – which is fine, or will be for a while, because the CEOs in these places tend to be in their mid to late sixties. But in Vaughan's case, strategy notwithstanding, the situation has become critical.

Client confidence is key here. It's not something you can afford to mess around with. The Global Equities Conference starts today, for example, and there are a lot of people in town, some of whom will be dropping by the office later on for a cocktail reception. And the Jimmy Vaughan of legend is one thing, but the Jimmy Vaughan of *yesterday*? That's another matter entirely.

So he really needs to know what's going on.

Howley turns and catches Angela's eye again. He brings a hand up to his ear and makes a phone gesture.

She nods.

He'll have a word with Meredith, try to get the point across. She's not the only one who can speak in code.

*

Leaving the Melmotte Room on the tenth floor of the Rygate Hotel, Scott Lebrecht turns to his assistant.

'This interview, Baxter? Where we doing it again?'

'The Wilson. It's uptown a bit. On Madison.'

'I know where the Wilson is.'

Baxter shrugs. They arrive at the elevators.

'So that went well.'

'No it fucking didn't.'

'What? You got a great reception.'

'Nah.' Lebrecht shakes his head. 'You know what it is? Most of these big equity guys are twenty years older than I am, more in some cases, and it's like they think of me as the *kid* or something. They talk down to me. And I hate that.' He pauses. 'What I hate is these events. I mean, a panel discussion? Come *on*. People here don't think I have better uses for my time than a fucking panel discussion? Please.'

The elevator doors open and they get in.

A lot of the delegates at the conference are from out of town and are staying for the full three days that it's on. In between sessions, and over dinners, they'll be discussing everything from how the industry needs to embrace change to the vexed question of going public.

Lebrecht can think of nothing worse.

Cutting out early like this, not sticking around, gives him some satisfaction. But now he has to face an interview with a business journalist.

In another hotel.

More convoluted questions, more evasive answers.

It'll be a welcome distraction if she's cute, but really, he has better uses for his time than that, too. Black Vine Partners is currently circling distressed European retailer Ballantine Marche, which fell into administration last month. Plus, they're trying to raise capital for a new mezzanine fund.

He has stuff to *do*.

The elevator door opens, and they head out across the lobby.

It's probably fair to say that Black Vine Media takes up more of his time than it should, but he's determined to make it work. If this movie comes together, Shem Tyner or no Shem Tyner, they could have a valuable franchise on their hands.

Young Adult Post-Apocalyptic meets High School Gross-out.

As they approach the exit, Baxter puts a hand up to his earpiece. 'You want to talk to Paris?'

Lebrecht stops. 'Yeah.'

This'll be Dan Travers, about Ballantine Marche.

'OK,' Baxter says, moving off. 'I'll be out at the car.'

'Dan the Man,' Lebrecht says, leaning back a little to look up at the lobby's soaring stained-glass dome. '*Comment ça va?*'

*

Sitting opposite a line of nervous-looking Japanese tourists on the downtown A train, Ellen Dorsey – sleep-deprived, but hopped up on java – is feeling pretty nervous herself.

It's a different kind of nervous, though.

She's decided to head down to the Herald Rygate hotel in midtown and then . . . assess the situation. She won't get past the lobby, because she's not registered, or accredited, to attend the conference.

So in all likelihood she won't get to see Scott Lebrecht.

But even if she did, if she pulled some ballsy reporter moves and got five minutes with him, what would she say? I'm running a story about an internet post that suggests you as a suitable candidate for assassination? I was wondering if you'd care to comment?

Yes, that probably is what she'd say. Except for one thing – she isn't running the story anywhere. Because that's all she's got and it isn't enough, and if she *were* to alert Lebrecht or the police, the story would get out at once and that'd be the end of any advantage she had.

Or might have had.

The train pulls into Seventy-second Street. The Japanese tourists get off and are replaced by three randoms – business guy in a suit, sultry teen boy and a woman about Ellen's own age but considerably better dressed.

And saner-looking.

The train rattles on.

Ellen doesn't really have any option here, does she? There's no obvious solution that presents itself. She's going to have to give this up.

Sultry teen boy stifles a sneeze, which seems to hurt. He then looks around scowling, as if it was someone else's fault.

She'll go into the *Parallax* offices and lay it all out for Max. She has a contact in the NYPD, and if it comes to it, she can make the call from there.

She stares down at the floor.

But first she'll swing by the Rygate.

Train pulls in at Fifty-ninth Street.

It can't hurt. She'll wander around for a while, see what's going on, play it by ear. Maybe inveigle her way into the conference.

She runs through a couple of scenarios in her head.

A short time later, as the train is pulling out of Forty-second Street, she looks up again, at the seats opposite. Only one of the original three randoms is left.

Her enhanced doppelgänger.

They both get out at Thirty-fourth Street, and as Ellen trails behind along the platform, she fantasises briefly about having this woman's life – the confidence to wear those clothes, the because-she's-worth-it hair, the Jell-O-on-springs gait. But as they approach the stairs weariness prevails, slowing Ellen down, and the fantasy fragments, disassembles.

The woman vanishes into the crowd.

Up at street level, heading east, Ellen regroups, sort of. Even if she were to change her mind about the Rygate, she could still pass close by it on her way to the *Parallax* offices. She wouldn't have to turn north for at least another few blocks.

But she hasn't changed her mind.

A little sunshine has broken through, and the city is wet and glistening from the earlier rain.

She walks on.

A few minutes later she turns a corner and there it is, on the other side of Broadway – the Herald Rygate, town cars and limos lining the kerb in front of it, drivers and doormen gathered under its awning.

Pedestrians streaming by.

Ellen pulls out her phone, checks the time, looks around and starts crossing the street.

*

'So, you'd say five, six feet?'

'Yeah, five, six.'

'Five or six feet at the *widest* point?'

'That's correct, sir. The widest point.'

'Which is at the bottom.'

'Yeah.'

'The bottom of the staircase?'

'That's correct, sir.'

Out on the floor, Frank Bishop has one eye on a row of flat-screen LCD units tuned to live coverage of the Connie Carillo murder trial and one eye on the door. Lance took the call about an hour ago. It was while Frank was dealing with a customer.

The regional manager, it seems, is going to be stopping by

for a brief unscheduled visit.

'On a Wednesday morning?' Lance said after the call. 'What's *that* about?'

Frank shrugged, his insides turning, Monday's conversation replaying one more time in his head. There's no doubt about it, he had a legitimate grievance. Those fifty LudeX consoles? Any manager would have been up in arms about that.

But how many would have called it a *fucking joke*?

On top of various other insults.

Pretty tense now, Frank is grateful for the intermittent distraction of the Carillo stuff on the store's multiple TV screens. In his second week on the stand, Joey Gifford, the so-called celebrity doorman, is being cross-examined by prosecution counsel Ray Whitestone. For reasons Frank is unclear about, questions are currently focusing on particular architectural features of the lobby in the Park Avenue apartment building where Gifford has worked for nearly forty years – and through which Connie Carillo herself is in the habit of passing every morning at seven with her two dogs.

'Now, Mr Gifford,' Whitestone is saying, 'would you please describe for the court the decorative brass radiator grille that is set in the wall of the lobby at the bottom of the staircase.'

As Gifford clears his throat to speak, Frank detects some movement from behind, and turns.

Walking across the floor, directly towards him, is Mike, the baby-faced regional manager, and another guy. Mike is in a suit, and the other guy, who looks even younger than Mike, is wearing a zipped-up leather jacket, but with a Paloma shirt on underneath it.

Frank can see the logo sewn into the collar.

'Hi, Mike,' he says, and then adds – as though responding to some Pavlovian trigger, unable *not* to – 'who's your little friend?'

Mike rolls his eyes. 'Say hello to Josh, Frank. He's the new manager here.'

'*Here?*'

Mike nods.

Of course. What was he expecting? Some kind of reasoned negotiation? A lively exchange of views? An *apology*? Letting it sink in, Frank just stands there and says nothing. Logically, this is where he should start grovelling, begging to keep his job, but he knows now that he's not going to do that.

After a moment, Mike says, 'You have fifteen minutes to get your stuff and leave.'

Frank looks at him. 'Or else?'

'No severance package. You'll be deemed to have acted in contravention of the regulations as set down in the employee handbook.'

'I see.'

'And can basically go fuck yourself.'

Frank nods, fighting a strong impulse here to lash out, with his fists.

But he doesn't.

'Good for you, Mike,' he says eventually, his stomach still churning. 'I was worried there for a moment that you'd left your balls back at head office.' Smiling, he turns and moves off in the direction of the storeroom.

Ten minutes later, out in the parking lot, under a thin veil of rain, Frank calls Lizzie.

He needs to hear her voice now. It's a matter of priorities, of perspective.

He waits.

She doesn't answer.

He squeezes the phone in his hand and represses an urge to fling it to the ground.

'I appear to be busy.' Her outgoing message. 'But say something if you want, after the beep.'

Languid and annoying, maybe, but it's all he's getting, and as usual he'll take it.

'Lizzie, it's Dad. Call me when you get a chance, will you?'

It suddenly occurs to him that this is probably the fourth or fifth time since Saturday evening that he's tried, without success, to contact his daughter. Which isn't normal. So should he be panicking? He tries to keep any trace of this out of his voice.

'Any time, sweetheart, OK?' He pauses. '*OK?*'

Not much success there either.

'Just call me.' He gazes around, at the desolate parking lot, at the overcast sky. 'I love you, Lizzie.'

*

The driver is leaning back against the car door, arms folded.

Baxter catches his eye and holds up an outstretched hand.

Five minutes.

The driver nods an acknowledgement.

Then Baxter looks left and right.

Broadway.

Torrents of people and traffic.

Not exactly ideal working conditions, but he stands there anyway, under the Rygate awning next to a doorman and a couple of other drivers, and takes out his BlackBerry. He checks for emails. As expected there are dozens, so he tries to block out the noise and starts scrolling down through them. In a matter of minutes he manages to clear six or seven, sometimes using only a one- or two-word reply. He's good at this kind of stuff, the guerrilla approach – not that Lebrecht would ever give him any credit for it, or thanks.

Baxter glances around.

It's funny what Lebrecht said earlier, that some of the older guys up in the Melmotte Room think of him as *the kid* – because compared to them, that's precisely what he is, a fucking kid. Baxter has worked for those guys, and they're very serious, very focused, very conservative. OK, Lebrecht is on a roll, making insane money, but none of it's *his*, and it won't last. He's too volatile, too unstable, and too attached to this notion of taking Hollywood by storm.

Which is just a fantasy.

He thinks he can do it, but Hollywood will chew him up and spit out the seeds.

Baxter's seen it before.

And he's not sure he wants to be around when it happens this time. The abuse he can put up with, because at the moment, with things going well, it's casual and flippant, almost unthinking. But when Lebrecht starts throwing real tantrums?

Forget about it.

Baxter clears two more emails and puts his BlackBerry away.

It might be time to move on, to look for something else.

But right now he could do with an espresso.

He steps forward a few paces and scopes out the immediate vicinity. Two blocks down there's a Starbucks.

He catches the driver's eye again. 'I need some coffee,' he says, over the sound of the traffic. 'You want something?'

The driver pushes himself forward from the car, clicks his tongue, and then says, 'You want *me* to go? I'll go.'

Baxter is about to take him up on the offer when the driver's eyes widen slightly and he nods at something – indicating to Baxter that he should turn around.

Lebrecht.

Shit.

The driver straightens up. Baxter turns, thinking *fuck it*, he'll get a coffee at the Wilson, and a proper one.

With real cream.

In that moment Lebrecht emerges from the revolving doors, and Baxter can tell he's distracted, sulky – complications with Ballantine Marche, no doubt.

He has that *look*.

But in the next second, the look changes. Everything does, the air, the weight of things, the density, the speed at which they move.

Lebrecht's arms go up, his whole body recoiling from . . . *what*?

Baxter turns to the right. There's a guy rushing towards Lebrecht, his arm outstretched, something in his hand. The doorman of the Rygate, a bulky streak of gold and red in his greatcoat, epaulettes and Pershing hat, intervenes. He deflects the outstretched arm, but wrestles the guy as well, the two figures then careening towards Baxter himself, who steps back in horror, arms up and out, glaring down at his shoes. But the entangled figures keep coming and a full-on collision is inevitable. It's like a football tackle, with Baxter suddenly deciding he has to resist, arms bunched in tight now, upper body pushing forward and over them. But on contact he loses his balance and falls, rolling off the doorman's back and onto the sidewalk.

There are voices, roars, shouts, but in all the confusion, as he clambers up, hand on the front of a town car next to Lebrecht's limo, Baxter has no clear idea of what he's hearing. Nor, when he turns around and manages to focus, does he have much idea of what he's seeing, either.

Because there on the ground, still struggling, are the doorman and what Baxter can only assume is a gunman, while a few feet away there appears to be a separate struggle going on, as two of the limo drivers try to restrain a second man.

Behind them, a stunned Lebrecht staggers backwards, stopping at the granite wall beside the revolving doors.

Baxter doesn't see any blood or obvious wound.

But then, why would he?

And it's only in that moment, as he hears the gunshot ring out, that he realises *why* he wouldn't –

Because there was no gunshot before.

There's certainly one now, though, and it's followed by a general recoil, a shocked pulling away, which loosens up the two nodal points of the skirmish. In the next couple of seconds the gunman on the ground, along with his accomplice, breaks free. They start running, but in different directions – one to the nearest corner, the other out into the traffic, where he proceeds to zigzag his way through the mid-morning chaos of Broadway.

Lebrecht's driver, standing next to Baxter, decides to give chase and slides over the front of the town car onto the street.

But he is immediately thwarted – blocked by a passing MTA

bus.

Baxter turns around again. Like everyone else here, he's in shock, and having a hard time processing what has happened – in particular the fact that when the gunman discharged his weapon a few moments ago someone apparently *took the bullet* . . .

It was – he sees now – one of the other drivers.

He's alive, still standing, but clutching his side, a fellow driver giving him support. The doorman, back on his feet, is there as well, and on a cell phone, wild-eyed, waving his free hand about, calling 911.

In a sort of post-traumatic slo-mo, Baxter then does a general pan of the area. No one is walking by the front of the hotel, they're going around it, actually stepping out onto the street to avoid the sidewalk. It's like some collective but unspoken agreement to preserve the crime scene. There *are* onlookers, but they've formed a partial cordon to the left and right – a no-go area also loosely defined from above by the perimeter of the hotel's awning.

Within this shaded rectangle of sidewalk, a handful of people stand, or move slowly, making eye contact with one another, shaking their heads in disbelief, waiting. Baxter glances over at Lebrecht, who's still at the granite wall, looking pale and shaken.

Their eyes meet.

Lebrecht raises an index finger and points it inwards, effectively poking himself in the chest, and mouthing, 'Me? That was meant for *me*?'

Baxter shrugs and emits the requisite degree of incredulity, but he experiences something else here, too, a flicker of . . .

what? Ambivalence? *Disappointment?* To deflect whatever it is he looks away, and that's when he sees her.

She's standing just inside the perimeter, to the left, staring at him, holding up her phone, a woman in her late thirties, early forties, dressed all in black.

Not just an onlooker, not just a bystander.

But what, then? *Who?*

With sirens filling the air, and getting louder, Baxter glances over at the wounded limo driver.

He's clearly in agony. No blood is visible, though.

Is that good or bad?

Baxter doesn't know.

As the first siren closes in, with multiple others coming up in the rear, he looks to his left again, still curious, but the woman with the camera phone is no longer there.

*

On the fifty-seventh floor, at the Oberon cocktail reception, no one will talk about anything else. There's wall-to-wall media coverage, too. He can see it from here, through the glass, it's on every screen and monitor – the Herald Rygate, Scott Lebrecht.

And the Twittersphere, apparently, is 'on fire'.

Not that Craig Howley gives a shit about that.

He's distracted enough as it is.

Without Vaughan here, it's like the meeting he chaired on Monday morning, only multiplied by a hundred. That event was an exclusively in-house affair, with just the heads of the various investment groups, whereas this afternoon's event is wide open, attended by some of the industry's biggest players, and with pretty much everything, Oberon's whole succession strategy (Vaughan conspicuous by his absence, Craig Howley clearly in charge), on display.

What he can't figure out is if all the attention on this shooting at the Rygate is a help or a hindrance. It'll be a help if it provides a little misdirection, takes some of the heat out of what's going on here, but if no one even notices in the first place? What use is that?

He circulates, floating in and out of different conversations.

'Well, of course, once is happenstance –'

'Yeah, but Scott's an arrogant little prick, I mean come *on* . . .'

'And how did this not get flagged?'

He actually wishes Vaughan were here.

'– twice is coincidence –'

'You'd imagine Homeland or the NSA'd be all over it like a rash, but Jesus H. Christ –'

'– thinks he's David O. fucking Selznick –'

The old man is so much better at this than he is.

'– and three times is enemy action.'

A pause.

'Who said that? Henry Kissinger?'

'Auric Goldfinger.'

Everyone laughs.

What worries him most is that Meredith might have taken him the wrong way earlier on, when he called. She was very quiet, which was unusual, so now he has visions of her whispering into Vaughan's ear like a Borgia, or some scheming harridan from Ancient Rome.

Don't listen to that awful man.

Get rid of him.

He framed what he had to say as diplomatically as he could. But did he play his hand too soon? Did he make the classic mistake?

'. . . you create value, and at some point, it's inevitable, you're going to want to *liquefy* it.'

'– it's a paradigm shift –'

'– but we're dropping the mandatory arbitration requirement for shareholder disputes, right?'

It's just as private equity issues are re-entering the conversational orbit like this that Howley looks up and sees Angela approaching.

'I'm sorry to disturb you, Mr Howley,' she says, holding a phone out to him. 'It's Mr Vaughan.'

Staged as he imagines this might seem to some of the guests here, Howley is genuinely surprised. As he takes the phone from Angela he hands her his glass.

'Jimmy,' he says, and in a louder voice than he intended. Out of the corner of his eye, he notices a sort of wave effect of turning heads. In the circumstances, should he have said *Mr Vaughan*? He's not sure.

'Craig, a word.'

'Of course, Jimmy.' He moves over towards the window, asking himself what this is about. The Rygate thing? The reception? What he said to Meredith?

He stands there, waiting, midtown nestled under a heavy blanket of grey cloud.

'I thought I'd be able to make it in today, but . . . I'm *tired*, Craig.'

Howley's eyes widen. He doesn't speak.

'I'm on these pills, it's a new treatment, sort of a trial really, some guys over at Eiben are working on it, but I'll be honest with you, Craig . . . I think it might be time to . . . you know.'

'*Oh*,' Howley says, his stomach jumping. Though he'll have to do better than that. 'Jimmy, I –'

'Look, we both knew this was coming. And you're practically running the show as it is.'

What does he say to that? He can hardly agree. 'Yes, but without *you*, without –'

'Yeah, yeah, stop it.' Vaughan pauses, then clears his throat. 'So, is this what they're all talking about there? Where's the old man? What's going on?'

'Actually, no, it's not.' Howley glances over his shoulder. 'This thing down at the Rygate has everyone pretty exercised at the moment.'

'Right. Well, sure, it's a big story. Three strikes. There'll be no getting away from it now.' A short silence follows. 'Craig, we'll make this quick. We'll set it up, put out a statement.'

Howley nods. 'OK, Jimmy.'

'Call me in the morning.'

'Yeah.'

'And in the meantime, I might send some stuff over for you to look at, some notes.'

'OK.' Howley furrows his brow.

Some notes.

When he turns around to face the room, he feels weirdly self-conscious, as though he has somehow pulled a fast one. But the feeling doesn't last. He hands the phone back to Angela and takes his drink again.

He joins a small group and within less than a minute has subtly steered the conversation around to the subject of bringing private equity companies public.

'So,' someone eventually asks, 'what about Oberon?'

'Well,' Howley says, as though the question had never occurred to him, 'I'm in two minds, really.' He raises his glass and drains what's in it. 'But not for long. One way or the other, I'll be making a decision about it very soon.'

Three

It was at a reception in Cardinal Spellman's residence prior to attending the Al Smith Dinner at the Waldorf Astoria in October of 1948 that William J. Vaughan was introduced to the young congressman from Massachusetts. The two were spotted later that night by Walter Winchell at El Morocco 'cupiding' a couple of girls from the chorus of *Brigadoon*.

House of Vaughan (p. 103)

7

On the way back uptown in a cab, Ellen replays what she has on her phone. It's blurry and chaotic, but it's all *there* – except for the first few seconds. It was only when she spotted Scott Lebrecht coming out of the revolving doors of the hotel that she lifted her phone, flicked it to camera mode and started recording – by which point, of course, the action was already under way . . . young guy rushing forward, arm outstretched, bulky doorman mounting a counterattack. But from that point on she pretty much caught the whole thing.

As the city blocks flit past outside now, she makes a couple of calculations. One, this surely confirms her theory. Whoever those guys were, they weren't professional, weren't military-trained, certainly weren't any kind of special ops. And they weren't jihadis, either. From what Ellen could make out they looked like . . . just two young white guys. One of them was wearing a grey zip-front hoodie and jeans, and the other one had on a heavier coat, jeans and a woolly hat.

Her second calculation is that she won't have been the only one back there who was quick on the draw with a camera phone. She might have been the first, but there'll have been others – and CCTV footage as well, no doubt – which means . . . no way this doesn't get out, no way this whole story doesn't undergo a serious retrofit.

Which in turn, of course, leaves her high and dry.

Because what else has she got?

Given how these two guys have left themselves so exposed – dozens of witnesses, cameras, possible forensics – Ellen can't imagine they'll be remaining free for very long.

That'll wrap the whole thing up. And with zero input from her.

She looks out the window.

At least she won't have to deal with the guilt of having allowed, or enabled – or, at any rate, *refused to prevent* – the killing of Scott Lebrecht.

She's assuming here that the limo driver makes it.

He was still on his feet. There was no blood.

Ellen decides to get out at Eighty-ninth Street and walk the remaining four blocks. As she's turning onto Ninety-third Street her cell phone rings.

'Hi, Max.'

'Holy shit, Ellen.'

'What?'

'You were *right*.'

'That was fast.'

'It's everywhere.'

'It only happened forty minutes ago.'

'They have footage of it, from someone's phone. It's on MSNBC.'

'I knew it.'

'What do you mean?'

'I was there. I got it on *my* fucking phone.'

'*What?*'

Standing outside her building, glancing around, she explains.

'Jesus, Ellen.'

'What?' Feeling defensive all of a sudden. 'You think I should have reported this? I was going to. I was on my way in to see *you*.'

'No, I mean you could have been *hurt*. Those guys had guns.' He exhales loudly. 'It's insane.'

She bites her lip. 'Did they mention the limo driver?'

'Er . . . not specifically. What –'

'There was a single shot discharged. One of the limo drivers took the bullet.'

'All they're saying is that one person was wounded, no details.'

'Wounded.' She pictures him standing there, the look on his face.

'You want to write this up, Ellen? We can put it on the website, upload your footage. Tweet the shit out of it. Maybe draw in a few hits.'

'Listen to *you*.'

Then she goes silent, thinking about it.

'Ellen?'

'How do I explain what I was doing there?'

'You were covering the equity conference.'

'I don't know, Max. Let me look at it again and I'll call you back.'

She heads inside.

The air is stuffy from last night. She opens all the windows and puts on some coffee. She transfers the footage from her phone to her iMac and watches it a couple of times. Then she turns on MSNBC to see what they've got. Alex Wagner and a panel of talking heads discussing payroll tax cuts. She goes to their website and sees the clip there.

Hers is better.

Longer, more detailed, clearer, less jumpy. But theirs is all right. It gets the point across. The report that goes with it is sketchy, but she can already see the shape of what's emerging.

Her version, basically.

Or what her version would have been if she'd managed to get it out there. But it's too late now. Because these guys will be in custody within hours. She's convinced of that.

She skips the coffee and lies down for a while, exhaustion catching up on her.

When she opens her eyes again it's after five.

Groggy and stiff, she rolls off the side of the bed and sits there with her head in her hands. What a weird, misshapen day it's turned out to be.

She gets up and checks the usual news sources.

No developments, just a heightened realisation that this is actually a huge story. The Yemen thing is mentioned again, and there are sidebars about corporate executives upping their security details. 'Citizen' journalism is dissected and the phone footage is shown endlessly.

She flicks around all the channels and websites, checks Facebook and Twitter, and aggregates the various reports in her head. The banner here is that Wall Street is under attack and no one seems to have the first clue who the attackers are.

Or no one is *saying*.

Because Ellen presumes the police are making headway with what they've got. It was Broadway, after all, and in broad daylight, so there'll be CCTV footage from every angle. Witness statements, ballistics, prints, fibres, particles.

A DNA deposit, maybe. On the doorman.

Somehow.

Fuck.

How did she let it all slip away?

She gets up from the desk, but immediately feels a little dizzy and has to reach for the back of her chair to steady herself. If she's going to stay on her feet, if she's going to keep working, she needs to eat something.

But not here.

*

There's something about this – being at home in the middle of the afternoon, on a weekday, when he's not sick or on vacation – that Frank *really* doesn't like.

It's weird and unsettling.

On his way back from the mall, he stopped off and bought a six-pack, and has put it in the fridge, but that's probably where it's going to stay. The alternative was a bottle of Stoli. That would have been too extreme, too fast, too downward-trajectory.

The six-pack isn't going to do it for him either, though. He can tell.

Too chill, too ball game.

What he needs is some serious anti-anxiety medication, a nice warm blanket of *Don't worry, that didn't just happen*, or of *. . . OK, even if it did, so fucking what?*

But he ran out of *those* pills a long time ago. After the divorce.

Another thing Frank is finding weird at the moment – now

that he thinks about it, now that he has the time – is the fact that he could even casually refer to this place he's in as 'home'. It bears so little resemblance to anywhere he has ever lived before.

Sitting on the couch now, he looks around.

Everything is stripped down, smaller, more compact.

Cheaper.

He hasn't put any kind of a personal stamp on the place. There's no art or interesting furniture, no design sense. There are no CDs or DVDs either. That stuff is all digital now anyway, invisible and hidden. He has a few books, but they torment him more than anything else. He started several in his first couple of months here, but lost his way with each one.

And it's not just books. His sense these days is of everything being fragmented, digitised, atomised. He can't stop at a channel on TV for more than a few seconds, can't decide what music he wants to listen to any more, can't read a newspaper. He can't pay attention to anything in front of him for long enough to even bring it into focus.

Sometimes he wonders how he ever managed to sit at a drawing board at Belmont, McCann and *work*, how he ever used modelling software, read contracts and building codes, how he ever steered a whole project through from initial concept to launch.

It's only been a couple of hours since he left, but now he's even beginning to wonder how he held down his job at the mall for so long.

How he spoke to people, interacted.

He reaches for the remote, hesitates, doesn't touch it. He considers standing up.

Or maybe stretching out on the couch.

There's really no move he can make here that's going to be the right one, is there? This is paralysis of the will, good and proper.

He stares at the blank TV screen.

The thing is, without the job at the Paloma outlet, there's no reason for him to *be* in this apartment, let alone in West Mahopac.

There's no money for it now, either.

So what's he going to do?

He's already cut his expenses to the bone. The move from working as an architect in the city to selling electronics out here in the boonies was about as much of a downsize as he could have ever envisaged being necessary. He did the math and made all the adjustments. The one thing he didn't factor in, he supposes now, was a sort of fatal, infantile compulsion on his part to eventually whine about it.

Deb would have factored that in.

Deb.

Deb-or-ah.

But then . . .

He stands up. Where's his phone? He gets it from the kitchen table and checks for messages.

Nothing.

He scrolls for Deb and hits Call. It's been a while since he's done this.

It rings. She'll be at work. Plenty of that for lawyers.

'What is it, Frank?'

Her tone. *Christ.*

'Have you heard from Lizzie?'

Stony silence for a second, then a panicky 'Why?'

'*Have* you?'

'No. Yes. Over the weekend. Saturday, I think. *Why?*'

He sighs. 'Nothing, it's just that I've left a couple of messages for her and she hasn't gotten back to me.'

'Jesus, Frank, is that all? She's got a life, she's busy. She's a *student*.'

'Yeah.' He stares out the window, at the car dealership across the street. 'I know.'

Then, in one of those classic Deb changes of pace – he can picture it, the lip bite, the head shake – she says, 'Frank, honey, are you all right?'

Honey?

There's no question of his coming clean here, about the job, not *now* – she'd link the fact that he's vulnerable with this sudden concern for Lizzie, and make a big deal out of it.

'I'm fine.'

And that's it. Nowhere left for either of them to go.

Didn't take very long, did it?

Afterwards, he remains in the same position, looking down, the phone in his hand.

He'll call Lizzie again, leave one more message.

He glances up.

And after that?

*

When they've all left, Craig Howley goes back to his office, sits at his desk and gazes out the window.

There are a lot of things that he's not.

He's not a sentimentalist, he's not a hedonist, he's not a *fool*.

But for a few moments now he thinks he can allow himself to feel just a little giddy. It's quite a sensation . . .

And he wants to mark it.

When he walked past Angela's desk on his way in here, he had an impulse to ruffle her hair, or to . . . to . . .

See?

He's no good at this.

He hasn't told Jessica yet. Should he call her now, or wait until later?

Chairman and CEO of the Oberon Capital Group.

Damn, that sounds good.

Ideas are already fighting for airtime in his head. There's so much to do, so much restructuring and reorganising that Oberon could benefit from.

He swivels in his chair.

And that'll be the first hurdle, now that he thinks about it. He's been the chief operating officer of the company for a year now, and in recent months something more than that, but the truth is there's still a lot about the place he doesn't know, information he's not privy to. And the reason for this is quite simple. The company, in a hundred different ways, is the very embodiment of its founder – a fact that, in turn, might help explain the culture of secrecy around here . . . the general reluctance ever to do interviews, for example, or to attend conferences, or to nurture any kind of a profile outside of financial and Washington circles. If a corporation is indeed a person, then no one can seriously doubt that the Oberon Capital Group *is* James Vaughan.

But all of that's going to have to change.

The old man may have spent decades preserving his

anonymity, but Howley will have no problem going on Bloomberg or Fox and talking the company up, talking the industry up – because that's what it needs right now, people like him to go out and tell it like it is.

He smiles, briefly amused by his own enthusiasm.

It's true, though. Private equity has an image problem – the predatory thing, the bonuses, a couple of lavish and regrettably high-profile birthday parties held in the last year or two – but Howley doesn't see why that trend can't be reversed.

He swivels around to his desk, reaches for a pen and a legal pad and starts writing.

Notes, headings, bullet points.

Not exactly a to-do list, not exactly a mission statement either – something in between, maybe.

At the very least, he wants to have his thoughts clear for when he next speaks to Vaughan.

He wants to hit the ground running.

After a few minutes, he checks the time. He and Jessica have a dinner later on with some friends. He'll tell her then, when he can see her reaction. It won't be a real surprise – she's been predicting this, or a version of it, for months – but she will be pleased.

When Howley looks up again, having jotted down another half page of notes, he is surprised to see that Jacqueline Prescott is outside his office. She's standing at Angela's desk. The two women talk for a bit. Then Jacqueline passes something – it looks like a file folder of some kind – to Angela.

Vaughan's office is on the other side of the fifty-seventh floor, and it's a fairly rare occurrence to see his PA over here. Despite her years, Jacqueline is still the old man's Praetorian

Guard, his firewall – everything that's directed to him, or that comes from him, must go through her first.

So what's *this*? Those notes Vaughan mentioned?

Howley studies Jacqueline for a moment, fully aware that out of the corner of her eye she's probably observing him, too. Quite the piece of work, she's soon gliding off down the hallway, that finishing-school deportment of hers, after nearly fifty years, still operating at full tilt.

Howley then makes a show of going back to his own notes. But he doesn't have long to wait. Angela comes in almost immediately, holding the file folder in her hand.

'Mr Howley,' she says, arriving at his desk and holding the folder out to him, 'Ms Prescott has asked me to give you this.'

'Thank you, Angela.'

He takes the folder and places it on his desk without looking at it. He's aware – from her expression, from her body language, even from a slight residue of tension in the air arising from Jacqueline Prescott's visit – that Angela knows something is afoot and wants to be briefed on it.

But he's afraid she's going to have to wait.

He freezes her out with a thin smile, and when he's alone again he looks down at the folder, closely studying its blank and slightly faded cream-coloured cover. This, if Howley is not mistaken, is one of James Vaughan's legendary 'black files'.

So called.

Vaughan is no slouch in the technology department, but when it comes to data storage – or the storage, at any rate, of *certain* data – he appears to have a preference for the non-digital, the legacy, which is to say, hard copies only, and kept in folders like this one.

For as long as anyone can remember – and generally that's nowhere near as long as Vaughan himself can remember – these cream-coloured folders have been a feature of life here at Oberon HQ. The old man often has one under his arm, he consults them at meetings, and there are always two or three on his desk.

Howley can't be sure until he looks, of course, but he's guessing that the folder he has in his hands right now contains some pretty interesting material. At the same time, it seems amazing to him that the old man would even let something like this out of his sight. Because for anyone wishing to arrive at a full understanding of the Oberon Capital Group, access to the contents of these files would surely have to be considered essential, the final piece of any puzzle.

Howley takes the folder in his hands and flicks through it. It's only about fifty or sixty pages. Some contain graphics, others just solid blocks of text.

So what's going on here? Is this some kind of a coded vote of confidence?

Howley has no other choice but to see it that way.

He smiles to himself and opens the folder at the first page.

*

It's after seven when Ellen sits at the bar in Flannery's on Amsterdam and orders an eight-ounce cheeseburger with smoked bacon, a Caesar salad and a pint of Leffe.

A sip or two into the pint and someone appears at her side.

'Hey, Ellie, what's up?'

'Charlie!'

Ellen comes to Flannery's quite a bit and has gotten to know a few of the regulars. Charlie here is a retired . . . something, she's never quite been able to establish what. But *he* knows what *she* does, and he enjoys analysing the stories of the day with her. Ellen enjoys this, too, because Charlie's taste in news, not unlike her own, runs to the conspiratorial, and it's a useful exercise every now and again to have to pull stuff back from the edge of crazy.

Not that *he's* crazy, but he's freer in what he can say than she is. His newsroom is the barstool, and standards there tend to be a lot less stringent. Tonight, though, she's surprised, and a little disappointed, to find that all Charlie wants to talk about is the Connie Carillo trial. For obvious reasons, she has missed the coverage today and isn't up to speed on developments. He gives her a quick rundown (more stuff about the lobby, how it's lit, footfall count, etc.), which he then follows up with a pretty incisive analysis of the subtle effects Joey Gifford's newfound celebrity seems to be having on both the content *and* the delivery of his ongoing testimony.

Interesting as Ellen finds this – and as she demolishes her eight-ounce cheeseburger – she does try to steer the conversation round to the shooting at the Rygate today. But to no avail. Charlie is dismissive of the whole affair, seeming to imply that it's all somehow way too obvious and predictable. Ellen would like to tease this out but knows she's not going to get the chance. In any case, they're soon joined by a few other people and the conversation opens up and at the same time, inevitably, dissipates.

Two pints and a shot of Jameson's later, Ellen finds herself heading out to smoke a joint with Charlie and a guy from the kitchen called Nestor. There's an alley two doors down from the bar and that's where they go. Nestor is probably twenty-two or twenty-three, a physics major apparently, and in his tight little cook's shirt and check pants – at least as far as Ellen is concerned – distractingly ripped.

As they pass the joint around, the conversation flits from one thing to another – the kitchen politics at Flannery's, the right ingredients for a Reuben sandwich, what the fuck a 'babyccino' is, and the routine abuse these days of the word 'quantum'. When they come out of the alleyway to head back to Flannery's, Amsterdam Avenue has notched things up a couple of gears in terms of sound level, colour display, pixelation, and Ellen herself now feels – the word bounces back into her head, on a curve, from earlier – *ripped*.

Distractedly ripped.

In the bar again, she starts into a pretty intense conversation with a friend of Charlie's about the bizarre rules governing Super PACs, but from where she's sitting the TV set at the end of the bar is in her direct line of vision, and she can't take her eyes off it.

They're showing the MSNBC clip from before, and it strikes her now that it's actually little more than a blur. You can see there's some kind of a tussle going on, just about. Then there's one clear shot of Scott Lebrecht looking dazed, another of the doorman being helped back onto his feet, and a very shaky few seconds of someone running out into the traffic on Broadway.

But we see this hooded figure from behind.

And that's it.

She visualises her own clip and it seems – from memory, through the prism of being stoned – to be so much more substantial, riper, brimming with texture and detail. From that moment on she can't get it out of her head. She needs to see it again, as soon as possible, and on a proper-sized screen. Within ten minutes, therefore, she has extricated herself from Flannery's and is floating up Amsterdam Avenue towards Ninety-third Street.

At Ninety-first something occurs to her and she takes out her phone. She's assuming Val Brady is on the story, so she calls him up.

'Ellen? What's happening?'

Dispensing with any niceties, she gets straight into it. What's he hearing? Basically. Is there much reliable CCTV footage? Do they have any kind of a fix on the perps yet? What are his sources in the NYPD saying? Are arrests imminent?

Val laughs, at her refined social skills presumably. Then he sighs. 'I wish I had something for you, Ellen, but the well is dry. As a fucking bone.' There are voices in the background. He's in a bar, or a busy newsroom, she can't tell which. 'The thing is,' he goes on, 'from what I'm hearing in the department? They've got nothing. And not publicly yet, but they've even stopped talking about it in terms of a regular terrorist threat. They're thinking more Beltway sniper now, with some kind of a twist to it, political maybe or . . . who knows. It's all just guesswork. The eyewitness accounts they have so far are pretty confused, and they're not holding out much hope either for the surveillance material they've managed to gather,'

'Holy shit.'

'Yeah, it's pretty weird, all right. And because this was the third hit, or attempted hit anyway, the story is just going to mushroom, you know. With everyone waiting to see what happens next. I'm telling you, watch what it does overnight.' He pauses. 'The cops are going apeshit, as well. I mean, this is *really* bad for the city.'

Ellen can't believe it. 'They've got *nothing*?'

'That's my understanding.' He pauses. 'I spoke to one senior detective on the case earlier this evening, and it was incredible, I'd never seen anything like it, he was putting his hands together, looking up and saying, *Just one lousy clue, Lord, that's all I ask, just one lousy fucking clue.*'

Ellen is stunned, but before Val has a chance to ask *her* any questions, she mumbles something and gets off the phone.

She makes it back to the apartment in about two minutes flat.

She goes straight to her desk, calls up the file and sits watching it with her jacket still on.

Adrenalin has cut a swathe through her buzz from the joint, and the clip isn't quite the lost Kubrick masterpiece it seemed like it might be back in Flannery's, but it nonetheless gives a much clearer idea of what happened outside the Rygate than the MSNBC version – the one that's been running for most of the day, and that the cops and the Feds are now presumably going through with a fine-tooth comb.

This one shows faces.

It's fleeting, but you can see them – two young guys, white, nondescript, sort of scruffy. They're like members of some indie band you've never heard of.

But who *are* they?

She watches it again.

The first thing you see is Lebrecht emerging from the revolving doors and then the uniformed doorman suddenly lurching sideways. He collides with Grey Hoodie; they entangle and in turn collide with another man, who falls over them and rolls onto the sidewalk. In the background, there's a melee as Woolly Hat struggles with a couple of suited limo drivers. There's a lot of shouting, but no words can be made out, and then there's a really loud bang, which everyone reacts to by pulling back – including Ellen, but only for a split second. In the confusion, Woolly Hat breaks free, Grey Hoodie struggles to his feet, and they both take off in different directions. Grey Hoodie heads straight out into the traffic. Someone then slides over the front of a car to follow him but this person is immediately blocked by a bus. When the bus moves on, Grey Hoodie has disappeared. In the stunned aftermath, one of the limo drivers clutches his side and another comes to his aid. The doorman pulls out his cell phone and barks into it as an ashen-faced Scott Lebrecht leans back against the wall, poking a finger – curiously – into his own chest.

Sirens are soon rising in the background, and as the first one closes in on the scene, Ellen withdraws.

The clip is jerky and blurry in parts, but enough of it is clear, in three- and four-second bursts, to make it feel like there's something there, something in it to be *seen*.

If you look hard enough.

She takes off her jacket and sits at the desk, hunched forward, leaning in close to the screen.

And watches it again.

And again.

She pauses, fast-forwards, rewinds. Plays it with sound, plays it without.

Eventually – after maybe the ninth or tenth replay – she does spot something. It's tiny, hardly a lead at all, and may well prove to be of no significance whatsoever, but at the same time it's the kind of thing she could imagine Val Brady's NYPD source zeroing in on.

She plays it over and over. Grey Hoodie is on the sidewalk, wrestling with the doorman, and at one point in the struggle – *for less than a second* – his zip-front jacket gets shoved up a bit, over his abdomen. Under the jacket he's wearing a dark T-shirt, and on the T-shirt something is printed, some lettering, a word or words.

She freeze-frames it.

The only thing she can make out, the only thing that's clearly visible, is a single letter, an upper-case A. It's in some weird font. The succeeding couple of letters are a complete blur.

And that's it.

She grabs the image, saves it and prints off a copy.

She holds up the page to study it.

A.

Significance? There can't possibly be any. It just *seems* like it might be significant because it's the only concrete, extractable, quasi-evidentiary element from the whole clip. There's no point at which the gun is visible, for instance. The two faces are visible, OK, but that's of no use to Ellen. It's not like she's got any face-recognition software and a database she can run them through.

So . . . just a fragment of something printed on a T-shirt, then?

Yeah. She sighs, and places the sheet of paper next to the keyboard on her desk. She leans back in the chair.

Either she stops this right here, or she takes it forward in some way.

But how?

For a few minutes, in the still silence of the apartment, staring into space, she mulls it over.

A.

A.

A.

She glances at the sheet of paper again.

The font *is* weird. Half Gothicky, half futuristic. What does she know about fonts? Not a lot.

She leans forward and reaches for the keyboard.

8

Frank opens his eyes. It's morning. He must have fallen asleep at some point, even though it felt like he was awake all night. He remembers lying there staring into the void, aware of each hour passing on the clock, his thoughts on a continuous loop but at the same time maddeningly, perpetually incomplete.

He tried to go over his finances, to calculate how long he might be able to string things out, but the figures kept dissolving and re-forming, refusing to compute into any comprehensible pattern.

He tries again now, sitting on the edge of the bed. Fully awake this time, he finds it just as hard, though for different reasons. He may have simplified everything – recalibrated his priorities, consolidated his accounts, cut down on his outgoings – but all of that was done in the context of paid employment. Now, with a negligible severance package and any prospects of new employment hopelessly compromised, the figures might compute, but not into any pattern he *wants* to comprehend.

He takes a shower and gets dressed.

His phone is on the kitchen table. He passes it on his way to the fridge.

OJ first.

But holding the fridge door open, about to reach in for the Tropicana carton, he hesitates. Then he turns quickly and picks the phone up from the table. Like an idiot, he's been putting this off, as though the delay were some form of Zen discipline.

He turns the phone on and waits.

Keys in his PIN.

Waits.

Fridge door still open.

No messages, no voicemail.

Fuck.

He goes back and rereads the various texts he has sent to Lizzie since Saturday. There are four of them, all short and to the point. Call me, basically. Plus, he's left her about three voicemail messages.

Again, *call me.*

Now. Here's a simple question. Is his daughter – as her mother seems to think – just a selfish, thoughtless little bitch . . . or is there something *wrong*?

He doesn't know, but neither does Deb – which is surely the salient point here. Because OK, maybe Deb would be right to see a link between Frank's current vulnerable state and his sudden concern for Lizzie . . . but if it turns out that something actually *is* wrong, how would that even matter?

In what universe?

He closes the fridge door.

Then he opens it again and takes out the OJ. He drinks directly from the carton, empties it, tosses it in the trash.

Coffee next.

This he drinks standing at the window, gazing out, distracted, but also thinking, making another calculation.

He could be up there in two hours.

What else has he got on today? He's unemployed.

After he finishes the coffee and rinses the cup he heads into the bedroom and gets a small holdall down from the top of the wardrobe. In reality, he could be up there in two hours, stay for another two and be back in time for a late lunch.

But what if he needs to stay?

What if –

He packs the bag. A change of clothes. Some stuff from the bathroom.

You can't argue with being prepared.

On his way down to the car, Frank is aware of a faint thrum of excitement running alongside the more regular and familiar rhythm of his anxiety.

He knows what it is.

He's been stuck in a deadening routine here – in this apartment, in this town – for many months, and despite the distressing nature of the immediate circumstances, despite the fact that he may well be *back* here in a matter of hours, it feels like he's escaping.

*

From the backseat of the car, cell phone in hand, Craig Howley gazes out at the Sixth Avenue traffic. After a good deal of hesitation, he calls Angela and tells her to cancel his appointments for the morning – two meetings, one at nine, the other at ten thirty, and a conference call at twelve. It's probably because he doesn't usually do this – has he ever? – that Angela asks him if he's all right, but he reacts to her perfectly reasonable question by snapping. 'I'm fine. Jesus. Just reschedule those, would you?'

Angela then reminds him, frostily, that he has a lunch appointment at one. It's at Soleil on Madison Avenue, with Gary

Wolinsky, and he can't possibly skip it.

'OK, OK.' He sighs loudly. 'I'll be there.'

When they've finished, he powers off his phone and slips it into his jacket pocket. As he does so, he looks down at the cream-coloured folder on the seat next to him, the faded, almost grubby appearance of the cover contrasting sharply with the shiny red leather of the upholstery.

He still can't believe what a high-risk strategy this seems to be on Vaughan's part. On the one hand, yes, it's a vote of confidence in Howley, but on the other . . . isn't Vaughan very deliberately goading him? It's like an act of loyalty and an act of betrayal.

Simultaneously.

The two things inextricable, but mutually exclusive.

And Howley can't even talk to him about it, because there's nothing to say, nothing to negotiate. He just has to make a simple decision – whether or not he's going to accept the job on these terms.

Howley looks up.

He certainly didn't see this coming – though he can hardly claim he didn't see the old man coming, can he? The old man's been there all along.

The old man's *always* been there.

Howley looks out the window. The traffic has been moving at a crawl up to this point, but suddenly there's a break and a spurt, and in no time they're at the Fifty-seventh Street lights. Howley tells his driver not to turn here, as he normally would, but to go straight on. When the lights change they surge forward and two blocks later they're turning left on to Central Park South.

Howley then tells the driver to pull over, that he needs to get out of the car and walk around for a bit. The driver pulls over, but can't stop for long, can't park. He looks into his rearview mirror, awaiting instructions.

Howley grabs the folder, and a bottle of water from the bar, and as he's reaching for the door he tells the driver to head on to the Oberon Building, that he's fine, that when he's ready he'll . . . get a cab.

Or something.

Once out of the car, Howley takes off into the park at a brisk pace and makes his way over to the Mall. Near the end of this tree-lined thoroughfare he stops and picks out a bench on the east side that is dry and relatively clean. He sits down and glances around. He doesn't know why, but he feels somewhat out of place here, in this little patch of virtual countryside. What is it? The smoothness of his silk suit? His pristine leather shoes? The scent of his cologne? Do any of these really sit well in the context, in this fresh, chilly environment he has so unexpectedly found himself in?

It's also been a while since Howley was actually *in* Central Park, and he can't believe how many people are out – strolling, jogging, walking dogs – and at nine fifteen on a weekday morning. Who are these people anyway, he thinks, and why aren't they at work? His weekdays are spent in offices and conference rooms, in elevators and hallways, in traffic, with all of the people around him busy too, engaged in similar work-related activities. *These* people, on the other hand . . . what, are they retired, independently wealthy, on vacation?

He opens the bottle of water and takes a few gulps from it. He wipes his mouth with the back of his hand and throws the half-empty bottle into a trash can next to the bench.

He picks up the folder and flicks through it, recognising certain pages – pages he has already read up to half a dozen times – and then he closes it again.

Holding the folder out in front of him, he stares at its cream-coloured cover, still surprised that Vaughan has entrusted him with this, because . . . it's just that the damn thing is so dangerous. It's like a live grenade in his hands, and if he were so inclined he could fling it out there, and do some serious damage with it . . .

Reputations, careers, *lives*.

But –

Even by the way he's holding it, the care, the hesitancy, it quickly becomes apparent to him that that's not what he's going to do.

Or anything like it.

Essentially, this is a cache of incriminating evidence – details, going back years, of Byzantine deals that could, at best, be described as unorthodox.

And at worst? Well, no point dwelling on it.

The takeaway message here is that the Oberon Capital Group is, and must remain, a private company. The disclosures that a public offering would entail, in relation to financial structuring, tax arrangements, salaries, options, profitability, and so on, are quite simply unthinkable.

Howley draws the folder in again and puts it under his arm. He stands up and looks around. What the hell is he doing in Central Park anyway? He needs to get back to the office. He needs to get this thing under lock and key – or, better still, back into the hands of Jacqueline Prescott.

Walking fast, he heads south. Before long, and as he glides under the shadowline of the skyscrapers on Fifty-ninth Street, Howley comes to the (perhaps now obvious) realisation that he was never really going to be in control of this process.

How *would* he have been?

Across from the Plaza, he stands at the lights, waiting. He could hail a cab from here, but the Oberon Building is only a few blocks away. He'll enjoy walking towards it, approaching and falling under *its* shadowline.

The lights change, and he moves.

Vaughan wanted to get this handover out of the way fast, so that's what they'll do. Tomorrow's Friday. They'll hold a press conference in the morning, get it done before the weekend.

Ba da bing.

As it were.

He should text Angela.

He takes out his phone and turns it on. He looks at his watch. He might even make it back in time for that ten-thirty meeting.

*

Watch what it does overnight.

Val Brady was certainly right about that. Thursday morning and it's everywhere, hysterical banner headlines screaming *Look out Wall Street!* and *Manhunt!* and *Who's Next?* It's the lead story in most major newspapers across the world. And why wouldn't it be? Investment bankers being targeted for assassination? Summary executions on the sidewalks of Manhattan?

Ellen puts on a pot of coffee. She then turns on her phone

and checks for messages. There are four, and all of them, to her surprise, are about the Ratt Atkinson piece she did for *Parallax*. She'd forgotten, the magazine is out today, and already, apparently, her piece is causing something of a stir.

Just as the coffee is ready, another call chimes in. She lets it go to message.

'Ellen, hi, Liz Zambelli, great piece today, I think there's going to be quite a buzz around this, give me a call.'

Liz Zambelli is a booking agent for a couple of the talk shows. One of the earlier voicemail messages was from someone on *The Rachel Maddow Show*.

But Ellen's puzzled. What is it? She's been so preoccupied with this other story for the last few days that she barely remembers what she wrote in the Atkinson piece. She's about to check online to see what people are saying when her phone rings again. This time she picks it up.

'Max.'

'Hi, Ellen.'

She waits. When he doesn't say anything immediately, she sighs. 'What is it, Max? I haven't looked yet, but there's obviously something there, something significant.'

'Well, *that's* debatable.'

Ellen rolls her eyes. 'Oh, just *tell* me.'

It turns out that what has caught people's attention is a passing claim in the article that Ratt Atkinson has been exaggerating his popularity on Twitter in order to make himself look good in the eyes of a potential electorate. She quotes one source inside Atkinson's own campaign as saying that eighty-nine per cent of the former governor's followers on the site are fake, and that up to half a million either inactive or dummy accounts have been set up, and maybe even paid for, in a spectacular act of what has now come to be known as 'astrotweeting'.

'*That's* the takeaway? Nothing about . . .' She pauses, thinking. 'Nothing about his . . . tax arrangements? The state contracts thing? No mention of that stuff about his wife and the soccer coach even?'

'Nope.'

'Jesus, that's depressing. Twitter trumps sex as material for a scandal? I wasn't even going to include that bit. If I hadn't been in such a hurry I would have cut it.'

'But it's kosher?'

'Oh yeah. It's all been fact-checked. Talk to Ricky. And I've got tons more about it, too, quotes from the search agency that crunched the numbers, there's a whole breakdown of his follower stats, but I dropped most of it, because . . . I just didn't think anyone would *give* a fuck at this point.'

'Well, a fuck they most certainly *do* give. I've had a dozen calls so far today. Listen, this may not be the Pentagon Papers, but it's exposure for us, OK, and we could use it.'

'I don't know, Max.' She looks over at her desk. It's strewn with loose pages, printouts of different typefaces, hundreds of them. She was up late again last night, chasing this . . . she hesitates to even call it a lead – especially since it led nowhere – but at least it felt like she was doing something serious. She did suspect she'd be giving up on it this morning, but if the alternative is appearing on cable news shows to talk about Twitter accounts with odd usernames and no profile photos, she's not so sure. 'I'm working on something.'

'What? Not Lebrecht? Not the shootings?'

'Maybe.'

'Do you *have* something, Ellen?' Pause, no answer. 'Because it looks like you were right about it not being a professional setup, but we all *know* that now. So what else do you have?'

'Nothing, not really, but –'

'Well, then.'

'Not *exactly* nothing. I need some time, Max. And I don't want to stop. I don't want to get distracted by this Twitter shit.'

He groans.

'Trust me, Max. If I get anywhere with this, anywhere at all, it'll be a whole lot better for the magazine than some pointless story about an ex-governor who's got no chance in hell of securing the nomination in any case.'

'That's a big *if*, Ellen. Have you seen how the story has scaled up? Every news organisation in the world is on this now. How do you compete with that?'

'I don't. I only compete with myself, Max.'

'Well, I hope one of you comes out on top, because –'

'Look, give me a couple of days, OK? The Twitter story can wait, it isn't going away. If I haven't made a breakthrough on this other thing by the weekend, I'll go on goddamn Bill O'Reilly for you.'

Max exhales loudly. 'Fine.' He'd clearly like to know more about where she is on the main story, but he knows not to push it.

They'll talk tomorrow.

Sipping coffee, standing at her desk, Ellen then glances over the stuff she printed out last night.

Hundreds of upper-case As.

Which was only a small sample of the literally tens of thousands she could have printed out if she'd wanted to. She'd still be doing it, of course, and that was the main reason she stopped.

Because what was the point?

The first half hour or so she spent researching the difference between a typeface and a font, then between serif and sans serif, then the general history and development of typefaces, after which she just started banging them out, in different point sizes, five or ten to a page, all upper case.

It took her another few hours to identify what specific typeface the A was.

Blackwood Old Style, apparently.

It was a meticulous examination and comparison process – tricky, hard on the eyes, exhausting – but she was pretty sure about it in the end. Reaching a conclusion felt good, too. But of course that was deceptive . . . because what did it mean? What did it *tell* her?

Absolutely nothing.

The typeface itself was designed in the 1920s by a former San Francisco newspaperman whom a local foundry had commissioned to come up with something they could sell to ad agencies. Not long after that, Blackwood Old Style made its first appearance – on a public billboard advertising the Culpepper Union Brewing Company – and over subsequent decades the typeface proved to be very popular.

But what was she supposed to do now? With drowsiness and near-paralysis taking hold, it occurred to her – as it should have done before she went off on this obsessive tangent – to make a list of categories where a typeface like Blackwood Old Style might be used in more recent times and then to search for examples. The most obvious one, given how young the two guys appeared to be, was colleges. Beers and breweries maybe? Rock bands. What else? Trucks? Automobiles?

But she was hanging on by her fingertips here, because even if she found something – a recent example of Blackwood Old Style – it would still most likely prove to be a dead end. The guy was just wearing a printed T-shirt, and the design on it was probably something totally random. It didn't have to be significant. It didn't have to be a coded message.

Conceding defeat, she went to bed.

But now this morning, feeling fresher, and spurred on by a desire to avoid getting caught up in this preposterous Twitter controversy, she re-engages. She sits at her desk and reviews the categories she came up with for her search.

And then it all happens in what feels like a flash.

Because again, the category most likely to yield results, it seems to her, is colleges. So she generates an initial list, confining it to ten East Coast states and eliminating anywhere that doesn't begin with the letter A.

Nineteen colleges.

She starts logging on to the websites for each of these, one after the other . . . and at number seventeen, she hits pay dirt.

Atherton College.

There it is, clear as day. Blackwood Old Style.

She stares at the screen for a few moments – at the typeface, at the initial letter – and it slowly dawns on her.

Fuck.

This *is* significant. It isn't random. It's a real lead. And why the hell didn't she do this last night?

After a moment, she hears the ping of an incoming email. The subject line is 'Ratt/Twitter'. She ignores it.

The thing is the guy was wearing a specific T-shirt. He was

wearing a T-shirt with the name of a college on it.

Was it *his* college?

Before she starts shooting holes in this, which she could do pretty easily, something else occurs to her – or, to be more accurate, she remembers something.

ath900.

Holy *shit*.

The phone rings. She ignores it.

That was the name attached to the comment in that blog post she found, the one that talked about 'popping the top guys'.

In shock, Ellen leans back in her chair.

Those two things combined . . . that's more than a lead, that's a . . .

Staring at the screen, she swallows.

That's a . . .

She's afraid to say it, or even think it, but that's a grade A, gilt-edged *scoop* right there.

Seriously.

She slides forward again and starts examining the college website, and as she's doing this, over the next half hour or so, two things become clear to her. One, she's going to keep getting phone calls and emails about this Ratt Atkinson situation, overtures that will only get harder and harder to fend off (especially if she remains here, in her apartment). And two, phone calls or emails *to* Atherton College simply aren't going to be enough, not given the gravity – not given the delicacy – of the situation.

There is a logical conclusion to this, and she reaches it pretty fast. Atherton is in upstate New York, probably less than three hours away. She could get a train to Albany and hire a car from there.

She looks down.

She'll probably need to get dressed first.

The phone rings again. As before, she ignores it.

Instead, she logs on to the Amtrak website.

9

Lizzie Bishop is reluctant to admit it, but this shit is addictive.

Beforehand, she'd have assumed that watching live coverage of a murder trial on TV would be like watching paint dry. OK, more than likely there'd be occasional ripples of drama, but the sheer tedium of it, day after day – the proceedings, the lingo, all that *ipso facto* shit, not to mention the endless analysis – just, *No, I'm sorry . . . no way . . .*

Who could possibly be into that?

Well, as it turns out, *she* could.

Because as it turns *out*, there's something sort of creepy and hypnotic about it, and from her curled-up perspective here on the couch – remote in one hand, can of Red Bull in the other – she's finding it hard to look away, to take her eyes off this prosecution guy, for instance, Ray Whitestone . . . who's not cute, or anything, Jesus, he must have Type 2 diabetes, at *least*, but he also has a commanding presence. And weirdly enough, too – it seems to Lizzie – the more banal the questions (and answers, of course), the more hypnotic the whole thing tends to become.

And it's not just Ray Whitestone, either. The witness on the stand at the moment, this doorman guy, Joey Gifford – he's something else. Curiously compelling is what one of the talking-head commentators has called him a few times, and that about sums him up. He's like a person you'd see on some ultra-tacky, cringe-inducing reality show, only more so.

Because this actually *is* reality.

'The awning, the one outside that covers the sidewalk,' Whitestone is saying, 'the canopy, that's . . . that's supported by four *brass* poles, am I correct?'

'Yes, brass . . . brass poles. I'm assuming it's brass, that's what it *looks* like . . . brass. It's the right colour.' Joey Gifford clears his throat. 'I mean, I'm no, what's the word, *metallurgist*, but –'

'Indeed, Mr Gifford, thank you.'

Not that Lizzie ever really watches reality shows, or daytime TV for that matter.

But –

A commercial break comes on and the spell is broken. She looks around, studying the apartment, these unfamiliar surroundings, for the hundredth time this week.

The place is small. In this room there's the couch she's sitting on, the TV, a shelving unit, a desk in the corner, and a longish rectangular table on which she has her study things laid out, textbooks, laptop, notebooks, pens. There's a window that looks down over a concrete yard with some scrubby trees in it and a dilapidated wooden fence that backs onto the yard of another, similar building. There's one bedroom, the door of which is always locked – during the day, at any rate. The kitchen and bathroom are tiny, really tiny, their poky windows giving onto the building's cramped air shaft, where all you can see is other mostly shuttered windows and red brickwork, darkened now and flecked by a century's deposit of bird shit and soot. There doesn't seem to be much soundproofing between the apartments either, because she can hear muffled voices, noises, random thuds, as well as the incessant clanking and hissing of the steam radiators.

Lizzie doesn't like it here. She doesn't feel comfortable on her own all day.

Not that it's much better in the evenings.

But to be honest, what she's really feeling right now is out of her depth.

And also a little stupid.

She takes a sip from her Red Bull.

The commercial break comes to an end, but instead of going back to the live feed from the courtroom, they start into a quick recap of the proceedings so far.

Most of which she has just watched.

She raises the remote control and flicks forward a few channels, stopping for a moment at a rerun of *House*.

'Sarcoidosis,' she shouts at the screen, then flicks forward again.

Nature documentary, insects.

She stares at it, not paying attention.

Out of her depth?

She takes another sip of Red Bull.

Stupid?

Why?

Because she doesn't know what the fuck is going on, that's why. And there's only so much of this crap that she can put up with. It's insane. No internet access? No going out or talking to people? No using her cell phone? No TV?

It's only supposed to be for a week – until tomorrow, in fact, and she did warn her friends about the impending radio silence.

But still.

Even the fact that she has slipped a bit – that wobbly call to her dad on the first night, putting the TV on this morning, and keeping it on – is surely telling her something.

That maybe she just doesn't care as much any more.

What she can't believe is that she actually felt disloyal this morning *turning on the fucking TV*.

For almost a week now – in what has admittedly been the most productive period she's ever spent as a student – Lizzie has been cooped up here in this apartment, reading, studying, but also assiduously abiding by these house rules, by this fucked-up paranoid off-the-grid communications blackout. And the thing is, she *gets* it, at least in regard to cell phones and social media. There's a real danger there of personal data being monitored, sure. So don't have them on.

Fine.

Being a fairly slack user of Facebook and Twitter herself, that aspect of it hasn't actually been hard at all.

But Jesus H. Christ . . . *the fucking TV*?

This morning it just seemed too ridiculous. She'd finished a long paper and prepared a detailed set of notes for her next one, and . . .

Enough was enough.

She was only doing it, in any case, to keep her boyfriend's *asshole of a brother happy*. So she turned on the goddamn TV, and started watching the first thing she came across, which happened to be live coverage of the Connie Carillo murder trial.

But now maybe she's had her fill of that. For the moment, at least. Now maybe – and for the first time since last Saturday – she's going to find a cable news channel and plug into what's going on outside in the wider world, the one beyond this shit-hole of an apartment on the Lower East Side of Manhattan.

Frank Bishop arrives in the small town of Atherton just before noon. The college is situated about a mile north of the town, so he decides to stop first and find a cheap restaurant or diner where he can sit for a while over coffee and gather his thoughts.

Atherton itself is pretty short on charm, mainly consisting of car dealerships, strip malls, fast-food joints and sports bars. He parks on a side street off Main and wanders around in search of what he soon realises is probably an elusive dream – the classic small-town diner with its chrome fittings, soda fountain and tabletop jukeboxes.

The nearest thing he finds is either a Wendy's or a Chicken Pit. Two years ago when he came here with Lizzie they had lunch at the Great Lakes Grill and Bistro, an indulgence he can no longer afford.

He chooses the Chicken Pit.

The coffee is undrinkable, the blueberry muffin he got to go with it inedible, but at least he can sit in his little booth, staring out the window, undisturbed.

And now that he's here, of course, he feels like an idiot. Because how uncool is this going to be for Lizzie . . . her old man turning up unannounced, and even – if he's not careful, if he can't keep a lid on recent developments – presenting as borderline unhinged?

At the same time, though, when he looks down at his cell phone on the table between his keys and coffee cup, Frank is reminded of why he decided to come up here in the first place.

It's perfectly simple.

Lizzie doesn't go this long without returning a call. It might be a chore, and *he* might be a pain in the ass – but she doesn't go five days, not when her old man is so clearly anxious to talk to her. And that's what he should have pressed home to Deb yesterday when they spoke.

That this has never happened before.

Not like this.

Formulating the thought makes Frank's insides turn.

He shuffles out of the booth and gathers up his keys and phone.

Out on Main Street, it occurs to him that he could have just called the college administration people and had them check up on her, but he's also pretty sure that Lizzie would have regarded that as a serious breach of trust.

Considerably worse than what he is about to do.

Because just showing up won't necessarily compromise or embarrass her. Anyway, he doesn't care, he's here now, and at this stage he actually *needs* to see her. It's an imperative. It's become that way.

He drives north out of Atherton and within a couple of minutes is approaching the sprawling campus. To the left there are residence halls, three of them, known locally as the Projects, and to the right there is the more severe, clean-lines administration block. Get past these and you enter a sort of sylvan grove, mostly single-storey buildings arranged on scenic, grassy quads and tree-lined courtyards that house the various academic departments, dining halls, libraries and student health and community centres.

He parks in a visitor's space in front of the Administration Building and gets out of the car. But standing there, he realises something. He feels weirdly self-conscious. It's as though he's guilty of something, or is about to be.

He looks around.

Where should he go first?

The easiest thing would be to wander the campus for a while and just randomly bump into Lizzie. Then he could be out of here in five minutes.

But that's a pretty unlikely scenario.

He looks over towards the residence halls, focusing on the middle one.

Is she in her rooms?

Maybe, but he can't just go in there, not without a security pass.

He needs to take this slowly. No one else is in a panic here. So he shouldn't be. Besides, it's lunchtime. Everywhere he looks, people are . . . having lunch.

On benches, on lawns.

He decides to wander around for a while anyway. He passes the Science Building and the main dining hall. He crosses the central quad, walks along by the Van Loon Auditorium and then makes his way over towards the tennis and basketball courts. At this point he stops at a bench himself and sits down.

But what is he doing?

Almost immediately he stands up again and walks back the way he came – quickly, straight towards the Administration Building.

He goes into the main office. There are two women working behind a high reception counter.

He feels he's blurting it out, but the information seems to get across, and within a minute the woman he's dealing with is on the phone. There's a brief exchange, and then some waiting.

Frank starts drumming his fingers on the counter, but stops himself almost immediately.

'There's no response from her room. I'll –'

The woman cuts herself short and hits another number. There's a second brief exchange, which Frank finds it difficult to hear, because a separate conversation is now taking place next to them.

When the woman has finished, she looks back at Frank. 'There'll be someone over to see you in a moment.'

'Who?' Frank says, a little too quickly.

'It's the house RA. She'll be able to help you.' The woman pauses. 'If you'd care to take a seat?'

Frank takes a few steps backwards and sits down.

She's not in her rooms.

That doesn't have to mean anything. She could be anywhere. In the library. At a lecture. Having lunch, like everyone else.

After a short while, Frank looks up and sees a young woman approaching. She's tall, thin and pale, with long red hair. She's dressed . . . half like a hippie and half like a corporate executive. This weird, mix-it-up dress code seems to be de rigueur on campus.

'Mr Bishop?' she says, extending a hand.

'Yes.'

They shake.

'I'm Sally Peake, the resident assistant in Lizzie's house.' She holds up her cell phone. 'I've just spoken with Lizzie's room-mate, Rachel, and . . . she says Lizzie is away for the week.'

Frank looks at her. 'Away? I don't understand. Away where?'

'Er, I don't know, Mr Bishop. Just away. That's all she said.'

'But –'

'Would you like to speak with Rachel yourself? I could take you over there right now.'

Frank pauses. 'Yeah. OK.' He nods. 'Thanks.'

A few minutes later they enter the third-floor hallway of Lizzie's residence. When they're about halfway along, a door opens and Rachel Clissmann appears, a good-looking, sun-blushed, sporty type in a floral-print dress and thick black-rimmed glasses. Frank met her once before, in the city, at some celebration. She looked different then and he barely recognises her now.

'Mr Bishop.'

'Rachel.'

She shows them in. Frank feels slightly out of place here, standing in this small room, with these two young women. But he glances around nevertheless, taking everything in – the bookshelves, the Shaker table and chairs, the candles and crystals and cushions, the implausible neatness, the scented atmosphere of wellness and moderation. He's prepared to bet that not all of the rooms on the third or any other floor here are like this.

He's prepared to bet that Lizzie's *bed*room is not like this. He looks over. The door is closed.

'Rachel,' he says, turning to her, taking a deep breath, 'Sally here told me what you said. Lizzie is away, is that right?'

'Yes, I –'

'I'm not checking up on her or anything. I –'

'No, no, I –'

'I've just been worried, that's all. She hasn't been returning my calls. Or texts.' He swallows. 'Or anything.'

'I understand, Mr Bishop, of course. She and Alex took off last Friday. It had been planned for a while, or . . . so it seemed.'

Frank stands there, looking into this girl's startling blue eyes, uncomfortable in his sudden awareness of her perfume, of the tone of her skin . . . and he feels a rising sense of how indefensibly ridiculous what he's about to say will sound.

'*Alex?*'

'Oh, oh, er . . . he's –'

'No, no, I didn't mean it like that. Please. Alex, Schmalex . . . whatever. But do you know where they went?'

Before she has a chance to answer he thinks, last Friday. That means that when he spoke to her on Saturday evening she wasn't here, settling in to finish a paper. She was somewhere else, with someone else, *doing* something else.

She was lying.

But again, fuck it, that's not the point. He sounds indefensibly ridiculous to himself now, when the only thing he's interested in, the only thing he cares about is . . . *is she OK?*

Realising then that Rachel has already answered his question, and that he wasn't listening, he says, 'Sorry?'

'I don't *know*, Mr Bishop,' she repeats, obviously bewildered at having to do so. 'Lizzie wouldn't tell me. I got the impression they just needed some time on their own.' She pauses. 'I'm sure she's fine.'

As Frank turns away, he catches a glimpse of Sally glaring at Rachel.

'Let me try her,' Rachel then offers, but not sounding too hopeful for some reason. As Frank stares at a framed She & Him album cover on the wall, he senses determined phone busyness behind him. After a moment, he hears 'Shit, voicemail,' a pause, and then, in a concerned monotone, 'Liz, Rach, call me.'

Frank turns back around.

A century on from two minutes ago, he looks at them both in turn, and says, 'OK, what do we know about this Alex guy?'

*

On the train to Albany, Ellen does as much background research on Atherton as she can.

A liberal arts college founded in the late 1870s, it was originally built on a twenty-five-acre site in the Sasketchaw Valley a few miles east of Atherton. The college moved to its present, much larger site a mile north of the town when it acquired the former Van Loon family estate in 1953. Most of the buildings currently in use on the campus were constructed in the 1960s, giving the place a curious feel, simultaneously contemporary and dated.

Atherton first admitted women in 1936, and today has a total enrolment of just under two thousand. It offers twenty-five majors leading to arts or science degrees, as well as pre-professional programmes in law, medicine, engineering and IT.

This takes Ellen as far as Yonkers. She then switches her focus to more practical matters.

As a school, Atherton is primarily residential, and most students live on campus. All of its three residence halls have common study areas, pantries, phone and cable connections and internet access. Suites are generally single-sex, but gender-neutral accommodation is available in the upper two floors of the third building. As an ex-Cartwright girl, Ellen is familiar with this kind of stuff, most of it, anyway – though she is certainly surprised by one thing, the range of food options available. Atherton's main dining hall has five different sections, the Globe Café (serving a selection of cuisines from around the world), the Cabbage Patch (salads and vegan), the Spoon (burgers, pizza), the Deli Zone (sandwiches, wraps) and the Juice Depot.

She looks up from the screen for a moment, and out the window.

Croton-Harmon.

And then back.

Atherton has all the usual other stuff as well, a Student Government Association that liaises with the college administration, an official student-run newspaper, the *Atherton Chronicle*, and a closed-circuit TV station (AthTV) that covers events on campus and in the surrounding area, as well as a highly respected and long-established college radio station (WKNT-92 FM) that broadcasts a mix of musical programming and various innovative talk-show formats.

Poughkeepsie.

In terms of security, Atherton is staffed by twelve full-time and six part-time professionals who are all state-certified security guards. The security staff also receive specialist training in first aid, CPR, conflict resolution, sex aggression defence techniques, cyber crime and diversity awareness.

Rhinecliff.

Ellen then spends a bit of time digging into the college's history, looking out for any tradition of student radicalism, or of anything politically sensitive at all, but there's really very little there. The late sixties and early seventies saw the usual reactions to Chicago, Kent State, Cambodia and so on, there were sit-ins and marches, but nothing exceptional. In 2007, a chapter of the recently re-formed SDS was opened at Atherton, but the main focus of activity here seemed to be either teaming up with wider anti-war protest networks or working to change the state education system.

Hudson.

In more recent years, there's been nothing of any special interest or note – no links beyond the obvious ones to the Occupy movement, and no discernible drift the other way either.

Ellen's impression is of a fairly insular place, self-satisfied and maybe even a little smug, probably not unlike hundreds of other colleges across the country.

So what the fuck is she doing up here?

As she gets off the train at Albany-Rensselaer, no new answer comes to mind – just the old one: it's all she's got.

She picks up the rental car she booked earlier and gets to Atherton in under an hour.

As she approaches the campus, she sees that it does indeed have a slight timewarp feel to it – angular grey concrete buildings, now partially streaked and stained but that must have once seemed futuristic and full of promise. Mitigating this somewhat is the landscaping, the well-kept lawns, flower beds and trees.

Ellen parks in front of the Administration Building and then has a quick think about how to proceed. Does she announce herself and spin some story about researching a piece on New York colleges, or does she wander around and wait until she gets busted by security?

She decides to wander around.

It takes her about thirty-five minutes to do a complete tour of the campus, stopping occasionally to inspect a building or to check out a sign or notice board.

She doesn't get busted, and nothing catches her attention.

Except some of the students.

She remembers being a student herself, and vividly – it wasn't *that* long ago – but these people here are like a different species. There's an air of confidence and self-assurance about the place that she's finding unfamiliar, and not a little strange. The crowd she ran with at Cartwright were all cocky and opinionated, no question about that, but this is not the same thing. This is like a sense of entitlement, or of ownership – and not ownership of property or material things, not even of position or privilege, but just of . . . *their own world.*

And its ways, whatever they may be.

Not exactly a formula for political engagement, she thinks, but maybe not a fair assessment either. Because she hasn't actually spoken to anyone yet.

It's early afternoon, sunny and cool, and quite a few people are out, some sitting on benches and lawns, others strolling around the various quads – most, it appears, in small groups, self-contained, cocooned.

Striking up a casual conversation out here isn't going to be easy, so she decides to head for the main dining hall. The logic isn't exactly airtight, but she imagines that standing in line for food could well generate an opening gambit or two.

Besides, she's hungry.

She heads for the Cabbage Patch. There actually isn't much of a line here, but she starts eyeing the salads on offer anyway.

'Check out the Avocado Wasabi.'

That was quick.

Ellen turns to her left.

'Good?'

'Oh my.'

The girl is early twenties, younger even, and quite geeky. She's in glasses, jeans and a T-shirt that has a cartoony graphic of a computer keyboard on it . . . geeky, that is, except for the small tattoo on the side of her neck, which Ellen now sees – as the girl turns around slightly – may well be part of a much bigger one all down her shoulder, or even her back.

Ellen takes the salad from the display and looks at the girl. 'Twenty years ago, when I was a student? *Wasabi?* I don't fucking think so. You do pretty well here.'

The girl draws back a little. '*Twenty* years ago? You're kidding, right?'

Shaking her head, but saying nothing, Ellen reaches for a bottle of water.

'Here?'

'No, at Cartwright.'

'Wow. I'm at the wrong *school.*'

Moving her tray along the counter, Ellen glances back. 'What are you studying?'

The girl pauses, maintaining eye contact and pursing her lips. 'You mean right now?'

Ellen feels like telling her there's a speed limit in this state, but she plays along, and within five minutes they've been joined at a table by two of Geek Girl's friends and Ellen is pumping them hard for information, so hard in fact that she eventually has no choice but to partially blow her cover and tell them she's a journalist.

One of them has heard of her and is wildly impressed.

But not a lot comes of it. She explains that she's researching student activism post-Occupy and would like to identify any sources of radicalism in the college. Not wanting to freak them out or scare them off, she quickly adds that she isn't looking for names or anything, which is a lie, of course, but she also gets the impression that if they had any such names, giving them out wouldn't necessarily be a problem for these girls, and not because of any latent McCarthyite tendencies they might have, but rather because it just wouldn't occur to them that anyone could possibly object.

Going by their ages, which probably average out at about twenty, it's a safe bet to assume that these girls have fully recorded and documented their lives online, at least from the start of adolescence, and that it's all still out there – every last confession, playlist and photo, and for anyone at all to see, at any time – on Xanga, Blogger, LiveJournal, Facebook, Flickr, Vimeo. It's the great fault line of the new generation gap, the end of privacy – and it's what makes Max Daitch (for example) such a dinosaur. He thinks, why would you do such a thing? They think, why *wouldn't* you?

It's just that right now, for Ellen, none of this is of any use, because it turns out that Geek Girl here and her friends are about as politically aware as, she doesn't know . . . the Smurfs. Or the Bratz.

One of them, however – the Smart One – does make a useful suggestion.

Ellen should check out a few past numbers of the *Atherton Chronicle*. She'll find a pile of them in the main library. And she should probably also listen back to some of the talk stuff they do on the college radio station – some of that shit, apparently, can get *very* political. She'll find it all archived online.

Before Ellen leaves the Cabbage Patch to head for the

library, she hoovers some personal details up from around the table – phone numbers, email and web addresses, usernames, handles, hashtags – info she may find useful later on, if it turns out she needs a quick route into the Atherton College social mediasphere.

The girls, of course, are only too willing to hand over anything she asks for.

*

'She did say one thing, now that I remember.'

Frank looks at Rachel. Whatever this is, she's pretending she's only just remembered it – Frank can see that clearly, and he's annoyed – but at this stage the information is what counts, nothing else.

'What is it?'

'Before she left, she said there'd be radio silence for a while. That's what she called it.'

'Radio silence.'

'Yeah.'

'Meaning?'

Rachel swallows, uncomfortable now. 'I guess that, yeah, she wouldn't be answering her phone, or tweeting, that kind of stuff.'

'Why not?'

'I don't know, Mr Bishop. She didn't elaborate. Lizzie isn't that forthcoming.'

He also finds it annoying being told what his daughter is supposedly like. 'You didn't ask?'

Rachel shuffles for a bit – in her bare feet, which Frank has just noticed – and then adjusts her glasses. 'No, I didn't. She's not big on social media, she's not an obsessive like I am, or like most people these days, so it didn't seem like such a big deal, you know? Things can get pretty intense around here, and I just figured she and Alex maybe needed to, I don't know, zone out for a bit.'

Alex.

She didn't have much to say about *him* either. Sally Peake is currently out in the hallway trying to see who she can scare up that might have a little more to say about him.

Frank feels he's getting something of a mixed message from these two. On the one hand, it's obvious they think he's a nut-job, and that he didn't get – or *read* – the memo about how his daughter going to college meant that SHE WAS LEAVING HOME. On the other hand, he senses a slight nervousness, especially on Sally's part, a desire to wrap this up, to contain it before security has to be called in.

'Around here,' Frank then says to Rachel. 'You said things can get pretty intense. You mean specifically at Atherton?'

'Yes. There's a lot of academic pressure, a lot of competitiveness.'

Frank nods. Now that he thinks about it, Lizzie is actually a very good student. She's always done well and gotten good grades. She's focused, and works hard. She got a part scholarship to this place.

So maybe she did just need a break.

And maybe her old man *is* a fucking nutjob, who could do with seeing a psychiatrist.

Sally Peake reappears in the doorway, again holding up her phone. 'Friend of Alex, guy who knows him pretty well? He's just coming out of the VLA, says he'll meet us at the Spoon in ten.'

Frank nods at Rachel and says, 'Thanks.'

She nods back.

As he's walking out of the room, he sees her lifting up her phone and starting to text.

The Spoon is a section of the main dining hall, which itself is more like a food court in a suburban mall, not unlike the one in Winterbrook, in fact – though seeing it again now Frank realises that this one is a tad fancier.

They approach a table near the front, where Sally Peake introduces him to a young guy named Claudio Mazza. Frank tries to get an instant fix on him, but is thwarted from the get-go. Despite his Italian name, Claudio Mazza has blond hair and blue eyes. Frank is also finding it hard to categorise him as a typical college kid. Is he a nerd, a jock, a hipster or a partier? None of these really seems to fit. He does have a book next to his coffee cup, but that hardly counts as a clue around this place. Probably nineteen or twenty years old, he's dressed with a nod to punk – or maybe it's punk-meets-goth – in dirty, wide-strapped, spiked boots and a pair of studded jeans that look like something from an art installation. But these are offset sharply by an almost foppish upper half – a tweed jacket and a plain white T-shirt.

What's *that* called?

Frank gives up.

With Sally Peake hovering in the background, he sits at the table and starts asking questions.

Claudio and Alex, it seems, are taking some of the same literature courses (Melville, Dos Passos, Coover) and that's how they know each other. Claudio says Alex is a really nice guy who doesn't drink or do drugs. He's very smart, very shy, very independent-minded, but he also has a naïve streak in him a mile wide. Thinks he can change the world. He has an older brother he's in thrall to, Julian, who was at Atherton a couple of years back and is a veteran anti-globalisation protester. Julian is apparently a streets guy. With Alex, it tends to be more cerebral. On hearing all of this, Frank finds himself simultaneously relieved and a little concerned.

He then asks Claudio about Alex and Lizzie.

It turns out the pair have been an item for several months now, and are rarely seen apart.

Or in the company of others.

'It's a very exclusive relationship,' Claudio says, 'and not just romantically. They tend to rely on each other in all sorts of . . . function-specific situations.' He reaches for his coffee cup, lifts it, then puts it down again. 'But it's an arrangement that seems to work pretty well,' he adds, 'given that neither of them has a lot going on in the old social skills department.'

Frank bristles at this, even though he knows it's true, at least in relation to Lizzie.

He leans back in his chair, unsure of what to think.

This Claudio seems fairly smart himself, and confident – though maybe a little too eager to showcase the Psych 101 stuff. Still, there's no reason not to believe what he's saying about Alex.

But where does that leave matters?

Deflating slightly, Frank glances around.

The Globe Café? The Juice Depot? This is *so* not like the food court at Winterbrook Mall. There are no obese people here, for starters. Everyone he can see is young and healthy. Look at Sally Peake, for instance – over there, pacing up and down, on her phone – the very picture of long-limbed, pink-cheeked, genetically unmodified youth.

Frank bends his neck slightly to get a look at the spine of Claudio's book.

And no one at the mall is reading Herman Melville's *The Confidence-Man*, that's for sure.

After a moment, he catches Claudio's eye and says, 'Do you have any idea where they are?'

'No, Mr Bishop, I don't. Alex wouldn't tell me, but he did mention they'd be gone for a week, and that means – what day is this? Thursday? – they'll probably be back tomorrow.' He shrugs his shoulders, as if to say, *Hey, problem solved.* Frank then half expects this nineteen-year-old to produce a small pad and a pen and to write him out a prescription for some Xanax.

But who's to say, maybe the problem *is* solved.

He pictures his precious girl, his Lizzie – little bit mousy, little bit mouthy – off somewhere with her shy, brainy, ideal-istic boyfriend, the two of them, what . . . going at it like jackrabbits?

Is that it? Is that *all*?

Does Deb know, and didn't want to tell him? Didn't want to point out that it's actually none of his business?

With what it's costing him, Frank could get worked up about Lizzie cutting school for a week, but . . . that's not going to happen.

Academically, she's doing fine.

He wants her to be happy, too, though. And if she is, well and good, who's *he* to interfere?

You're only young once.

He stares into space for a while. When he refocuses, he realises that both Sally Peake and Claudio Mazza are staring at *him*.

*

Walking along the High Line, towards the exit at Thirtieth Street, Lizzie feels sick to her stomach. She also feels sort of hollowed-out, and paralysed.

Not to mention scared.

She wonders if, when she gets back to street level, she shouldn't just keep heading towards midtown. Because then she could stop by the law firm where her mother works. She could submit herself to *that*, and all it would entail – the machinery of the law, the machinery of her mother's disapproval.

She doesn't know which machinery would be worse.

Although they're both pretty much unthinkable, really.

Like every other option she's come up with in the last three hours. Which is how long she has been out and about in the city, wandering aimlessly, having hot flashes, hallucinating (as good as), and dry crying.

When she saw it – the clip, the footage from outside the Herald Rygate – *fuck*, it was like getting whacked on the head with a baseball bat. Because at first she had to piece the story together, the references and images, which were all rapid-fire, all seemingly random and out of sequence, it wasn't breaking news any more, but an aggregate, a mosaic, an accumulated and already absorbed narrative.

Jesus, listen to her, she sounds like fucking Julian.

But now she understands. That's the difference. Now she *gets* it. And she's been going over it all, the past week, reassembling it in her head, reinterpreting every word spoken, every testy exchange, every weird glance and inexplicable mood swing. Now she understands why Julian was so unhappy about her tagging along – the politically illiterate pain-in-the-ass girlfriend that his brother couldn't bear to be separated from even for a lousy few days.

How could she have been so *stupid*?

Actually, she knows how. Because go over the signs, go over the timeline, and it all fits . . . even if it doesn't make any sense, even if it doesn't connect on an emotional or a gut level, even if it's literally *un*believable – the idea that Julian could plan and carry out an operation of this magnitude. But go over the *footage*, study those two familiar, spectral figures, the way they move, the body language, and suddenly it all makes perfect sense.

To her at least.

But don't ask her to explain it.

She walks down the steps of the cutoff to Thirtieth Street and keeps going. She crosses Tenth Avenue and heads for Ninth.

She's wearing jeans and a sweater, but there's a chill in the air, and it's probably going to get chillier. Also, her feet are sore. She left the apartment in a hurry, not giving any thought to what she was doing, certainly not to what shoes she should wear.

She brought her phone, but the damn thing needs to be charged.

She has maybe twelve dollars and some loose change in her pocket. She's hungry, but won't go in anywhere because the thought of having to deal with people makes her feel even more nauseous than she's already feeling.

At Sixth Avenue, she turns left and heads uptown.

So far she has covered most of downtown, the East Village, SoHo, Tribeca and the West Village. Then she made her way up to Gansevoort Street, where the High Line starts.

There's a lot to process in what has happened, no question about that, and she's in a daze, but there's also something nagging at her, tugging at her, some other level of this that she's resisting.

What is it?

Block after block passes and her mind refuses to settle. When she gets to Forty-second Street, she wanders into Bryant Park, finds an unoccupied bench and sits down.

There's a simple, recurring question here: how could she not have seen what was going on? Was she blind? Lizzie's understanding of the situation up to now has been that Julian is the radical in the Coady family. He's involved with various protest groups and firmly believes in direct action – city marches, shutting down bridges and ports, so-called black bloc rampages, that kind of thing. He also believes, at some level, in the use of actual physical force. She hasn't given much thought to this, but if she does, what comes to mind? Pushing, shoving, shouting stuff like 'Fuck the cops.' Maybe throwing stones or broken bottles. All of which leads, of course – according to Alex – to police brutality, tear gas, pepper sprays, Tasers, stun grenades. And beyond that to mass arrests, trumped-up charges, surveillance, infiltration, raids. And then, inevitably, on to more cycles of resistance.

But if Julian is the radical activist in the family, then what is Alex? The armchair strategist? Lizzie isn't sure, because Alex plays his cards very close to his chest, even with her.

Lizzie's understanding of the situation this week in particular was that Julian had asked Alex to come down and help him organise some big street protest that was in the offing. She wasn't surprised that Alex agreed, because she knew that Alex would do anything for Julian. But she also knew from experience not to ask too many questions, and was content instead to imagine the two of them – it's preposterous *now*, she realises – hand-cranking out leaflets on a small printing press, or unpacking bulk consignments of Anonymous masks.

But then Alex asked *her* to come as well. She was into it at first, a mix of flattered and intrigued, but that was when her exposure to Julian hadn't extended beyond a single face-to-face meeting over a pizza, a few Skype calls she happened to be in the room for, and Alex's many stories about him.

Five days of the real thing has pretty much taken the shine off *those*.

But Lizzie's focus in all of this is not – and never has been – on Julian. In a way, he's the mad, fucked-up older brother in the background, like a secondary character out of some sitcom that got cancelled after its first season. No, the focus for Lizzie, obviously, has always been on Alex – innocent, whispery, logical, weirdly sexy, on-the-fucking-*spectrum* Alex.

And Alex doesn't get cancelled, not lightly.

Which is when it hits her. Like a second whack of the baseball bat.

That *thing* that's been nagging at her.

Within a minute, Lizzie is on her feet, digging into the pocket of her jeans for the crumpled-up ten and two ones. Walking along Forty-second, she looks back over her shoulder. Sixth goes up, right? And Fifth down.

She's not a native here, not any more.

She approaches the front of the New York Public Library, the steps, the stone lions. She'll get a cab downtown, as far as the meter will take her, and walk the rest.

She has no choice now. She has to go back. It would be an act of disloyalty not to, and as the cab whittles down through the midtown cross streets, below Fourteenth, down to Washington Square Park and over to Broadway, she realises she doesn't feel sick any more. She's not anxious, or scared, either.

She doesn't know what she is.

But one thing she does know – as she gets out of the cab, surrendering her twelve bucks, with fifteen or so blocks outstanding, and as she replays that clip in her head – one thing she *alone* knows, and knows for sure.

It wasn't Julian, it was never him.

The shooter? OK, outside the Rygate, the *potential* shooter – but the shooter on Columbus Avenue? The shooter in Central Park? She's prepared to lay even money now, not that she has to, because it's just come to her, in a flash, from the clip, the woolly hat, the grey hoodie, which was which.

Who was who.

The shooter wasn't Julian.

The shooter was Alex.

*

Ellen comes out of the library with a name.

Julian Robert Coady.

It was actually pretty easy. Five minutes of sweet-talking her way into a temporary reader's pass, forty minutes of flicking through a pile of *Atherton Chronicle* back issues, and then another twenty, twenty-five minutes online, cross-referencing names that appeared in the paper with names from the college radio station's website – specifically from the page for its headline talk show, *What Up?*

The paper is a weekly and doesn't have an online edition, but it didn't take Ellen long to familiarise herself with the layout and to identify likely page locations where strong political views might be expressed. She also started from a year ago, more or less around the time of that blog post with the comment thread that threw up the 'ath900' handle. She got through over fifty issues – a quick riffle, literally, for each one – before coming across anything of interest. This turned out to be a semi-regular column called 'The Eyeball' that railed pretty consistently against the bankers and their gigantic criminal conspiracy. Nothing unusual in that, of course, it's practically a new art form – indignation porn, you find it everywhere – but the tone here was quite peculiar.

The byline on the articles was Caligula.

In one of them, reference was made to an academic called Farley Kaplan, who had apparently given an interview the previous week on a small local cable news show, the *Stone Report*, in which he stated that 'leading bankers should face a firing squad'.

When Ellen went online and did a trawl of names on the WKNT website – guest lists, programme hosts, production assistants – she quickly came across the name Farley Kaplan again. He appeared on an edition of *What Up?* a couple of months after the 'Eyeball' piece and did a ten-minute interview in which he expanded on his firing squad comment.

What Up? is a half-hour show that goes out on Saturday afternoons and covers political and environmental stories mainly culled from alternative media sources. Ellen pulled the Kaplan interview from the archive and listened to it. It was standard stuff, with the firing squad remark definitely coming off as facetious rather than sinister, but towards the end of the ten-minute slot he did repeat it, adding that there should be enough bullets to go around 'for a representative from each of the three Wall Street crime syndicates, investment banking, hedge funds and private equity'.

Ellen was still trying to process this when the presenter signed off by thanking Kaplan for coming on the show, and also 'our sound engineer, the *Chronicle*'s legendary Caligula, for enticing him to come on'.

It didn't take Ellen more than a couple of keystrokes to establish that the *What Up?* sound engineer around that time was one Julian Robert Coady.

Was Coady the guy? Was he ath900? Was he one of the shooters?

Maybe, maybe not, but as she emerges from the library, Ellen has a keen sense that she's on to something, certainly that she has something to work with – names (Coady, Kaplan) and possible places to check out (the WKNT office, the residence halls here at Atherton, wherever the *Stone Report* operates from).

She decides her next stop should probably be the Administration Building, but as she's crossing the main quad in front of the library, she spots Geek Girl and her posse occupying a bench on the east side, under a maple tree, all of them looking in her direction.

'Hey there,' Geek Girl says, and waves.

Ellen stops, shakes her head and walks over.

'What, you guys have nothing better to do,' she says, 'no classes to go to?'

The Smart One holds her hand out, indicating the now sun-drenched quad. 'What could be better than this?'

'Besides,' Geek Girl says, 'we're intrigued.'

Ellen looks at her, holding her gaze, saying nothing.

'You *know*.'

'Do I?'

'A reporter on campus, a *real* reporter. There must be something . . . afoot.'

'*Afoot?*'

'Yeah, you like that?' She pauses. 'Newspaper girl.'

This chick is something else. Ellen has been hit on by women before, but not – as far as she can remember – by a twenty-year-old, and not outside the dim and noisy confines of a bar.

'I don't work for a newspaper.'

'Oh, that's right,' the Smart One says, holding up her phone. '*Parallax* magazine. I Googled you.'

'Yeah, well,' Ellen says, deciding she might as well get started here. 'Whatever. But listen. Speaking *of* newspapers, do any of you guys actually read the *Chronicle*?'

This is greeted with a collective hoot of derision. Bulldozing through it, Ellen adds, '"The Eyeball"? Caligula? Ever hear of those? It's a . . . column.'

But from two years ago, she suddenly remembers.

So pretty unlikely.

This is confirmed by a few head shakes and some murmuring.

'Julian Robert Coady?' she tries, throwing it out there.

A silence follows, and then, '*That's* weird.'

This from a girl standing at the back. She's short and pale, gothy, impossibly young-looking.

'Why so?'

'Well,' the girl says, not making eye contact with Ellen, 'I just got this text from a friend of mine, Alicia? It seems you're not the only one around here asking questions today.'

Everyone turns and looks at her, waiting for more.

'Well?' Geek Girl says. 'Spill it, Morticia.'

Morticia flips her one and then says, in a conspiratorial whisper, 'Lizzie Bishop's old man is here. He's looking for her and ... no one can find her.'

'*What?*'

'Everyone's talking about it. Texting, tweeting.'

There's a collective grab for phones.

Ellen stands there, watching them all juice in. She gives it a few moments. After the first couple of message tones, she says, 'So, what has this Lizzie whatsit got to do with ... Julian Robert Coady?'

The Smart One looks up from her phone. 'Lizzie's going out with Coady's brother, a guy called Alex.' She pauses, consulting her device again. 'And no one can find *him* either.'

Ellen's heart skips a beat.

Alex ... and Julian. Two brothers? One of them a radical-minded student at Atherton from a couple of years back, the other one still at Atherton, but currently *missing*?

Caligula and ath900?

The Atherton T-shirt?

She stands back now, swaying slightly from side to side,

looking on as the girls work their phones, foreheads all screwed up in concentration, fingers hopping and dancing like they're in some demented jazz ensemble.

So this story, the shooting of Wall Street bankers? Has she just fucking *cracked* it? That's the way it seems, but she has to keep her nerve here. Because what she's got is still based on speculation. She needs to go one more round and come up with some concrete evidence.

There is a fresh wave of message tones.

'My friend Trish?' Geek Girl says, looking up from her phone. 'She spoke with Sally Peake. That's the RA in Lizzie's house. She says they've been gone since last Friday.'

Ellen nods along. Each new thing.

'But apparently,' the Smart One says, 'Lizzie did tell her roommate she was going, and that's why no red flag was raised.'

'So . . . do we know where they went?'

A pause, and then a ripple of shaking heads.

Ellen considers this for a moment. 'The girl, Lizzie,' she says. 'Her dad. Is he still here?'

Morticia gets on the case, clickety-click.

'So,' Geek Girl says, 'you going to put us on the payroll?'

Ellen smiles. 'I just might. You guys have been a real help.'

'Wow.'

'What?'

'She *smiles*.'

A moment later, Morticia's phone makes its pinging sound. As she's reading the message, she raises her arm and points. 'He's over that way,' she says. 'Other side of the VLA. In front of the Admin Building. Talking to someone. They've been there for over half an hour.'

Ellen leans forward. 'And under surveillance the whole time? Jesus, have you guys thought of applying for jobs with the NSA?'

'Not too much happens around here,' the Smart One says. 'This is an event.'

A couple of minutes later, Geek Girl and Morticia accompany Ellen as far as the front of the Science Building, where they meet another girl, a Morticia clone, who points out Lizzie Bishop's father.

He's about fifty yards away, on a tree-lined pathway between the Admin Building and the parking lot. From here he looks mid-forties or so. He's slim, medium height and casually dressed. He's talking to an older man. The older man is holding a leather satchel and has an academic look to him.

'Anyone know his name?'

'I think it's Frank,' the new girl says.

'And the guy he's talking to?'

'Don't know,' Geek Girl says. 'I've seen him around. He's an associate professor of . . . something.'

'Something? Nice. Is that what *you're* studying?'

'I've taken courses in it.'

The Morticias trade eye rolls.

A little more time passes, and they just stand there, the four of them – in silence now – watching the two men.

'OK,' Ellen eventually says, glancing around. 'You know what? Why don't I take it from here?'

Geek Girl pouts. 'We're being dismissed?'

'The next phase of the operation might be a little delicate. I don't want to scare him off.'

But as she's saying this, Frank Bishop and the Associate

Professor of Something shake hands and separate. Bishop heads for the parking lot.

By the time Ellen gets halfway there he's already in his car and driving away.

Ellen then veers left and heads for her own car.

As she's reaching for the door, she looks back over at the Science Building. Geek Girl is still standing there.

They exchange nods.

Ellen then gets into the car and follows Frank Bishop out onto the main road that leads back into the town of Atherton.

*

Frank orders a Stoli on the rocks. He's driving, but he really needs a drink.

Just the one should do it.

As with the search for a diner earlier, he's ended up having to settle for considerably less than he hoped for. This place, the Smokehouse Tavern, is the only bar he could find on Main Street. He knows from his previous trips to Atherton that there are a couple of big sports bars over on Railroad Avenue, but he'd never be seen dead in either of those, and besides, he figured there might be a more mood-appropriate dive bar here on Main, an old-school joint with sawdust on the floor and a faint smell of puke in the air.

Turns out there isn't.

Instead, it's the bland, musty Smokehouse, a place that makes Dave's Bar & Grill back at the mall look like the Stork Club.

It'll do, though. It's almost empty, and the barman isn't a talker.

Actually, middle of the afternoon now and Frank doesn't feel too bad. At least he's coming away with something, a plausible scenario, Lizzie and Alex on the road, off the grid, Bonnie and Clyde-ing it around for a few days – but without the bank robberies, or the erectile dysfunction.

He tried Lizzie's phone again, and of course there was no answer, so he's decided he's going to find a motel room and stick around until tomorrow, wait for her to show up. He's not going to be pissed off or anything. He just wants to look at her and make sure she's OK. Tell her he loves her. Tell her to answer her fucking phone once in a while.

Then he'll be out of here.

There's another reason he doesn't feel too bad. That encounter he had just now with Leland Bryce. Frank found it pretty refreshing, because what they talked about, and almost exclusively, was architecture. Now an associate professor at Atherton, Bryce used to teach at Columbia, and Frank took some of his courses. It was weird bumping into him again after all these years, and in these circumstances, but apart from mentioning he had a daughter at Atherton, Frank didn't say anything at all about what was going on. Instead, they reminisced about Columbia for a bit and then got into a thing about the latest addition to the lower Manhattan skyline, F. T. Keizer's controversial new residential tower, 220 Hanson Street. Not yet complete, and already the subject of extensive litigation, 220 Hanson has notoriously divided architectural opinion in the city. It's been in the news a lot, and Frank has read about it, extensively, but he was still sort of surprised to find that he had an actual opinion on the matter – as if he'd somehow forfeited the right to have one of *those* by losing his job.

Nevertheless, this felt like the first grown-up interaction he'd engaged in for quite a while, and as a result he left the campus feeling a good deal less anxious.

But he still needs this drink. And might actually need a second. It's not as if one adult conversation is going to solve all, or indeed any, of his problems.

He takes a sip of Stoli. As he's putting the glass down, he looks into the mirror behind the bar and sees movement – someone emerging from the shadows of the Smokehouse Tavern's dimly lit vestibule area.

It's a woman. She's fortyish, small and slim, with short, dark hair. She's dressed all in black – in jeans, a T-shirt and a jacket.

She approaches the bar and pulls out a stool three along from where Frank is sitting. She lays car keys and a phone down in front of her.

The barman comes up from the far end where he was stacking some glasses and looks at her, eyebrows raised interrogatively.

'Club soda, please.'

She sits down, picks the phone up and starts . . . whatever, texting, tweeting.

He takes another sip from his drink.

The barman places a glass of club soda with ice and lemon in front of the woman and wanders off.

There is silence for a while, the thick silence of a slow-moving, aimless afternoon.

Then, 'Frank . . . isn't it?'

He turns. 'Sorry?'

'Frank Bishop, right?'

The woman is looking directly at him. He's puzzled. Does he know her? Is he supposed to recognise her?

'I'm sorry . . . have we met?'

'No.' She shakes her head. 'Someone pointed you out to me. Back there . . . on the campus. One of the students.'

Frank shifts on his stool and turns, studying the woman's face for a moment. She has smooth, pale skin and dark, penetrating green eyes.

Then something occurs to him.

'Did you *follow* me here?'

She nods. 'Yes, I'm sorry. But I needed to talk to you. My name is Ellen Dorsey. I'm a journalist.'

Frank swallows, a hundred things racing through his head at once, but principally, *What the fuck . . . a journalist?*

This is also – he's now aware – what the look on his face is saying, and it seems to make her uncomfortable, maybe even a little uncertain. As the seconds pass, he keeps staring at her. It's as though she's weighing something up and needs more time. But he doesn't feel like giving her any.

'Come on,' he says, 'you've got something to tell me? What *is* it?'

She wipes away an invisible speck of dust from the bar before looking at him. 'I'm not sure how to say this, Frank, but I think your daughter might be in serious trouble.'

*

Not exactly how she planned it.

But in the few moments she was sitting there, the reality of the situation, the complexity of it, overwhelmed her. If she thinks about it now, even for a second, one thing is clear. This man in front of her isn't just a source, a provider of the next link in a chain of information.

He's involved.

She remembers talking about this to Jimmy Gilroy, about how you get involved – when a story goes a certain way, when you get out of the house and meet people, look them in the eye. It can all get a bit knotty. Ambivalence creeps in.

She looks him in the eye now.

He says, 'I *beg* your pardon?'

Ellen adjusts herself on the stool. 'I'm still working on it, OK, but I've been investigating something, a story, and a certain name has come up, Julian Robert Coady. The thing is, I think the guy your daughter is involved with, Alex, might be this guy's brother.'

Bishop's eyes screw up as he tries to process this. In his obvious bewilderment and desperation he does his best to formulate another question, but all he can manage is 'Story? *What* story?'

Ellen takes a breath and pauses. She can't get straight into it, can she? Not without some prepping. And besides, it's beginning to feel a little flimsy to her – a T-shirt, a comment made on a radio show?

What is she doing?

'I'll get to that,' she says, 'but . . . do you have any idea where they are now? Lizzie and Alex?'

'No.' This isn't quite shouted, but it's close. 'That's why I came up here. I can't reach her. She's not answering her phone.' He raises his left hand, holds it up for a moment, almost threateningly, and then, in frustration, slaps his thigh with it, and really hard. 'It's been almost a *week*.'

'Right.'

It's sudden, but the sense hits her now – ineluctable, inarguable – that this is over. The situation has reached critical mass. There's simply no way she can contain it, or hold out for more. 'Look,' she says, 'I may have it wrong, I may be putting two and two together here and getting five, but . . .' She exhales and looks down at the bar, at her keys, at her phone.

How to say this.

'*What?*'

She looks up at him again. 'These recent shootings in Manhattan? The Wall Street guys? It's my belief that Julian Robert Coady is . . . involved. Actually maybe both him *and* his brother.'

'What the *fuck?*'

This he does shout. The barman turns, looks over, but Ellen lifts a hand to keep him at bay.

'Look,' she says, half in a whisper now, 'I've only literally just put this together myself. It's still circumstantial, but . . .'

A pale Frank Bishop stares at her for a second. Then, as though he's forgotten something, he turns to the bar, picks up his glass, drains it and puts it down again.

He turns back to face her.

'What did you say your name was?'

A tremor in his voice.

'Ellen Dorsey.'

'Well, Ellen, you're going to have to explain all of this to me, and you'd better make it fast, because my head is just about ready to explode.'

So she does. She explains it to him, quickly and efficiently. No point doing it any other way. But passing the story on like this also means it'll very soon be out of her hands. Because really, in the circumstances, what does she think Frank Bishop is going to do with it?

'Jesus Christ.'

His voice is calm now, quiet. He reaches into his jacket pocket and takes out his cell phone. He holds it up.

'I – I have to call . . . . Lizzie's mother.'

He gets off the stool and takes a few steps away from the bar. There is a slowness to his movements, an exaggerated steadiness, a concentration, as though he is drunk and trying not to show it. He's actually in good shape, and handsome, sort of, with tight-cropped, greying hair. But he has a weary look to him as well, tired eyes, tired posture.

When he is far enough away, Ellen turns to her own phone and checks for messages, emails, tweets. Then she uses some of the co-ordinates she gathered back at that table in the Cabbage Patch for a quick data sweep through the Atherton social mediasphere.

With one eye on Bishop, who's managing to keep his voice under control – though not his body language, *that's* becoming increasingly agitated – she worms her way through half a dozen Twitter accounts.

It's all anyone is talking about. A localised micro-trend. Lizzie Bishop, her old man, that journalist.

Alex Coady.

Those two guys this morning.

Ellen stops, rereads that one.

This is getting a little creepy now. And those two guys asking questions this morning? Feds #noquestionaboutit

Ellen feels a weird sensation shooting down her spine.

Feds?

She quickly finds Geek Girl's number and sends her a text.

There were two guys asking questions this morning?

It's a long shot. Or maybe it isn't. She'll find out soon enough.

Frank Bishop turns around and looks at her, real fear in his eyes now. He walks the few steps back to the bar and reaches out to his stool for support. 'My wife, *ex*-wife, is freaking out. Of course.' He swallows loudly. 'She wants to know who *you* are.'

Ellen nods.

'Because she – Deb's a lawyer – she says the cops'll have been getting hundreds of crank calls on this since it started and we'll need something to get their attention. To break through the firewall. And that's you.'

Ellen nods again. 'I know. And I know who to call.' She pauses. 'I was going to do it anyway, but I wanted to talk to you first.'

The message alert on her cell phone pings.

She puts a hand out to pick it up, but then pauses. 'I'm going to look at this,' she says. 'OK? It might be relevant.'

He nods.

She reads the message quickly.

Just heard about this from someone else. Two suits, this morning, but asking about Alex Coady not Lizzie Bishop xxx

Ellen looks back up.

'Seems the cops are already on it,' she says.

*

Twenty minutes after Lizzie gets back to the apartment, she hears the key in the door. She's sitting at the table, textbook

189

open in front of her.

Trying to appear normal.

Heart racing.

She doesn't know what she's going to do, or say – she just has this overwhelming sense of needing to see Alex, to envelop him, to let him know that she knows, *and that it's OK*. All week there has been this poisonous tension between them that she's hated, silences, sighs, deflected looks, things half spoken. She didn't understand what it was, and attributed it to Julian's influence over him, to the force of Julian's toxic personality. She feels awful now, realising that it was more than likely the unimaginable pressure that Alex had put *himself* under, and that she certainly wasn't helping by being needy.

Also, she's not allowing herself, at least for the moment, to dwell too much on what Alex has done, and what it might mean – other than what it says about his relationship with Julian.

Because – to her mind – it reverses things.

It puts Alex in charge, which is where she's always thought he belongs. Julian is noisy and pushy, but Alex is the quiet stillness at the centre of things. When Julian launches into a rant about the bankers or whatever, all she wants to do is scream or run away. When Alex talks about the same thing, in his subtler, more measured tones, she listens, and is soothed, seduced, won over.

The door opens now and when she looks up, she sees it immediately – it's in their faces, in their body language. No doubt it was there all along, but for her this is a realignment, a correction, and she wants to make amends.

Julian comes in first, lumbering to the table and heaving his backpack onto it. He grunts something at her, sits down and starts stroking that ridiculous, barely noticeable goatee of his.

Alex glides in behind him.

Lizzie catches his eye and smiles. He doesn't smile back, but that's OK. He sits on the arm of the couch, leans forward and starts massaging his temples.

On the other days when they've come in like this, exhausted, hardly able to speak, Lizzie has remained quiet herself and stayed out of their way.

Not this evening. She wants to know where they've been all day, and what they're planning next. She wants to open this up and let them know whose side she's on – let Alex know it's all right, let him know that more than anything else *they're* all right. But just as she's about to speak, Julian looks over at her, brow furrowing, and says, 'There's something different about her.'

Alex raises his head. 'What?'

Lizzie feels the air thicken around her.

'She knows,' Julian says. 'Look at her.' He stands up slowly, and points. 'She's been out. She *knows*.'

Alex stands up as well, rising from the edge of the couch, and glares at her.

Lizzie pushes the chair she's sitting in back a little. What is it? Are her cheeks flushed from all the walking? Is she still perspiring?

'Yes,' she says, a crack in her voice, 'I went out, so what? I know what you've been doing.' She gets up from the chair. 'I watched some TV earlier, they showed that clip on the news, but listen –'

Julian bangs his fist on the table. 'Jesus *Christ.*'

'Lizzie,' Alex says, his tone calm, but also direct and clinical, 'have you spoken to anyone? Have you *told* anyone?'

She looks into his eyes. 'Oh, Alex . . .' She pauses, lips parted. If only they could stay like this forever, and let everything outside their line of vision, everything else in the room, in the world – that table, Julian's backpack, Julian himself, New York, the *news* – dissolve to nothing. 'No,' she says at last, but softly, in a whisper, still maintaining eye contact.

Julian shakes his head. 'Dumb-assed *bitch*.' He turns and scowls at Alex. 'I told you a hundred times this was a bad idea.'

There is a pause. Then Alex says, calmly, without redirecting his gaze, 'Shut the fuck up, Julian.'

'*What?*'

Lizzie swallows, and once again the room begins to spin.

But then it stops.

Because there's . . . a creaking sound.

They all turn towards the door, then freeze.

'What was that?' Julian says, in a loud whisper.

Alex looks at him. 'Someone's there.' He reaches for the backpack on the table. Then he turns to Lizzie, eyes widening, and nods at the door.

She moves swiftly towards it, and senses equally swift movement behind her. At the door, she narrows her right eye in on the peephole – imagining for a second, she doesn't know why, that it's her father she'll see, a dreamlike Frank in fisheye, standing there, shuffling anxiously, waiting. What she sees instead – as a *rap*, *tap* sounds on the door, followed immediately, almost stopping her heart, by a shouted 'POLICE, SEARCH WARRANT, OPEN THE DOOR' – is a retreating mass of black that quickly forms into the shape of a man, revealing behind *him* a hallway lined with other men, all in black, all heavily armed.

Lizzie spins around.

Julian has his back against the wall and is straining to see out of the window. Alex is standing in the middle of the room with a gun in his hand.

'Jesus,' Lizzie whispers, all her limbs starting to tremble, 'there's a fucking SWAT team out there.'

Alex nods his head again, to the side this time, indicating for her to move.

She hesitates, but then slides over towards the kitchen.

'We're armed in here,' he shouts. 'We've got explosives. Back off. *Back off now.*'

From this angle just inside the kitchen door, Lizzie stares at Alex, and the only thing in her head, the only thought she can process, is that she's never heard him shout before.

Four

When it became apparent in April 1913 that newly elected President Woodrow Wilson was ready to do the unthinkable and concede ground on union recognition, the industrialist, banker and Vaughan family patriarch Charles A. Vaughan was quoted in the *New York Journal* as saying, 'It would be nice if some day we could have a real businessman as president.'

House of Vaughan (p. 164)

10

Out on Main Street, in front of the Smokehouse Tavern, with Frank Bishop standing next to her, Ellen finds the number and calls her contact in the NYPD. She lays it out for this guy, a homicide detective, just as she did for Bishop inside at the bar, but this time she does it faster, and almost in a sort of code or shorthand. The contact listens, interjecting only once with a low whistle of disbelief. This is when she mentions that the Feds might already be involved. He says he'll run it up the line and get right back to her.

Then Ellen suggests to Bishop that they return to Manhattan without delay. The shootings took place there, and if there's going to be another one, or any development at all, that's more than likely where it'll happen. Any Atherton-based information about the Coadys they can get by phone or online.

Bishop is still in a state of shock, and Ellen has to prod him into a response. They eventually come to an arrangement – Ellen will drop her rental off locally, and then they'll head back together in Bishop's car. Ellen offers to drive, but Bishop says he's fine, that it'll be a distraction.

Within half an hour they're on I-87.

Ellen isn't great at making small talk, so she just fires questions at him as though it's an interview. She can't take notes – or at least can't be too blatant about it, not in these circumstances – but if something significant comes up she can always use the phone in her hands to record the conversation.

Bishop is forthcoming on most things and speaks, in fact, as though he *were* being interviewed. It's something Ellen has noticed before – how without declaring your hand up front you can establish a sort of determining rhythm to a conversation. In any case, she finds out quite a lot about him, and also about his daughter, Lizzie – whom Ellen pegs at once as a likely piece of collateral damage in all of this.

After about an hour on the road, they pull in at a rest stop to get some coffee. Ellen stays in the car and takes the opportunity to call Max Daitch. She exchanged a few texts with him back at the Smokehouse Tavern, during which they agreed that Ellen should call her NYPD contact ASAP. But with Bishop now occupied she's able to explain in more detail what's been happening.

'Why didn't you tell me all of this before?' he says.

'Because I've only just put it together myself. What I told you yesterday was guesswork. It's taken me until now to flesh it out.'

'OK, OK.' He sighs. 'Look, I'm trying to get clearance from legal to see what we can post online right now, if anything. Because by tomorrow morning, maybe even by tonight, this'll be everywhere.'

'I know. My NYPD contact said he'd get back to me. I'll text you as soon as he does.' She checks the time. 'We should be back in the city by about seven. This guy here, the girlfriend's father, I'm talking to him all the time, so at least we're ahead on that angle if we need it.' She looks up. 'OK, I've got to go.'

Bishop gets back in the car and they sip their coffees in silence for a while. It's grey and murky out, and the relentless whipsaw of the passing traffic out on 87 is giving Ellen a head-ache.

Did she really use the word *angle* to Max just now? We're ahead on that *angle*?

She fucking did, didn't she?

That *is* where this is going, though – she knows that, they're not carpooling here for convenience. She's going to have to broach it with him, and it'll depend on how things play out, but exclusive access is the prize.

It's what she's after.

She looks at her half-reflection in the windshield and rolls her eyes.

Then Bishop says, 'This is going to be rough, isn't it? If it's true, I mean. If these . . . brothers, these pricks, if they're the ones, and Lizzie's with them, it's going to mean a lot of attention, media attention, isn't it? A lot of intrusion?'

Ellen turns and looks at him. 'I hate to be the bearer of bad news, Frank, but what the fuck do you think *I'm* doing here?'

'Yeah.' He exhales and half smiles. 'I know. It just . . . doesn't feel like that. Not yet, anyway.' He pauses. 'And I meant it more from Lizzie's point of view.'

'Well, if it is true, and let's face it, that's the way it's looking, yeah, it *is* going to be rough. On her, on you, on her mom.' Ellen shifts in the seat and leans forward a bit. 'So look, this is where I make a reasonable pitch for you to give me exclusive access, and in return I do my best to minimise your exposure, minimise the bullshit you have to put up with. Protect you.' She pauses. 'But the thing is, Frank, there is no protect. There's only exposure. And that's a beast *no one* controls.' She clears her throat. 'If you want my honest pitch, here it is. One way or another, I'll be writing about this. It's what I do. But I have a pretty decent reputation, so I won't write anything that's a lie, I won't exaggerate and I won't withhold anything from you.' She pauses again. 'That's it.'

'OK.'

'OK what?'

'*OK*. Presumably you know people. Cops. You have contacts. You can find out stuff. You understand the system. I'm going to need that.' He looks at her and waves a hand between them. 'You know, give and take.'

She nods. 'Yeah. Sure. Of course.'

He puts his coffee down and starts the car.

After about ten minutes back on the road, Ellen's phone rings.

It's her NYPD guy.

She sits in silence and listens. He explains that the situation has moved on somewhat. Those guys at Atherton this morning were indeed Feds and right now in fact, together with members of the New York Joint Terrorism Task Force, they're involved in a siege situation in an apartment on the Lower East Side of Manhattan with three suspects, two male, one female. The situation is extremely volatile and there's even a possibility that explosives might be involved. This news, he says, is barely fifteen minutes old. It hasn't gotten out yet, and he's only telling her now because the info she provided earlier gave *his* guys a little leverage with the Feds and the JTTF.

Ellen swallows. She wants to ask questions, she wants clarification, but not with Frank Bishop sitting next to her driving the fucking car.

She gets off the phone and starts texting.

'What was that?'

'Nothing.'

Look at her, withholding already. Didn't take long.

She sends a quick text to Max Daitch and another one to Val Brady. There's not much she can do, stuck here for the next two hours. Val might as well get a jump on things. Maybe relay some details to her later.

Give and take.

She leans back, takes a deep breath. She glances over at the shoulder.

Then she turns to Frank.

So she can tell him to pull in and stop the car.

*

'*That's* a relief.'

Craig Howley looks up from his laptop.

'What is?'

Jessica is standing in the middle of the room, hand on hip. She nods at the TV. '*That* is. They've caught those guys.'

From his position on the couch, Howley looks at the screen for a moment – a tenement building downtown somewhere, police cars, armed officers – and then he reads the crawl. 'They haven't exactly *caught* them, though, have they?' he says. 'A siege? What I'd be asking is how they let that happen.' He turns back to his laptop. 'I thought they had these things down to a fine art.'

On the screen of his laptop there's a sequence of market data charts showing previous private equity IPO performance levels. He scrolls down through them, stopping occasionally to study this or that one more closely for a moment.

He's looking for ammunition.

And the evidence here, as far as *he's* concerned, is pretty encouraging. On an each-way bet it's still a negative benefit outcome – because they either flatline or they tank. Which is just as well, because as Vaughan has so subtly illustrated with his 'black file', the idea of Oberon opening its books to public scrutiny is a non-starter anyway.

Howley closes the laptop and looks back at the TV screen.

There is a panel discussion going on and it's getting quite animated. 'Look, it's *very* clear,' someone is saying, 'check it yourself, it's Title Eighteen of the United States Code, section thirty-one oh nine . . .'

'What are they talking about?' Howley says.

Jessica turns around. She's still standing there in the middle of the room with her hand on her hip. She does that some-times. It's her slightly haughty, non-committal way of watching TV – watching, but ready to drop it and walk away at a mo-ment's notice. 'Oh, they're discussing the, what did you call it, the *fine art* of how to execute a search warrant.'

'Arrest or search?'

'Search. That's what they said. Why?'

'Because they're different. With a search you're obliged to . . . knock and announce, I think they call it.'

'How do *you* know that?'

'The curse of a photographic memory. I read it somewhere. Who can say?'

'Well, one of these guys is arguing exactly that, he's saying they followed procedure, and the other one is saying they'd have been within their rights to just barge in there unannounced.'

'Uh-uh.' Howley shakes his head. 'Though it's a pity they didn't. Because look.' The street scene from earlier is on again. 'The city doesn't need this.'

Jessica turns back and looks at it.

'No, it certainly does *not*.' She shakes her head as well. 'With the benefit coming up? Please.' She clicks her tongue. 'They'd better resolve this fast, that's all I can say.'

The benefit is a Kurtzmann Foundation fundraiser, a gala event Jessica has been working on for months.

She turns around again. 'Shouldn't you be getting ready, darling? The Lowensteins will be here in an hour.'

He nods, *yes, yes*.

When she leaves the room he opens the laptop again. His statement for tomorrow is still a little rough round the edges, but he'll keep chipping away at it. There are certain subtle points he needs to make, ideas he needs to implant. A lot of people will be paying attention.

Though *on* that, something occurs to him.

He glances up at the TV again.

If this siege thing has any legs at all, it'll swamp the next couple of news cycles, at least, and there's one person he knows who'll be happy about that.

James Vaughan.

People know the Oberon name, the brand, but very few people have actually heard of Vaughan himself, and that's how he'd like to keep it. Howley can well imagine how much Vaughan is dreading the public nature of this handover tomorrow – especially if it's going to be presented in the context of his failing health.

So any distraction will be welcome.

And this one certainly seems to be shaping up nicely.

Vaughan won't be at the press conference himself, but he'll be referenced endlessly, and his office will be inundated with media requests.

Howley closes the laptop again and puts it down beside him on the couch. He looks around for the remote but can't find it.

He gets up and stands there, Jessica-style, staring at the screen.

This is crazy stuff.

But however it pans out over the next six, twelve, even twenty-four hours, he's pretty sure that with words like 'explosives' and 'evacuation' now creeping into the narrative, Vaughan won't have a whole lot to worry about in the morning.

*

When he looks up, and around, and sees that they're at a Hundred and Tenth Street already, Central Park just over to the right, Frank realises, remembers, that he hasn't been into the city for months, three or four at least. But gliding down Fifth now, he feels nauseous, dizzy, as though he's being delivered to his own execution.

Ellen Dorsey is driving.

He turns to his left and looks at her. She's staring straight ahead, both hands on the wheel, arms rigid.

Tense, silent.

The last two hours have been like this, neither of them wanting to speak – he, for obvious reasons, and she . . . well, who knows? Maybe she's embarrassed. Maybe she's out of her depth. Maybe she's calculating how much money she can make out of this.

He doesn't know.

He's glad she's driving his car, though.

Because *he* couldn't.

He stares out the window now, the cross streets clocking down like a ticking bomb . . . Fifty-seventh, Forty-second, Thirty-fourth, Twenty-third.

She takes a left at Fourteenth and gets onto the FDR Drive.

The Lower East Side is a part of town that somehow seems abstract to Frank, as they approach it – doesn't seem like a Lizzie sort of place at all. What comes to mind, if he does think about it, is the Tenement Museum . . . immigrant families, old photographs, vintage storefronts, fire escapes, raggedy kids playing around a water hydrant, that street panorama from *Godfather II*. He knows these are stereotypes, but it's not as if he ever had occasion to come down here, when he was working in the city.

Which was midtown. Mostly.

Uptown, a bit.

Mostly where he lived was Brooklyn, and that, he thinks, definitely *is* a Lizzie sort of place, the house they had in Carroll Gardens, for instance . . . up the stoop, in the door, take the stairs two at a time and over to the right . . . her *room* . . .

So vivid.

What he hopes here, for this, the ideal outcome, is that he arrives on Orchard Street just as they're parading the three of them out of the building, perp-walking them out the door, the two brothers first, whatever they look like – he doesn't know, *or* care – and then the girl. He's standing there, he looks up *and it isn't her* . . .

It's someone else, someone taller, skinnier, darker, it doesn't matter, it isn't Lizzie, and this is all a mistake, a misunderstanding.

Wires got crossed.

Ellen Dorsey here got her facts wrong.

Slumped in the car seat now, staring down, he replays this scene multiple times in his head.

'Are you ready, Frank?'

'*What?*'

He looks up and around. They're on Grand Street.

'We're just coming to Orchard now,' she says.

Before he has properly refocused, they're turning right and facing north again. He was certainly right about the fire escapes. And up ahead, two blocks, he sees it – the crowds, the police barriers, the blue lights rotating. He can't see beyond that. Because this is just the periphery.

'*There's* a space,' he says, pointing. 'We're not going to get much closer than this. We can walk.'

Ellen Dorsey nods and pulls in.

Quickly, they get out of the car and start moving.

Frank's heart is pounding. Earlier he was concerned about media intrusion, journalists, photographers. He was also concerned for a while about seeing Deb. But now he feels he'll be able to bypass all of that. Because the only thing he's concerned about right now is Lizzie, and the idea that she's somewhere in the middle of this circus.

They come to Delancey, and it starts there, on the far side – the barriers, the onlookers, the cops, the outside broadcast units, the camera operators, the booms, the cables and tripods and mikes, the reporters.

Frank turns to his left. Ellen Dorsey has her phone out.

'Wait,' she says to him. She then obviously sees the panic in his eyes and takes him by the arm. 'Just wait a second, I'm going to call someone, OK?'

He waits, standing there, staring ahead.

'Val? Ellen. We're here. Anyone there you can talk to?'

The next ten or fifteen minutes float by in a headachy haze, as they are met by men in dark suits and uniforms. They are then guided forward – cameras clicking and whirring behind them – through the barriers and on to a second set of barriers just before the next intersection. At one point it takes Frank a few seconds to realise that he is standing beside Deb. She looks just as shell-shocked as he feels, and it takes them another few seconds to acknowledge each other, to react, to embrace.

Interviews follow – interrogations, really – with representatives from different law enforcement agencies. These take place in the back of a large van, or maybe it's a trailer, Frank isn't sure of anything that's happening. He answers whatever he's asked, but doesn't feel that any of the questions make sense. He asks several questions of his own – though they're all the same question, really – but no one will give him a straight answer.

More time passes.

Then Frank finds himself back outside, standing next to Deb again, looking from behind a barrier at a long, deserted section of the street – no people, no cars, not even parked ones. It stretches all the way to a corresponding barrier just beyond Stanton Street. And there appears to be another one beyond that again, on East Houston.

What worries Frank is that no one here seems to know what's going on, or is even prepared to say what they *think* is going on.

He looks around.

Almost without him noticing it, night has fallen. It's dark now, city dark, an orange wash from the streetlights suffusing everything. There is an eerie silence, too, with a muffled backdrop of normal sounds – distant traffic, distant sirens.

Then something occurs to him. Where's Ellen Dorsey? He hasn't seen her for a while and doesn't see her anywhere now.

He looks at Deb. They don't know what to say to each other. But they're here, and they're together, and they're waiting.

It's not just them, though.

Everyone is waiting.

*

Lizzie is drowsy. She's been drifting in and out of sleep for some time now, in and out of actual dreams, too . . . little narrative passages that for all their weirdness and anxiety-laden expansiveness have been a welcome respite from – she opens her eyes – from *this*, the silent, musty, horrible, box-like, *coffin*-like little apartment they are trapped in.

She is sitting on the floor in the kitchen, leaning back against the wall, under the window, in the tiny space between the table and the cupboards, and she's been here . . . since this started.

Forever, it feels like.

Though still, it must be what, nearly five hours already?

What time is it?

She doesn't have a watch, and her cell phone is out in the other room.

There's no clock in here.

What gets her is the silence, the virtual silence anyway. She can hear traffic, and the occasional siren, but she can't hear any of the regular building sounds, no flushing toilets, no muffled voices, or creaking floorboards from upstairs.

But she knows why. It's because they've evacuated the building, isn't it? Probably the whole street, and the buildings behind as well.

It was that one word Alex used, *explosives*. Otherwise, she's sure they would have stormed in by now, with tear gas or stun grenades or whatever the hell it is they use in these situations.

But the thing is, Lizzie doesn't know if Alex and Julian actually have any explosives. Alex grabbed that backpack from the table pretty fast. Was it just to get his gun? Or was there something else in it? Does Julian have anything stashed in his bedroom?

Lizzie didn't make a decision to stay in the kitchen like this, on the floor – not consciously, anyway. It just came about. For the initial twenty minutes, or half an hour, she stood a couple of inches inside the kitchen door and didn't move a muscle, barely even took a breath. Neither did Alex or Julian; they just stood where they were, frozen, waiting for something to happen, for someone to make a move.

Then the phone rang, the landline.

Julian and Alex flinched. Alex gestured for Lizzie to *move*, to get back, as though the phone itself were about to explode.

Lizzie did move back, into the position she's in now.

She sat there, trembling, and listened, as first Julian and then Alex tried their hand at . . . negotiation? Is that what it was? She couldn't make out everything they were saying, but she heard enough to know that either they didn't know what they were doing or they didn't care.

A few more quick phone calls followed, and then . . . nothing at all. Obviously some sort of a waiting game. For her part, Lizzie waited where she was, thinking Alex might come in and tell her something, try to comfort her – she wanted him to, and was prepared to wait for *him* – but it's as if she wasn't even there.

Through the kitchen door, over the next couple of hours, she could hear them whispering, conspiring, strategising, or so she imagined. But there were also moments when the exchanges sounded harsh, as if Julian and Alex were bickering or snapping at each other. Occasionally, she could see shadows and some movement, but not a lot, and then for the longest time all she could make out was Julian's boots, positioned horizontally – so she took it that he was sitting on the floor, too, legs outstretched, leaning against the section of wall next to the living-room window.

No sign of Alex.

After that, time just passed. She considered crawling over to the door, or whispering something out, but the more the hours drifted by, the harder it became for her to imagine doing anything at all, even moving. It got dark as well, and no one turned on any lights, or tried to turn on the TV. Was this because the electricity supply into the apartment had been cut? Maybe. She didn't know. Though if it *was* the case, it probably meant that cell phone and internet connections had also been blocked.

Eventually, the drowsiness came, and Lizzie started letting her head slump.

Now she's in a weird in-between state.

'*Lizzie.*'

She focuses. It's Alex. He's in front of her, crouched down, but with one hand holding onto the table, for balance. In the dim light, his face is only partially visible.

'*Alex*,' she whispers, leaning forward suddenly, reaching a hand out to touch him, as though they haven't seen each other for months.

'Listen,' he says, moving sideways, avoiding her hand. 'We need coffee, if we're going to stay awake. So make some, will you? But keep as quiet as you can.'

Lizzie stares at him. 'Alex, what's happening? *Talk* to me.' Her eyes fill up with tears. 'What are we going to *do*?'

She puts so much effort into saying this last word that it's like a release. And now that she's finally asked the question, she can't help feeling that an answer – full, satisfactory, game-changing – will come spilling out of him. But all he says is 'I don't know. I don't *know*.'

'You *must* know.'

'Look, this wasn't part of the plan, OK?' He says the words slowly, his tone very deliberate. 'Now. Will you please make the coffee.'

Lizzie feels sick all of a sudden. She doesn't know what's going on here. It seemed like they were almost in tune back there, before this started, in the other room, like they had a chance of connecting again – but only for all of, what was it, five or six seconds? And that was *it*? Now she's supposed to just make coffee? In normal circumstances, Julian wouldn't let her touch anything in his precious kitchen, now she's the fucking *maid*?

Fully awake again, she starts thinking more clearly than she has done in a while.

'OK,' she says, wiping her eyes with the sleeve of her sweater, 'it wasn't part of the plan, but that was then, what's the plan *now*?'

Alex sighs, shudders almost. 'There isn't one. I mean . . . Julian . . . he can't take this, he's falling apart in there. I don't know what to do.' Now *his* eyes fill up. 'I'm sorry, Lizzie. I shouldn't have gotten you involved in this, in our family *shit*. I just . . . I wanted you around –'

'Oh, Alex,' she says, her heart swelling, 'I love you.' She reaches out to touch his face again, and this time he lets her. After a moment, she whispers, 'What did you tell them . . . when they called? What happened?'

He looks confused. 'I . . . I don't really remember. We just talked bullshit. Julian was incoherent. I told them to fuck off, and that if they didn't, we'd . . . you know . . .' He stops, exhales, unable to finish putting the thought into words.

Lizzie uses her other sleeve to wipe his tears away.

'Listen to me,' she says, adrenalin starting to pump through her system now. 'We really need to focus. This is not the time to be incoherent. You guys did what you did for a *reason*, OK? And you were very focused when you were doing it. So that's what you've got to hold on to here. What *we've* got to hold on to. And when they call back, which they're bound to do sooner or later, you articulate that reason, over and over, hammer it home, show them you're not just a pair of crazy fucks, that there's a way out, a route to the other side.' She pauses and swallows, unsure where any of this is coming from. 'And then, when we get out of here,' she goes on, 'that reason, that rationale, whatever it is, even if it's fucked up or hopelessly deluded, it'll be a platform, and a passport to *some* kind of public sympathy. It won't be much, but what else is there?'

Alex stares at her, then nods his head. 'Yeah,' he says, in a loud whisper, 'yeah, you're right.'

'So go back in there. Talk to Julian. Work something out. The phone might ring in the next five minutes. It might not ring all night. But you have to be ready.'

She leans forward and kisses him on the forehead.

Moments later, he's back in the other room, and she hears their voices again, Alex whispering to Julian, Julian whispering to Alex.

Then she looks up at the cupboard where the coffee is. She looks at the stovetop. It's dark in here, but not completely. How hard can it be?

With her heart still racing, Lizzie breathes in, reaches for the edge of the table and slowly pulls herself up.

*

It's in a bar on Norfolk Street – at around 5 a.m., while having a quick drink with Val Brady – that Ellen Dorsey decides she's had enough of this whole story and should really go home. It's been a long night of huddled conversations with other journalists, of rushed phone calls and livetweeting, of trying to make contact with Frank Bishop again but being blocked at every turn (she'd given him her number but somehow, stupidly, in the confusion, hadn't taken his), and ultimately of realising she's lost all control of the story, that it's moved ahead without her, that she works for an outlet where breaking news just doesn't figure in the mission.

Not that she didn't know this already, but she'd certainly been trying to ignore it in recent days.

She looks across at Val now.

There's an early edition of the *New York Times* spread out on the table in front of him. This is his first ever page-one byline and he can't stop staring at it. He also hasn't been able to stop thanking Ellen for texting him the previous afternoon and giving him the jump on everyone else.

She knew there was no point in trying to get anything up on the *Parallax* site, or even on her own page – because, to be honest, who would see it in time? This needed to be addressed head-on, and within minutes, literally. So while she might have been trapped in a car on I-87, texting Val meant that he could be the first person on the scene.

And she has to admit that he did a great job, because not only was he the first one to publicly name the Coady brothers, he also managed to dig up some pretty electrifying background material on their father.

At one point during the evening he offered to share his byline with her, but for various reasons, political, logistic, whatever, that was never going to happen. She didn't mind, though. *He* got to break the story, and that's how it goes.

But man, thinking about it now, at 5 a.m. with a drink in her hand . . .

'So you don't get to do this,' she says after a while, 'but I think I'll slink off to bed.'

'No fair.'

'Fuck you. Do your job. That means no sleep for the next twelve, twenty-four, thirty-six hours, whatever it takes.'

Val already looks shattered – bleary-eyed and coffee-jagged – but it's what he signed up for.

'Come on,' he says, 'why don't you stick around?'

'Because I don't have to, that's why. I can read about it in the paper' – she flicks the *Times* with the back of her hand –

'or online, or watch it on TV, with much better pictures and angles.' She picks up her drink, releasing a long sigh. 'I'm done here. My last thread to this was the girlfriend's old man, but they won't let me near him, and besides, he's probably signed a movie deal already.' She drains what's in her glass. 'Plus, there's no point, I don't work for a daily newspaper. What am I going to do? Fucking *livetweet* developments all day? I'm a journalist, not a civilian.'

'Right.'

'I just need to look for a new job, that's all.' She puts her glass down. 'But that's not going to happen today. Plus, *plus*, I have this Ratt shit to deal with.'

Val laughs and is about to say something when his phone pings. He whips it up and reads the message, starting to slide out of his chair as he does so. 'Er, I have to get back. There's been a –'

Ellen holds up a hand. 'No, don't tell me. I'll read about it. Just go.'

He hesitates, knows not to say thanks again, half smiles and leaves.

A few minutes later, she leaves herself, gets a cab on Delancey and within half an hour is at home and in the shower.

She's tired and tries to sleep, but isn't able to. After a while she moves from the bed to the couch and considers turning on the TV. She decides not to and throws an eye instead over the Ratt Atkinson article with a view to arming herself for later. There won't be as much interest in it as there was yesterday, but she likes to be prepared.

At what she considers a reasonable hour – reasonable, that is, for her sister, a mother with two school-age kids – Ellen calls

Michelle and slips into their familiar routine . . . or at least tries to, because as it turns out all that Michelle wants to talk about is this horrible siege thing up in New York. When Ellen, with some reluctance, fills her in on a few of the background details, Michelle is transfixed. The point of the call, however, gets lost and can't be retrieved.

When she puts the phone down, Ellen is more tired than ever, but even less likely to be able to sleep. Stretched out on the couch, staring up at the ceiling, she pictures that deserted block on Orchard Street, pictures a small second-floor apartment. It's been nearly fourteen hours now. What the fuck is going on in there?

In some ways it's a classic siege situation. They've been through the initial phase and are now in the more fluid negotiation, or standoff, phase. Conventional wisdom says that the longer a siege of this type goes on the more likely it is to end peacefully, so the negotiators are probably dragging it out deliberately, employing various well-worn tactics. But it's unclear so far what demands, if any, the Coadys are making. None of that information had trickled down from police sources to any of the reporters Ellen spoke to.

There was plenty of speculation, though, as more information became available about who they were, about the older brother's previous activism, and about the circumstances surrounding their father's death.

There was also plenty of speculation about the explosives – about whether or not they really had any, and about what kind these were most likely to be if they did.

Ellen figures that this is the key point on which the whole thing will turn.

She also figures there'll have to be a development soon. It's gone on long enough, and with Friday morning kicking into gear a four-block-radius shutdown of *any* part of the city is pretty much unsustainable.

She could turn on the TV for an update, but again she decides not to.

Why?

Because on reflection she doesn't really want to know. It's not her story any more.

If she turned on the TV now, it'd be as a civilian.

It'd be prurience.

So she keeps staring up at the ceiling, unable to stop running stuff through her mind, though.

It's weird, the one person she feels particularly bad for is Frank Bishop. He was a nice guy, strangely guarded, or repressed or something, she doesn't know, but what he must be going through at the moment is unimaginable.

Ellen eventually starts getting drowsy, and by a little after 9 a.m. she has fallen asleep.

*

Thanks to an endless supply of bad coffee and high-grade adrenalin, Frank has managed to stay awake all night and well into the next morning.

There's a strange feel to the new day. All the fire escapes and shop signs on Orchard are glistening and sun-dappled in the early light. But simultaneously, at street level, a deathly stillness radiates from the deserted, locked-up bodegas and nail salons, the leather goods stores and discount boutiques.

Frank finds it disturbing and weirdly calming at the same time.

But really, he's been through so many phases of this thing already that it's hard to tell, from one moment to the next, just *what* he's feeling.

Once he got past his own initial phase late the previous evening – pure terror eventually yielding to a slightly less intense cocktail of anxiety and confusion – he found that talking to people, the police officers, the FBI guys, the negotiators, anyone who'd engage with him, was as good a way of steadying his nerves as any. And these people did allow a certain amount of information to filter out. Initial phone contact, for example, revealed an apparent degree of confusion on the part of the Coady brothers. Seasoned negotiators regarded this as a positive, because it indicated amateur status – it meant the brothers didn't really know what they were doing and would therefore be easier to manipulate. A long – and no doubt calculated – standoff phase ensued, and during this time detailed profiles of the Coadys were drawn up, not just by the various law enforcement agencies involved but also by the media, with the online edition of the *New York Times* first out of the gate. And by this stage, too, late into the night, Frank and Deb were both glued to their respective devices, monitoring news and Twitter feeds, text messages and emails.

As a result, it wasn't long before there was something approaching full disclosure on Alex and Julian Coady. Frank found this extremely difficult, even humiliating – hearing in detail, along with everyone else, about a boyfriend of his daughter's he hadn't known existed until yesterday.

It appears that the Coadys, originally from Florida, are a

wealthy, well respected family – or at least *were* until six years ago when old man Jeremy L. Coady slit his own throat in a Manhattan hotel room after being indicted by a federal grand jury on twenty counts of fraud, conspiracy and money laundering stemming from his alleged role in a $4.7 billion Ponzi scheme. In the subsequent trial of his business partner, it emerged, or was claimed, that Coady had been unaware of what was going on in the company and was driven to suicide by the shame and ignominy heaped on him after the charges were made public. This was the narrative that his family – certainly his two sons, and especially the older one – chose to embrace. Julian was 'radicalised' by what had happened and embarked on a so-called crusade against the bankers and financiers of Wall Street – individuals and institutions *he* saw as being responsible for the culture of greed and excess that had ultimately destroyed his father. Younger brother Alex, the quiet, impressionable one, was perceived to have been led astray by Julian.

References to Elizabeth Bishop, the 'girlfriend' – incorrectly assigned to Julian in some reports – were cursory and light on detail, a fact that Frank found irksome, as if they were somehow giving her short shrift. But at the same time it was a relief, and it also meant that no reference was made at this stage (early morning, first editions) to either him or Deb. This was almost an even bigger relief, as far as Frank was concerned, though he didn't expect it to last.

At around 5 a.m. there was a second flurry of activity.

A phone call was made to the apartment.

As one of the cops, a Detective Lenny Byron, explained to Frank later, this was strategic, a very deliberate move, the idea being to disorient the Coadys after hours of silence, to shake them up, maybe even to *wake them up*.

But what nobody expected was that the negotiator would be greeted with a coherent shopping list of demands.

And that these would be delivered by the girlfriend.

It took both Frank and Deb a good while to bounce back from this. Lizzie was the difficult one of their two kids, the one who required inordinate amounts of cunning and guile to deal with, and who gave it all back in spades – so on one level this didn't *really* come as a surprise . . .

But –

It still did.

Plus, it also led to an unfortunate and inevitable shift in focus. Because for the next editions, for the online news updates, for the TV breakfast shows, and for fucking Twitter, it was no longer a question of who are these geeky boys, and more a question of who is this nineteen-year-old *girl*?

America going, 'Hey Nineteen'.

Skate a little lower now.

Frank's heart bursting and ripping itself into bloody shreds inside his chest.

Then, by eight o'clock, on discussion panels all across the networks, professors of behavioural psychology were namechecking Patty Hearst and wondering if this mightn't be another classic case of Stockholm syndrome. Deb was distraught at the very idea, as it seemed to bring home to her just what a circus the whole thing had become. She'd been fairly composed for most of the night and had spent a lot of it on the phone to her second husband, Lloyd, either out at the barrier or sitting in one of the NYPD trailers. She and Frank had been civil at first, united in their horror at what was happening, but they'd pretty quickly run out of things to say to each other. By morning, a combination of sheer physical exhaustion and the weirdness of this enforced proximity had led to a palpable tension between them, with contact soon limited to the occasional wordless look or cryptic shrug.

Now, just before ten o'clock, that tension escalates in a way that catches Frank off guard. Deb emerges from one of the trailers and comes towards him with her BlackBerry held up.

She looks great, as usual, elegantly dressed and with that commanding, lawyerly presence. She walks right up to him and waves the BlackBerry in his face. 'You weren't going to tell me?'

'What?'

But he knows. *Fuck.* Winterbrook Mall. It seems like a thousand centuries ago.

'You lost your job? You got fired? From a *Paloma* store? Because you couldn't keep your *mouth* shut?'

'But –'

'And now it's all over the internet?' She waves the BlackBerry in his face again. 'On *Gawker*? "Like Father, Like Daughter? Does This Man Need Anger Management Classes?" *Jesus*, Frank.'

He wilts.

Frank hadn't mentioned anything because . . . why the fuck would he? The focus was on Lizzie, as it should have been. He and Deb were here for *her*, not to exchange pleasantries or career updates.

But this is being wilfully naïve and he knows it. Exposure of some kind was inevitable. In fact, Deb is being naïve if she thinks they won't go after her, too. No one controls this stuff, isn't that what Ellen Dorsey had said?

'It's *my* business, Deb, mine only. I can't help it if these bastards have no scruples.'

'Well, have you talked to anyone else?'

'What do you mean? I haven't talked to anyone at all. Certainly not to anyone at Gawker. They're the ones who probably talked to someone at Paloma, or at the mall. And don't think they won't be sniffing around up at Pierson Hackler either.'

Deb's law firm.

She stares at him, and he sees a crack. 'We've had a few calls,' she says, 'from . . . the cable news shows, looking for an interview . . . just something short.' She pauses. 'Lloyd thinks we should do it.'

Lloyd.

He's a lawyer, too, of course.

Then Frank suddenly leans in towards her. 'We? You mean *us*, right?'

Deb falters, and he sees it coming. 'No, Frank,' she says, 'I don't. I mean me and Lloyd.'

*

Lizzie isn't sure, but she thinks Julian might be dead. Either that or he's slipped into a convenient coma. He's over in the corner, on the floor, curled up in a foetal position, not moving or making any sound.

Alex is on the couch, staring blankly at the blank TV screen.

Lizzie is at the table, an open book in front of her that she's no longer even pretending to read.

Between the three of them they've drunk all the coffee in the apartment. They've eaten a pack of rice cakes, a bag of sunflower seeds, some cold cuts, a chunk of Swiss cheese, a few apples and two bananas.

They've each used the bathroom at least twice.

They've each come close to having full-blown psychotic episodes – though Lizzie *sort* of felt she was faking hers, that hers was more an attempt to make Alex feel better about his. Julian's, on the other hand, was the real deal, hysteria uncoiling slowly down to virtual catatonia – and unless something happens soon, they may have to unload him.

On medical grounds.

Which would make things a little easier for her. Relatively speaking. But it's been nearly eighteen hours already, so surely something will have to happen soon anyway?

The police, the FBI, whoever is in control of operations – they're clearly playing a long game here. From what they said on the phone earlier, Lizzie understood that they're waiting for an uncle of Alex and Julian's to show up from Florida, that they think this guy's presence will shift the dynamic sufficiently to break the impasse. Though she also got the impression that *her* taking the call was something of a surprise to them.

Maybe they'd been assuming she was a hostage.

Not any more.

The thing is, when it came to it, Alex just froze. It was really early, just before five, dawn breaking. The phone rang, and he picked it up, but then he held it out in front of him, as though he didn't know what it was for. After a few agonising seconds, Lizzie grabbed it from his hand, simultaneously reaching over to the table to pick up the list of demands they'd compiled.

'Hello?'

There was a pause. Then, 'Good morning. Who's this?

Lizzie? Is that Lizzie I'm talking to?'

'Yes.'

'Hi. I'm Special Agent Tom Bale. Listen, Lizzie, is everything all right in there? How are the guys doing? You got enough water? Have you had something to eat?'

Soothing, eminently reasonable, all-things-are-possible negotiator voice.

'We're all doing fine,' Lizzie said. 'Feeling a bit cut off maybe, communications-wise.'

It turned out that they did have electricity in the apartment, but the TV and internet connections had been blocked.

'Well, you know how it is, Lizzie. These are standard procedures. But let me see what I can do, OK? It's just that . . . I mean, the thing is . . . we're all naturally a little concerned out here, considering what Alex said and all, at the outset of this thing. He was very clearly distressed, we understand that – but we're not sure if . . . you know . . .'

Never having undergone this process before, Lizzie found it surprising how transparent and predictable it seemed. She knew exactly what Special Agent Bale was up to and didn't even have to think about how to respond.

'Well,' she whispered, 'you *heard* what he said, the word he used, right? It was pretty unambiguous.'

She left it at that.

It was then that Bale mentioned the uncle who was supposed to be on his way up from Florida. Lizzie didn't react. Though she did wonder, and not for the first time, about her own folks. Were they here? Standing outside the building? *Next to each other?* She found that thought a little disquieting and decided to get on with the business at hand.

'We have a list,' she said. 'These are the things that we want.'

'Lizzie, that's great, it is, but I must –'

'Just shut up, OK? And *listen*.'

Micro beat.

'You got it.'

Then she started reeling them off. Nothing about food here, or tampons, or money, or safe passage out of the building – these were hardcore political demands.

'. . . end the carried-interest tax break for hedge fund managers . . . reinstate the Glass-Steagall Act . . . impose a zero-point-one per cent tax on all trades of stocks, bonds and derivatives . . .'

And as she read these out – her eyes darting from the page to Alex, then back to the page again – Lizzie felt the peculiar, transgressive thrill of knowing that while she sounded in control here, the truth was she barely understood a word of what she was saying. She had *some* knowledge of this stuff, from listening to Alex over the months, but she was extremely vague on the specifics.

'. . . mandate a new separation of the banks into investment and commercial by repealing Gramm-Leach-Bliley . . .'

So once she got off the phone – having lobbed the ball firmly into the FBI's court – she decided it was time to get with the programme and just *bone up* on the specifics. Energised, she gathered a few of the books and papers Julian had lying around the apartment, spread them out on the table and started reading.

This was important.

That's what she told herself.

There was a whole language here she needed to learn, a

language that both she and Alex, when they found themselves caught up – as they soon would, make no mistake – in the flaming crucible of global media attention, could use to . . .

To what? To *what*?

Looking back now, a few hours later, she can see that *that* was the high point – before, during and immediately after the phone conversation with the FBI guy. It was the high point in terms of energy levels and enthusiasm, the high point in terms of being in love with Alex, of being exquisitely deluded, of being in the throes of a mindless, giddy, tingly, bring-it-on, romantic *death* wish, whatever . . . *that* was the fucking crucible right there.

But it didn't last, it couldn't, and after half an hour or so of reading about fiat currencies and the gold standard, the air went out of it all.

Literal deflation.

She persevered, but there wasn't much point, and the next few hours were like the comedown from an acid trip – or, at least, never having done acid, what she imagined that would be like.

The mention of a Coady uncle didn't help matters. As far as Julian and Alex were concerned, the prospect of this man maybe standing down on Orchard Street with a bullhorn and *saying things* certainly seemed to put a dampener on the proceedings, and might have even been the catalyst for each of their subsequent 'episodes'.

In any case, Friday morning lurching towards its midpoint, here they are, the three of them, one slumped in a chair, one on the couch, one on the floor.

All waiting.

But for what? The internet connection to boot back up? Some cable news channel to come on the TV (with an update on the Carillo trial)? An amplified voice from outside to start pleading with them to surrender? The door to be kicked in, followed by the blinding, deafening flash of an M84 stun grenade?

This all feels a lot smaller than it did before – the possible outcomes more limited, the future more boxed in.

It's the new torpor, and Lizzie doesn't like it one little bit.

She looks at the guys and wants to scream at them.

But the thing is, what would she say?

*

The media conference is being held in the Amontillado Suite at the Wilson Hotel on Madison Avenue.

Announced at such short notice, and considering what else is going on in the city, it'll be a low-key enough affair, but that's fine. The event will be reported, recorded, livestreamed and blogged. The message will get out, and there'll be plenty of opportunity for follow-up. Howley will read his prepared statement, introduce his new COO/head of global infrastructure, and then answer a few questions.

And that'll be that.

The takeaway here – he hopes – will be the phrase 'effective immediately'.

Everything else will be noise and interference.

And heading up to the Wilson now for a midday kickoff, Howley pretty much knows what kind of noise and interference to expect. The more seasoned business hacks – the ones with a genuine sense of history – will want at least some return on the Vaughan angle. How is the old man? *Where* is he? What are his plans? Others will be focusing more on the succession process, and others again, predictably, will be fishing for any hint of an IPO announcement.

The succession narrative is fairly well established by this stage. For several years, whenever the subject came up, the names of a few high-profile contenders from within the company would be trotted out, but then Vaughan took the decisive step of bringing in an outsider as *his* new COO, a move widely seen as an unequivocal appoint-and-anoint. It was designed to end the speculation – that much is clear – but it also had the effect of emphasising just what a one-man show the Oberon Capital Group really was.

Today's announcement will bring an end to all of that.

As for an IPO, Howley intends to put that issue to bed next week, on Thursday or Friday, when he appears on Bloomberg to do an in-depth interview.

The final arrangements have yet to be made.

Approaching Seventy-first Street now, Howley leans back in his seat and takes a deep breath.

This is the big one, the pinnacle of his career.

Five or six years at the helm of Oberon and he can think about retiring. It's incredible. Only seems like yesterday that he was moving to DC to work as a consultant at the Defense Department.

The car pulls up outside the hotel. Howley gets out, and as he's standing there on the sidewalk he feels his phone vibrating in his pocket.

He pulls it out and looks at the display.

Vaughan.

He's been expecting this. They went over the statement very briefly last night and everything was in order, but it was a business call and neither of them made any reference whatsoever to the significance of what was being set in train here. Howley is no sentimentalist, but he has a strong sense of occasion and would like to see this particular one marked in some way.

Or at the very least acknowledged.

He understands that Vaughan probably has mixed feelings, as well as a degree of trepidation about the publicity side of things – but on that score, just as Howley predicted, all eyes this morning are on Orchard Street.

On this Lizzie Bishop.

Whose fifteen-minute allotment of fame, as far as Vaughan is concerned, has come at just the right time.

Glancing around at sunny Madison Avenue, Howley raises the phone to his ear. 'Jimmy?'

'Craig, how are you? Listen, meant to say last night, I'm thinking of heading out of town for a while, give you a little breathing space.'

'No, no, Jimmy, come on, that's not necessary, you don't have to –'

'No, I don't. But I might anyway. Spend some time at the house in Palm Beach. Relax, do a bit of sailing –'

Sailing?

'– play some golf. That'd be the *real* reason, if you want to know the truth.'

'Would you . . .' Howley doesn't know how to phrase this. The Jimmy Vaughan he saw earlier in the week was a very sick man. 'Would you . . .'

'Would I be *able* to, you mean? Well, listen, this new medication I'm on – the one I told you about, that the boys at Eiben are working on? – it's *amazing*. It's finally kicking in, and I actually feel pretty good for a change.'

'Holy shit, Jimmy.' Howley isn't sure what to make of this. But one thing does occur to him. *The boys at Eiben?* Isn't that a little weird? Given the history, given –

Then he sees Dave Fishman, Oberon's director of corporate affairs, coming through the hotel's revolving doors, and he gets distracted. 'Er . . . that's great, it really is . . .'

'Don't worry, Craig,' Vaughan says. 'I'm still going to die.'

'*Jesus*, Jimmy –'

'No, I just mean I mightn't have such a miserable time doing it.'

As Fishman approaches, eyebrows raised, pointing at his watch, Howley feels a flicker of panic, of uncertainty. It's as though he has lost his bearings all of a sudden. 'Er, listen, Jimmy,' he says, 'I have to –'

'Go, go, you're fine.' That was whispered. But what Vaughan says next is much louder. 'You know what, I might just stick around. This could be interesting.'

'Good . . . yeah, OK.'

'And Craig?'

'Yeah?'

'Don't fuck this up on me, you hear?'

*

It's nearly one o'clock and Frank has an uneasy sense that something is under way. But he has no idea what it is and no one will talk to him.

There's a lot of coming and going, a lot of huddled, urgent-looking conversations taking place between busy, important-looking people.

He keeps glancing around to see if he can spot that detective he spoke to a few times during the night. What was his name? Lenny Byron. *There* was a man you could deal with – open, direct, reluctant to just peddle any old line from the department.

But Detective Byron doesn't seem to be here any more.

It's not that *no one* will talk to Frank – there are liaison officers and trauma counsellors and all kinds of spokespeople available and willing to talk to him, but what they really are is a sort of buffer zone.

Right now he wants to talk to the important-looking people.

Because he has his suspicions.

Gleaned from various conversations and from things he's overheard.

For instance, it's Frank's understanding that there is considerable FBI scepticism about the explosives. Apparently, what led them to the apartment in the first place was a tipoff from an informant inside the protest movement regarding a firearms trail. All they had was a search warrant for this address. They had no idea what they were stumbling upon, and it was only the simultaneous tipoff from Ellen Dorsey that enabled them to get on top of things so fast.

But a subsequent trawl of their intelligence has turned up nothing that would indicate any explosives capability on the part of the Coady brothers.

What worries Frank is that if the FBI and JTTF think the explosives claim is a bluff, then they might do something reckless.

His second suspicion about what might be going on has to do with this much-rumoured uncle who is supposed to be arriving from Florida. First, if it's true, then where the fuck is he? It's been over twenty hours already since this thing started, and last time Frank looked Florida was about a three-hour plane ride away, not nestled somewhere between Australia and New Zealand. And second, there seems to be a serious disagreement about the advisability of using this guy even if he does arrive – it has to do with some bullshit psych assessment of the family dynamics.

Frank's third suspicion arises from that conversation he had this morning with Deb. She wouldn't say anything more about it, wouldn't elaborate or confirm, but the idea seemed to be that she and her husband – fucking Lloyd Hackler – would go on TV and *talk* about the situation.

Lloyd would talk about Lizzie.

His daughter.

Deb and Lloyd have been married for three years, and for two of those Lizzie has been away at college. So what's he going to say about her?

It's absurd.

And it's not just the humiliation of being excluded. Frank feels *that* for sure. It's also the question of motivation.

Why would Deb do this?

He doesn't know.

She's kept her distance all morning, spending most of it on the phone – but now, just in these last few minutes, Frank has noticed a slight increase in the levels of activity around her, and he can't help thinking this is it.

She's going to do it.

When Lloyd Hackler appears a short while later, it's pretty much confirmed, and Frank's stress levels skyrocket. Agitated, and only a few yards away, he looks on as a little group forms, Deb, Lloyd, a man he guesses to be some high-ranking TV executive and Victoria Hannahoe, the preternaturally radiant anchor of a cable news show he can't remember the name of. He watches as these people talk among themselves, smiling, throwing hand gestures around, and even, on occasion, laughing.

A few moments later, they begin to move away – where they're going, Frank doesn't know, but he starts to move as well, to follow them.

His heart pounding.

At which point an arm shoots across his chest and blocks his path.

'Frank, don't.'

He turns to his left, and exhales in defeat. It's Lenny Byron.

'Detective.'

'That look on your face, Frank. Bit of a giveaway. I'd stay here if I were you.'

'Yeah . . . OK.'

Byron lowers his arm.

Frank nods his head, indicating Deb and the others. 'Where are they going exactly?'

Byron turns and watches as the group recedes down the street. 'One of the trailers back there on Delancey. They've set up a temporary little, I don't know, it's like a little . . . studio or something. But –'

He pauses and makes a pained face. Byron is in his late thirties. He's dark and handsome, but he looks overworked. He could also do with a shave and a haircut and a new suit.

'Yeah?'

'There's something you should know. It's not just going to be an interview with Victoria Hannahoe, they're going to do it like a . . . sort of on-air appeal, and they're going to run it directly into the apartment.'

'*What?*'

Frank feels weak, faint, as if his body is suddenly remembering it hasn't slept in over thirty hours.

'It's another . . . strategy,' Byron says, speaking almost under his breath now, and glancing around, 'not necessarily what *I'd* do, but the Bureau's running the show here.'

Frank tries to steady himself. 'But what about *me?*' he says, with great effort. 'I'm her father.'

'I know, Frank, I know.' Byron looks at him directly and maintains eye contact. 'It's a calculation on their part. They feel . . . they feel Lizzie is somehow in control in there now. That's not based solely on the phone call, they have partial sightlines in through the various windows as well, and that's just how they're reading it. Julian has more or less folded. Apparently. And Alex is next.' He pauses. 'So they think a direct appeal to Lizzie might work.'

'Appeal? Coming from Deb, maybe. But from *Lloyd?* You've got to be kidding me. She hates that prick. It'll . . . it'll backfire, if anything.' He breathes in hard, suddenly fighting back tears. '*I* should be doing this with Deb.' Then he says it again. '*I'm her father.*'

Byron nods, doesn't look away. 'Listen, Frank, I don't know how up to speed you are on what's been happening over the last few hours . . . out there.' He waves an arm in the air, indicating . . . what? The city? The world? 'I'm talking about the internet,

Frank. You've been pretty much crucified. This guy you worked for, this Paloma guy, the area manager or something? Man, you must have really pissed him off, because he's been bad-mouthing you a *lot*, and it's caught on. Now you're like some kind of fucking Bruce Banner character, I don't know, some kind of ticking time bomb, and that's *not* who they want in that trailer doing their little live broadcast.'

'But –'

Frank stops. What's the point? This is a nightmare.

'Look, man,' Byron says, 'I don't know you from Adam, OK, but I know *people*, and this is clearly bullshit. You still have to be careful, though. So let me give you a piece of advice.'

Frank looks at him. He's bewildered.

Advice?

'There's going to be more of this,' Byron says. 'One way or the other. And if you want to come through it, you'll have to get some help. To mount a counterattack.'

'I don't –'

'A press agent, someone in PR, a journalist who's got your back, I don't know. But right now, Frank, you're a sitting duck for these people.'

A few minutes later, standing at the barrier, still numb from this latest shock, Frank starts patting down his pockets, then searching them one by one.

Ellen Dorsey gave him her card, and he took it. He didn't throw it away. He put it somewhere.

He eventually finds it in his back left pocket.

He holds the card up to read the number on it. He takes out his phone and calls her.

The phone vibrating on the glass coffee table is what wakes her. She turns her head, looks at it and lets it go to message. The phone is on silent, but it makes this low buzzy sound on a hard surface when it vibrates. She reaches out for it, groaning from the effort, and then sits upright on the couch. She looks at the display, doesn't recognise the number.

She checks to see if there's a message. There is. It's from Frank Bishop.

There are messages from other people, too, five in total – that one just now from Frank, one an hour ago from Val Brady, one just before that from Liz Zambelli, and two much earlier from Max Daitch.

Everyone agitated.

But Frank the most, naturally.

All he said, in his shaky, tired voice, was 'Ellen, this is Frank Bishop. Please call me.'

It occurs to her that she has no idea what's going on. The last she knew of anything was some time after 5 a.m. when she was in that bar on Norfolk Street with Val Brady.

She checks the time on her phone.

1.25.

That's eight hours.

Is it finished? What happened? She slides off the couch, picks up the TV remote, points it and flicks. Then she goes over to her desk and taps a key on the keyboard.

Before she calls him back she'd better get some kind of an update.

Stiff from sleeping on the couch, she hobbles into the

kitchen and puts on some coffee.

Over the next ten minutes, sipping espresso and dividing her attention between the TV and the computer, she updates herself comprehensively.

The first shock is that it's still going on. The second is that Lizzie Bishop has supplanted the Coady brothers as the focus of everyone's attention. And in what seems to be something of an unfortunate sideshow, Frank Bishop himself has come in for a bit of a hammering.

Does that have anything to do with why he called?

She needs more coffee. She goes and makes some. Then she has a pee. Then she takes a quick shower.

Putting it off.

Because what's she supposed to tell him? What can she do for him? She's not in a position to do anything.

When she finally calls him, she does it standing at the window, looking out onto Ninety-third Street.

'Frank? It's Ellen.'

'Hi. Er . . . just a second.' She hears some sounds in the background, muffled voices, shuffling. Then he's on again. 'Sorry. Thanks for getting back to me.' He pauses. 'I . . . I didn't see you anywhere last night, after we got here, I –'

'They wouldn't let me through,' she says. 'I guess you got swept up into it all, but I was held back at the first barrier. And I didn't have your number. I tried to get a message to you, but . . . the general atmosphere was pretty crazy. I stayed most of the night, but eventually I just came home.'

'Right.' There's a pause here as he considers this. 'OK.'

With that settled, sort of, he goes on to tell her about the upcoming Victoria Hannahoe interview and Lloyd Hackler's involvement and how fucked up it all is. There's an occasional crack in his voice as he speaks, but there's a steely quality to it as well.

'So look,' he says in conclusion, 'I could use some help. In return, you get exclusive access. Your phrase.'

This time it's Ellen's turn to pause and consider.

She'd given up on the story, and with good reason, but it's funny how things can change in the space of a few hours. Because this is no longer *news*. That part of the process is over, almost. Now it's morphing into something different, something that needs to be coloured in and dissected and explained before it's filed away in the public consciousness, archived as the Story of the Wall Street Killers, or the Siege of Orchard Street. With exclusive access to Frank Bishop – and, all going well, to Lizzie – there could be a substantial long-form piece in this.

Pretty much Ellen's métier.

And it'd be perfect for the next issue of *Parallax*.

'Yes,' she says, 'of course. Give and take. *Your* phrase.'

The second she's off with Frank here, she'll call Max.

'Good. Thanks.' He pauses. 'Where are you now?'

She tells him and says that she can be down there in twenty minutes, half an hour.

He tells her that he'll arrange for an NYPD detective named Lenny Byron to let her through the security barriers. That she should ask for him.

Ten minutes later, chewing on a last bite of stale bagel, she's out on Columbus Avenue hailing a cab.

*

When the phone rings, Lizzie's heart lurches sideways and she stands up at once from the table. Julian shifts slightly on the floor in the corner and groans, as if the sound of the phone is disturbing his sleep, but not enough to wake him up. On the couch, Alex turns his head. That's all. He doesn't say anything, doesn't say, 'You getting that?'

Doesn't need to.

Because she's *getting* it.

Picking it up, clearing her throat.

Loudly.

She has no script this time, no list, and a lot less adrenalin than she had the last time. The truth is, the waiting has been awful and has effectively drained the life out of her. She knows it's probably been a deliberate strategy to undermine morale in here, and boy has it worked, but little do they know how fragile morale was to begin with.

'Hello?'

'Hi, Lizzie. It's Tom.'

Tom.

This pretence of friendship is annoying. It's patronising. Standing at the table, next to the chair she's been sitting in for hours, she sways from side to side.

She actually has nothing to say.

'Lizzie?'

'Yeah, I'm here. Have you reinstated Glass-Steagall yet?'

'Er...'

She closes her eyes. Shit, that was stupid. It was flippant. She wasn't going for flippant. She's tired. Tired isn't even the word for it. She opens her eyes. Alex is looking up at her. She shrugs and turns away.

'Well?'

She's not backtracking now.

'Lizzie, let's take it one step at a time, OK? But I *do* have movement on something you asked about earlier, the communications situation?'

'Yeah?'

'Yeah, we'd like to get your TV back on. There's something we'd like you to watch.'

Oh fuck.

'What?'

'You'll find out in a –'

'Jesus, Tom –'

'Look, bear with me, Lizzie, OK?'

He pauses.

She can picture him, Special Agent Tom, huddled over his equipment. What she imagines his equipment to be. She doesn't know, headphones, recording panels, displays with dials and gauges. He'd love to move in for the kill here. She can hear it in his voice. She's not stupid. A little bit of veiled flirting, some white empathetic noise, and then *bam –*

Lizzie, we know we can count on you, and we know you're under pressure in there, we do, so tell us, quick, the explosives . . .

She exhales loudly down the phone.

'It's an interview,' he says, almost whispering. 'I think you'll respond to it. You will.' Before she can say anything, he adds, 'Turn the TV on in about two minutes, OK? Fox News.'

And then he hangs up.

There is silence, and stillness, for probably most of the two minutes. Then Lizzie puts the phone down on the table. She walks around to the front of the couch and looks for the TV remote.

'What?' Alex says, looking up, as though he's stoned but making an effort.

And then, shit . . . holy *shit* – it occurs to her – these mother-fuckers *are* stoned, on pills, sedatives, diaza-, diazap-, benzoap–

Whatever the fuck those things are called.

She's seen them in Julian's medicine cabinet.

What else would explain –

'*What?*' Alex repeats, shifting a little on the couch.

Lizzie rolls her eyes. This has been going on for nearly a whole day, a whole twenty-four hours, but she feels like she has aged ten years in that time, more – aged and changed and moved on, shed personas, past lives, complete versions of her-self . . . grown, expanded, *aged*, calcified, atrophied.

In a quiet voice, she says, 'They want us to turn on the TV. There's something they want us to watch.'

Alex shifts again on the couch, wriggles for a moment and reveals that he has been sitting on the remote.

There is another lurching movement from the corner, as Julian rolls over to face the room for the first time in many hours.

Oh, what? The promise of a little TV is enough to cut through the chemical molasses here? To raise these bozos from their self-administered inertia?

'Turn it *on*,' she says.

Alex picks up the remote and flicks it.

'What channel?'

Lizzie looks at him. 'Fox.'

'Of course.'

The screen pops into life with a commercial for some anti-ageing cream. Alex flicks forward through basketball, a sitcom and a couple of soaps before getting to the cable news channels. He stops at Fox.

It's *America Unbound with Victoria Hannahoe*.

'What *is* this shit?' Julian says.

Lizzie watches as he drags himself over to the couch, crawls onto it and sits beside his brother.

There's an item about Iran on at the moment, a filmed report. It seems to be coming to an end.

'Why are we watching this?' Alex says.

'I don't know. Just . . . wait.'

They wait.

Then it cuts back to the studio. It takes Lizzie a moment to focus and to realise that the background graphic, which has the word *siege* emblazoned across it in jagged red letters, is a treated, filtered image of Orchard Street.

In the foreground sits glamorous Victoria Hannahoe, with her extravagant red hair and striking blue eyes.

'We return now to our top story,' she says, 'the ongoing siege of a downtown New York City apartment in which three radical students believed to be in possession of bomb-making equipment and a quantity of explosives are caught up in a now nearly *twenty-four-hour* standoff with the New York City Police Department, the FBI and members of the Joint Terrorism Task Force.'

Lizzie can barely process this. It seems unreal.

'The three radicals – students of Atherton College in upstate New York – have issued a wide-ranging series of demands, which, if carried out, would amount to an effective restructuring of our entire financial system.'

'*Yesss.*'

'Two of the three – brothers Julian and Alex Coady – are also believed to be responsible for the recent murders of two Wall Street bankers, Jeff Gale and Bob Holland, and for the attempted murder of another, Scott Lebrecht. However, it is now emerging that the leader of the group, and the ideological driving force behind it, may well be the third student holed up in the Orchard Street apartment, one Elizabeth Bishop.'

'What the *fuck* –'

Julian struggles to turn around on the couch.

Alex remains completely still.

Lizzie stares at the TV screen in disbelief.

'Elizabeth – or Lizzie – Bishop is the one who issued the demands and is also, according to police sources, understood to be the most in control and proactive member of the group.'

Julian throws his arms up. '*This is . . . this is BULLSHIT!*'

'In an attempt to further our understanding of these events – events that are unfolding before the eyes of the world – we are now going to speak exclusively to the mother and stepfather of Lizzie Bishop, Deborah Bishop-Hackler and Lloyd Hackler –'

'*Oh Jesus, oh no.*'

Lizzie staggers back towards the wall as the camera pans right to reveal . . . her *mother*? And Lloyd fucking *Hackler*? Sitting together like teenagers, looking all attentive and concerned? This is horrendous, and where's . . . where's *Frank*?

Lloyd isn't her fucking *father* . . .

'. . . and let me ask you as well . . .'

Wh-what was that? Lizzie didn't hear the first part of the question. She's finding it impossible to concentrate.

'. . . as a child, growing up . . .'

'*Fuck* this,' Julian says, and starts getting up off the couch. Alex turns and looks at Lizzie, the weirdest expression on his face – this pale, sickly, confused stare – and then he lurches to the side and throws up, a liquid hurl of vomit landing in a splat on the floorboards next to the couch.

'You *bitch*,' Julian says, one eye on Alex as he comes round the end of the couch, and then directly towards her, 'I should have fucking –'

'. . . what you might call *emotional* intelligence . . .'

But he stops . . . just as – or just after – Lizzie hears a dry *phwutt* sound. Julian's eyes roll upwards, he stumbles to the left, and the red mark on the side of his head bubbles and spurts into a sudden and rapid trickle down his cheek.

Lizzie tries to scream but nothing happens. Her throat is dry and her chest seizes up in pain. When Julian falls to the floor, she notices a tiny cracked hole in the window behind him. In the next moment she hears a second *phwutt* sound and an identical hole appears beside the first one. By the time she turns and looks down at Alex, whose head is now resting on the edge of the couch, the trickle of blood on *his* cheek has already started mingling with the vomity mucus around his mouth.

Directly ahead of Lizzie, her mother is on the screen, leaning towards the camera, words coming from her mouth, only some of them getting through, only some of them comprehensible.

'. . . a mother's perspective . . . . here now to implore my little . . .'

Lizzie leans against the wall behind her, stretching her arms out, pushing back hard, tears in her eyes. She looks to the right, at the window, at the two holes, waiting . . .

But it doesn't come.

Then she slides quickly to the floor, out of the sightline of the window, facing the table and the back of the couch.

She feels like throwing up herself now, but manages to hold it in.

She's no longer able to see the TV, but her mother's voice continues to fill the room.

'. . . and for that reason, and that reason only, I know that Lloyd and I –'

Then it stops abruptly and is replaced by a low hum.

The connection cut.

The sudden stillness is terrifying. A few feet to her right is Julian's crumpled body. To her left, on the floor next to the couch, she can see the glistening, lumpy peninsula stain of vomit – Alex himself unseen, but so close, slumped on the couch in front of her.

Dead.

Poor, sweet Alex.

In her worst imaginings this ended with handcuffs and a televised perp walk and orange jumpsuits and a vague, inexact, drawn-out *process*, including lots of photographers and clips gone viral and trendings and . . .

She's ashamed now to think how little she thought it all through, and angry at how stupid she's been – or *was*. Because she could have done something. She could have gone along with the guy on the phone, for instance. She could have found *some* way to neutralise the situation, to wind it down peacefully.

She wipes her eyes and nose with her sleeve.

So now what?

Is the phone going to ring? Will there be a gentle rap on the door?

Seconds pass, each one unbearable, each one hijacked by images and thoughts and emotions she has no way of resisting or fighting off. She thinks of her mom on the TV, a tracker scout calling back at her from the hostile, oxygen-thin media landscape. She thinks of her dad; she'd earlier imagined seeing him through the more intimate medium of the apartment-door peephole. When she got back from her long walk yesterday afternoon and plugged in her phone to charge it, she saw that he'd left voice messages and texts, so many of them – which had made her smile. She should have called him then.

If she had, all of this might have been different.

She thinks of her brother, John. She should have –

Jesus.

What?

Is that all she's got left? A fucking catalogue of *should haves* . . .

Shoulda this, shoulda that, shoulda the other.

The phone rings.

She lets it go for a bit, but then leans forward. As she's reaching up to get the phone, she notices Alex's backpack under the table. She pulls it out, realising that she has no idea what's in it. It doesn't feel heavy. It could be just a few books.

She doesn't know. She doesn't open it. She puts it on the table.

She picks up the phone. She doesn't say anything.

'Lizzie?'

She avoids looking at Alex, but notices that on the couch next to him – and next to the remote control – is the gun he had yesterday.

'Lizzie? *Lizzie?* You there?'

'Yeah.'

She stretches across the table, over the back of the couch, and reaches down for the gun.

The window is to her right.

She must be plainly visible.

'Lizzie, listen to me very carefully, OK?'

'Have you done it yet?'

'What . . . sorry?'

'Glass-Steagall. Have you reinstated it yet?' She pauses. '*You stupid motherfuckers.*'

She drops the phone on the floor. She raises her other hand, points the gun at the window and pulls the trigger. The sound is alarmingly sharp, and in the recoil her arm and shoulder yank back really hard. Unlike the earlier and more discreet incoming shots, this one shatters the windowpane completely.

Lizzie's shoulder is sore and she rubs it for a moment with her free hand.

When she's done, she picks the bag up from the table. She walks over to the door and kicks it a couple of times, grunting loudly.

Then she opens it.

Holding the bag up and pointing the gun directly in front of her she heads out into the narrow hallway and the oncoming steel-grey blur of Kevlar vests, ballistic helmets and M4 assault rifles.

*

In the cab on the way down, Ellen tries to plot out the next three weeks in her head. The first one – assuming this siege thing doesn't drag on too long – will be talking to Frank Bishop and, hopefully, to Lizzie. The second week will be back up at Atherton, excavating the Coady connections and gathering local detail, and then *maybe*, if it becomes necessary, a Coady-related schlep down to Florida for the rest. The third week will be at home on an intravenous coffee drip getting the story written for the next *Parallax* deadline.

Her agreement with Frank Bishop – informal, and yet to be tested – will be key here. To make it work she'll have to help *him* first.

Devise some kind of a strategy.

As the cab turns onto Delancey Street, her phone pings. It's a text from Max.

You watching Hannahoe?

She composes a reply – *No. In a cab.* – but then decides not to send it. She doesn't want to be distracted by calls or texts. She'll get back to Max after she's met with Frank.

At the barrier on the corner of Orchard she asks a uniformed officer if she can speak to a Detective Lenny Byron. The officer turns away and relays the request into his radio. After a few moments he turns back and tells her that Detective Byron will be along to see her in a few minutes.

She thanks him and looks around.

Traffic is passing normally on Delancey, but there are a lot of extra parked vehicles – squad cars, trucks, trailers. There is a large group of people gathered on the sidewalk, too, mostly civilian onlookers, locals, the evacuated. There's a good deal of curiosity and neck-craning and disgruntlement. She can see up Orchard Street, and there's another, smaller group of people at the next set of barriers, just before Rivington. These are mostly cops, Bureau and Homeland personnel, journalists, tech crews.

After a couple of minutes, a guy in a crumpled suit and an invisible cigarette sticking out of his mouth wanders down.

Ellen has met a lot of NYPD detectives in her day, and they tend to fall into fairly set categories: the assholes, the plodders and the ones you can actually have a decent conversation with. Only problem is you can never tell beforehand. Unless you have an indication. The fact that Frank Bishop apparently has this guy on his side is indication enough for Ellen.

And that's how it turns out.

A minute or so later, they're both strolling back in the direction of Rivington and parsing recent testimony in the Connie Carillo murder trial. The sun is nudging its way out from behind a passing cloud bank, and Ellen has already spotted Frank Bishop.

It is a moment of virtual tranquillity.

And then a shot rings out.

It's somewhat muffled, but it's unmistakable.

Byron runs on, everyone else moving at the same time, sucked forward.

But just as quickly, all movement ceases and there is an eerie silence.

The scene suspended, everyone left hanging.

Frank Bishop leans over the barrier, his head in his hands, Byron at his side now.

Ellen stands watching.

Then the silence is broken, this time by a sustained burst of gunfire. It comes from the same direction, from inside, and is louder, fuller, more comprehensive.

Still only a couple of seconds.

But enough to change everything.

11

Walking from the door of the building over towards Frank, Detective Lenny Byron gives a quick shake of his head. He's pale and his eyes look hollowed out.

He mouths, 'I'm sorry.'

Frank stares at him in disbelief, barely able to breathe now, his chest like a brick, his gut twisting into knots. He holds onto the barrier with both hands, squeezing so hard it feels as if either the metal or his bones should crack.

There is a moment when his voice comes close to making a sound, to releasing something, a scream or a howl, but the moment passes. And then it's too late. Frank knows what this is, even if he can't control it – his systems are shutting down, his emotions seizing up, grief and despair retreating, burrowing into dark, silent recesses.

Almost immediately, too, stuff begins to happen around him, distracting stuff, like the Rivington and Stanton Street barriers being pushed aside to make way for the extra personnel that are now appearing – technical units, crime scene, bomb disposal, paramedics – a whole security apparatus whose function, it seems, is to disassemble, to debrief.

To obliterate.

Frank and an openly howling Deb soon get swept up into a separate debriefing process that involves being talked to, or talked *at*, in various locations, at various times – and, most disconcertingly, in various tones – by a parade of uniformed officers, special agents and PTSD counsellors. What the process does *not* involve, however, is any kind of response to their repeated requests for information.

For confirmation.

For a chance to see their daughter's body.

That – it soon becomes apparent, as they are drawn ever farther away from the scene – is simply not going to happen. And despite whatever armoury of legalistic-sounding bullshit Lloyd Hackler is able to draw on, the firewall phrase 'national security concerns' proves to be impenetrable.

But what strikes Frank about this – about the notion of juxtaposing that phrase with his daughter's name – is just how preposterous it seems.

A part of him wants to laugh.

Which actually feels like something he might be able to do, in the absence of other, more appropriate responses – crying, say, howling, trembling uncontrollably, lashing out.

He doesn't laugh, though, or do any of these things. Instead, he moves through the hours like a zombie, dealing with the authorities, with Deb and Lloyd, talking on the phone to John (after Deb calls him), accepting Deb's invitation to stay with *them* tonight (because where else is he going to stay?) and ending up in their apartment on Eighty-sixth Street, with people dropping by all the time, people he knows vaguely, people he doesn't know at all, then watching Deb break down, watching her recover and watching her break down again.

Unable to sleep that night, he stares at the ceiling for six hours.

At around noon the next day, he and Lloyd drive out to

JFK to pick up John. This forty-minute car journey should be awkward and emotionally charged, as it's actually the first time the two men have ever been alone together, but instead it's nothing. It's preceded by a testy encounter between Lloyd and some of the photographers and reporters camped out on Eighty-sixth Street, and is followed by an interminable wait in the overcrowded arrivals area.

John is understandably distraught when he appears, but after a long silent hug, Frank leaves most of the talking, and explaining, such as it is, to Lloyd.

And in this way Saturday rolls on and folds into Sunday.

The media barrage in the morning is relentless, the papers, the talk shows, but Frank ends up being shielded from a lot of it – and again, here, thanks are due to Lloyd, whose crisis management skills are operating at full tilt.

But what Frank realises after a while is that he doesn't want to be shielded from it, because in the absence of being able to *feel* anything, he finds that all he can do is think, and to do that he needs input, he needs information.

In the apartment, there is a lot of walking on eggshells, and whispered conversations, and tea drinking, and Frank knows he won't be able to bear this for much longer. On Sunday evening, therefore, he has a quiet word with Deb, an even quieter one with John, and then he takes his leave. He borrows a coat and hat of Lloyd's, so that when he exits the building he's able to slip by the photographers unnoticed.

He's not sure what he's going to do, though.

He doesn't want to go downtown to retrieve his car – doesn't want to go anywhere near *there*, not yet. Besides, he'll have to stick around town for a few days, to find out what's going on.

To find out about the release of the body.

So he wanders aimlessly for an hour or two, and eventually checks into a cheap hotel, the Bromley, in midtown, near Seventh Avenue. For a cheap hotel, the Bromley is still fairly expensive, but Frank doesn't care. He has a credit card, and *some* money in the bank.

Not that any of that matters any more.

He settles into his room, which is musty and could do with a lick of paint and a change of carpets, and turns on the TV.

He flicks around the channels looking for any reference to, or analysis of, the events of Friday. Incredibly, it seems that the story has already receded somewhat, and other stuff has come to the fore. But he does find a bit of coverage, which he watches with mute incomprehension – and as soon as it's done, he flicks on through the channels to look for more elsewhere.

He's also very hungry, he realises, but he does nothing about it.

Eventually, he falls asleep on the bed, in his clothes, the remote control in his hand.

*

'Well, I wasn't paying attention. I was actually pretty busy on Friday.'

'Yeah. Guess I called *that* one wrong.'

It's Sunday night and Ellen is at the bar in Flannery's having a drink with Charlie. She raises her glass and says, 'You might not have been the only one.'

Charlie nods. 'Quite the spectacular fuck-up, wasn't it?'

Ellen doesn't say anything. She can still hear the gunfire in her head, and feel the resultant knot in her stomach. She's had the weekend to get over it, to digest what happened, but it now appears that that's not going to be enough.

'Three dead kids?' Charlie goes on. 'That's a bad day's work, no matter what the circumstances. OK, this wasn't Kent State or anything. They shot those banker guys, I get that. But still.'

Ellen doesn't know how old Charlie is exactly, but his casual reference to Kent State as a sort of touchstone for this says a lot.

'Anyway.' She doesn't really want to talk about Orchard Street. It's not that she doesn't have anything to say on the matter. She does. That's the trouble. She wouldn't know where to start. 'So, counsellor,' she says, upbeat, 'what's going on? What's the latest?'

Charlie's obsessive interest in the Connie Carillo murder trial is almost as amusing as the trial itself. It's like a soap opera for him, something to watch and then ironically tear apart and analyse in the bar with his co-retirees and anyone else, like Ellen, who'll bother to listen.

'OK,' he says, 'on Friday morning Joey Gifford finished up, so after lunch they called the next witness.' He glides a hand through the air, as though conjuring up something magical. 'Enter Mrs Sanchez, the housekeeper.' He lets that sink in for a moment, but when it doesn't get the reaction he was obviously expecting, he hammers the point home. 'It means we get our first glimpse *inside the apartment*. And even if Mrs Sanchez is no Joey Gifford, she's going to have a lot more to dish up on the day-to-day stuff chez Carillo.'

Dutifully, Ellen raises her glass again. 'What's not to like?'

'Exactly.'

But as Charlie goes on with his account of Friday's proceedings in the courtroom, Ellen finds her mind wandering back to Orchard Street, and to an image she has of Frank Bishop standing alone at the barrier, stooped, motionless, waiting for Lenny Byron to reappear.

She and others were shunted away at that point.

Near the outer barrier she had a quick word with Val Brady, and then stood around on Delancey for a while before wandering off and eventually – once again – heading home.

Here there were more voice messages and emails inviting her to address Twittergate – or, as it should perhaps more generously be called (it being the only -gate he's ever likely to get) Rattgate – but she ignored them. She turned on the TV, went online, grabbed her phone and started following the Orchard Street story across as many platforms as she could handle. Unlike earlier, she accepted now that she was a civilian where this was concerned. But she was a committed one and wanted answers.

She wanted to understand.

And over the course of Saturday and Sunday she *has* come to understand quite a bit, even managing to piece together for herself a plausible-ish picture of how and why the whole thing happened. Unsurprisingly, though, certain key questions remain unanswered – questions about the different guns the Coadys used in the shootings, about whether or not there actually *were* any explosives in the apartment and about the exact sequence of events at the very end. She knows from experience that when these issues come up for official processing they'll either be dealt with head-on and honestly, or they'll be fudged, spun and subjected to such extensive redaction as to be rendered meaningless.

But in the meantime there's plenty of speculation and theorising and opinion, endless rivers of the stuff, in fact – and of every colour and shade. Today alone, for example, in the papers and online, the Coadys and Lizzie Bishop have been vilified, lionised, psychoanalysed, diagnosed, caricatured and satirised. Members of their respective families have been followed, hounded and photographed. Ellen even found herself watching a brief YouTube clip of Frank Bishop standing outside an apartment building with a couple of other people on the Upper East Side somewhere.

What was the point of that?

Who knows? *She* doesn't.

What she does know, however, is that she liked Frank Bishop, and she feels for him. On the drive down to the city from Atherton they talked a lot, at least for the first part of the journey, and she got a real sense of what makes him tick, of how he thinks, and especially of how important Lizzie was to him. Maybe that last part is to state the obvious, but it certainly puts things into perspective for Ellen.

As she listens to Charlie talk now about the Carillo trial, she feels no real connection to any of the key players in it. Sure, Connie is on trial for her life, and may well be innocent, but as a semi-public figure of some years' standing – socialite, opera singer, mob wife and politician's daughter – she's been so mediated and filtered already, *before* this, that she doesn't come across as authentic or relatable in any way.

Frank Bishop, by contrast . . .

Who'd ever heard of *him* before last Friday?

No one.

This is an ordinary guy who's suddenly living the unimaginable nightmare of having his personal life – family tragedy, professional failures, character flaws, the lot – projected onto the Jumbotron screen of public consciousness.

From total anonymity to full-spectrum media blitz in a matter of hours.

There's no comparison.

She looks into her glass.

Not that it's a competition or anything.

Later, walking back to her apartment along Amsterdam Avenue towards Ninety-third Street, Ellen wonders how Frank is doing. He still has a story to tell, that's for sure – a unique perspective, at the very least, and to put it at its most neutral, on a significant public event.

She's not going to call him, though.

She *should*.

If she was doing her job right.

But maybe that's the problem. Maybe she doesn't know what that is any more.

*

For most of Monday morning Craig Howley avoids going anywhere near Vaughan's office. He knows that it has already been vacated, divested of all traces, and that he's free to rearrange the furniture in any way he sees fit, but still, there's something very final, very Rubicon-esque, about this, about stepping over the threshold.

It isn't so much like taking over the Oval Office after a previous incumbent's four- or even eight-year term – a better analogy, Howley thinks, would be how L. Patrick Gray must have felt in 1972 taking over as director of the FBI following J. Edgar Hoover's nearly *four decades* in the job. Howley doesn't know if Gray occupied the same physical space as Hoover, if he took over his actual office, but man, he must have been feeling the pressure.

Howley himself is certainly feeling it.

At least when a four- or eight-year term is up, it's up.

At least Hoover was *dead*.

In any case, Howley chairs the usual 8 a.m. meeting of senior investment directors in the conference room. He then spends an hour or so floating around the hallways, popping into other people's offices and engaging in a form of banter that ends up being slightly awkward and forced. He also stands around reception for a while making calls and sending texts.

Displacement activity.

At around midday, just before he's due to go for lunch with Paul Blanford, the CEO of Eiben-Chemcorp, Howley makes his way over to what has traditionally been thought of as Vaughan's personal corner of the fifty-seventh floor. He couldn't count the number of times in the last year that he has sat outside this office, waiting for the nod from Jacqueline Prescott. But now, suddenly, here's Angela, already in place at her new desk. He has a few words with her before making his way into the main office.

He stands inside the door and closes it behind him. The layout and design of this huge space are pretty much old-school, lots of mahogany panelling and red leather furniture, carpeting, blinds, a big, solid desk, anonymous artworks. Vaughan had the conference room renovated six months ago, but hadn't gotten around to doing his own office yet, even though he'd apparently been talking about it for some time.

Howley will do it now, though – gut the place and start from scratch.

He has a few ideas.

Brushed steel and travertine, custom fabrics and smoked glass. A couple of really big fishtanks, a walk-in humidor, a bocce court. Indulgent, yes, to a certain degree. He figures he's earned it, though. This may well be the last office he ever occupies, so he's determined to put his personal stamp on it.

But the truth is that there's a lot more to be rearranged around here than the furniture. It's something that has become plain to him over the last few days.

What it is, essentially, is a matter of survival.

He walks across the room to the big desk and sits behind it. He looks out on all that James Vaughan – up until last week some time – surveyed. He thinks of the decisions that have been made from behind this desk, the deals struck, the strategies devised, the vast web of Oberon-related *business* that has been conducted. Howley has even been involved in some of it himself – over the last year, obviously, but also before that, from the other side of the fence. He and Vaughan were instrumental in setting up a supply chain out of Afghanistan of the precious metal thanaxite, an essential manufacturing component used in advanced robotics. More specifically, it was needed for a program called the BellumBot – an autonomous battlefield management system – that was in development at Paloma Electronics.

All of which is perfectly fine, but if Howley is really to succeed here on his own terms, he's going to have to be more assertive, more proactive.

He swivels from side to side in the chair.

He's going to have to do something about James Vaughan.

Because despite all of Vaughan's good wishes and declarations of support, and despite his various health problems, as long as the man has a breath left in his body he will continue to run things – at *some* level, consciously, unconsciously, whatever, it doesn't matter.

He was at it the other day, making that call just before the press conference, blowing hot and cold, actually trying to undermine – or so it seemed – the whole event. And it was the same up in his apartment that time, the way Howley was ushered into the fucking kitchen and then more or less dismissed after twenty minutes.

Mind games.

The ultimate example of which, of course, is this business with the 'black file'. Howley has wondered on more than one occasion recently if Vaughan wasn't in the grip of some form of creeping dementia, but not after that.

It was too calculated and controlling.

However, there *was* one thing about the other day that puzzled Howley and that he thought about a lot over the weekend. He even discussed it with Jessica.

The boys at Eiben?

This new medication Vaughan is on?

It was the second time the old man had mentioned it, and it seemed to be something he was genuinely excited about. It also seemed to be something that was outside his normal arena of calculation and control – this despite the glaring fact that Eiben-Chemcorp was actually one of the companies listed in the file.

It was almost as if mentioning this new medication he was on had been a slip of the tongue, and therefore, in Howley's view of things, a demonstration of weakness. Possible demonstration, at any rate. It was certainly worth looking into, certainly worth rearranging his first official lunch for.

As he's leaving the office to meet Paul Blanford at the Four Seasons, Angela tells Howley that a producer from Bloomberg has called to schedule a meeting for tomorrow morning. Howley is pleased about this. Putting down his marker as Oberon's new leader in a TV interview – something Vaughan would never have done – seems to him the right way to go about things.

He sets a time for the meeting with Angela. Then, just as he's turning to go, he asks her to draw up a list of interior designers who specialise in executive office suites.

*

It's not the dingy rooms, or the long soulless dingy corridors, or the oppressive rattling dingy elevator cars, Frank doesn't mind those, but he wishes he'd picked a different hotel, in a different neighbourhood. The Bromley is rube central, the obvious place you'd pick on the map if you were heading to that New York City for the first time and had tickets to see a show.

But he's not going to change hotels now. It'd be too much hassle. Not that it actually would be any hassle. All he's got by way of stuff is the few things he accumulated this morning on a quick trip to the nearest Duane Reade.

It'd be a hassle in the sense that *breathing* is a hassle.

But the relative anonymity is working.

Because who'd think to look for him here? And apparently

people *are* looking for him. He's had voice messages on his cell and on his phone in Mahopac, all from journalists and TV booking agents wanting to get him to open up and *talk*. He's also spoken to Deb more than once today, and each time the subject was raised – Victoria Hannahoe wants to do a follow-up interview and thinks maybe *this* time Frank should come on.

Frank tries really hard to make his 'no' not sound like a primal scream. Also, he doesn't have any idea where to begin trying to understand what Deb is thinking.

So he doesn't.

The only reason he's keeping the channel open is because he needs the information – what's going on, what are the FBI saying, when will the body be released.

Lloyd has been the point man in all of this, and Frank is grateful to him. He's always hated Lloyd, resented him, been unable to bear the sight of him, and now he just thinks, thank fuck for Lloyd.

When he got up this morning, Frank quickly found himself entangled in the illusion of being busy. He took a shower and shaved. He went out to get something to eat. He bought that stuff at the Duane Reade. Every few minutes he stopped and checked his phone. At a newsstand he picked up a *New York Times* and a *Post*. He walked around looking for somewhere to go through them. He found a place, a bench in Bryant Park, and sat down. He scanned the papers and read anything in them that was relevant. And just beneath the surface of all this – in his mind, in the pit of his stomach – there was a faint, constant thrum of expectation.

But expectation of *what*?

It didn't take him long to realise that nothing was going to happen, at least nothing that he might *want* to happen. And he was going to have to keep reminding himself of this. Because otherwise, he'd go insane.

By the middle of the afternoon, however, he feels that he already has. The shapelessness, the lack of purpose, is inescapable. On the way back to his room, going through the lobby of the Bromley, he passes a group of German tourists. They look like intrepid explorers, with their maps, windbreakers, moustaches and accents – confident, curious, ready for whatever lies in the undiscovered country ahead.

And yet *he* feels like the visiting alien.

In the elevator, alone, he presses the button for ten. On the way up, he doesn't know what it is, maybe it's the motion, maybe it's a combination of that and the disorienting effect of the infinity mirrors, but something seems to dislodge deep inside him and he lurches sideways, simultaneously whimpering and gulping, unsure if he's going to fall over, cry or puke. He does none of these, but when he gets out of the car, escaping the mirrors, and is hobbling down the corridor towards his room, doors flickering left and right, he feels sure there'll be *some* toll to pay for this, and a physical one.

When he gets to his room he hesitates, standing just inside the door, but then rushes into the bathroom and throws up. He spends the next twenty minutes sitting on the toilet, eyes closed, head in his hands, squirming, grunting in pain, as his insides twist and coil.

He imagines, when he's finished, that this was some kind of psychosomatic delaying mechanism.

Because it was either his tear ducts or his gut.

And, at some level, an executive decision was taken.

Avoidance, repression.

Misdirection.

Except that he knows what's going on. He understands how it works. It's just that he can't control it.

He *could* stage an intervention. Raid the minibar, infuse some alcohol into the equation. That would loosen things up.

But is it what he wants?

Because he knows that if he goes from thinking to feeling, if he hits *that* switch, there'll be no turning back, and no telling where he'll end up.

Talk about an undiscovered country.

He comes out of the bathroom and lies on the bed. He stares up at the ceiling. What he *thinks* he wants, before he surrenders, is to properly understand. And right now he doesn't. Right now, despite the blanket nature of the media coverage, everything he sees or reads seems hopelessly superficial, each fact and opinion recycled, mediated, memed, so that he never feels any of it is actually about his daughter . . .

He can't relate to the person they're describing.

And he needs to.

Because where's *Lizzie* in all of this?

Probably what Frank needs to do is talk to the people who were close to her, the friends she hung out with, the ones who knew what she was like and what she was into – the ones who can tell him if she really was, if she'd really turned into, some kind of extreme . . . militant activist.

The only problem is, that will mean going back up to Atherton, and he isn't ready to do that yet.

After a while, a thought strikes him.

Who did Ellen Dorsey meet when she was up there? What, if anything, did she find out? She told him some stuff in that bar, but he can't remember any of the details. And in the car on the way down here, *he* did most of the talking.

He slides over and sits on the side of the bed.

What does she know? What can she tell him?

*

It's early evening, neither of them particularly wants a drink, so they meet in a diner. It's on Ninth Avenue between Fifty-fourth and Fifty-fifth, a real dive, but Ellen knows the owner, the food is actually good and they won't be disturbed.

'What can I get you?'

Frank looks up at the waitress with something like mild panic in his eyes. It's as if he's never been in this situation before and he doesn't know what to do.

'Er . . .'

He drums his fingers on the table.

Ellen studies him. He looks awful. Tired, pale, shaky. It occurs to her that he probably hasn't slept or eaten much in the last couple of days.

'The grilled chicken sandwich is good,' she says, to move things along, and on the basis that a grilled chicken sandwich will more than likely fit the bill.

He nods.

'Two, please,' Ellen says to the waitress. 'And an iced tea.' She looks at Frank again, and he nods again. 'Two.'

They surrender their menus.

The place is nearly empty. They have a booth by the window,

looking out onto Ninth.

'Thanks for agreeing to see me.'

'No problem.'

He explained to her on the phone that obviously things had changed since the previous time they'd spoken, that the help he'd needed then was not the help he needed now. That what he needed *now* was just to ask her a few questions.

Fine by her.

On the way down here she tried to anticipate what those questions might be, but she couldn't really settle on anything. What did he expect from her? As soon as he starts, though, it all begins to make sense. He talks for five minutes straight, articulately, and through his obvious exhaustion and *pain*, mapping out in detail what he refers to, with sphincter-grinding restraint, as his 'dilemma'.

His need to understand before he can grieve.

Their food and iced teas arrive. The waitress distributes plates and glasses. They murmur their thanks.

Ellen welcomes the brief interval.

She's curious. Frank hasn't actually asked his questions yet, even though it's clear to her now what they will be. But the thing she's wondering is, doesn't he have anyone else to talk to? She gets it about the ex-wife. But doesn't he have any friends he can confide in, the way he's just confided in her? She's good at talking to people, at getting them to open up to her, she knows that, but this is hardcore.

Reaching for his iced tea, Frank looks at her, and it's as if he can hear what she's thinking.

'I'm sorry,' he says.

'For what?'

'This. The long preamble. I haven't really been able to *talk* to anyone. Since the other day.' He sips the tea. 'It's funny, you know. When I was working – as an architect, I mean – all my friends were architects, or in that world, and when you lose that, the work, when you get kicked out on your ass, you lose the friends as well. No one wants to get infected. And hanging out with other people who got canned isn't much of an option either.'

She nods along. 'I know. It's more or less the same with journalism. I've seen it happen.'

'Yeah. So. Anyway.' He puts the glass down. 'Here's the thing. That's not my daughter I've been reading about for the last two days. Political activist? Militant?' He shakes his head. 'Lizzie was a bright kid, but she . . . I never once . . .' He seems reluctant to pin it down. 'She wasn't interested in politics.'

'Maybe so,' Ellen says, 'but this was a lot more than politics. Plus, she was at college. Shit happens at college. People change, they get into stuff.'

'I know. I know. But –' He looks out the window, and then back at Ellen. 'That's what I wanted to ask you. Who you spoke to up there, what you heard, if you met anyone or saw anything. I know you told me some of this stuff at that bar, but I wasn't exactly at my most focused.'

She thinks about this for a moment. The thing is, Ellen's understanding of what happened is that Lizzie became central to events only when she spoke to the negotiator. Up to then it was all about the Coadys. They were the ones who carried out the shootings, who had a backstory and a supposed motive. Lizzie was just the girlfriend. She barely figured. But then she spoke, she read out those demands – this girl, this *kid* – and suddenly the story lit up like a fucking pinball machine . . . out here, in the media, but maybe *in there* as well, in the apartment. Maybe Lizzie's real involvement started right at that point, when she answered the phone, and once she *got* involved there was no route back. Once she voiced those demands, it was an easy next step to picking up the gun and pulling the trigger. Though why she was the one who answered the phone in the first place, and read out the demands, is – and probably forever will remain – a mystery.

But is that what Frank Bishop wants to hear?

Probably not.

In any case, it's only a theory – pieced together from her conversations with Val Brady and others, from what she's read and from her general feel for these things, her instincts as a journalist.

And she may be wrong about all of it.

Besides, he didn't ask for her opinion.

'Well,' she says, deciding to simply lay out the facts for him, 'I did speak to a few people at Atherton. But remember, when I went there I didn't have any names, and Lizzie's only came up at the very end, which is why I went chasing after you.' She stops and glances down for a second at her grilled chicken sandwich. 'It was what I found in the library, and in the archives, that led me to Julian Coady's name. And this was stuff that more or less underpinned what they were about, what they *did*. In an ideological sense.'

Frank looks at her. 'Ideological? *Really?*'

'Well . . . yeah.' Ellen is aware that a lot of the big-name protest groups have been dissociating themselves from anything to do with the Coadys and Lizzie Bishop, almost as if the whole thing were an embarrassment to them. Much has been made – in certain quarters – of the list of demands and how naïve or generic or even just derivative it was. But actually, on reflection, there was nothing that Ellen came across in the *Atherton Chronicle* pieces, in the radio interviews, in the opinions expressed on the *Stone Report* or by Farley Kaplan, that was in any way inconsistent with mainstream activist thought. The only dividing line – apart maybe from tone and register and levels of paranoia – was the question of whether or not the use of violence could be justified, and *that* question was as old as the hills. She turns and looks out the window, at a passing limo, a black streak of light on the avenue. 'I don't know,' she then says. 'They certainly put a lot of thought into what they were doing.'

'*They?*'

Ellen hesitates, then picks up her sandwich and takes a bite out of it.

'Yes,' she says, chewing and nodding. 'Look, there were three of them. They were in that apartment together, and for a *week*. During which time two, nearly three, assassinations were carried out. That didn't just happen. They talked about this stuff, they planned it. And probably for months.' She puts her sandwich back on the plate, realising that she's straying here from hard fact, drifting back to opinion. But it's difficult not to do. 'Alex and Lizzie were a couple, Frank. And Alex and Julian were brothers. In and out of each other's lives. However misguided it was, what they did was planned. It also didn't come out of thin air, it was based on . . . stuff they were exposed to. Ideological stuff. They weren't just going around shooting people randomly. This was a programme.'

'What do you mean?'

Ellen pauses, thinking. She picks up a French fry.

Dips it in ketchup.

He's staring at her, waiting.

In all the coverage of the shootings she's read, seen or heard, the victims have been referred to simply as Wall Street bankers – they've been lumped together into one easily identifiable, monolithic group.

But –

Her coverage, if she'd gotten to do any, would have been more specific, more nuanced.

'What do I mean?' she says. 'They had a programme worked out. Of assassinations. They weren't just randomly shooting bankers. They wanted one from each of the three pillars of the system . . . one guy from an investment bank, one guy from a hedge fund and one guy from a private equity firm. They got two and narrowly missed the third, the private equity guy.'

She pops the French fry into her mouth.

Frank continues staring at her. She wants to nod at his chicken sandwich and say, *Come on, eat up*, but the moment isn't right.

'How do you know this?' he says quietly. 'Are you guessing?'

'No.'

She's guessing to *some* degree – about the dynamics in the apartment, about what went on between Julian and Alex and Lizzie. But she's not guessing about their overall plan. She explains to Frank about ath900 and Farley Kaplan's interview on *What Up?*

He seems stunned. It's a level of detail he hasn't heard from anyone else.

'The cops,' he says, 'the authorities, the FBI, they've all been really cagey about telling us *anything*.'

'That's pretty normal, I'm afraid. But this is stuff I came across by myself.' She picks up her iced tea and takes a sip. 'The FBI possibly doesn't even know any of this yet. They came to the case by a different route. They had an informant, apparently. Inside the group Julian was associated with. We just happened to converge.'

There's a lengthy silence here, during which Frank, head down, seems to be processing what Ellen has told him.

'Come on,' she says, taking her chances. 'Eat up.'

He glances at the sandwich and shrugs.

'You look like shit, Frank. If you don't take care of yourself you're going to get sick.'

He raises his head. 'The private equity guy?'

'Yeah?' She gives a quick, puzzled shake of her head. 'What about him? Scott Lebrecht. Black Vine Partners. The one that got away.'

'Black Vine Partners. What do *they* do?'

Ellen is the one who shrugs this time.

'I don't know. Private equity. LBOs. Asset stripping. They buy companies with debt, fire the employees, dump their pension funds, suck all the cash out and then . . . skedaddle. It's not how *they'd* portray it, but . . .'

There is another silence. She studies his face, his eyes. He's lost in thought.

She nudges his plate across the table, just an inch or so.

'Don't want to sound like your mother, Frank, but Jesus, *eat* something, will you?'

He looks at her, then nods. 'Yeah, OK.' He lifts the sandwich up off the plate and takes a bite.

She does the same.

They eat in silence for a while, chewing solemnly, gazing out at the passing traffic on Ninth Avenue.

*

The next morning, Howley has his meeting with the producer from Bloomberg, and they set things up for late on Friday afternoon. It'll be a wide-ranging interview with, by agreement, no holds barred but no real surprises either. He intends to mount a general and fairly robust defence of private equity, he'll talk up some deals that are in the pipeline and he'll lay out his position vis-à-vis any prospect there might be of an IPO. He's done TV before and knows what they want, knows what tone to adopt. He's not one of the flamboyant guys, he's not charismatic, so it'll be a question of slipping his message in under a cloak of unprepossessing middle-aged baldness and cautious, dense, meandering syntax.

It's a reflex thing, but Howley feels he should be running all of this by Vaughan.

He's not going to, of course. They've moved beyond that – or, at any rate, are in the process of doing so.

Apropos of which, lunch with Paul Blanford yesterday proved to be very interesting. Howley knew Paul years ago through a Pentagon connection, and although they hadn't been friends exactly or done any formal business together, enough of a mutual impression remained for Howley to be able to get Blanford's attention and then bear down fairly heavily on him. The fact that Oberon once owned Eiben-Chemcorp certainly made things easier – but without the personal link Howley wouldn't have been able to cut *quite* as straight to the chase with Blanford as he did. He circled the issue for a while and then dived in by expressing 'deep concern' about a possible breach of protocols at Eiben that had just been brought to his attention. It was in relation to a particular set of clinical trials, he said, and this was especially worrying in the light of a recent DOJ investigation into how pharmaceutical companies were carrying out these very sorts of trial.

Blanford was dumbfounded and wanted to know more. He wanted to know exactly what Howley was talking about.

Howley wasn't about to oblige at this point, but what he did was remind Blanford that Eiben-Chemcorp was no stranger to this kind of thing. There were various instances he could have cited here, most of them taking place long before Blanford's time. In the early days of Triburbazine, for example, there was a damaging product liability trial involving a Massachusetts teenager who murdered her best friend and then killed herself; there was the botched takeover of Mediflux amid allegations of research results being suppressed; and there was the more recent scandal of widespread résumé fraud at a CRO hired by Eiben. But what Howley chose to cite instead was something he himself had read about just days earlier in Vaughan's 'black file' – those disturbing rumours from about ten years ago of a so-called smart drug called MDT-48 being leaked onto the streets with rather alarming consequences. The reason Vaughan had brought this story, among others, to Howley's attention was to illustrate what a bad idea going public would be. Back then the Oberon Capital Group had sold Eiben-Chemcorp in the full knowledge that these rumours were about to break, and had then brazenly shorted the buyer's stock – hardly the kind of trading practices that would bear much public scrutiny.

The reason that Howley was now bringing the story to Blanford's attention, however, was quite different. In the current climate, any hint of another such scandal could easily destroy a company like Eiben, and at the very least they'd be stung for a couple of billion in fines.

So what he wanted to do was scare the shit out of him.

Phase one.

And it worked.

As far as Blanford was concerned the whole thing had come out of the blue, leaving him not only scared but also confused and compliant, which was just what Howley wanted, because without having to offer an explanation or mention Vaughan by name, he was then able to suggest that Blanford take a close look at any clinical trials Eiben might be conducting on new drugs for geriatrics.

And get back to him on it ASAP.

Simple as that.

Howley isn't even sure where this might lead, but he feels he's being proactive. He doesn't want any surprises.

He doesn't like surprises.

The Bloomberg guy leaves, and Howley calls Angela in. He has a few minutes before his next meeting and he wants to see how far along she is with her list of office designers.

I 2

By Tuesday evening Frank has skimmed through most of the books he bought. They're lying on the bed or in small piles on the floor, probably about fifteen in all. He acquired them in three separate spurts of enthusiasm (or delusion?) – each trip out from the hotel to the Barnes & Noble on Fifth Avenue a desperate attempt to shore up his developing but still fragile understanding of the financial crisis, each new title he came across a hit from the crack pipe, an opening up of possibilities, a tingling promise of illumination. On his last trip out he also stopped off at a liquor store and got himself a bottle of Stoli.

Promises, promises.

The one book he keeps coming back to – although there's no real prospect that he'll get to grips with it right now, or possibly ever, because the damn thing is over 850 pages long – is Murray Rheingarten's *The Dominion of Debt: Financial Disambiguation in an Age of Crisis*. Over and over he reads the blurb and the press reviews and the introduction and the chapter headings, he flicks through its capacious, deckled pages, its dense, labyrinthine prose, catching random names and phrases, picking up the sense each time, tantalisingly – like having a word on the tip of your tongue – that deep inside here somewhere, if only he could find and unravel it, is the key to the whole thing, the answer. He feels if he could only persevere and concentrate and *focus* he could extract from these endless blocks of print an explanation of what happened to everyone that will explain what happened to Lizzie.

Some of the other books are easier, or seem so at first – *Wall Street Crash (And Burn)*, *Money Down*, *Goldman Sachs and the End of the World* – but with most of them it doesn't take Frank long to see that they're too specialised, too technical, too detailed in an area he doesn't *quite* need to go to. These books vie with one another for the accolade 'clearest account so far of the crisis', but twenty pages into each one and you're predictably neck-deep in jargon and graphs, in credit default swaps and bogus triple-A-rated securities.

What got him started on this was something Ellen Dorsey said the other night. They were standing outside that diner on Ninth Avenue, about to go their separate ways, when he remarked one more time that he just didn't understand what Lizzie had been thinking.

'Maybe it wasn't such a mystery,' Ellen said. 'I mean, look at that list of demands they made. They were pissed off at the bankers and the money guys. Like a *lot* of people. And once you follow that stuff, or try to understand it, which Lizzie and the others had obviously been doing, it's hard not to . . . *respond*. I guess it's just a question of how you choose to do it.'

Walking back to the hotel, Frank turned this over in his mind. Is that really what Lizzie had been thinking? She was angry? She was *indignant*? It was hard for Frank to see his daughter in this way – as someone who was independent, informed and politically aware. Possibly because of the divorce and the years of minimal contact, his image of her was stuck back in the early teen years.

She was his little girl.

Sweet, smart, spiky . . . vulnerable, but also belligerent – a dangerous combination, but what Frank had to face now was that these were characteristics Lizzie had obviously carried with her into adulthood, and that if he wanted to understand her, it would have to be on *her* terms.

The other thing he realised walking along Fifty-fourth Street was that he himself wasn't really angry or indignant. This was probably because he knew next to nothing about the financial crisis. Sure, he'd read the papers and watched the news and shared a certain amount of received indignation, he'd rolled his eyes and passed remarks like everyone else, he'd been appalled at the numbers, he'd seen the ripple effect in the economy, he'd lost his motherfucking *job*, for Christ's sake – but he hadn't ever focused on what had actually been happening, he hadn't tried to figure any of it out. When he was at Belmont, McCann he'd been too busy working, trying to hold on to his job, and after he got laid off he'd been too busy feeling sorry for himself and scrambling around to find a new source of income. In other words, like a lot of people, he'd been too inward-looking and self-absorbed to pay attention.

So when he got near the hotel he went into what was now his local Duane Reade and bought a few magazines, business titles – *Forbes, Fast Company, Bloomberg Businessweek, The Economist* – with the vague intention of boning up on the crisis. But it didn't take him long – back in his hotel room, flicking through these glossy, ad-heavy mags – to understand that there was a closed lingo here, that a lot was taken for granted, and that he'd have to dig a little deeper. His laptop was in the apartment in Mahopac. There were one or two internet cafés near the hotel, but they seemed really busy and touristy and he couldn't see himself sitting in one of those for too long – or in the business centre here in the hotel lobby. What he did was go out and head for the Barnes & Noble on Fifth Avenue, where he stood for a while in front of what turned out to be a dedicated section, a display actually called 'Understanding the Crisis'.

The weightiest and most hyped book here seemed to be *The Dominion of Debt*, so he picked that one up first, along with *Money Down* and a copy of Galbraith's *The Great Crash, 1929*. Back in his room, he started reading, but was soon switching from one book to another, growing ever more impatient, constantly suspecting that he was reading the wrong one, that the books he'd *bought* were the wrong ones, that all the learning and illumination were happening somewhere else.

The next morning he went back to the Barnes & Noble, to the now altar-like 'Understanding the Crisis' display, and loaded up on more tomes with urgent-sounding titles such as *Financial Catastrophe 101* and *Buddy, Can You Spare a Trillion Dollars?* The same thing happened, and he made a third trip in the afternoon – stopping at that liquor store on his way back.

Now, as evening settles in, he feels simultaneously gorged and empty. He admits he's learned *some* stuff, but really, more questions are raised by what he's been reading here than answers. He detects in himself a growing resentment, too, an anger even, about what he's discovering. But there's a muffled quality to it, a reticence. What's driving him first and foremost is this obsessive curiosity, this burning need to know what Lizzie knew.

To see what Lizzie saw.

He hasn't opened the Stoli yet, and he mightn't.

He looks around the room.

These books and magazines are all very well, but what he could really use here is internet access, high-octane hyperlinks to take him where he needs to go. Someone mentions Bretton Woods? Glass-Steagall? Jekyll Island? Fine, he can go there, follow the thread, not be confined to the impenetrable thickets of some forty-page chapter on collateralised mortgage obligations. Because it seems to Frank that the financial crisis of 2008 – its origins stretching back over decades, its aftermath unfolding into the foreseeable future – is a huge, unwieldy subject, a web of interconnecting narratives that cannot be contained in a single text or contemplated at a single glance.

He thinks about this for a while and then just heads straight out. There's a place he's passed on Forty-eighth Street called Café Zero, and that's where he goes. With so many free wifi hotspots around now, these dedicated internet cafés are becoming a thing of the past – but this one is still pretty busy, and although he's not comfortable here, he settles in at a table and starts surfing.

He goes to Google and types in 'Glass-Steagall Act'.

In less than a tenth of a second more than two million results come up.

*

It's a foggy night in the spring of 1865 and he's crossing the Brooklyn Bridge on foot – vaguely aware somehow that construction of the bridge will not in fact be commencing for another five years – when he bumps into a tall, gaunt man in a frock coat and a shiny top hat. Then, curiously, and without any warning at all, it's 1915 and the two men are in an IRT train, rattle-tattling, lights flickering, hurtling over the bridge, the president fumbling in his pocket for a greenback –

Vaughan says, 'Sir, I – I –'

'Sshhh . . . listen to me now, don't . . . don't tell anyone about . . .'

Hhhnnn.

'Don't –'

Hhhnnnn.

He opens his eyes. Looks around. *Shit.* That was intense.

He shakes his head.

Vivid, lucid, almost hyper-real.

It was like . . .

He glances around the room, at the red leather armchairs and the bookshelves, at the Persian rug and the Matisse. He holds up his old, soft, mottled hand and stares at it.

Like *this* . . . like reality itself.

But it's not only his dreams – ones he might have dozing off for ten minutes in the library, say, as he's just done now, or denser, longer ones fresh in his head after waking in the morning – it's his *memories*, too. These are more directed and rational, which is hardly surprising, but they're just as vivid and cinematic. He can glide back over past times and recall details he would never normally have access to. In the last couple of days, for instance, he's had a flood of memories from the late 1950s – that office he had in the Century Building, with its art deco fittings, walnut and ebony throughout, and those baggy double-breasted suits he used to wear. And that sterling silver cigarette case he had, that Kitty gave him . . . with the ribbed pattern on the outside and the gilt yellow swirled finish on the inside . . .

Shit.

When was the last time he thought about *that*?

In a reverie now, he stares into space.

Transported back.

Of course, in those days he was constantly at war with the old man.

He can just see him, striding into the office in his vicuña overcoat, declaiming, waving his cigar around.

The generally held view back then was that William J. Vaughan was a great man, a business titan of the old school who'd be a hard act for his son to follow. But really, what was so great about him? Apart from his one big coup in 1929, what did he ever achieve? The fact is that all through the thirties, forties and fifties William J. oversaw the steady decline of the family business, undoing through recklessness and negligence everything his *own* father had ever done to build it up (before dropping dead during a recital in Carnegie Hall in 1938). And yet because he was this big personality who played golf with cardinals and fucked movie stars he was perceived by everyone to be an amazing success.

Vaughan sighs.

Enough.

He stands up out of the chair and straightens his jacket.

The ironic thing is that this . . . this *clarity* has only kicked in over the last few days, a week at most. It's ironic because that's more or less when he decided to call it a day. He'd been so tired, and sick most of the time, that it seemed pointless to continue. Everything was in place, and all he had to do was set things in train.

Which he did.

But then, as arrangements for the press conference were being finalised, this new medication he's been on suddenly started to work – the dreams, the vivid memories, but also renewed energy and a general feeling of well-being. He wasn't really going to go sailing in Palm Beach, that was just to yank Craig Howley's chain, nor was he serious last night when he hinted to Meredith that he wouldn't say no to a blowjob – *but* . . . these ideas didn't come out of thin air either.

He *is* feeling better and stronger.

And he doesn't care one whit that the medication is untested and possibly dangerous.

It's worth it.

Because we're all going to die, so what difference does it make? When he first got sick in his mid-seventies he figured, not unreasonably, that his days were numbered, that death was probably just around the corner. But it proved to be a long, wide corner, a half-moon crescent of a thing that just wouldn't quit – and now, nearly ten years later, here he is, still alive, still breathing, still on various medications. The thing is, most of his friends and contemporaries are dead, he's attended a lot of funerals, looked into a lot of graves, but if anything, his sense of his own mortality has blurred somewhat and dimmed. It's like, *all right, already*, he's gone through the scary phase, worrying about it day and night, shitting himself over it – and now he's come out the other side. If he's still here, then he's still here. He doesn't want to have to waste any more time thinking about it.

So, about a month ago, when he had a chance conversation with Jerome Hale, former head of research at Eiben-Chemcorp, Vaughan decided he was going to take some positive action.

Hale was talking about what he believed Eiben currently had in the pipeline, a suite of in-development products that were offshoots of MDT-48, a designer smart drug that had nearly destroyed the company about a decade earlier when a batch was siphoned out of the lab and found its way on to the streets. MDT was way too powerful and dangerous a drug ever to find a place in the mainstream commercial market, but researchers at Eiben had been trying ever since to develop second-generation and much toned-down versions – one of which, apparently, according to Hale, was targeted at geriatrics and was reputed to combat a range of conditions, including extreme fatigue and dementia. He added that this was still years away from even going to first-phase clinical trials, *but wasn't it interesting?*

By which he meant, *given their own involvement in these events all those years ago* – his as head of research and Vaughan's as proprietor of the parent company.

Vaughan nodded in agreement, yes, for sure – but he actually found it much more interesting than that. Without telling Jerry Hale what he was doing, he proceeded to track down an old contact who still worked at Eiben, and then, using a combination of arm-twisting, outright intimidation and eye-watering amounts of money, he managed to coax a sample out of the Eiben lab.

First he was warned about possible side effects. Then he was told that the formula required a build-up in the system and not to expect any results for at least a week. But when nothing had happened after two, and with his general condition deteriorating rapidly, Vaughan resigned himself to the inevitable and triggered the succession process with Howley.

And then, go figure, the medication kicked in.

Originally given enough for a month, he now has less than a week's supply left.

Which is an issue he'll have to address very soon.

Vaughan wanders out of the library. He went in there to take a quick nap. Normally at this time of the day, after lunch, he'll go to bed for at least an hour and sleep soundly. He'll then spend another hour fighting grogginess and trying to reconstitute himself so he can function for the remainder of the day. Recently, though, he's finding that ten minutes in an armchair is all he needs, and that no recovery time is required either.

The only problem *now* – given that he's officially, ironic air quotes, retired – is that he doesn't have anything to do.

As he moves along the floor of the hallway, with its mother-of-pearl-encrusted black marble tiles, he taps out a quick, slightly giddy soft-shoe shuffle.

He'll have to see about *that*, though, won't he?

*

On his way to the Bloomberg studios on Friday afternoon, Craig Howley flicks through his notes. He likes to be prepared, to have a sprinkling of figures and statistics at the ready. It won't be a hard interview, in the sense that he won't be asked any particularly tough questions, but he does want to get certain points across, and that can sometimes be difficult to do without coming off like a used-car salesman.

He also flicks through his diary. Normally at this time of year he and Jessica go to the country on weekends, but with the Kurtzmann Foundation benefit happening on Monday night, Jess is up to her eyes in last-minute arrangements, so she's staying put. He will, too.

Maybe catch up on some reading.

He glances out the window. They're on Lexington, the Tower just a couple of blocks away.

As he's gathering up his notes and papers, his phone rings.

It's Paul Blanford.

Howley's done a little extra homework since their lunch earlier in the week – on Eiben-Chemcorp, on its board, on the sector in general – and he's fairly sure now that he's got Blanford by the balls. As CEO, Blanford has been perfectly adequate, but with the company's $47 billion in annual sales built on blockbuster drugs such as Narolet and Triburbazine – drugs whose patents are due to expire in the near future – the board is, well, pretty jumpy. What's more, Howley knows of at least three members who are said to be unhappy with the CEO's performance. Any public hint of another R&D leak, therefore, and it'd be curtains for Blanford.

'Paul?'

'Craig. How are you?'

'I'm good. Any luck with that thing?'

'Not yet, but I'm all over it, believe me. I just need another couple of days.'

The key thing here is, while Howley can ostensibly hold out knowledge of this leak as a threat, what he really wants is the same thing Blanford wants, for the leak to be plugged. But as long as Blanford has no idea what Howley's interest is, and as long as he's reluctant to ask about it, which he clearly is, Howley feels he has the advantage. Full disclosure – i.e. any mention of Vaughan's involvement – would transfer some of that advantage back to Blanford, and while this is probably inevitable, it's something Howley wants to put off until the last possible moment.

First, however, they need to find the leak.

'Why is it taking so long?' he asks.

'Well, R&D is our biggest division, Craig, and I can't just charge around the place making accusations. You know that.' Blanford has a rep for being non-confrontational, so this can't be easy for him. 'I mean, I have put out some feelers, but it's a tricky one.'

This isn't the way Howley would handle it, but he doesn't have the time to argue his point now. 'You know where to reach me, Paul.'

The car pulls into the public plaza of Bloomberg Tower, Howley is met by the producer and a couple of assistants and they all head inside.

He is shepherded through makeup and then onto the set for a quick sound check. After a few minutes, the show's host, Rob Melrose, appears and they chat briefly. The atmosphere is relaxed, the studio bright and spacious, unlike pretty much every other studio Howley's ever been in.

Someone adjusts his mike, and before he knows it the interview has started.

Rob Melrose's style is direct and quite dynamic, but he's also respectful – and, in Howley's case, maybe even a little deferential.

The first few minutes they spend on private equity and its image problems.

'There's no denying it, it's a tough time for the industry,' Howley says in his now almost trademarked whisper. 'Because the fact is, Rob, not all deals work out, and it's pretty easy to highlight the ones that don't and make a song and dance about them, but really, the numbers should speak for themselves. I'm talking about the number of jobs created, proportion-wise compared to in the general economy, three point nine per cent compared to one point two per cent last year alone, I'm talking about returns for investors and pension funds, and about availability of growth capital for new companies, I mean it just goes on and on.'

'But the negativity *is there*,' Melrose says, swivelling on his stool and flicking the back of his hand at his silver laptop, as if to indicate all the hard data he has on his screen, 'so what effect is that going to have on the Oberon Capital Group, what effect is it going to have on Craig Howley?'

'Well, you're right, Rob, there is negativity, and unfortunately, for a time, that's going to make it harder for companies like Oberon to raise funds and to buy companies and ultimately to create new jobs . . .'

And . . . yadda, yadda, yadda.

OK, Howley can admit it to himself, he was slightly nervous coming on to do this interview, but sitting here now, under the lights, large bot-like cameras hovering on the periphery of his vision, he suddenly feels totally relaxed.

He *knows* this stuff.

There isn't a single question Rob Melrose could put to him that he wouldn't be able to answer – comprehensively, and with more wit and depth than they could ever have time for on a show like this. All he needs now is a nice little segue into his IPO spiel and his work here will be done.

'Let me throw something else at you,' Melrose then says. 'This whole question of going public, it's pretty much a hot-button issue at the moment, to file or not to file, pitching to investors, how much stock to offer, how low or high to set the price, the whole crazy rollercoaster ride. Where does Craig Howley stand?'

'Well, Rob,' Howley says, looking directly at him now, and smiling, 'I'm glad you asked me that . . .'

*

'. . . because it's been on my mind a lot recently, but you know, having a stock ticker isn't necessarily a panacea. Sure, it's a good way to raise cash, but to be frank, that wouldn't be one of our core concerns right now. And I like the idea of being able to stay agile, especially in the current climate –'

'Keeping it lean and mean.'

'Maybe not the term I'd use, Rob, but yes, and there's a certain tyranny about the quarterly report, you know, about having to meet analysts' expectations and forecasts, where you end up romancing the markets instead of looking after your LPs . . .'

'*Romancing* the markets? Fuck *you*, you prick.'

Frank takes another swig from the now half-empty bottle of Stoli and replaces it on the bedside unit.

The arrogance of this motherfucker on the screen, with his barely audible, breathy delivery, is something else.

Romancing the markets?

If it wasn't so tragic, it'd be funny.

But a word like that certainly sticks out, because most of the time what you hear on these business cable shows – the language they use, the jargon – is impenetrable. It's also mind-numbingly boring, and this is probably deliberate.

Because they . . .

They obfuscate.

That's the word.

He burps and pats his bare chest.

They operate in secrecy and darkness and hide behind arcane terminology.

'. . . more or less what you get when credit spreads blow out, when correlations go to one . . .'

Listen to him.

Laid out in front of Frank on the bed are a couple of books open at specific pages, some magazine pieces and printouts from the various websites he's been visiting. A part of him expects all of this material to pull into focus suddenly, to coalesce into a neat revelation, a mathematical formula almost. But another part of him knows it's not going to happen, that this stuff is too diffuse, the connections too tenuous, the hunger for order and meaning – *his* hunger – too acute and voracious to possibly accommodate any degree of reasoned argument or criticism, any anomalies or pieces of the puzzle that don't fit.

The truth is, over the last two days, much of it spent in Café Zero, Frank has been sliding into a quicksand of unverified and largely unverifiable . . . what? He hesitates to describe it as information.

White noise?

All he was looking for was an answer, an explanation, a grand unified field theory, something or someone to focus on and *blame*. What he got instead was an ever-widening gyre of speculation and paranoia – from Alan Greenspan to Ayn

Rand, from the securitisation of subprime mortgages to the payment of German war reparations, from LIBOR to Jekyll Island . . . from JFK's infamous executive order skewering the Fed to Abraham Lincoln being assassinated by a cabal of international bankers because he insisted on printing his own debt-free legal tender to pay for the war.

From the New World Order to the Book of Revelation.

He didn't know how or where to stop and ended up with a splitting headache, stomach cramps and a sore back. Some time late in the afternoon he gave up and came back to the hotel. He stripped and crawled into the shower.

When he got out after about twenty minutes he checked his phone, which he'd left in the room all day. He had half a dozen messages from Deb, a couple from Lenny Byron and one from Ellen Dorsey. He didn't reply to any of them.

He didn't feel up to it.

Wearing only boxer shorts, he flopped back onto the bed and stared up at the ceiling for a while.

Then he got off the bed, grabbed the unopened bottle of Stoli from the dresser, *opened* it and took a slug.

Deciding that surrender wasn't an option, he sorted once again through the books and magazines he'd bought and the articles he'd had printed at Café Zero. He spread some of them out on the bed, trying to conjure up a pattern, a meaning.

He continued taking belts of vodka directly from the bottle.

At one point, in need of further sensory stimulation, he reached over for the remote and flicked the TV on. He whipped through a few channels, dismissing each one in turn. But then he found himself pausing and staring at *this* guy, Craig Howley. It wasn't so much the Boring Middle-aged White Guy in a Suit thing that caught his attention, or the awful financial jargon. It was more the words on the screen: DEFENDING PRIVATE EQUITY ... which, after a couple of seconds, did actually coalesce into something of a revelation, and quite a neat one, too. Because for all of this time, since last weekend, Frank has been interested in only one thing: finding a wormhole into Lizzie's mind, and what he suddenly suspected he had here was a wormhole *out* of it. It's what Ellen Dorsey was talking about the other night in that diner. The three pillars of the system. One guy from an investment bank, one from a hedge fund and one from a private equity firm.

They got two and narrowly missed the third.

But knowing how much thought and effort were involved here, knowing how much planning and commitment there was, *knowing Lizzie* ... Frank can't help thinking that this narrow miss must have preyed on her mind, and that as the siege progressed it must have assumed an ever greater significance for her. Because however she felt about their list of demands – which had surely been improvised, and could only ever have been aspirational anyway – their plan, their statement, their grand gesture ... was incomplete.

Did that rankle with Lizzie?

He bets it did.

It's funny, but when he thinks of her now, he sees a different person. It's as if she has changed, morphed into someone else. It's as if she has grown in stature.

He reaches for the bottle of Stoli on the bedside unit and takes another hit from it.

Then he looks at the screen again, at this Craig Howley guy, CEO and chairman of ... what are they called? The Oberon

Capital Group?

'. . . the spreads are pretty high and the base rates are low, so you're picking up a lot of return, basically, for a lack of liquidity.'

It cuts to the host of the show, a handsome, chiselled little prick in his early thirties. 'And how about real estate, Craig? Tell us about the opportunities you're seeing in the sector right now.'

'Oh, this is just an incredible time to be in real estate, Rob.'

'Why?'

'Well, you've got all these CMOs that aren't going to roll over, you've got overpriced properties and distressed sellers . . .'

Frank squeezes the neck of the bottle. He doesn't understand what Craig Howley is talking about here, not exactly, but he's picking up a tone, a hint of contained glee, of dog-eat-dog exuberance. Distressed sellers? Cool. Let's kick these motherfuckers while they're down.

'. . . and then you're streaming into that attractive investment-grade credit market we mentioned earlier.'

'So share with us, Craig, how much has Oberon put into real estate so far this year?'

'I don't have an exact figure, Rob, but it's probably several billion, four perhaps, four point five.'

'Wow!'

Fuck.

Frank raises the bottle to his lips again.

'Look, it's a large part of our business. We're known as a private equity company, but really we're a bit more diversified than that.'

'Sure, private equity, real estate, debt and asset management, financial advisory, credit, it's a long list.'

'It is, and people often think that investment by a company like Oberon means focusing only on short-term returns –'

'The classic strip and flip.'

'Yeah, well,' Howley laughs here, but there's an edge to the laugh, 'again I'd use different language, not that it's even true *any*way . . . but no, I mean, take an example . . .' He pauses. 'Take any company in our portfolio.'

He stops to think for a moment.

Frank breathes in deeply, his head spinning ever so slightly. Half a bottle of Stoli? Straight up? If it weren't for his accelerated adrenalin flow, his extra nervous energy, he'd be unconscious by this stage, or in a pool of his own vomit. He glances down at the bottle in his hand and feels his stomach lurch.

Oh, Jesus.

No self-fulfilling prophecies, please.

'Yes,' Howley says, nodding, ready to continue. 'I mean, consider a company like Paloma Electronics, for instance –'

Frank looks up.

'Great company,' the host says, 'consumer electronics, but a lot more besides, am I right? Military and defence contracting, IT, consulting, security.'

Frank is stunned.

'Absolutely, and don't forget biotech, and robotics –'

'Of course.'

'So yeah, they're just a super, super company, and we at Oberon are committed to helping them develop and grow, but here's the thing, Rob, that's *over the long term*.'

Frank leans forward on the bed and gulps, reflux vomit coming up into his mouth. He manages to swallow it back.

'Right. Though there *have* been job losses at Paloma recently, if I'm not mistaken, and a lot of cost-cutting?'

'Oh sure, but with any effort to drive stronger performance you're going to get *some* element of rationalisation.'

It happens again, but this time Frank just lets it out, splats of clear liquid – he hasn't eaten today – landing all over the bed, on the books and the magazines. In a sort of daze he lets go of the bottle, the remainder of its contents glugging out over his bare leg and making a deep stain on the polyester bedspread.

Fuuuck.

He wipes his mouth and looks back at the TV screen.

He's focused now, though.

And the first thing he notices is that, OK, Howley's suit is fine, expensive-looking and all, but at the same time . . . who chose that fucking shirt? And the *tie*? The second thing is that this is Ellen's – *Lizzie's?* – Ellen's . . . this is the guy that got away.

This is the private equity guy.

The third pillar.

He's not *the* guy, OK, he's not Scott Lebrecht. But that doesn't matter any more. He's actually a better pick – a point that Frank would like nothing better than to be able to hammer out with Lizzie . . .

He clears his throat and coughs up some grainy, charcoaly phlegm.

Spits it out.

'. . . in point of fact turmoil is *good* for private equity . . .'

And the supreme irony of the situation is that until a few days ago, until a week ago, maybe a bit more – he can't remember exactly, until *whenever* – but it turns out that this bland, calculating, vicious, badly dressed bastard on the screen *was his boss* . . .

'. . . but ultimately, I think, to solve the deficit problem, governments in Europe, and here, governments everywhere –'

All Frank wants to do now is tell Lizzie that, discuss it with her, dissect the irony.

That's *all* he wants to do.

'– are going to have to move to the printing presses . . .'

But what he does instead is pick the empty Stoli bottle up, raise it high and fling it hard at the flickering TV screen.

Five

It was while working in 1878 as an ill-paid scrivener at a dingy law office on Wall Street that Charles A. Vaughan first encountered the fabulously successful financier and speculator Gilbert Morley.

House of Vaughan (p. 212)

13

The reference to Paloma Electronics is what gets her.

It's weird, she thinks, how all of this stuff seems connected. The only reason she's watching an overcaffeinated cable news channel like Bloomberg in the first place is because she received an email out of the blue yesterday from Jimmy Gilroy in which he mentioned that Craig Howley was taking over as the new CEO of the Oberon Capital Group.

Not *really* out of the blue, then.

Which is her point.

Jimmy Gilroy has been researching James Vaughan and Oberon for the last eighteen months, ever since he and Ellen covered the Rundle brothers story together. That was big enough in itself – one of the most spectacular cases of a presidential candidate falling from grace in US history – but Jimmy knew that Rundle's withdrawal from the race was only the outermost ripple of a much darker and more complex set of circumstances. The Rundles' business in the Democratic Republic of the Congo, for instance, involved the setting up of an illegal supply chain of thanaxite that led all the way to a robotics plant in Connecticut. But when it became apparent to Jimmy that behind *that* story was a large and very active private equity firm, the Oberon Capital Group, the focus of his interest shifted. It shifted again when he became aware of Oberon's founder, James Vaughan – of his wide-ranging influence in Washington and of his long, serpentine family history.

So what started out as a proposed series of background articles for *Parallax* has gradually morphed into a book-length project with the provisional title *House of Vaughan* – a book that will apparently cover a period stretching back over nearly a century and a half. The only problem is that the project seems to have turned into something of a black hole, and one that Gilroy himself has more or less disappeared headlong into.

Ellen occasionally gets emails from him – yesterday's was the first in several months – but she's heard other stuff, stories from people in the business, rumours that Gilroy doesn't have a publisher or any kind of a contract, that he has encountered all sorts of obstacles in getting research done, that he's been subjected to subtle forms of intimidation and even manipulation, that he's had to sell his apartment in Dublin to keep going, that he's had a nervous breakdown, that he hasn't actually written a single word.

Ellen liked Jimmy Gilroy, and she got on well with him over the few weeks that they ended up working together. But he was young and relatively inexperienced, even a little callow, and when he took off on his initial research jag to the Congo she wondered if he'd ever be heard from again.

The occasional emails she got from him were reassuring, but they didn't reveal much.

Yesterday's revealed a bit more than usual.

It turns out that he's been living in Brooklyn for the last three months, working in a bar and trying to patch his manuscript together.

But *go figure* is what he seemed to be saying in the email yesterday.

Just as I'm getting somewhere with this book, James Vaughan retires? What, is he going to die on me next? Rendering the book even less relevant than it apparently already is? And his replacement is this boring-as-shit Craig Howley guy? Seriously? Watch him on Bloomberg tomorrow and you'll see what I'm talking about.

So here she is, watching, and what is it that catches her attention? Craig Howley's mention of Paloma Electronics is what. This is the company that uses thanaxite to manufacture its military robots in Connecticut. But it's also the company that Frank Bishop had a retail McJob with until very recently – before he shot his mouth off and got fired, and was then catapulted to national attention when his daughter . . .

Ellen shakes her head.

She doesn't know. You see weird connections all the time. They don't have to mean anything, and they usually don't. But the result of this particular connection is that she is now thinking about both Jimmy Gilroy and Frank Bishop, and it's giving her the strangest, weirdest feeling. She doesn't believe in intuition, not really, except when it shows results, and even then it's more often than not because you worked pretty hard to achieve those results *anyway*.

But sometimes . . .

She hasn't answered Jimmy's email yet. She gets up from the couch, goes over to her desk, opens up a reply and starts typing. She says it's great to hear from him and that they should meet up soon for a drink – that she has some stuff she wants to talk to him about.

What that stuff might be specifically, what form it might take, she's not quite sure herself yet. But she's not worried about it.

She presses Send.

Then she picks up her phone.

She called Frank earlier in the day and left a message. He never got back to her.

When she saw him on Monday evening he was in pretty bad shape, but there wasn't much she could do about it, apart from answer his questions. She hadn't met him to get a story or anything. *He'd* called *her*. Besides, as far as she was concerned the story had played itself out – and as for a human interest angle, the grieving father in the aftermath of a tragedy? That held no interest for her whatsoever.

So why did she call him today?

And why is she about to call him again now?

She doesn't know.

Intuition?

She waits.

'Yeah?'

'Frank? Hi, it's Ellen.'

'Ellen.' Pause. 'Hi.'

He doesn't sound any better. Though why would he, she supposes. After all, he *is* a grieving father in the aftermath of a tragedy. A few days isn't going to make any real difference.

'How are you, Frank?'

'I'm OK. I was pretty drunk a little while ago. Then I got sick. Not drunk any more.'

'Oh . . .'

'Yeah, I was watching TV. A thing with, an interview with . . . what was his name again?'

Still sounds a *little* drunk.

'I don't know, Frank.'

'Craig Howley. That's it. One of these big fucking . . . private equity guys.'

Ellen's heart stops. '*What?*'

Frank Bishop takes a deep loud breath. 'Private equity guy. Even turns out I used to work for him. What do you think of that?'

'But . . . how did . . . ?' She knows how *she* came to be watching the interview with Howley on Bloomberg. But Frank?

'Huh?'

'How come you were watching *that?*'

'I've been watching all the business channels, Ellen, reading business magazines, business *books*. I'm an expert now. On the financial crisis. I couldn't *explain* any of it to you, but –'

He stops. There is silence for a moment and then he starts coughing.

Definitely still drunk.

Ellen stares at the floor, waiting.

This is her fault. He was trying to make sense of what had been going on in Lizzie's head, and *she* more or less told him that to have any chance of succeeding he'd have to . . . do what he was apparently doing. It was outside the diner on Ninth Avenue. They were standing on the sidewalk. She doesn't remember her exact words, but –

'– it'd make no difference anyway,' Frank says, recovering. 'These people are just carrying on regardless. I mean, you ought to hear what this guy was saying, he –'

'I know, Frank,' she cuts in. 'I saw him, I was watching it, too.'

'Sorry . . . *what?*' He seems confused. '*You* were watching it?' He takes a moment to fold this information into his argument.

'Well, then, you know what I'm talking about, right? Because
. . . this motherfucker, he's like the one that got away. In fact,
he's *worse*.'

Ellen feels something creeping up on her here, a chill. That
phrase he's just used, *the one that got away* – that was also from
their conversation the other night. She just can't remember the
exact context, and which of them used it first.

She looks up and across the room.

It's more likely to have been her, though.

'What do you mean, Frank?'

'Nothing. *Nothing*. I don't know. It just struck me that –'

He's trying to be cagey now.

'*What?*'

'That . . . that I wish I was still drunk.'

She has a knot in her stomach.

'Where are you, Frank?'

'I'm in this shitty hotel, the Bromley. Deb says the FBI are
being difficult. They told her we're not going to see the body . . .
see Lizzie . . . until at least . . .'

There's a long pause here. She stares at the back of her couch.

'Frank?'

'Until –'

He makes a loud gulping sound. It's followed by another
one, even louder, and some heavy sniffling.

Then the line goes dead.

'*Frank?*'

She tries the number again immediately, and a couple more
times after that. It goes to message each time.

She puts her phone down.

Poor bastard.

She sits there swivelling from side to side.

She shouldn't have called him. Why did she call him?

After a moment she hears the ping of an incoming email. She turns to the keyboard. It's from Jimmy Gilroy. He says yes, let's meet up, he has tomorrow night off, how about then? She writes back, OK, and suggests a time and a place.

She hits Send.

Connections.

Then she sits there, still swivelling in the chair, staring out across the room. At nothing in particular. But this strange, weird feeling she's got? This chill?

She can't shake it.

*

He sees the absurdity of the situation, the irony, he gets it – he's an old man and he's acting like he's some young kid trying to score a dime bag, if that's what they still call them. And not just any old man either, an old man who used to *own* the very pharmaceutical company that's developing the drug he's so desperate to get his hands on.

It's ridiculous.

At least he can do it over the phone. He doesn't have to hang around on a street corner, waiting.

'You going to bed, sweetheart?'

'In a minute. I have a call I need to make.'

He heads for the study.

Though it's barely ten o'clock, he and Meredith are just back from dinner at Dick and Maria Wolper's. This was a big deal for the Wolpers, apparently – to have him there. And they'd obviously been briefed about timing and procedures. The old man has his medication regimen. Needs his sleep. No dairy or gluten. As for wine, French only, and don't stray too far from Bordeaux. Whatever. But the thing was, Vaughan felt he could have outpaced anyone there. He was seated next to Felipe Keizer, the architect who designed 220 Hanson Street, and they were having this great conversation, Keizer talking about the litigation he's currently involved in, Vaughan reminiscing about his dealings with Mies van der Rohe in the early sixties and the construction of the Snyder Building. It was a process, he told Keizer, that he found awe-inspiring in its speed and complexity. It was like time-lapse photography – the derricks and cranes appearing, the steel skeleton climbing up into the midtown skyline, the pipes and ducts sliding into place, followed by the partitions and suspended ceilings. It was pure magic. Keizer agreed, and then quizzed him about Mies. What was he like to work with? Was he difficult, approachable? Vaughan was happy to answer these questions, but before you knew it the whole table was listening in.

Not an experience Vaughan has had for a while – being at the centre of attention, and firing on all cylinders – but he liked it. And he wasn't too happy when a clearly terrified Maria Wolper started shunting them out the door at nine thirty.

Anyway.

He's only got a few of these pills left and he's having a hard time getting in touch with his contact at Eiben. This guy, Arnie Tisch, who's now an executive vice president in charge of worldwide business development, used to run R&D projects under Jerry Hale in the Oberon days. He was an easy enough mark – but now what, he won't take Vaughan's calls?

He's left three messages already.

Sitting at his desk, he tries him again.

'Hello?'

'Arnie?' A miracle. 'Jimmy Vaughan.'

'Oh, Mr Vaughan, good evening. I'm so sorry I didn't get back to you sooner, I –'

'You *didn't* get back to me, Arnie. That's the whole point. It's what, ten o'clock on a Friday night, and *I'm* getting back to *you*?'

'Oh? Oh yes, of course. Sorry.'

'And you know why I'm calling, don't you? I need you to get me some more of those pills.'

When he says it like that it sounds sort of pathetic. Not so much a kid looking to score a dime bag as a degenerate lowlife junkie pleading for his next fix.

Like his degenerate lowlife junkie *son*.

When was that? Jesus, 1981? Feels like a century ago. Feels like yesterday.

'The problem, Mr Vaughan, is that –'

'No, no. There *is* no problem. This is a repeat prescription, my friend.' If this bastard wants to be difficult, Vaughan will instigate proceedings to buy Eiben-Chemcorp *back*. Which he could do. In a heartbeat. 'Just see to it that what we did last time happens again, OK? You know the terms. They're very generous. So I'll expect to hear –'

'But, Mr Vaughan –'

'I'll *expect to hear from you on Monday or Tuesday*. Thank you.'

He hangs up.

That has agitated him a little, and he doesn't like it.

This drug works, it's as simple as that, and he wants more of it. He heard all the scare stories ten years ago about MDT-48, and he wouldn't have gone near the stuff with a ten-foot pole. But now? Now he's *old* and he doesn't give a damn. Besides, this is clearly MDT-lite.

Very lite.

His doctors are amazed – and baffled – at his improved condition, so why would he back away from this? Why would he not take advantage of it? He's been involved with companies developing innovative products and services all his life, in pharmaceuticals, electronics, communications, the agri and energy sectors, you name it, and when has he *once* benefited personally or exploited his position in any way?

He gets up from his desk and leaves the study.

He should go to bed.

Instead he goes in search of Meredith. He finds her down the hall, in the main living room, splayed out on a couch with a soda in one hand and the TV remote in the other.

He steps into the room and stands there, looking at her.

The way she's positioned, all languorous . . . her skirt pulled up a bit, lots of stocking showing, one shoulder strap slipped off and –

He feels –

'What are you watching?' he says.

He's got a *hard-on*.

She looks up, distracted, and presses Pause on the remote. He turns and glances at the screen.

Connie Carillo, frozen in sober grey, staring out over the courtroom.

'I DVR'd it,' she says. 'It's *so* depressing.'

'Then why are you watching it?'

She takes a sip from her drink. 'I don't know. It's *Connie*.' She pauses. 'I still can't believe it. I mean, she stabbed him in the chest with a *carving knife*.'

Hard-on's gone.

'*If* she did it,' he says, only for something to say. He's grown bored with the trial and hasn't followed it for days.

'Of course she *did* it.'

Attempting to sit up now, Meredith gets a splash of soda on her dress.

'Jesus.' She reaches down and puts the can on the floor. Then she inspects the stain. 'Shit. They'll *never* get this out.'

'Well,' Vaughan says, 'I'll leave you to it. Good night.'

He goes to bed and falls asleep pretty quickly, but after maybe an hour something wakes him, a passing siren maybe. He stares into the darkness. He was in the middle of a dream . . . Ray Whitestone cross-examining Connie Carillo in the kitchen of their house in Palm Beach, asking her how many ladles and soup spoons and pepperpots she had, and if she could describe them.

It was extremely vivid.

But also stupid and meaningless.

He turns over and tries to go back to sleep.

*

When he's leaving the room, Frank puts the Do Not Disturb sign on the door handle. There's a big fat crack on the plasma TV screen from the Stoli bottle and he doesn't want to have to deal with *that* today. He may be coming back here, he may not be, he doesn't know. He's paid through till Wednesday. It was the easiest thing to do.

He gets a cab outside the hotel and tells the driver to head downtown.

This is something he *really* doesn't want to do, but what choice has he got?

They're on Seventh Avenue, and when they get below Fourteenth Street, he tells the driver to go east. Then, when they get to Orchard Street, he gets him to crawl along, says they're looking for a car – but that if they reach Delancey to turn left, and on *no* account to go straight on. It's bad enough being down here, but he doesn't think he could bear going right past the building. Looking around, what strikes him first is how ordinary everything is, how there's no . . . there's no trace of what happened. But why would there be? It was a week ago, which is the second thing that strikes him . . . the relentless, forward-moving, unidirectional, fuck-you nature of time itself. There was before, there was the event, and now there's afterwards. If you've got a problem with that, then . . . you've got a problem.

Car's not here.

They turn left on Delancey.

'No car, sir?'

'No.'

Parking's pretty crazy in New York, with times, alternate side regs, etc. Also, he can't remember exactly where he parked, if it was at a hydrant or a loading zone.

'They boot your car, probably.'

'Yeah, but I didn't see it. It'd still be there. Let's spin around one more time.'

They loop back onto Grand and then onto Orchard again. It's definitely not there.

'When you leave it, sir?'

Frank exhales. Yeah, it's kind of obvious now, isn't it?

'Week ago,' he says, knowing what's next.

'Ah, even if they boot it, sir, after two days it gets towed. You want to go to the pound.'

Pier 76.

West Thirty-eighth and Twelfth.

'OK.' He rolls his eyes. 'Let's go.'

On the way there he calls Deb. He doesn't want any surprises at the pound, like alarm bells triggering when he hands over his credit card or anything. She's left him multiple voice messages over the last few days, but he hasn't actually spoken to her.

So this isn't going to be easy.

'Jesus, *Frank*.'

He gets it out of her pretty quickly that he's not being sought for further questioning, at least not yet. She says that Lloyd has been fielding all of that stuff, and that, as she said in one of her messages, the FBI are refusing to give them a release date.

Frank swallows.

He looks out at languid, sunny Twenty-third Street, quiet Saturday morning traffic cruising by.

A release date.

He asks how John is.

John went back to California two days ago. He has stuff to do at college. He'll be back again, though.

He'll be back when . . .

Yeah.

'But how are *you*, Frank? I'm worried about you.'

The reflex response here would be *I'm fine*, but he's not fine, so he isn't going to say it. He mumbles something and turns it around by asking her how she is.

'I *guess* I'm fine, but counselling helps. It really does, Frank. You should consider –'

'Are there still media people outside your building?'

'Erm . . . no. They've moved on. The damn world has moved on. I can't even *watch* the news any more.' She pauses. 'Frank, where are you? Why don't you come and see us? Let's talk. Come for dinner. Come tonight.'

'I can't.'

'Well then, how about –'

He makes a vague commitment for early next week some time and gets off the phone.

Pier 76.

Oh God.

The waiting room is more than half full. It's hot and stuffy, and peopled by the hungover and the dispirited. It doesn't take too long, though. He gets called to the window after about twenty minutes. He's allowed to go and get his registration and other documents from the car and then after another maybe ten minutes he's paying with his credit card and being handed a retrieval slip.

Another ten minutes again and he's heading north on the West Side Highway.

The drive back to West Mahopac passes in a dreamlike rush, and it's only when he gets near his apartment building that he starts feeling weird, and actually a bit sick. That's when he realises he hasn't eaten in . . . how long? He can't remember. Eating seems like a sort of weakness, a betrayal, a surrender to the future.

Anyway, once inside the apartment, he makes straight for

the bathroom and throws up, or spends a couple of minutes trying to, at least – retching and groaning.

There's nothing he'd eat in his fridge or in any of the cupboards, and he doesn't want to go out again, not just yet. Eventually, he finds a couple of granola bars, which he tears open and eats standing at the sink. Then he makes some coffee.

He gets his laptop out, sits on the couch with it, and for the next several hours reads anything and everything he can find on Craig Howley and the Oberon Capital Group.

*

When Ellen sees Jimmy Gilroy coming through the door, she gets quite a shock. He's put on a little weight and has a beard. The callow look is gone. He surveys the room, and when he spots her sitting at the bar his face lights up.

They embrace, double take, re-embrace and then get settled, Jimmy doing a quick survey of the taps and bottles before ordering a Theakston XB.

Ellen is fine with her Leffe.

It's early Saturday evening, so the place isn't too crowded. She'd been going to suggest Flannery's, but she knows too many people there and they'd never be left alone. This place – the Black Lamps, on East Sixteenth – is small, dark and rickety, with a tiled floor and worn oak fixtures. It's perfect for a quiet reunion like this.

They spend a few minutes doing catch-up, during which Ellen reacquaints herself with Jimmy's Irish accent. She also sees definite flickers of his earlier self, but her main impression is of someone who is tired and a bit desperate, someone who has been backed into a corner and can't see any way out. His pursuit of James Vaughan seemed logical at the outset, given that Vaughan owned most of the companies, most of the *players*, involved in the original affair – Paloma Electronics, Gideon Global, the Rundles – *and* given that he'd been around for, if not directly complicit in, the very event that kickstarted this whole thing in the first place, a helicopter crash at a conference in Ireland that resulted in the deaths of six people. But the very idea of pursuing Vaughan for a specific crime, for any wrong-doing at all, in fact, soon began to seem ridiculous, quixotic even. The corporate and legal firewalls surrounding a man like him were impenetrable. So Gilroy decided to focus instead on Vaughan's business empire, in a general sort of way, and then on his family.

Which was fine, but there were two slight problems here. Three, really.

One, the subject matter was vast, octopus-like, and it expanded exponentially the more he researched it. And two, who gave a fuck? No one.

Which is still the case. Because the simple fact is, no one outside of business or political circles has ever really heard of James Vaughan. So who's going to want to buy, let alone read, a book about him?

Which leads neatly on to the third slight problem.

In a scenario like this one, how do you pay the rent?

Well, it turns out that Gilroy did indeed sell his apartment in Dublin. He also has that bar work he mentioned. But how does any of this promote . . . the career?

'It doesn't,' he says. 'The career is in a sort of holding pattern at the moment.'

Ellen looks at him, brow furrowed. Though she knows what he means, because really, her own career as a journalist is in a holding pattern, too. At least *he's* got something to focus on, something to be passionate about.

'The thing is,' he continues, 'as long as Vaughan is alive, he, or people in his organisation, will block this any way they can, and they've made things very difficult already, believe me.' He pauses and reaches for his XB. 'When Vaughan dies, though? That's it. Window closed. I mean, all the work I've done? It'll be of historical interest, sure, at *some* point . . . but that's not what I signed up for.'

She nods. 'What about the stuff that's going on at the moment? These shootings. The kids down on Orchard Street. The protest movements, the marches, Occupy. Bain. Isn't there a renewed interest in the whole private equity thing arising out of all that?'

'Yeah, I suppose,' he says, 'but there's a hell of a lot more to James Vaughan than just private equity. He's managed to fly under the radar for years, but the fact is he's involved in virtually everything – finance, domestic and foreign policy, intelligence, the military. My basic problem is I've written a biography of someone fascinating who no one has really heard of. Don't get me wrong, they *should* have heard of him, but they haven't, and there isn't much I can do about that. No one's interested. It's too long for *Parallax* or any other magazine, and publishers just shrug and say who's James Vaughan?' He pauses. 'I suppose I could self-publish, do it as an ebook, but I can't make the leap. Psychologically. I want someone to make me an offer for it. I want to bloody well get *paid* for my work.'

'I know,' Ellen says, 'I know.' But she's surprised. 'You've actually finished it?'

'Pretty much. A full draft, give or take. It's not Robert Caro or anything, it's fairly succinct. But I knew if I didn't nail it, and soon, the damn thing would kill me.'

'*House of Vaughan*?'

'Yeah.' He smiles, sheepish. 'You want to read it?'

'Nah.' She shakes her head. 'Of *course* I do, you moron.'

He reaches into his pocket and takes out a flash drive. He puts it on the bar and slides it across to her.

'I'm paranoid about sending this kind of thing by email. My account has been hacked too many times.'

'Tell me about it.'

She takes the drive and slips it into her pocket. 'Thanks. I look forward to reading it.'

And she genuinely does. Because she hopes it amounts to a lot more than what *she's* done in the last year and a half, which is a dead-end series of articles about failed presidential candidates, followed by this recent, seemingly never-ending attempt to break into a story that has just persisted in eluding her.

She doesn't relish the prospect of talking about it, though, of telling him about her various interactions with Frank Bishop over the last week or so – but she will, because there's actually a small part of her that suspects this story can't go on eluding her forever.

'So,' Jimmy says, shifting on his stool. 'Ellen Dorsey. What have *you* been up to?'

14

After chairing his third consecutive Monday morning sit-down of the senior investment directors, Craig Howley is beginning to feel that he has some sort of a grip on things. The Bloomberg interview was a triumph, and he's been getting texts and messages of congratulation ever since – even more, weirdly enough, than when the actual takeover announcement was made. It's the power of media exposure, he supposes, something that Vaughan himself would have done well to learn about and try to harness years ago. Howley plans on doing more interviews and has scheduled a meeting for later with Beth Overmyer, Oberon's vice president of communications, to sketch out a new media strategy. As a direct result of tonight's Kurtzmann benefit at the Waldorf Astoria, photos of him and Jess will be appearing on multiple platforms across the mediasphere, and it seems sort of crazy not to already have a strategy in place to take advantage of that.

It's funny, but even a couple of weeks ago – at that cocktail party in the Hamptons, say – he couldn't have foreseen how quickly, and how far, things would progress.

As he gazes out over the office now, mentally stripping away the mahogany panels and ripping up the pile carpets, Howley gets an alert from Angela that he has a call, and that it's from Vaughan.

He reaches for the phone. What the fuck is *this* about?

Vaughan is the last person he wants to talk to today.

'Jimmy?'

'Yeah. I was thinking.' Good morning to you, too. 'A bidding war? Is that really what we want to get into with Tiberius? Because the numbers don't make a lot of sense to me, Craig. We're at twenty-three dollars forty-five a share, they go twenty-four fifteen, we counter with twenty-five something or twenty-six something, then it's a war of attrition, no one's happy, and six months down the road we're not talking to each other, when we *need* to be, and all over some crappy retail chain that's over-priced to begin with?'

Howley can't believe this. And they were only discussing it earlier, at the meeting. As it happens, Vaughan's analysis is probably correct, but what does he think he's doing?

'Jesus, Jimmy, I . . . I don't understand, what happened to *I'm going to play some golf*? I thought you were supposed to be taking it easy.'

'I *am* taking it easy. But the old batteries are recharged, you know, and I . . . I can't help it. I see stuff like this in the papers, what do you want me to do, sit around and *watch*?'

Yes.

Howley leans far back in his chair and glares up at the ceiling. His batteries are recharged? Holy shit, two weeks ago, less, the man was practically an invalid.

'I don't know what to tell you, Jimmy.'

'Tell me you agree. Then I'll set up a lunch with Chris and get him to back off.'

Oh Jesus.

Chris Beaumont, chairman of Tiberius Capital Partners.

'That's not a good idea, Jimmy. I mean, really.'

'Why not?'

He has to *explain* it?

'You know what, Jimmy,' he says, 'let me think about it and I'll get back to you, OK?' Then he blusters his way off the phone, saying he's heading into a meeting.

Unbelievable.

It's clearly this trial drug Vaughan is on, and something has to be done about it. So less than a minute later Howley is through to Paul Blanford and using some fairly explicit language. The CEO of Eiben-Chemcorp practically has a nervous breakdown on the other end of the line. Howley can hear him hyperventilating.

'I'm doing what I *can*, Craig, Jesus. What *is* this? Tell me what you know.'

Howley swivels in his chair. He's not far from hyperventilating himself. 'Whatever this new drug is,' he says, squeezing the receiver, 'there's someone very high-profile who has access to it, OK? And they're fairly, let's say . . . volatile. So when this person eventually loses it, which they *will*, and it gets out that they were hopped up on your untested product, ten years ago will seem like a stroll in the fucking *park*, do you hear me?'

Blanford goes silent, and Howley can almost hear the cogs turning in his brain.

Who? *Who?*

It's the obvious question, but Blanford won't ask it, not here, not on the phone. It's only a matter of time in any case. They're talking about a drug for geriatrics, that much was established in their last conversation, so surely all it will take for Vaughan's name to come up is one whisper from the rumour mill – one hint of erratic behaviour on the old man's part.

Howley breaks the silence. 'You and Cassie are coming this evening, right? To the benefit?'

'Yeah,' Blanford says, though it's more of a grunt.

'OK. We'll talk then.'

Howley hangs up. He gets out from behind his desk and walks over to the window.

He doesn't feel like laughing exactly, but the idea that Vaughan could go to lunch with someone like Chris Beaumont and just get him to *back off*, and probably with nothing more than a few coded remarks – it's really quite impressive. Like many of his contemporaries, Howley himself wields a certain degree of power and influence, but it is prosaic, featureless, a function of structure and hierarchy. This is something else entirely. This is something based on the force of personality that is almost occult and mystical. OK, turning Chris Beaumont so easily would be a very minor manifestation of this power, but at the same time it would serve as an unwelcome reminder that it still existed.

After all these years.

Howley turns from the window and goes back to his desk.

Because his feeling is that Vaughan's power belongs to a different era, and that these last twitches of its corpse cannot and must not be allowed to distract from Oberon business going forward.

*

Frank keeps the gun – along with an old pocket watch of his father's, a couple of fountain pens and a folder of documents and photos – in a large brown padded envelope. He keeps the envelope under his mattress. Not exactly a high-tech security system, but so what. He used to have a safe when he lived in the apartment in the city, and they had one in the Carroll Gardens house, too, one that was bolted to the floor.

And this is what he has now.

A fucking padded envelope.

He pulls it out from under the mattress and spills its contents onto the bed.

The watch, pens and other items he ignores. They each in their way have the power to lure him into what would become a vortex of memory and emotion, especially the photos, but he can't let himself get near any of that stuff now. He picks up the gun, turning it in his hands as he walks away from the bed. It's a .40 calibre semi-automatic pistol, a Glock 27, Gen 3. It's got a standard nine-round magazine in it, with a small extension to improve grip.

He's used it at a firing range, plenty of times, but not for a few years.

He slips it into his jacket pocket.

The concealed-carry handgun of choice.

Or so he was told when he bought it.

He takes it out again and puts it on the kitchen table beside his keys.

He didn't sleep well last night, if at all, and now he feels really tired. His head was full of the stuff he's been reading since he got back here on Saturday – an indiscriminate, unfiltered feed of Wikipedia entries, blog posts, PDF files and quarterly reports. Halfway through yesterday he lost all sense of what he was doing, but he couldn't stop and just continued reading. By the time he lay down he knew that he'd reached saturation point. He also knew that no amount of information was going to make any difference to what he thought or to what he was going to do.

He looks over at the laptop on the couch.

Is there any point in taking it with him?

Not really.

It's too late for all that now ... checking stuff, cross-referencing, verifying. None of it made sense to him at the time anyway. He was just stalling.

He goes into the bathroom and checks himself again in the mirror. He straightens his tie. He looks respectable, as if he's about to attend a meeting or make a presentation.

He flicks his wrist up to check the time.

10.38 a.m.

He feels like screaming.

He turns away from the mirror, leaves the bathroom and goes into the kitchen. He gathers up his keys, and the gun, from the table and puts them into his jacket pocket.

He looks around the apartment one more time and leaves.

It's early in the day, and he's got plenty of time – too much time – but he can't stay around here, in the apartment, in West Mahopac, any longer. So he gets in the car and hits the road.

If it comes to it, he can spend the afternoon staring up at the ceiling of his room at the Bromley.

*

After a shower and some breakfast, Ellen opens the *House of Vaughan* file and picks up where she left off. She started reading it late last night, having delayed for nearly twenty-four hours, and now she really wants to finish it. As Jimmy Gilroy said the other evening, the book is succinct – just over two hundred pages – but it covers a lot of ground. Not only the story of James Vaughan himself, it's also about his father and grandfather, and consequently could be – and probably *should* be – four times as long. Some day it may well be, but the brevity of this current version gives it an urgency and punch that Ellen has rarely come across in a standard biography.

But she can see where the problem might lie. While *House of Vaughan* possesses the energy of really good investigative journalism, that's not what it is. It actually *is* history, in that it doesn't deal with any of the shit that's happening right now, or tell us who the James Vaughan of today is. Another aspect of the book that's challenging, and perhaps wilfully so, is that it is written in reverse. It moves backwards in time, taking us from the early 2000s right back to – she *thinks*, she hasn't gotten that far yet – the late 1870s. It's as though Gilroy were hacking and chopping his way through the decades, through dense fields of inexplicable effects, looking for some ultimate and explicable cause – some original sin that would explain all the others. He clearly subscribes, at the very least, to the notion that a good understanding of the present requires a forensic dissection of the past – which is fine, but at the end of the day unless James Vaughan himself emerges from the grey shadows of his anonymity and agrees to become a judge on *American Idol* then not that many people are going to be interested in reading a book about him.

Ellen is interested, but that's because she's both a news junkie and a history nerd. She sees the connections to her own work and the work she did with Jimmy Gilroy. She's also fascinated to learn about Vaughan's personal tragedies, stuff she'd never heard before – how his third wife (of six), the mother of his two children, died in a car crash thirty years ago; how his only son, an aspiring musician, died of a heroin overdose a couple of years before that; how his older brother was killed in Korea.

What surprises her, though, and what seems to be emerging as the central theme of the book, is the number of key moments in recent history where one or other of the Vaughans seemed to play a role, either at the heart of things or on the periphery, but always there, always involved, and how this recurring role, this active participation, tells us something about the . . . the secretive, conspiratorial and frankly compromised nature of our . . .

She looks away from the screen.

Of our *what*?

She was going to use the D word, wasn't she? Weary now, and jaded – jaded because she's back here again, back at *this* point, the point she inevitably reaches with so many of the stories she covers – Ellen gets up from her desk and walks over to the window. She stands there for a while looking out onto Ninety-third Street.

These last few days her thoughts have been yo-yoing between Jimmy Gilroy and Frank Bishop, and it's happening again now – an easy, natural transition from one to the other, only this time the contrast is sharper and more unsettling. Jimmy has had a tough time over the last year and a half researching and writing this book. He told her the other night about some of the obstacles Vaughan's people had put in his way, how he'd been intimidated by lawyers, hounded by private investigators, had his accounts hacked, even been physically threatened. But the fact is, no one asked him to do it, to get involved. Frank, by contrast, has had an infinitely tougher time over the last *week* and a half, and none of it by choice. Yet there is common ground. The two men share something.

Ellen turns and goes back to her desk. She picks up her phone.

They share an obsession – a feverish need, albeit for different reasons, to understand what it is about money and power that gnaws away at the human soul. Jimmy's obsession is borderline, on the cusp between professional and certifiable, whereas Frank's is over the line, no question about it.

Jimmy's is focused. Frank's is shapeless, directionless and dangerous.

She gets through to his voicemail, but doesn't leave a message.

Where did he say he was staying again? The Bromley? That's a huge pile down on Seventh Avenue, midtown somewhere. She looks up the number.

He's still registered at the hotel. There's no answer from his room, though.

When she gets off the phone, Ellen paces back and forth for a while, going from the window to the desk, then from the desk back to the window.

But enough.

She grabs her jacket and keys and heads out. She flags down a cab on Columbus Avenue and within fifteen minutes is walking into the lobby of the Bromley Hotel. There is a large group of tourists, along with all of their luggage, gathered in front of a fountain in the centre of it. Two of their party are at the desk engaged in some sort of negotiation, or argument even, with an attractive young receptionist in uniform. Standing behind the receptionist, also in uniform, is a slightly older guy, late thirties maybe, who seems to be observing the scene but not participating. Ellen catches this guy's eye and indicates to him that she wants to talk. He silently leaves his colleague and moves along the desk, past a fake marble pillar, to a quieter section at the end.

'Good morning, ma'am. Welcome to the Bromley. How may I help you today?'

'Hi, I need to speak to a guest. A Mr Frank Bishop. I don't know his room number.'

The receptionist smiles, does a few strokes on his keyboard and then reaches for a phone.

Ellen knows there probably won't be an answer, but she waits anyway.

'Ma'am, I'm afraid that Mr Bish–'

'Yeah, I figured,' she says, interrupting him. She glances left and right, then leans in slightly. 'You see, I, er . . . I think there might be a problem here.'

'I beg your pardon?'

Ellen lays it on fairly thick. She's concerned about her ex-husband. Hasn't been heard from in days. May have stopped taking his meds. The name Bishop has been hard to avoid recently, but she's hoping, gambling on it, that the receptionist doesn't make the connection.

He looks concerned, even slightly alarmed. He works his keyboard a little more, then makes another discreet call, turning away and speaking in a whisper. He looks back at Ellen. 'Hmm. Housekeeping haven't been into Mr Bishop's room since Friday.' He taps his fingers on the desk. 'That's not *necessarily* unusual, of course –'

'I know, but . . .' Before he starts talking about strict protocols and informing his superiors, Ellen decides to go for broke. She glances at his name tag. 'Look, Luis, all I want to know is that poor Frank isn't lying there in the bathtub with his wrists all slit open and blood everywhere, OK?'

Luis winces and his eyes widen, but he's still wavering.

Ellen shrugs. 'How about this? I'll give you fifty dollars. All you have to do is open the door and look in. I don't even have to be there. I just want to know that he's OK.'

Luis glances around. Then he looks back at Ellen and nods. Despite what she said about not having to be there, Ellen follows Luis and he doesn't seem to object. They take the elevator in silence. As they walk along the corridor to Frank's room they pass an elderly Japanese couple.

At the door, which has a Do Not Disturb sign on it, Luis clears his throat. Then he raps on the door and says, 'Management.' He does this twice more and when there is no response he takes out a card key and without looking back at Ellen or referring to her in any way he opens the door, steps in and flicks on a light.

Ellen steps in behind him.

The room is a mess, but a weird mess. There are books and magazines strewn everywhere. The air is heavy, the bed is unmade and there are some clothes lying around . . . but it's mainly the books and magazines that catch the eye.

'Holy shit.'

Ellen looks up. Luis is staring at the wall-mounted plasma TV screen, which is blank but has a long crack or gash in it. On the floor in front of it, there is an empty vodka bottle, also cracked.

Suddenly remembering why he's here, Luis rushes over to

the bathroom, pushes the door open and reaches for the light switch. Somehow, Ellen knows that Frank won't be in there and that the bathtub will be empty, so for the few seconds that she's alone here in the main room, and not hearing any gasps of horror, she throws her eye over some of the book titles.

From what she can make out, they're mostly what Frank said. Business books.

Money Down.

The Dominion of Debt.

Luis reappears. 'Mr Bishop isn't here,' he says.

Ellen holds out her hand. There's a fifty-dollar bill in it. 'Thanks,' she says.

Luis swallows. 'You know what?' He holds up his hands, palms outstretched. 'I'm good.'

He looks pale, almost as if he *has* seen a bloody corpse in the bathtub.

'Take it, Luis.' She stuffs the bill into the breast pocket of his jacket. 'I'm relieved he's not in there, believe me.'

Back outside, as Luis is closing the door, Ellen hears the ping of the elevator down the hallway and turns to look.

A moment later, Frank Bishop appears.

Shit.

He walks for a few yards in their direction before he focuses and sees Ellen.

'What the –'

'Hi, Frank.'

Luis seems horrified but also conflicted. That TV is going to have to be accounted for.

Frank shakes his head. 'Were you in my fucking *room* just now?'

'Sir,' Luis says firmly, 'please stay calm. I can explain.'

Ellen holds up a hand. 'I was worried about you, Frank. You weren't answering my calls. You haven't been –'

'What are you, my *wife*?'

She avoids looking at Luis and studies Frank instead. He's wearing a suit and a tie. He's clean-shaven. Has she missed something?

'Look, Frank . . .' she begins, but then stops. She turns to Luis. 'I think we're OK here, Luis. You know? Thank you.'

Luis hesitates. Then he addresses Frank. 'There is the question of the TV, sir. I'll have to –'

'You have my credit-card number, right? Buy a new TV with it. Knock yourself out.' He pauses. 'OK?'

Luis nods. 'Very well, sir. Ma'am.'

He takes off down the corridor.

Frank closes his eyes for a moment. 'Ellen,' he then says, almost a tremor in his voice, 'you had no right to come snooping around here. If you want –'

'I wasn't snooping. I told you. I was worried about you.'

'Worried about me? You don't even *know* me.'

'I know you a *bit*. Enough to be concerned.'

'Well, don't be.'

She nods back towards the room. 'That's quite a collection of material you have in there.'

'I told you.' He shrugs. 'I'm an expert now.'

'No one's an expert, Frank. Isn't that part of the problem?'

'Maybe, but I'm not interested in the problem any more. Just the solution.'

She looks at him. 'And what's that?'

He holds her gaze for a moment. 'Ask my daughter.'

Ellen swallows and looks away. She wonders again about his suit, his tie, this clean-cut appearance. Maybe that's how he usually looks. Or maybe he looks this way because he's just come back from seeing his daughter's *body*? And this intrusion, this presumption on her part, is the last thing he needs? Is that it?

'I'm sorry,' she says. 'I shouldn't have come here.'

She starts to walk away.

'Don't worry about it, Ellen. For what it's worth, I'm sorry, too.'

'For what?'

'I wasn't of much use to you, was I? In the end?'

Ellen doesn't know what he means by this – if he's being honest, or deeply sarcastic, or if he's just confused.

'I don't look at it that way, Frank.' It's the only answer she can think of.

'Well, who knows,' he says, 'maybe we'll get one last shot at it.'

He's definitely confused.

'I wish you all the best, Frank.' She raises a hand and gives it a gentle wave. 'Take care of yourself.'

On the way down in the elevator, she curses herself for getting up this morning.

*

Normally, Howley doesn't mind this getting-ready period at home prior to going out. Jessica isn't one of those obsessive, neurotic women – and Howley has known a few – who make a production number out of it, parading all their insecurities, fussing over clothes and hair, soliciting opinions and then dismissing them instantly. Jess is level-headed, and rightly confident in her looks and how she dresses. But this evening is a little different. The Kurtzmann gala benefit is the culmination of several months' work, and although she has an excellent staff and committee who appear to be on top of everything, Jess is understandably on edge.

Howley is, too, as it happens, though it's got nothing to do with the benefit. He feels he's under siege. Vaughan has called him twice this afternoon, and both times Howley refused to take the call. He's never done that before, not even once, and he somehow doubts that anyone else has either. But he can't go on doing it.

Nor does he want to have *the conversation* – the one where he tells Vaughan, in whatever ingenious formulation of words he can summon at the time, that he's effectively being an interfering pain in the ass and must *stop*. Howley's only hope here is that Paul Blanford will come up trumps by cutting off the supply of this new medication, and thereby, he doesn't know, slow Vaughan down, return him to the seemly and steady decline to which they had all . . . happily . . . become accustomed?

Whatever.

But the problem *now* is that Paul Blanford won't return *his* calls. They said at the end of their conversation this morning that they'd talk at the benefit, but soon after he put the phone down Howley remembered what a control freak Jessica can be at these events and that a discreet, private confab with a colleague might actually be hard to arrange.

So he called him back, after lunch.

Twice.

It's now nearly seven o'clock, they're heading out in ten minutes, and Blanford hasn't returned the call yet. Howley is irritated as a result, because this is really not the frame of mind he wants to be in this evening. The benefit, which is being held in the Grand Ballroom of the Waldorf Astoria, will be his first major social engagement as the new head of the Oberon Capital Group, and he's determined to make the most of it. It's a culmination of months of work for Jessica, sure, but it's more than that – it's also a culmination for *them*, as a couple. This is a pinnacle of sorts, an arrival.

Looking stunning, Jessica eventually emerges from her lair – leaving behind, he's in no doubt, a deeply frazzled team of stylists and cosmeticians. She's in a ravishing Tom Ford dress and nude leather Christian Louboutin pumps. Her strawberry-blonde mane is embellished with a beautiful floral headband. She's clearly nervous, but not letting it get the better of her. Holding hands, they take the elevator down, then float – pumps notwithstanding – out through the marble echo chamber of their lobby to the waiting car on Sixty-eighth, assistants hovering, security on point, every detail in place.

It's still earlyish, Manhattan's electric background thrum carrying everything, carrying them all, into a warm, familiar crepuscular embrace. They settle loose-limbed into the back of their spacious limo and then break out their devices.

The driver hums forward and quickly angles right onto Park.

They have eighteen or so blocks to go. The driver – his name is Pawel – knows what he's doing, he's wired into the system, hyper-aware that the timing of arrivals is choreographed to within an inch of, if not his, then *someone's* life, and consequently he's working the traffic – the flow, the pacing, the lights – like a smacked-out bebopper on a *serious* roll.

Howley is sending a text to Angela when he gets a call alert. He answers it.

'Mr Howley, it's Vivienne Randle, from Mr Blanford's office.'

Howley sits forward. Jess looks up from her iPad, but only for a second.

'Put me through to Mr Blanford.'

'I'm afraid Mr Blanford is indisposed.'

'*What?*'

'He was taken ill this morning, at the office.'

Howley rolls his eyes and then turns to look out the window, all too aware that they're probably gliding past Vaughan's building right about now. 'Is it serious? Is he in the hospital?'

'No, Mr Blanford is at home. He's receiving medical attention there.'

'What was it, his heart? No, not his heart, he wouldn't be at home if it was his heart.'

'I believe it was some stomach problem or intestinal issue.'

Yeah, right. A fucking ulcer. We all have those, sweetheart.

'OK, thanks.'

Jess glances up at him again. 'Who was that?'

'No one. Paul Blanford. Don't worry about it. Just one name off the list.'

She returns to her screen.

They stop at lights.

Howley is seething now, furious. He feels like jumping out of the car, storming over to Vaughan's building, grabbing the old bastard by the throat and throttling him to death.

That'd cure any stress-induced ulcer right there.

The lights change and they whoosh forward.

As Frank walks east along Forty-ninth Street, he feels his heart thumping in his chest. He feels other things, too, elsewhere in his body – minor sensations, twinges, darts of pain or discomfort. These are mild and intermittent. But he does wonder if he's having some form of coronary, or pre-coronary. He doesn't eat well and doesn't get enough exercise, and even though he's lucky to have the kind of metabolism that means he generally doesn't pack on the pounds (and looks fairly OK as a result), the reality is, he's almost fifty years old and could well be in the grip of various conditions and diseases *already*.

Without knowing it.

He's a prime candidate. Plus, the stress he's under at the moment is of a level and intensity he has never experienced before – the kind he imagines you ignore at your peril.

Perfect storm, sounds like.

Nevertheless, he wonders if it's possible, by sheer force of will, to delay something like this, a heart attack – if that's what he's actually having – to hold it off, to keep pushing, until you get over some . . . line.

Real or imaginary.

At Sixth, he waits for the lights to change.

In this case, the line is very real, and very close, three blocks away.

People gather on either side of him, in front, behind, waiting. The lights change. He pushes forward, across the avenue, and then on towards Fifth.

He catches his reflection in a store window.

Anonymous man in a suit.

Denizen of the city.

Architect.

For so much of his life that's how Frank defined himself, which meant that he never had to struggle with his identity. It was simple – the world, and his place in it, consisted of angles and forms, of light and space. It was the ordering of the infinite into the quotidian, the perfect marriage of art and science. For a quarter of a century, as a student and then as a professional, but also as a husband and as a father, he needed no other terms or rules to live and breathe by – that is, until one Friday afternoon two years ago, in the Belmont, McCann conference room, when he got laid off and had to surrender his identity . . . simply give it back, then somehow carry on *without* it, making do with whatever ramshackle alternative he could piece together from the Help Wanted section in the paper and the weird looks he got from, among others, his precious daughter, Lizzie . . .

But –

But.

Crossing Fifth.

He was going to *say*.

It was always this part of town that made him feel most like an architect, midtown – with its soaring towers and vertiginous canyons, its expanses of glass and steel, its mullions and spandrels . . . the mongrel skyline rising from an ordered grid, this great aggregate of the revolutionary and the dandified, the conservative and the radical . . .

Skyscrapers.

Like that one up ahead there, with its granite base, its limestone facade, its bronze-clad cupolas. He comes to the foot of the squat Colgate-Palmolive Building on the corner of Park and Forty-ninth and stops. It's just over there, on the other side of the avenue, the one with the anchored canopy, and the cars lining up outside, and the flashing lights, and the barriers, and the security, and the photographers, and the crowds . . .

He crosses to the grassy median and waits, gazing over at this iconic art deco masterpiece.

One of his favourites.

The Waldorf Astoria Hotel.

*

Something is bugging her, and by early evening Ellen needs to get out of the apartment, she needs a drink, or a couple of hits of a joint, anything that will lead to an altered state of consciousness. Because the one she's currently in is tired, used up, polluted with the contorted syntax of all the emails she had to write this afternoon turning down offers to talk or blog about Ratt Atkinson and his bogus Twitter accounts.

She can't believe *that's* still going on.

A call to Michelle would normally be a reliable route out of the mental ash cloud, but recently Michelle has been too news-focused in her chat, too eager to engage with the stories Ellen needs a little respite from.

But still, that's not what's bugging her.

This thrum of anxiety has been with her since she left Frank Bishop earlier – left him standing outside his room in the Bromley Hotel on Seventh Avenue, left him in that wide, desolate corridor, on that ugly multicoloured carpet, with its vertigo-inducing geometric patterns.

Frank Bishop is what's bugging her.

His demeanour, his suit, the things he said and maybe didn't say . . . his hotel room, the books and magazines, the cracked TV screen and the empty vodka bottle.

How would *she* have reacted, and behaved, in his position? There's no saying.

Not that it's any of her concern any more.

If it ever was.

She heads down to Flannery's, which is pretty much empty. This is because it's early and it's a Monday, which suits her just fine. She orders – and it's almost perverse, because it's not what she normally drinks, or ever drinks, in fact – a Stoli on the rocks. The barman gives her a look. She shrugs. What? She has to explain?

I'm looking to break a code, to enter someone's mindset.

Right.

Not that it works, of course. The Stoli. As a *drink* it does, sure, but that's all.

She'd probably be better off if she had someone to talk to. Charlie's not here, which is a pity, because she watched some of the Carillo trial earlier and feels that she's maybe ready to re-engage. After more than a week, Mrs Sanchez is still on the stand and Ray Whitestone is getting her to deconstruct the household, its comings and goings, its rhythms and routines, and in quite staggering detail.

She'd like to get Charlie's take on it.

But he's not here.

The gorgeous Nestor is, though. She sees him emerge from the kitchen, obviously finished his shift and heading off. He spots her at the bar, makes a discreet toking gesture and flicks his head in the direction of the alleyway up the street.

She's all over it.

A few minutes later they're passing his joint back and forth and discussing why teleportation as seen in *Star Trek* is technically impossible.

Looking into Nestor's eyes, and not entirely without irony, Ellen says, 'Beam me aboard, Scotty.'

'Never going to happen, because . . . think about it –'

'Yeah, I am.'

'You've got to obliterate the human body, which is ten to the power of forty-five *bits* of information, and then reassemble all that shit somewhere else without so much as putting a single itty-bitty molecule out of place. I don't *think* so.'

Ellen is wondering how Nestor would react to being hit on by a forty-one-year-old woman when something occurs to her.

Reassembled bits of data.

She passes the joint back, exhaling thick smoke, and looks away. Various corollaries of the thought that has just struck her seem to be forming now in clusters around her brain.

The bottle of Stoli and the cracked TV screen . . . when did he throw one against the other? And why? Isn't it suddenly *obvious*? It was just before they spoke on Friday, when he was drunk and watching Craig Howley being interviewed on Bloomberg. And the solution? He said he was no longer interested in the problem, only in the solution, but when she asked him what that was, he told her to ask Lizzie.

Ask my daughter.

The last thing he said was that maybe he and Ellen had one more shot at this.

What did *that* mean?

She leans back against the alley wall.

Then there was the suit and tie, and the clean-shaven look, which she took to mean . . .

But –

Maybe she misread that one completely.

'You cool?'

Ellen turns back to Nestor. 'Yeah. Yeah, I am.' She takes out her phone. 'I'm sorry . . . to do this, but . . .'

Without finishing her sentence, she turns away again and wanders out of the alley.

Standing on Amsterdam, she stares down at her phone, trying to work out what to do.

A fire truck rushes past, siren screaming.

It's Craig Howley, isn't it? Private equity, Paloma . . .

But *what*?

She Googles him. Goes to News.

The first few stories are about him taking over the Oberon Capital Group, his appearance on Bloomberg, his press conference. Then there's a story about something called the Kurtzmann Foundation. She clicks on it.

Ellen hates using her phone for looking stuff up on the internet. The screen is too small, the keys too fiddly. But she enlarges the text and reads.

Gala benefit . . . Jessica Bowen-Howley . . . Monday evening . . . 7.30 . . . the Waldorf Astoria Hotel . . .

She looks up and gazes out at the passing traffic.

Stoned, but not stoned.

Unconvinced, disbelieving, *tired* of all this.

She looks back down at her phone. What time is it? Just after seven.

Shit.

She turns around. 'Sorry, man.' This to Nestor. 'I have to go.'
Nestor shrugs and rolls an index finger.

Next time.

Ellen walks to the corner and flags down a cab going east.

*

They cross Park at Fifty-seventh Street.

Still seething, Howley is hunched forward, neck and shoulders all tense, switching his phone from one hand to the other. He's desperately anxious to move this situation forward.

Fifty-fifth.

In just a few blocks Pawel will be swinging to the left, around the median, and they'll be pulling up at the Waldorf.

He can't hit the red carpet like this, can he? Looking distracted, angry, a scowl on his face? It wouldn't be fair to Jessica. There will be A-list celebrities here, Hollywood actors, sports stars, senators and congressmen, people who know how to smile in public, schmooze, work the big room.

Professionals.

He needs to get with the programme.

He looks over at Jessica and smiles, or at least tries to.

She's about to say something when her phone rings. She rolls her eyes and answers it.

As she's talking, he decides to try Blanford's cell one last time.

It goes to message.

Damn.

They're at Fifty-second.

'Paul?' He looks over at Jessica. She's still talking. He turns to the right, facing the window. 'Paul, it's Craig,' he whispers. 'What the fuck is going on? Are you really sick or has he gotten to you? It's Jimmy Vaughan I'm talking about. But you had to have known that, right? Well, let me tell you *this.*' Rapid flick of the head towards Jess, then back. 'If Jimmy goes on being allowed to take this stuff, he will fucking *eat you alive*, do you hear me? He'll end up destroying your company, or worse, buying it back. And believe me, Paul, you do *not* want Jimmy Vaughan in your life, running things. Find this leak, find it now, and *plug* it.'

He presses End Call.

Shit.

He overplayed his hand there, didn't he? But the pressure of all this is getting to him.

He puts his phone on silent and slips it into his jacket pocket. He reaches a foot over and nudges Jessica in the leg. She looks at him and nods.

'Gotta go, sweetie,' she says into the phone. 'See you in a bit.' She puts the phone away and looks out the window.

They're swinging around the median.

'That's quite a crowd,' she says, beaming.

Howley looks out the window, too, at the flashing lights and the photographers, at the security guys and the onlookers.

'Damn right,' he says, the red carpet just sliding into view now.

He reaches a hand out to Jessica.

'You ready?'

*

On the periphery there is mild curiosity. A few people in a passing MTA bus crane to see. A man in a car, stopped at lights, beeps his horn. Pedestrians on Forty-ninth and Fiftieth glance, then glance away.

Closer in, under the canopy, it's a different story. On either side of the red carpet, which leads from the kerb through the central entrance and right up into the lobby, there are security barriers. These are draped in white. Thickset guys in black with earpieces parade up and down, scanning the area for trouble, never smiling, exuding a kind of dumb, steroidal menace. Behind the barriers, on either side, there are photographers and onlookers. The real action for the photographers – as far as Frank can make out – is probably inside, in the main lobby. That's where the posing and the interviews will take place, the serious media work. The photographers out here, he's guessing, are bottom-feeders, only a notch or two above the onlookers.

People like him.

As each car pulls up – all either SUVs, town cars or limos – there is a directed flurry of attention. The assembled photographers and onlookers wait to see who gets out, then react accordingly. If it's some middle-aged couple, tanned and moneyed-looking, as most of them have been so far, the reaction is muted. If it's anyone with the remotest whiff of celebrity to them, the reaction tends to be pretty wild.

'This way! Over here!'

'Look at me!'

In the ten minutes he's been standing at the barrier – having slowly wormed his way in, the nudge of an elbow here, an *excuse me* there – he has barely recognised anyone.

Which is a cause for concern.

He thinks he saw Ray Sullivan, secretary of the Treasury, and he's fairly sure he saw one of the lesser Bush brothers, Marvin or Neil. He saw the actress Brandi Klugman, who caused quite a stir, and a Fox News guy whose name he can't remember. There were one or two others he half recognised, as well as several he didn't.

And they keep coming...

But standing here now, Frank is feeling a little anxious.

A little anxious? A *lot* anxious.

What if he misses his opportunity? What if Craig Howley doesn't show? What if he got here early and is already inside?

Every muscle in Frank's body, every atom, is tensed up and ready for this. It's all that's left of himself, he realises, as he eddies ever farther out to sea, beyond reason or logic, any access to his emotions long since abandoned. But it's OK, because when the broad-shouldered security guy who's been standing directly in front of him for the last few seconds moves to the right, it's like a curtain being drawn back.

And there he is...

The door of the limo opens and out steps tall, balding, moneyed-looking Craig Howley, unmistakable from his TV interview and a hundred magazine and Google images. By his side is the elegant Jessica – the driving force, apparently, behind this whole event.

Some short, stocky guy in a tux is there to greet them. There's a little banter, a little glancing around, and then the couple join hands and turn, with Howley on the right, to head inside.

As they move forward, each second shattering in his mind like a pane of glass, Frank reaches into his jacket pocket for the

Glock. He draws it out, inserting his finger right in over the trigger to make sure that he's ready – to make sure that the various safety mechanisms deactivate when he pulls it.

He looks up.

Howley is nearly level with him now.

Given the crowded, confined space he's in, it's sort of an awkward manoeuvre, but Frank brings his arm up to his chest and then quickly extends it, all the way out, aiming at Howley's head.

He fires once, then a second time.

The loud cracks are followed almost instantly by a collective intake of breath, and in the nanosecond before he is mobbed to the ground, Frank sees a streak of something, it's red and stringy, spurt from the side of Howley's bare head, which itself jerks and twists awkwardly off to the left.

Pinned to the ground now, face down, Frank closes his eyes. With both arms yanked back almost to breaking point, with a knee lodged sharply between his shoulder blades and with voices roaring in his ear and everywhere, he offers no resistance.

There is a degree of pain in all of this. He surrenders to it.

*

Even from three or four blocks away, Ellen can see the revolving lights of the police cars.

And of an *ambulance*.

There's one crossing Park now, arriving east on Forty-ninth.

She's ready to throw up, but fights it really hard, taking deep breaths and rolling down the window.

After another block, with the traffic ahead starting to get

backed up, she thinks . . . what's the point?

'Pull over, please,' she tells the driver. 'Now. Here's good.'

She pays and gets out.

At Fifty-first Street, she crosses to the east side of the avenue. The tension in the air here is palpable and as she moves closer to the scene, the hubbub of a few hundred animated conversations soon begins to overwhelm even the roar of the traffic. She gets to the edge of the crowd, which has extended back now to the corner of Fiftieth, and just stands there, trying to see what's happening.

She pretty much knows what *has* happened, though, doesn't she?

No need to be told.

She makes eye contact with someone, a woman in a business suit, and throws her an interrogative look.

The woman shrugs. 'Don't know. Some guy got shot?'

Without turning, someone else, a lanky kid in front of them with a huge pair of cans around his neck, says, 'Yeah. One man down. They got the shooter.'

Ellen nods, still feeling the urge to throw up.

A few minutes later, the ambulance takes off, followed shortly thereafter by at least three police cars.

The crowd begins to disperse.

She spots one or two reporters she knows, already on the scene, notebooks and recorders out.

Big story.

She turns around, eye out for a cab.

If she's going to throw up, she wants to do it in the comfort and privacy of her own bathroom.

15

It seems like the logical solution.

To reassume control of the company.

If *he* doesn't step up to the plate, what are they going to do? Bring in an outsider? Pick someone from the Oberon gene pool who'll cause all sorts of resentments and destabilise everything?

Nah.

This is the right thing to do.

Besides, he's up for it, and has never felt more motivated or energised.

From the moment Vaughan enters the Oberon Building early Tuesday morning, he picks up on the reaction – heads turn, there are audible intakes of breath, he hears murmurs, people whispering. The elevator ride to the fifty-seventh floor is a solemn affair and passes in silence, but once he steps into reception – at least as far as *he's* concerned – it's business as usual.

Craig Howley's death last night, at the hands of a madman, was an appalling tragedy, and tribute will be paid to him in due course, recognition for his contribution to the company, there's no question about that – but Craig would be the first to acknowledge that you can't let your guard down, that the show must go on, and must be seen to go on.

Back in his office, behind his desk, Vaughan firefights his way through a fairly cluttered agenda. It seems to be just one crisis after another. They're relatively minor ones, but he works his magic on them nonetheless, mostly over the phone. One key meeting he sets up is with Beth Overmyer, Oberon's vice president of communications. She's coming in at eleven to discuss how this whole thing should be dealt with from a media perspective.

On a more personal level, the situation with Arnie Tisch at Eiben-Chemcorp is a real worry for Vaughan. He needs to refresh his supply of this new medication, because he has only two pills left, but the trouble is . . . he's been feeling so damn good that he hasn't given any real thought to what might happen if, or when – and it's now looking increasingly like when – he runs out.

So just before Beth Overmyer shows up, he spends a few minutes on the phone trying to reach Arnie Tisch.

But Arnie Tisch, it would appear, is unavailable.

Vaughan looks around the office, and over to the window. He hates being thwarted like this. He leaves a message – a message that is unequivocal in its grumpiness.

Moments later, Beth Overmyer is shown into the office. She approaches and takes a seat in front of Vaughan's desk.

Initially, he's distracted by how attractive she is, in her satin blouse and slim-fitting skirt, with her shapely legs and peep-toe shoes. Her sparkly eyes. Like a young Meredith.

Like a *what*?

Jesus Christ. Did he just think that? He did. Rather than feeling excited by her presence, though, or aroused, he feels irritated.

He nods at her to go on.

She starts by expressing her condolences and shock on the

347

death of Mr Howley. Vaughan nods at her again – yes, yes, now *go on*.

She outlines the media coverage of what happened last night. The main focus so far, without a doubt, is on the father–daughter angle, the high drama of all that. Howley is getting some attention, but it's cursory. In a way, he's little more than a piece of collateral damage.

'Which is good, isn't it?' Vaughan says. 'For us, I mean.'

'Sure.' She clears her throat. 'But there could be some fallout from . . . well, from you being here. Today.' She pauses, indicating the desk. 'Like this.'

'What? The man's barely dead twelve hours and someone's replaced him already? The unseemly haste of it, is that what you're talking about?'

'Yes, but –'

'Yes, but it's *bullshit*. Clearly. Because it's *me*.' He pats his chest. 'That's the beauty of it. If it was anyone else, maybe, but –'

'The beauty, OK, but also, just maybe, the problem. It puts a spotlight on you, Mr Vaughan.'

He freezes.

'And my understanding is that –'

'Yes, yes, OK.' He holds up a hand to silence her.

She's right.

God*dammit*.

The 'understanding' she referred to there is an unspoken company policy of always striving to protect Vaughan's privacy and even, where possible, his anonymity. Coming in like this today was certainly a bold move on his part, but also one that was bound to attract attention. By any standard, therefore, it was a serious error of judgement.

348

However, it is perfectly clear to Vaughan, now that he thinks about it, that the *real* error of judgement here was Craig Howley's. There's already been speculation in the papers and online that Howley was targeted because he ran a private equity company, and that this deluded character, this Frank Bishop, was supposedly carrying out the wishes of his own deluded daughter. But if Howley hadn't gone on television and done that interview, if he hadn't been so stupid as to place a value on that kind of exposure, on having a so-called high profile, maybe Bishop would have ended up going after someone else.

Who knows?

But why take the risk?

Beth Overmyer drums her fingers on the side of her chair. 'Mr Vaughan, may I be frank?'

It's barely perceptible, but he nods assent.

'I think you should go home. This . . . *visit*. We can describe it, if we have to, as a gesture of solidarity with the staff. By the company patriarch. At this terrible time. But any announcement we make about a successor to Mr Howley, or about whatever temporary arrangements we're putting in place . . . it really shouldn't have your name on it anywhere. In fact, you shouldn't *be* here a minute longer than is necessary.'

Vaughan makes a face, petulant now.

But she's right. Again. Maintaining privacy has been a priority throughout his life, partly fuelled by a distaste for his father's flagrant disregard of it, and partly necessitated by certain commercial sensitivities. But it has now reached the stage where it's probably close to a pathology. So this carelessness of his today, this recklessness . . .

It's taken him somewhat by surprise.

Maybe it's due to the medication, he doesn't know, but –

'Mr Vaughan,' Beth Overmyer says.

He needs to keep his eye on the ball a bit more.

'Er . . . yes?'

'There *is* one other thing. It has come to our attention that Jimmy Gilroy has resurfaced.'

Vaughan leans forward on the desk and buries his head in his hands. This is the little bastard who broke the J. J. Rundle story and then spent the next year or so nosing around for a follow-up story on Vaughan himself. He was discouraged gently, and then not so gently. Obstacles were put in his way, incentives too. Vaughan thought he'd been taken care of.

He looks up at Beth Overmyer.

Now what?

'Well, he has apparently finished this book of his, and although no one seems to want to publish it, which is a good sign, he has just recently met up with Ellen Dorsey again.'

'Oh, *please*.' Vaughan slaps his hand on the desk.

'My concern, therefore,' Beth Overmyer goes on, 'is that with this dreadful business of Mr Howley's death, there will inevitably be increased focus on Oberon, even on you . . . and that this might increase Gilroy's chances of finding a publisher.'

Vaughan leans back in his chair. Initial intelligence reports on what Gilroy was putting together were pretty horrifying – a full family history, no less. But with confidentiality clauses, libel laws, insiders sworn to secrecy and so on, he was never going to get very far.

That was the understanding, at any rate.

'No,' Vaughan then says, shaking his head. 'This situation cannot be allowed to develop. It is *not* acceptable.'

Beth Overmyer nods in agreement. 'Absolutely.' She pauses and straightens out a crease in her skirt. 'What would you like me to do about it?'

Vaughan thinks about this for a while, swivelling in his chair. But there's only one thing he can do, isn't there?

'Don't worry about it,' he says eventually, standing up from the desk. 'I'll take care of this.'

'O-K.'

'But in the meantime can you get me a copy of the damn thing? Of this stupid *book*?'

'It should be possible, yeah. But Mr Vaughan, is that really a good idea –'

'Yes. It is. I want to see what he's written.'

'Very well. I'll send it to you as soon as I get my hands on a copy.'

'Good.'

He remains there for a moment, distracted, gazing at her legs.

'Mr Vaughan?'

'Er, yes.' He looks into her eyes. 'Thank you. That'll be all.'

She stands up, but seems reluctant to move.

'OK, OK,' he says to her. 'I get it, I get it. I just have *one* phone call to make and then I'm leaving.'

*

Ellen spends a lot of Tuesday on the couch in front of the TV, flicking between analysis of the Frank Bishop story and live coverage of the Connie Carillo murder trial. When the analysis becomes unbearable, either too convoluted or just too close to the bone, she switches to the murder trial. And when the trial becomes too much, with its longueurs and its overreliance on trivial detail – Ray Whitestone's signature technique – she switches back.

She feels bad for Frank. She feels she should have seen this coming and done something. She did see it coming, in fact, but not soon enough. And anyway, what *could* she have done?

This has all just compounded her general sense of uselessness. The thing is, instead of vegetating on the couch, she should probably be working on her next piece for *Parallax*, the one on West Virginia congresswoman Jane Glasser. But it's not happening. There's nothing in the tank to kickstart *that* story.

'Now, Mrs Sanchez, could you kindly describe for the court the exact layout of the kitchen?'

Ray Whitestone is getting closer here, finally, to the heart of the matter. This is where the murder took place. Or at least it's where Howard Meeker's naked body was found.

In the kitchen, on the floor.

A lot of people will be relieved that the prosecution's case seems to be entering its final phase – though no one is quite sure yet where this massive accumulation of detail Whitestone has built up is leading. So far no motive has been established, no tearing apart of Connie's character has taken place – there's been no real drama, in fact. The appeal of the trial, weirdly, appears to lie in its very banality, in this slow-burn, slightly soporific, almost tantric quality. It's as if the promise of an explosive resolution is what has been carrying everyone forward.

Appropriately drowsy, Ellen stares at the screen.

There are only three fixed angles allowed in the courtroom. One takes in both the prosecution and defence teams, with

Connie Carillo herself sometimes visible, sometimes obscured, at the far end. The second angle is of the witness box, which provides virtual close-up shots of those giving evidence, and the third angle is of the bench and of the fifty-eight-year-old presiding judge, ex-Olympic shot-put silver medallist J. Shelley Roberts.

'Well, first off, Mr Whitestone, let me tell you, it's a *big* kitchen, 'specially when you got to clean it . . .'

Ellen flicks over.

'. . . to be honest, what this sap did, what his daughter did – and I'm not condoning it, obviously, God forbid – but I don't understand why there hasn't actually been *more* of it, because when you look at the situation, when you consider the *scale* of what's been perpetrated on the American people . . .'

And back.

'. . . the countertop, that part of the island, it's of marble, I guess, I don't know, a kind of dark, black marble, and it has these light fixtures hanging over it, they're made with copper, I think . . .'

'. . . I mean really, were we all asleep at the *wheel* when these bozos passed the bill in 2000 exempting toxic assets like CDOs, repos and swaps from regulation? Were we smoking *crack* when the ratings agencies declared that junk mortgages were as safe as Treasury bonds? I mean come *on* . . .'

After a few more rounds of this, Ellen has had enough and flicks the TV off. She goes over to her desk and calls up the *House of Vaughan* file.

She's not sure if she's ready for this either, but she wants to finish it. The last chapter she read was a vivid account of how James Vaughan's grandfather, Charles A. Vaughan, was one of the seven men who met in secret at a remote hunting lodge on Jekyll Island off the coast of Georgia in 1910 to plot the creation of the Federal Reserve System. The book's final chapter then takes the reader back to Vaughan's youth decades earlier and describes how he effectively came out of nowhere and got started in business.

The really surprising thing, as far as Ellen is concerned, is the detailed account of an incident that Gilroy chooses to close the book with, an incident that seems to identify – and with pinpoint precision – the very beginnings of the Vaughan family fortune. As she's reading it, fully awake now and engaged, two aspects of this strike her as significant. One, the story is nothing short of incendiary – but kind of deceptively so, as it describes something that happened way back in late August of 1878. And two, in the unlikely event of the book ever being published and sparking controversy, debate or even litigation, Gilroy has built a pretty solid and impressive firewall around it in the form of multiple primary and secondary source citations. These include newspaper reports and contemporary eyewitness accounts.

The incident in question, which was quick and brutal, involved Charles Vaughan himself and Gilbert Morley, a renowned Wall Street speculator, as well as, indirectly, Arabella Stringham, the daughter of dry-goods magnate 'Colonel' Cyrus T. Stringham.

When Ellen has finished the book, she gets on the phone and calls Gilroy up.

'Hi, Ellen.'

'Jimmy.' She whistles. 'I've just finished *House of Vaughan*.'

'Oh.' Flicker of insecurity, standard issue. 'And?'

She gives it to him straight – largely positive, one or two things she's not sold on, one or two editorial suggestions. But her most enthusiastic comments she saves for last. The closing section of the book, she tells him, is fantastic, an absolute bombshell of a thing. She quizzes him for a few minutes on his methods, how and where he managed to dig up this material and how confident he would be about defending it.

Completely, he says. The ironic thing is that Vaughan's subtle and not so subtle attempts to sabotage the project effectively drove it underground, causing a shift in focus and steering Jimmy's gaze ever deeper into the past – so that instead of trying to research and interview contemporaries of Vaughan's, he ended up bunkering down in various basement libraries and trawling through, for the most part, old newspaper archives.

They then discuss the killing of Craig Howley and all the publicity surrounding it, but Jimmy guesses that for most publishers the link with Vaughan and his family history would still be too tenuous to justify acquiring the book and putting it out there. Vaughan *really* needs to stick his head above the parapet, Jimmy says, and that's pretty unlikely at this stage.

But he's fine with it.

The relief of getting the book finished has been liberating, and he's looking forward to moving on.

'OK,' Ellen says, 'but you're not giving up, right?'

'No. Certainly not. The way I see it, you know . . . it's a long game.'

Yeah, Ellen thinks, as she's putting the phone down a few moments later, you can say that again.

*

'Can I make another call?'

His first one, last night, at Central Booking, was to Deb. Not to apologise exactly, or even to explain, it was just to connect. And he has to give Deb her due, she let him. After the initial shock, she didn't launch into an attack or go off on a rant or anything. In fact, she spent most of the time trying to persuade him to let Lloyd bring in a partner from the law firm to represent him.

Seymour Collins. Here now in the cell.

'Yeah,' he says, 'we can arrange that. Who to?'

Collins is businesslike, very direct, no bullshit. He's mid-fifties, well fed, well dressed, well groomed, but he clearly knows what he's doing, knows his way around the system and talks everyone's language. At the arraignment this morning, even though he must have known it wouldn't be granted, he made very convincing arguments for bail. When the judge then ordered that Frank be transferred to Rikers Island for his pre-trial detention period, Collins successfully argued that given the high-profile nature of the crime his client should at least be granted protective custody.

Which means that Frank is being kept in the West Facility and away from the prison's general population.

So again, thank fuck for Lloyd.

But as for who Frank wants to call? Well, Collins has just spent the last hour telling him about what's in the papers today and what's being said about him on TV and online. Frank Bishop, domestic terrorist, sick ideologue . . . epic fuck-up as a father, epic fail as a man. Can't even hold down a shitty job in retail. *If this guy doesn't plead insanity*, one blogger wrote, *then he's obviously insane*. Now, while one part of Frank agrees with all of this, and wholeheartedly, another part doesn't – the same part that insisted on entering a plea of not guilty at the arraignment. That's the position he's taking. He's prepared to admit that he shot and killed Craig Howley, but not that he's guilty. This is why he's being kept on remand, and why there's going to be a trial, and why – given the nature of the coverage – he's going to need an ally, someone to tell his side of the story.

'Ellen Dorsey,' he says.

Collins does a double take. 'The journalist?'

'Yes.'

Frank has no real reason to trust Ellen Dorsey. But he has no reason to distrust her either. All he has to go on is his instinct.

'You sure that's a good idea, Frank? I think maybe you ought to let –'

'No. Believe me, it's a good idea.'

Actually, what Frank isn't sure of right now is how long Seymour Collins might want to stick around. Because who knows, for a firm like Pierson Hackler this whole thing could very easily turn into a PR nightmare. Deb's initial impulse to help could become a liability. They could lose clients.

But something tells Frank that with Ellen Dorsey it'll be different, that she's just too fucking stubborn to turn her back on this, and that consequently any chance of a fair hearing in the media lies with her. And he means a fair hearing not just for himself – maybe not even for himself at all, in fact – but for Lizzie. Because really, that's what he wants to see, something written about *her* that's honest and that tries to make sense of what happened without resorting to lies and hysteria.

'How well do you know this person? Can you trust her?'

This person.

He and Ellen drove down from Atherton together. A week later they sat in a diner for about an hour. They've spoken briefly a couple of times since. It's not much – but not much is all he's got left.

'Yes, I can.'

Collins paces back and forth. The cell isn't very big. 'OK, so what do you have in mind?'

Frank explains. He keeps it simple. The idea is to enlist the support of someone with a bit of integrity who can set the record straight.

Can't hurt, can it?

'Very well,' Collins says. 'Be careful what you say, though. The call will be recorded.'

A while later, as Frank is being escorted to where the phones are in the recreation area, he wonders what he really meant when he used the phrase *set the record straight*.

Because Lizzie was involved in two murders.

And *he* carried out a third.

What could be straighter than that? All the rest is noise, and will soon be forgotten.

Just like he'll soon be forgotten.

And this is a thought that occurs to him now with clock-work regularity. It's like a new heartbeat, dull, thudding, relentless. Prison is all he will know for the rest of his life – damp walls like these, and awful smells, and shitty food, and restricted access to everything, and constant, gnawing fear. He'll never again make eye contact with that Asian woman who works at the Walgreens, never again experience that frisson of excitement as a possible future opens up before him.

Never be free of self-pity, either.

The guard escorting him indicates which phone Frank should use. He goes to it, picks it up and huddles in.

This is potentially something, though, isn't it? A chance to talk, to remember, to put it all down for posterity.

A link with the past, a link with the future.

He has Ellen's number written on a piece of paper. He punches it out and waits.

*

Thursday is Vaughan's first day in a month without this new medication. He took the last pill yesterday and spent a good part of the morning walking in Central Park and most of the afternoon sorting through some old archives. But his irritation at not being able to contact Arnie Tisch – who has apparently been transferred, or has had himself transferred, to Eiben's main office in Beijing – is mitigated slightly by a determination not to let himself be ruled by this.

It's only a stupid pill, after all.

He's James Vaughan.

But he's not giving up on it, either. If he has to, he'll go straight to Paul Blanford, Eiben's CEO, and find some way to scare the living daylights out of him. Because what's the big deal? It's not like they're conducting illegal clinical trials in some third-world hellhole and are afraid of getting caught. He's *volunteering* to take it. You'd think they'd be happy to get the feedback.

By ten o'clock, however, and despite his determination to brave it out, Vaughan has to admit that he's feeling pretty lousy. Energy levels are noticeably down on recent days, and all of a sudden he's aware, as he hasn't been for ages, of various bodily aches and pains.

And he's not *doing* anything, apart from shuffling aimlessly around the apartment. He doesn't want to panic, though, so he makes a real effort to engage. He goes into his study and sits at his desk. He places a call to Paul Blanford. After a few moments, he's informed that Mr Blanford is unavailable. Wheezing a little now, suppressing a cough, he just about stops himself from barking *Do you know who I am?* into the phone. What he does say is that it's imperative Mr Blanford gets back to him.

Then, feeling a bit sick, he goes in search of Meredith.

He finds her, as he does most days now, sitting at the counter in the kitchen, drinking either coffee or a soda and staring up at live coverage of the Connie Carillo murder trial on the wall-mounted TV. Sometimes Mrs R is around, sometimes not. Today she's not, and Mer is alone, in jeans and a T-shirt, no makeup, hunched forward over the counter, can of soda next to the remote.

It all seems to have become a little obsessive of late.

Vaughan doesn't say anything. He just stands in the doorway – watching her, then watching the TV for a bit, alternating between the two, in a sort of daze himself.

Mrs Sanchez is still on the stand, and Ray Whitestone is continuing the very thorough and forensic dissection of the housekeeper's cleaning regimen that he began yesterday. Vaughan read about it online earlier this morning, how jury members had been shown a selection of cleaning solvents taken from the kitchen of the Park Avenue apartment, and had then been treated to detailed readings from their labels. Whitestone argued that the presence of one product in particular, Erodon

10, a highly unusual and industrial-strength cleaning solvent, was inconsistent with the defence counsel's claim that Mrs Sanchez was scrupulous in regard to safety. No one seems to know where this is going, and Judge Roberts hasn't shown any inclination to intervene.

Unbelievably, Whitestone is still chiselling away at the same point this morning.

'Mrs Sanchez,' he's saying, 'is it not true that Erodon 10 is a singularly inappropriate substance to use in an everyday domestic setting?'

'Objection, leading.'

'Overruled.'

'Mrs Sanchez?'

'Yes, normally. I suppose.'

'And yet you had it there, under the sink, in among the washing powders and grease-stain removers?'

'Yes, sir, but –'

'Mrs Sanchez, are you aware that Erodon 10 is used in heavy industry, and that it is even used by the military?'

She pauses, obviously irritated by the line of questioning. 'No, sir.'

Vaughan looks at Meredith. She is engrossed, mesmerised.

'So you are not aware that it is essentially a commercial by-product of a chemical weapons R&D programme?'

'*Objection.*'

'Mr Whitestone?'

'Bear with me, Your Honour.'

Judge Roberts exhales, waves him on.

'Mrs Sanchez, did you never once read the safety warnings on the label?'

'Yes, I did, but if I could –'

'So despite the alarming nature of those warnings, as we saw here yesterday, *you* saw fit to keep a container of the stuff in the defendant's *kitchen*?'

'I had –'

'Mrs Sanchez, please, you must answer the question. Did you consider it appropriate to keep a container of Erodon 10 in an ordinary domestic setting? Yes or no?'

Mrs Sanchez rolls her eyes. She hesitates, sighs, seems to be looking for a way out.

'Mrs Sanchez, *did* you consider it appropriate?'

'*Yes.*'

'I see. May we ask why?'

'Why? You want to know why?'

'Yes, Mrs Sanchez.'

She leans forward in the box, clearly agitated now. 'Because of Mr Meeker's *girlfriend*, that's why, she kept spilling her stupid cherry soda –'

The courtroom erupts.

'– it was that Dr something, Diet Cherry, and I don't know how many times she spilt it on the kitchen floor, on the tiles, and *nothing* gets that stuff out, *nothing*, believe me, I've tried –'

The defence counsel jumps to his feet. '*Mrs Sanchez!*'

'– then someone told me about this Erodon 10,' she goes on, 'that it was good for getting out tough stains, but without damaging the tiles, because you know with terracotta –'

'*Mrs* Sanchez, *please.*'

Judge Roberts calls for order.

'– because you have to . . .' She is looking around now, obviously bewildered by the reaction. 'You have to be careful . . .'

With the commotion continuing in the courtroom, Vaughan turns, as though in a dream, and looks at Meredith. She is leaning back from the counter now, her mouth open in shock. She raises a hand to cover it. 'Oh my God,' she whispers – it's just about audible – and then turns in Vaughan's direction.

Their eyes meet.

A wave of exhaustion washes over him. He's confused, but also suddenly quite focused.

Meredith shakes her head and then, slowly, they both look down at the counter, at the can of soda in front of Meredith.

It's the one she always drinks, the one that anyone who knows her knows she drinks.

It's Dr Thurston's Diet Cherry Cola.

*

The word she's seeing most is *frenzy* – as in 'media frenzy' or 'frenzy of speculation'. Because everyone is asking the same question. Who is she? Who is Howard Meeker's quote un-quote girlfriend?

'Please tell us,' one blogger writes, 'because we gots to know . . .'

On the train back from Atherton, Ellen has just put away her notes and taken out her phone. And it's all over Twitter – this first serving of real drama in the Carillo murder trial. Mrs Sanchez is trending, Ray Whitestone is trending, *#mysterygirlfriend* is trending.

Ellen checks a couple of news sites to get the lowdown. It seems that Whitestone's laborious and painstaking technique of intense engagement followed by sudden deflection has paid off, providing the trial with something it has conspicuously lacked up to now, a motive.

She watches a clip of a panel discussion on MSNBC. The studio backdrop is a graphic depicting the scales of justice superimposed on a photo-montage of Salome's veils, the Dow Jones logo and a dead fish wrapped in newspapers.

'Yes,' one of the panellists is saying, 'we now have a motive, and it appears to be sexual jealousy.'

'Which, of course,' another panellist says, 'is quite in keeping with the operatic dimensions of this whole case.'

'Indeed. But who is this other woman? The only thing we know about her is that she drinks some kind of . . . diet soda.'

'And appears to be a little clumsy.'

This prompts a laugh.

'We're also getting reports in that Mildred Sanchez is now claiming she doesn't know who the girlfriend is, or at least doesn't know her by name, but that this person was a frequent visitor to the apartment, especially when Connie was away on tour.'

'And now the hunt is on to find her.'

'Extraordinary. An absolutely extraordinary development in court today.'

They then show the relevant exchange.

And it *is* extraordinary.

But how many times, Ellen wonders, will they be rerunning it in the coming days and weeks?

She puts her phone away, leans back and gazes out the window, pondering the extraordinary development there has been in her own circumstances.

The call on Tuesday from Frank Bishop came as a real

surprise, but when he made his proposal she didn't hesitate for a second. Because it all seemed to make sense now. She was no longer racing against the clock to crack a story that kept getting ahead of her. The story was already there, and she was being given the chance to tell it, comprehensively and more or less from the inside. When she got off the phone with Frank, she called Max and they worked out a strategy right there and then – three parts over three months, once the trial was out of the way.

Ellen got on the case without delay by going through all of her notes. She then took the train up to Atherton College to re-establish some of the contacts she'd made first time around, and to make a few new ones. She stayed until this morning so she could interview as many people as possible.

Travelling back this afternoon, she feels energised, her head brimming with ideas on how to approach this. From Penn Station she takes an A train uptown, but instead of going straight home she decides to stop off at Flannery's first for a quiet drink.

Settled at the bar, one beer in, she looks up and sees Charlie approaching.

'Hey, Ellen.' He takes the stool next to her. 'You been following it, right? Please tell me you've been following it.'

'Carillo? Not exactly.' She plays with her phone, twirling it slowly on the bar. 'I've been working. I heard, though.'

'Something else, isn't it?'

'Yeah, the mystery girlfriend. You couldn't make it up.'

Charlie rears back. 'What? You're behind the curve, sweetheart. Mystery's been solved.'

'What?'

'Yeah, things are moving pretty fast. Someone squealed, apparently, about an hour ago. On Twitter. Of *course*. And now it's everywhere.'

'Oh.' She takes a sip from her glass. 'So who's the little charmer?'

Charlie catches the barman's eye and orders a drink. He turns back. 'Who is it? Well, her name is Meredith Vaughan. Seems she's married to some much older –'

Ellen's jaw drops.

Charlie looks at her. 'What?'

'Meredith *Vaughan*?'

'Yeah.'

'*Holy* shit.'

She slides off the stool, simultaneously grabbing her phone from the bar.

'*What?* Ellen. Jesus.'

'Give me two minutes, Charlie.'

She heads for the door, moving quickly, phone held up in front of her, looking for Jimmy Gilroy's number.

Outside, there is a warmth in the late afternoon air, a sort of thickening.

'Hi, Ellen.'

She feels excited.

'Have you heard?'

'Meredith? Yeah. It's just unbelievable. The whole thing has ignited. I'm online right now, and one of the questions people are asking is, who is James Vaughan? It's like . . . it's . . .'

'Like Christmas has come early.'

'*Yes.*'

'You've got to resubmit the book to publishers, Jimmy.' She watches an MTA bus glide by. 'Do you still have an agent?'

'No, but –'

'I'll talk to mine.'

'Thanks. I just want to do some edits, a few days, and then –'

'Yeah, let the momentum build. This story isn't going away any time soon.'

Jimmy laughs. 'You know what, Ellen, I'm supposed to be heading out to work in a few minutes, but how am I going to get through this shift without cracking *something* open, and preferably a bottle of champagne?'

'Uh-*uh*, you save that for when I'm there.'

She tells him about the Frank Bishop development. They discuss the overlap, and how it might mean they could end up working on the same story again.

'For our sins,' Jimmy says.

'Yeah.'

'Fine by me, though.'

'Yeah, me too.' Ellen looks around. 'OK, Irish, you get your edits done, I'll talk to my agent tomorrow, and we'll meet up early next week.'

She puts her phone away, breathes in a lungful of Amsterdam and heads back inside.

*

It's four thirty when he wakes definitively. Doesn't mean he's going to get up, but he certainly won't be going back to sleep. That last little passage of dreamtime was enough to seal *that* deal – him and LBJ in a corridor somewhere, Johnson blocking the way, won't let him get by, exhorting, cajoling, breathing in his face. 'I'm tellin' ya, son . . .'

The reality was quite different, though, because Vaughan

famously clashed with LBJ – had the temerity to *defy* the man – and then went to work for Barry Goldwater.

It was in the summer of '64.

Famously?

If *that* isn't a relative term.

Now that he's sufficiently awake, yesterday comes flooding back to him in all its horror. First, the screaming, mostly from Meredith, who was all defensive and passive-aggressive, trying to say it *didn't mean anything*, which if he hadn't been in such physical pain by that point he would have laughed at. And then the dramatics, the bag-packing and the flight from the apartment, ostensibly to save his 'feelings', but in reality because she knew damn well that if she stayed here, she'd end up – once the cat was out of the bag – becoming a virtual prisoner in the building. And it wasn't long before said cat *was* out of the bag and roaming free, claws out. It was a few hours at most.

Some time late in the afternoon his phone started ringing and it didn't stop.

He refused to take any calls.

He also resisted turning on the TV for a while, but he eventually gave in. What he saw unfolding before him on the screen, and later on his computer in the study, was deeply traumatising. He had never experienced anything like it before.

It was his ultimate nightmare.

Exposure.

Every mention of the word *Vaughan* felt like a stab wound. Every photo they showed – and they were mostly from the archives – felt like a laceration. As the evening progressed, he also felt sicker and weaker. This was, presumably, the effect of his withdrawal from the medication, which in turn, presumably, was responsible for the gradual unmasking of his various underlying conditions. After a while, it became hard to tell them apart, these two forms of pain – one imposed from outside, one pulsating from within.

Painkillers helped.

But painkillers only help in the short term. In Vaughan's experience, they usually end up killing a lot more than just the pain. He tried Paul Blanford again, without success, so he now pretty much accepts that with all this media stuff going on he hasn't a hope in hell any more of continuing with the medication.

He gets up at seven and slowly makes his way to the bathroom.

It hurts to piss now.

He has a quick, awkward shower, using the handheld unit. He dries himself off and puts his robe back on.

As he's coming out of the bedroom, he realises that he's alone in the apartment.

Mrs R will be here shortly, as will his doctor. He dismissed his full-time nurse a couple of weeks ago. Didn't see the point of having her. In the old days he used to employ a permanent domestic staff, but Meredith changed all of that.

Clutching his side, which is really sore now for some reason, he walks along the hallway towards the kitchen.

A few minutes later, as he's preparing to make coffee, or trying to, he spots the remote control on the counter and curses it.

He holds out for about thirty seconds.

When he flicks the TV on, the *first* image he sees, if only for a brief moment, is the exterior of his own apartment building. There are clearly reporters and photographers down there, but

Billy the doorman is under strict instructions not to interact with them.

It then cuts back to a studio and another panel of primped and preening morons. Mostly what they seem to be talking about is Meredith and that whole social scene she's involved in. Despite his vested interest in this, Vaughan quickly grows restive and changes the channel.

But it's more of the same.

On yet another channel, they're showing a photo of Vaughan in a white linen suit and a Panama hat, standing next to poor Hank Rundle. They're in front of an enormous construction site – it must be in the Middle East somewhere, one of their great engineering projects from the early seventies. It's followed by an even older black-and-white shot of Vaughan's father, William J., taken at the Stork Club with Lana Turner. After that – Jesus *wept* – there's one of his grandfather's funeral procession on Fifth Avenue from, what, 1938?

Where'd they get their hands on *that*?

Vaughan's sense of invasion, of violation almost, is acute. How can this be relevant in any way? How can these people possibly justify this stuff?

That's why he had to take the steps he did with that young journalist. This thing with Meredith is temporary, and with any luck it'll blow over and be forgotten, but not a *book* . . . not a book with goddamn chapter headings and footnotes . . .

'Mr Vaughan.'

He turns around.

It's Mrs R. He didn't hear her coming in.

'Good morning.'

'Good . . . Mr Vaughan, what . . . what are you *doing*?'

'Nothing . . . I . . .'

He looks at the counter, at the mess he's made, spilled coffee beans, the grinder on its side.

He got distracted by the TV.

But that doesn't explain the look on her face. He glances down and sees that his robe is open, and that he forgot to put his boxers back on after the shower.

Damn.

He then sees his reflection in one of the glass cabinets, tousled wisps of grey hair, two-day stubble.

Pale as death.

He stands there, not entirely unaware that several seconds have already passed and he hasn't closed his robe yet.

What is *wrong* with him?

'I'm sorry,' he says, closing the robe, the room starting to spin slightly – a glimpse of Meredith up on the TV screen, eyes shining, lips ruby red.

A kaleidoscope.

He reaches out for the counter to steady himself and starts coughing.

'*Mr Vaughan?*'

It takes him a few moments to get it under control, but he does eventually, and when he looks down at the marble countertop he sees that it is speckled with blood.

*

The call comes on Monday morning. Ellen is at her desk, keying in notes from her Atherton interviews.

She reaches for the phone, her *hello* as distracted as they come.

'Is this Ellen Dorsey?'

'Yeah.'

'My name is Detective Oscar Rayburn from the Seventy-seventh Precinct in Crown Heights in Brooklyn. Are you acquainted with a James Gilroy?'

'Yes.' She sits up. 'Is he OK?'

'No, ma'am, I'm afraid he isn't.' She tenses. 'Mr Gilroy was found dead in his apartment yesterday afternoon. We believe he took his own life.'

'*What?* But that's –' Her incredulity, instant and all-encompassing, prevents her from going on.

'Ms Dorsey?'

'That's . . . not possible. He was –' She wants to mention the champagne, how he talked about cracking open a bottle of champagne, the word exploding like a supernova in her brain – *champagne, champagne* – but she doesn't, she *can't*, and resorts instead to a dense, slow, loaded 'Oh . . . my . . . God.'

'I'm sorry, Ms Dorsey.' He pauses. 'How well did you know Mr Gilroy?'

'Not *that* well. We worked together. I'm a journalist, and so was he. We were colleagues, *and* friends, but . . .'

She's babbling.

'The reason I called you, Ms Dorsey, is because it appears the last person he spoke to on his cell phone was you.'

'Yeah, on Thursday. Thursday evening.'

'Can I ask what you guys talked about?'

'Er . . .' Ellen pauses and swallows. She stares at a page of scribbled notes on the desk, her mind beginning to glaze over. Then something kicks in, some kind of professional survival mechanism, where gears shift and extra adrenalin is pumped into the system. She leans forward on the desk. 'I'm sorry, Detective, did you say the Seventy-seventh Precinct? In Crown Heights?'

'Yes, I –'

'Are you there for the next while, the next hour or two? Because frankly I'd prefer to do this face to face.' She swallows again and winces, as though there's suddenly something toxic in the air. 'I think I'm probably going to have as many questions as you have, if not more.'

'That won't be neces–'

'Yes, it will.'

They tussle over it for a bit, but Ellen's determination wins out. She gets the impression that this case is only one of many on Oscar Rayburn's roster, that he hadn't figured on it needing anything more than a phone call, and that she has blindsided him, maybe even inconvenienced him.

But what, she's supposed to *give* a fuck?

It's his job.

She puts the phone down and the next short while, the time between ending the conversation with Rayburn and getting into the back of a cab on Columbus Avenue, goes by in a blur – no coherent thoughts, just bathroom, jacket, notebook, phone, keys, stairs, street. Sitting in the cab, though, city flickering past, is a different story. Here the thoughts are all too coherent and they revolve around a single, awful word, *suicide* – in most cases awful for the obvious reason, in a certain few cases awful for a less obvious one. In these few cases, the victim is usually a journalist, or a whistleblower, or a troublemaker of one kind or another. In these few cases, it's suicide as a weapon.

But, of course, in these few cases it's not suicide at all.

And that's her most coherent thought, the one that's keeping others at bay, the one that's keeping emotion at bay.

Or not.

She tightens her fist into a ball, squeezes it hard. It doesn't work. She starts crying.

The little *bastard*. He stormed into her life one afternoon, out of the blue, walked into her apartment, sat down and started talking, unspooling this incredible web of intrigue and malfeasance, of corruption and venality. He was almost ten years younger than she was, but he had none of the arrogance or sense of entitlement you often get with guys that age, journalists that age, who think the world owes them an era-defining scoop, and are themselves defined, chiefly, by impatience. He wanted her help and he was respectful, because all he *really* wanted was to make sense of what he had in front of him and to write it up.

They were thrown together by necessity – she had the experience and connections, and he had the story – but people she knew, people in the business, were shocked to find that the notoriously uncooperative and prickly Ellen Dorsey was actually collaborating with someone.

It was easy, though.

Because the guy was basically a sweetheart. He was good-looking and kind of cute, but there was never anything between them. He felt like a really smart kid brother that she could boss around and –

She was going to say *protect*.

But that could never be part of the equation, not in this job. She's not so sentimental as to think that *that's* why she's crying.

She's crying because she liked him and respected him, and now he's dead.

She sniffles and gets out a tissue. Blows her nose, sighs, says *fuck* a few times under her breath.

Looks around.

Driver taking in the show, surreptitiously, through the rearview.

She goes back to her most coherent thought.

Why would Jimmy Gilroy want to kill himself? No discernible reason. Plus, he was talking about cracking open a bottle of champagne and *celebrating*. Why would someone else want to kill Jimmy Gilroy? For a very discernible reason. Plus, he'd already been threatened.

There's a depressing, all too familiar pattern here. She could list off other cases, Danny Casolaro, Steve Kangas, Gary Webb, half a dozen more. She doesn't know if these people were murdered or not, but the official line on each of them is the same – they were depressed, they drank too much, life closed in on them . . . nothing to see here, please move along. Meanwhile relatives are baffled, and files go missing, and legitimate lines of journalistic enquiry dry up.

Thing is, it's an airtight method, it's foolproof, because anyone who cries foul can easily be dismissed as a conspiracy theorist . . . and a fool.

And Ellen *doesn't* know. She's ambivalent. Believing isn't enough, and people do commit suicide.

She looks out the window, the cables of the Brooklyn Bridge rippling past in the sunlight.

She knows where Barstool Charlie would stand, and that always gives her pause. But at the same time she has to steel herself here, because even from this distance, she can feel it coming, feel it in her bones . . .

The dreaded *official line.*

It comes sooner than expected, and not from Detective Oscar Rayburn, either.

When she gets to the Seventy-seventh Precinct, she announces herself and is asked to sit in the waiting area. She takes her phone out and does a quick internet trawl. To her surprise, there are already several reports of Gilroy's death. Unsurprisingly, there's a uniform, sort of planted feel to them. James Gilroy, the journalist who broke the Senator John Rundle story a couple of years back, has been found dead in his Brooklyn apartment, a bullet to the head, suspected suicide . . . sources say he'd been depressed and drinking, that his career had gone off the rails . . .

Sources?

She deflates in her hard plastic chair.

Poor Jimmy.

Ellen's interview with Rayburn doesn't help.

He's distracted and uninterested. Mid-forties, heavyset, sad and unhealthy-looking. Probably underpaid and overworked. When he asks his question again and she gives him an edited version of what they spoke about, adding that Jimmy was happy and untroubled and looking to the future with real enthusiasm . . . he barely reacts.

Ellen asks him about the weapon used, about ballistics and positioning. He answers each question, without looking at her, by consulting pages and folders on his desk.

She asks him about the state of Jimmy's apartment, about his computer or laptop.

Rayburn looks up at her and then back at his pages. He flicks through them, reads something. Checks another page. Then he looks at her again and shakes his head. 'He didn't have a computer.'

'What the –' Ellen stops and composes herself. 'He didn't have one, or you didn't find one in the apartment, because you people –'

Rayburn raises an index finger. 'Steady, ma'am.'

'Detective, he was a single male, thirty years old, he was a *journalist*. Are you seriously telling me he didn't have a computer? How did he send emails?'

Rayburn shrugs.

'And I'll tell you something else, Detective. It's a hell of a lot less likely that he owned a *gun*.'

Rayburn shuffles through a few papers and then holds something up. 'State of New York,' he says wearily. 'Licence to own a handgun, premises only.'

Ellen nods, her weariness matching his.

She asks about who found him, and about next of kin.

Seems he has a cousin who lives in Queens. And yes, there'll be an autopsy. Funeral arrangements aren't yet known.

Ellen gets the cousin's number.

Rayburn then indicates that time's up, that he's *really* swamped here.

He stands up. She stands up too.

They shake hands and she leaves.

*

In bed, propped up with pillows, Vaughan clicks his way

through the pages of the document. He catches words, phrases, *names* especially, but he can't focus enough to read any more, not properly. A sentence or two at a time is about all he can manage.

Nevertheless, it's infuriating – the idea of some little shit snooping around his affairs like that, talking to people, asking elaborate *questions*, looking up archives, scrolling down through endless sheets of microfiche in some musty old library basement.

Like a rat.

On a treadmill.

And of course he's Irish.

Vaughan doesn't have a great history with the Irish. Got held at gunpoint once in Dublin, on a construction site, on the forty-eighth floor of a new build, albeit by an extremely attractive young woman.

The file arrived this morning as an email attachment, sent by Beth Overmyer.

House of Vaughan.

He nearly got sick.

Sicker than he already is.

He's been in bed since Friday, hooked up to drips and machinery. He refused to go to the hospital. His doctor argued for it, harangued him about it, but Vaughan resisted. What's the point of having fifteen billion dollars if you can't tell your doctor to go fuck himself?

He's also refusing to see visitors, even though they're apparently lining up outside.

Who are these people, anyway, but ghosts? Some of them, *most* of them, not even born when he was in his prime.

He looks out over the room, the machines beeping, the BP values fluctuating.

That doesn't make *them* ghosts, though, does it? Isn't *he* the ghost?

Whatever.

He's made sure – as much as these things are possible – that this outrage, this so-called book, will never see the light of day.

Containment.

He's set it in train. It's a respectable policy and has a long and fairly rich tradition behind it. It's been shown to work in the past, it'll work again.

He comes to the last few pages of the file and tries really hard to focus.

. . . but instead, Charles Vaughan's decision to short-sell his Union Pacific stocks only served to further provoke Gilbert Morley . . .

A pain throbs behind his eyes and he has to look away from the screen for a moment. There's a Pissarro out there, on the wall opposite, it's usually a soothing presence, comforting, but he can't see it right now. Everything's a bit of a blur.

He reads on.

. . . in addition to which Vaughan's attentions to Arabella String-ham, Morley's fiancée, were to prove intolerable to the fusty and straitlaced Wall Street speculator. Undeterred, Vaughan pressed his advantage with the beautiful young dry-goods heiress . . .

This is the one and only Charles A. Vaughan he's reading about, his grandfather, whom he vaguely remembers from when he was a kid – the mid-1930s it would have been, all those visits to the cottage in Newport, the stiff formality of the man, his grey beard, his tortoiseshell cane with the carved ivory handle.

He was the architect, the great begetter, the patriarch.

But *this* version of him? The brash young nobody on the make . . . the schemer, the conniver, the hustler?

It's a travesty.

Vaughan clicks on to the last page.

. . . and then early one Thursday afternoon in August of 1878, as he made his way along Broad Street, Vaughan spotted Morley emerging from a tavern . . .

And farther down.

. . . but witnesses then report the conversation taking a somewhat violent turn, with Vaughan grabbing the other man by his lapels and shoving him backwards . . .

Vaughan simply cannot believe what he is reading, but he pushes on, increasingly horrified, knowing that if this material ever *were* to be made public, the humiliation, the exposure, would kill him, and outright – much faster, in fact, than the multiple, advanced, late-stage cancers riddling his body that he has been reliably informed over the last two days are killing him now.

*

On Utica Avenue, outside the Seventy-seventh Precinct, Ellen wants to scream. Is this how Jimmy ends up? Is this what he's reduced to? A half hour of inconvenient paperwork on the desk of some stressed-out, overworked cop?

That's how it seems.

But contrasted with this is an image in her head now that she can't shake. Jimmy slumped on his couch, gun in one hand, arm twisted back, brains daubed on the wall behind him.

Alone.

But not alone.

A spectral figure, maybe two, gliding around his apartment, placing items, removing items, subtly determining in advance the shape and direction of what will appear in Detective Rayburn's paperwork.

What makes her sick, and a little dizzy, is the apparent ease with which this can be done. So it's not something she can let lie. She's going to have to pursue it, extract more information from Rayburn, dig deeper – maybe get Val Brady to look into it.

But then something occurs to Ellen, a thought that grows – mushrooms, in fact – as she walks the six blocks to the Crown Heights–Utica Avenue subway stop.

If she is right, and this has happened because of Jimmy's book, it would be logical to assume that Jimmy was under surveillance. Wouldn't it also then be logical to assume that *she* is too, given her history with Jimmy and their recent meeting at the Black Lamps?

Is that a stretch?

To remove any trace of Jimmy's work, they took his computer. Presumably, they've also hacked into his accounts to delete whatever material he might have had stored remotely on iCloud or on Dropbox.

But do they know that *she* has a copy?

They must realise that publishers have seen it, that a digital file, pretty hard to eliminate completely, is *out there*. But they would also know, or suspect, that Ellen is the one person most likely to want to use it.

Or would they? And, for that matter, who *are* they?

Standing on the platform now, waiting for a 4 train, she looks around, a little uneasily.

Who are they?

The Oberon Capital Group owns Gideon Global, a private security and intelligence company with massive resources. What more do you need to know? This isn't a stretch at all.

The train arrives and she takes it to Fulton Street, where she gets a 2 train uptown.

All the way home, Ellen feels nervous, and increasingly so as she approaches her building. She's been the subject of surveillance in the past, while working on stories. She's been hacked and she's been subtly intimidated. But she's never feared for her actual safety before. She's never felt that she had to scan the other passengers on a subway car or look over her shoulder walking down the street.

She looks over her shoulder now.

But there's no one there.

Weirdly, that makes her feel more nervous.

As she walks up the stoop to her building and goes inside, she thinks she might throw up. She also becomes convinced that she's going to find something unpleasant when she gets into her apartment.

But what?

She gets to the fourth floor and stands there, with her key in her hand, not *quite* hyperventilating.

Fuck this.

She unlocks the door, pushes it open and looks inside.

Nothing. It's just as she left it.

She goes in and locks the door behind her. She goes over to the window and looks down onto Ninety-third Street.

After a while her breathing returns to normal. But she also realises something. This isn't just paranoia on her part. It's real. And it isn't going away, either.

Standing there, she takes out her phone.

'Yep?'

'Max, are you at the office?'

'Hi, Ellen, yeah. Where else would I be?'

'Stay there.'

She gets ready, gathers a few things and goes. Approaching Columbus Avenue, she finds herself almost breaking into a run.

She flags down a cab.

Fifty blocks south, then a few more east.

When she walks through the door of the *Parallax* offices, she feels a distinct release – it's physical, and could be expressed as a scream or a manic laugh or even fifteen minutes of uncontrollable sobbing. But she holds it in check and walks the long hallway that leads to Max's office.

Sitting behind his desk, hair unkempt, eyes out on sticks, Max looks like he's inches from a caffeine heart attack.

'Hey, Jimmy Dorsey, what's up?'

It's a formula he's used before. She doesn't know how to tell him that it's not funny, not any more. But neither does she want to.

Not now.

And yet. She's a reporter. She has to report.

She stands in front of his desk. 'Those IT geeks you had in here once,' she says, 'are they still around?'

'And good morning to you, too. Yeah, of course.' He looks at her, picking up on the tone. He adjusts his position in the chair.

'Ellen. You're scaring me. What's going on?'

She takes Jimmy Gilroy's USB flash drive from her pocket and places it gently on the desk.

Max leans forward and studies it. 'So. What have we got here?'

She keeps it brief.

Jimmy's dead. She explains how – or, at least, how it seems. Then there's his book here, the one about James Vaughan and his family. She explains more or less what's in it, and how it finishes with a charming tale of Vaughan's grandfather, who one afternoon as a very young man was witnessed, near the corner of Broad Street and Exchange Place, getting into an altercation with another man, one Gilbert Morley, pushing this man into an adjacent construction pit and then bashing his brains in with a lead pipe. Evading prosecution, Charles Vaughan subsequently married his victim's fiancée, and not long after that effectively inherited his new father-in-law's substantial fortune, which in turn became the financial basis for his own railroad, steel and mining empire.

Max listens, first with shock on his face, then alarm.

'So what I think we should do', Ellen goes on, pointing at the flash drive, 'is upload that onto the *Parallax* website.' She pauses. '*Today*.'

Max exhales, shaking his head, trying to process what she's told him. 'Jesus, Ellen. This is a lot to take in.'

She remains standing there, impassive, waiting.

Max thinks about it for a minute.

'I don't . . .' He's struggling. He looks at her directly. 'I don't get the point of putting it on the website today. What's the hurry?'

'OK,' Ellen says, 'let me tell you. One, you want to save this magazine, right? Best way to do that, as we both know, is by ramping up your web presence. How do you achieve that? Do something spectacular, get everyone's attention. With James Vaughan not just in the *news* right now but halfway to being a fucking celebrity, this book is a heat-seeking *missile*. Two, Jimmy deserves it. He did the work, so this means he won't be forgotten. And you don't have to worry about making any allegations that won't stand up, because the context will do it for you. Some straight reporting on how Jimmy died – I'm going to get Val Brady working on it – and *this*, his book, which is fully sourced and referenced, will speak for itself. And three . . .' She stops and sits down, pulling herself in closer to the desk. She puts her hand over the flash drive. 'And *three*. Once this is out there, clocking up hits, I'm safe again.'

'You're not safe now?'

'Look what happened to Jimmy. These people have to know I was in touch with him.' She leans in even closer. 'So let me tell you something for free, Max. I'm not leaving the building until you upload this thing onto the website.'

Max sits back in his chair and swivels. 'OK, let me read it first. Then we'll get the tech guys in, and legal, too.' He swivels some more. 'If we go ahead with this, you'll have to write something, an introduction.'

'Of course,' Ellen says. 'Absolutely. I'd want to.'

Max sighs. He picks up the flash drive and studies it. 'It's going to be a long day.'

Ellen shrugs. 'There's plenty of coffee, isn't there?'

'Sure.' Max looks at her for a while. 'Are you OK, Ellen?'

She gets up from the chair. 'I don't know. We'll see.'

She takes out her phone and walks over to the window.

Standing there, she makes a few calls, the first one to Val Brady, the second to Jimmy's cousin in Queens and a third to her sister, Michelle.

When she can't talk any more she finds a free desk and gets down to work. It takes her a couple of hours to write the introduction. After that she goes over her Atherton notes. Then she spends another couple of hours preparing questions for the interview she's doing later in the week with Frank Bishop.

During all of this, in the background, people come and go, suits, guys in beards, phone calls are made, facts checked, opinions sought.

Ellen even manages to fall asleep for a while.

Some time late in the afternoon, Val Brady shows up.

He has a piece on Gilroy ready to go. He's been out to the Seventy-seventh and has met the cousin. He says that if *Parallax* goes ahead and posts *House of Vaughan* on their website this evening, his piece will make page one of the *Times* tomorrow, which in turn will send a lot of traffic back the magazine's way.

This revives Max, who's been flagging somewhat. He then heads off for another round of consultations. Twenty-five minutes later, he reappears and says, 'OK, looks like we're good to go.'

Ellen isn't sure she's heard him right.

'Yeah.' He sinks into his chair. 'It's all been cleared. The guys have set it up. They've previewed it. They're using, I don't know, WordPress or something. Anyway, one click and we're done.'

A weary Ellen turns to Val. 'I haven't eaten all day. Are you hungry?'

Val's eyes widen. He nods and says, 'Yeah, sure, but I'm buying.'

Ellen then gets up and walks over to Max's desk. She goes in behind it, stands next to him and looks at the screen.

Max drags the cursor over to the Publish icon. He withdraws his hand from the mouse and glances up at her.

'You want to do it?'

Ellen takes a deep breath. She reaches down, clicks on the icon and waits. 'That's it,' she says, after a couple of moments. 'We're live.'

Also by Alan Glynn

ff

Bloodland

Ireland AM Crime Fiction Book of the Year

Corruption. Collusion. Conspiracy.

A private security contractor loses it in the Congo,
with deadly consequences.

The ex-Prime Minister of Ireland struggles to contain
a dark secret from his time in office.

A dramatic news story breaks just as a US senator
begins his campaign to run for office.

What connects them? Seemingly nothing – until a young journalist,
investigating the death of a tabloid star, finds himself caught up
in an ever-expanding web of lies.

'A cracking conspiracy thriller worthy of Le Carré.'
Sunday Independent

'Ripped from tomorrow's headlines, *Bloodland* is irresistible.
An exhilarating thriller from the dark heart of the global village.'
Val McDermid

'Scarily plausible . . . I've not read such a multi-layered, expertly
plotted portrayal of arrogance, greed and hubris for a long time.'
Guardian

ff

Winterland

One Night. One Name. Two Bodies.

One death is a gangland murder, the other, seemingly, a road accident. But when family member Gina Rafferty starts to look into it, she refuses to accept the official line.
Told repeatedly that she should stop asking questions, she becomes more determined than ever to reveal the truth.

'Timely, topical and thrilling.' John Connolly

'An enthralling and addictive read.' *Observer*

'A page turner in the best sense of the word . . . The plot never lets up for a moment and the three set-pieces of the story are as good as anything I've read in contemporary crime fiction.'
Irish Times

'A heavyweight, grown-up thriller . . . Told in wonderfully fluent prose, *Winterland* is a gripping tale of a world of greed and secrets.' *Guardian*

ff

Limitless

The #1 Box Office hit movie, starring Bradley Cooper, Abbie Cornish and Robert De Niro.

Imagine a drug that made your brain function
to its full potential.

A drug that allowed you to pick up a
foreign language in a single day.

A drug that helped you process information
so fast you could see patterns in the stock market.

Just as his life is fading into mediocrity, Eddie Spinola comes
across such a pill: MDT-48 – a sort of Viagra for the brain.
But while its benefits materialise quickly, so do certain
unwelcome side-effects. And when Eddie decides
to track down other users, he soon discovers that
they're all dying, or dead . . .

'Fast, clever and horrifying.' *Daily Mail*